P...
Fourth Grave Beneath My Feet

"The fourth entry in Darynda Jones's wildly popular Charley Davidson series is every bit as solidly successful as the first. In fact, this might be the best yet. *Fourth Grave Beneath My Feet* continues to blend paranormal, romance, and mystery better than any other contemporary work out there . . . At its heart, Charley is still perfectly Charley, well-adjusted PI/grim reaper, and one of the elements that works so well is that right strike of outrageous humor one moment and teeth-chattering suspense the next."
—Heroes and Heartbreakers

"A great book . . . snappy writing and quirky dialogue . . . one of my favorites."
—Fiction Vixen

Third Grave Dead Ahead

"Jones perfectly balances humor and suspense."
—*Publishers Weekly* (starred review)

"Wickedly witty . . . will delight aficionados of humorous paranormals."
—*Booklist* (starred review)

"Charley Davidson is one of the most fun characters I have had the privilege to read. She is witty, independent, and lives a little on the crazy side of life."
—Dark Faerie Tales

"Absolutely amazing . . . a thrill ride from the very first page until the very last."
—Red Hot Books (5 stars)

P9-EFJ-583

"A hilarious, wickedly sexy, action-packed mystery that will have you howling with laughter . . . A strong character-driven series, this urban fantasy takes you on a crazy laugh-filled adventure with strong emotional story lines, multiple subplots, charismatic characters, and witty dialogue." —Smexy Books

"Love!" —Oh My Books! (4½ stars)

"A barrel of laughs mixed with some intense action. Jones's trademark humor makes this series a must-read for urban fantasy readers who like a good laugh with their suspense. Jones gives readers some of the most entertaining characters to come along in a long while." —Debbie's Book Bag

"Hilarious, engrossing paranormal mysteries with absolutely no vampires or werewolves . . . with an easy-to-root-for heroine." —Quirky Girls Read (A+)

Second Grave on the Left

"Jones perfectly balances humor and suspense in [this] paranormal thriller featuring grim reaper, PI, and 'all-around badass' Charley Davidson . . . It's the distinctive characters, dead and alive, and the almost constant laughs that will leave readers eager for the next installment." —*Publishers Weekly* (starred review)

"This is an amazing book and a fantastic series! In a lot of ways it is similar to Janet Evanovich's Stephanie Plum series, only ten times better!" —*Night Owl Reviews*

"A saucy sequel . . . Readers will be captivated by Charley's near-death adventures." —Associated Press

Also by Darynda Jones

Fifth Grave Past the Light

Darynda Jones

St. Martin's Paperbacks

This is a work of fiction. All of the characters, organizations, and events portrayed in this novel are either products of the author's imagination or are used fictitiously.

FIFTH GRAVE PAST THE LIGHT

Copyright © 2013 by Darynda Jones.
Excerpt from *Sixth Grave on the Edge* copyright © 2014 by Darynda Jones.

For information address St. Martin's Press, 175 Fifth Avenue, New York, NY 10010.

Library of Congress Catalog Card Number: 2013009880

ISBN: 978-1-250-04338-2

Printed in the United States of America

St. Martin's Press hardcover edition / July 2013
St. Martin's Paperbacks edition / January 2014

St. Martin's Paperbacks are published by St. Martin's Press, 175 Fifth Avenue, New York, NY 10010.

10 9 8 7 6 5 4 3

For Luther and DD.
You are wondrous and heroic
and my favorite kind of strange.

Acknowledgments

Wow, five books in and I still can't get enough of Charley Davidson. She makes me look forward to waking up. Each book is a little more fun to write than the last and I owe it all to you, dear readers, for allowing me this opportunity. And, as always, my heart and gratitude go out to my fantabulous agent, Alexandra Machinist, and my extraordinary editor, Jennifer Enderlin. The good news is, we made it through another installment. The other good news is, that nervous twitch I gave you by pushing this deadline just a little further than I probably should have will disappear soon. Promise. You might try an ointment. Or therapy.

And while we're on the subject, my copy editor, Eliani Torrcs, is kind of amazing. I am so fortunate to have you. A humongous thank-you to Stephanie Raffle for our simultaneous versions of the Vulcan mind meld. I'm telling you, great minds, baby. And to the incomparable Cait Wells, the bestest beta reader in the world. (I know you're dying to correct that.)

To my gorgeous niece, Ashlee Duarte, for letting me use a story straight out of her childhood. So, dear readers, when you come to it, the story where Amber signs a sentence incorrectly really and truly happened, word for word, only it happened to my niece when she was about nine. You'll soon find out why I treasure that story so much.

Thank you ever so much to the Grimlets! You guys are the best. And to my assistant, Dana, for her tireless efforts, and our very own Mama Grimlet, Jowanna. There are so many people I would love to thank. Every book I am able to write is a gift. I am honored and humbled there are actually people who want to read them. Thank you all so much!

Fifth Grave
Past the
Light

Chapter One

Ask me about life after death.
—T-SHIRT OFTEN SEEN ON CHARLEY DAVIDSON,
A GRIM REAPER OF QUESTIONABLE MORALS

The dead guy at the end of the bar kept trying to buy me a drink. Which figured. No one else was even taking a second look and I'd dressed to the nines. Or, at the very least, the eight-and-a-halves. But the truly disturbing part of my evening was the fact that my mark, one Mr. Marvin Tidwell, blond real estate broker and suspected adulterer, actually turned down the drink I'd tried to buy him.

Turned it down!

I felt violated.

I sat at the bar, sipping a margarita, lamenting the sad turn my life had taken. Especially tonight. This case was not going as planned. Maybe I wasn't Marv's type. It happened. But I was oozing interest. And I wore makeup. And I had cleavage. Even with all that going for me, this investigation was firmly wedged between the cracks of no and where. At least I could tell my client, aka Mrs. Marvin Tidwell, that it would seem her husband was not cheating on her. Not randomly, anyway. The fact that he could've been meeting someone in particular kept me glued to my bar stool.

"C-come here often?"

I looked over at the dead guy. He'd finally worked up the courage to approach and I got a better view. I figured him for the runt of the litter. He wore round-rimmed glasses and a tattered baseball cap that sat backwards on top of muddy brown hair. Add to that a faded blue T-shirt and loosely ripped jeans and he could've been a skater, a computer geek, or a backwoods moonshiner.

His cause of death was not immediately apparent. No stab wounds or gaping holes. No missing limbs or tire tracks across his face. He didn't even look like a drug addict, so I couldn't tell why he'd died at such a young age. Taking into account the fact that his baby-faced features would make him look younger than he probably was, I estimated him to be somewhere around my age when he'd passed.

He stood waiting for an answer. I thought "Come here often?" was rhetorical, but okay. Not wanting to be perceived as talking to myself in a room full of people, I responded by lifting one shoulder in a halfhearted shrug.

Sadly, I did. Come here often. This was my dad's bar, and while I never set up stings here for fear of someone I knew blowing my cover, this just happened to be the very same bar Mr. Tidwell frequented. At least if it came to a knockdown drag-out, I might have some backup. I knew most of the regulars and all of the employees.

Dead Guy glanced toward the kitchen, seeming nervous before he refocused on me. I glanced that way as well. Saw a door.

"Y-you're very shiny," he said, drawing my attention back to him.

He had a stutter. Few things were more adorable than a grown man with boyish features and a stutter. I stirred my margarita and pasted on a fake smile. I couldn't talk to him in a room full of living, breathing patrons. Especially when one was named Jessica Guinn, to my utter mortification. I hadn't seen her fiery red hair since high school but there she sat, a few seats down from me, surrounded by a group of chattering socialites who looked almost as fake as her boobs. But that could be my bitterness rearing its ugly head.

Unfortunately, my forced smile only encouraged Dead Guy. "Y-you are. You're like the s-sun reflecting off the chrome bumper of a f-fifty-seven Chevy."

He splayed his fingers in the air to demonstrate, and my heart was gone. Damn it. He was like all those lost puppies I tried to save as a child to no avail because I had an evil stepmother who believed all stray dogs were rabid and would try to rip out her jugular. A fact that had nothing to do with my desire to bring them into the house.

"Yeah," I said under my breath, doing my best ventriloquist impersonation, "thanks."

"I'm D-Duff," he said.

"I'm Charley." I kept my hands wrapped around my drink lest he decide we needed to shake. Not many things looked stranger to the living world than a grown woman shaking air. You know those kids with invisible friends? Well, I was one of those. Only I wasn't a kid, and my friends weren't invisible. Not to me, anyway. And I could see them because I'd been born the grim reaper, which was not as bad as it sounded. I was basically a portal to heaven, and whenever someone was stuck on Earth, having chosen not to cross over immediately after death, they could cross to the other side through me. I was like a giant bug light, only what I lured was already dead.

I pulled at my extra-tight sweater. "Is it just me, or is it really warm in here?"

His baby blues shot toward the kitchen again. "Hot is m-more like it. S-so, I—I couldn't help but notice you t-tried to buy that guy over there a drink."

I let my fake smile go. Freed it like a captured bird. If

it came back to me, it would be mine. If not, it never was. "And?"

"You're b-barking up the wrong tree with that one."

Surprised, I put my drink down—the one I bought myself—and leaned in a little closer. "He's gay?"

Duff snorted. "N-no. But he's been in here a lot lately. He l-likes his women a little . . . l-looser."

"Dude, how much sluttier can I get?" I indicated my attire with a sweep of my hand.

"N-no, I mean, well, you're a l-little—" He let his gaze travel the length of me. "—t-tight."

I gasped. "I look anal?"

He drew in a deep breath and tried again. "H-he only hits on women who are more s-substantial than you."

Oh, that wasn't offensive at all. "I have depth. I've read Proust. No, wait, that was Pooh. *Winnie-the-Pooh*. My bad."

He shifted his nonexistent weight, cleared his throat, and tried again. "More v-voluptuous."

"I have curves," I said through a clenched jaw. "Have you seen my ass?"

"Heavier!" he blurted out.

"I weigh— Oh, you mean he likes bigger women."

"E-exactly, while I on the other hand—"

Duff's words faded into the background like elevator music. So Marv liked big women. A new plan formed in the darkest, most corrupt corners of Barbara. My brain.

Cookie, otherwise known as my receptionist during regular business hours and my best friend 24/7, was perfect. She was large and in charge. Or, well, large and kind of bossy. I picked up my cell phone and called her.

"This better be good," she said.

"It is. I need your assistance."

"I'm watching the first season of *Prison Break*."

"Cookie, you're my assistant. I need assistance. With

a case. You know those things we take on to make money?"

"*Prison. Break.* It's about these brothers who—"

"I know what *Prison Break* is."

"Then have you ever actually seen these boys? If you had, you would not expect me to abandon them in their time of need. I think there's a shower scene coming up."

"Do these brothers sign your paycheck?"

"No, but technically neither do you."

Damn. She was right. It was much easier to just have her forge my name.

"I need you to come flirt with my mark."

"Oh, okay. I can do that."

Nice. The F-word always worked with her. I filled her in and told her the deal with Tidwell, then ordered her to hurry over.

"And dress sexy," I said right before hanging up. But I regretted the sexy part instantly. The last time I told Cookie to dress sexy for a much-needed girls' night out on the town, she wore a lace-up corset, fishnet stockings, and a feather boa. She looked like a dominatrix. I'd never been the same.

"S-so, she's coming?" Duff asked.

"Possibly. She's watching hot guys on TV. It all depends if her daughter is there or not. Either way, she should be here soon."

He nodded.

As I sat waiting for my BFF, I took note of all the women in the bar that night. Calamity's was kind of a cop hangout. Women certainly came in, just not by the droves. But this place was packed and noisy, and at least 75 percent of the patrons were women. Which was odd.

I'd been coming to the bar for years, mostly because my dad owned it, but partly because my investigations office was on the second floor, and in all that time, I'd never seen the place so disproportioned in favor of the feminine mystique except that one time I talked Dad into bringing in a male revue. He'd agreed for two reasons. One: I'd batted my lashes. Two: He thought a male revue was a guy who came in, tried the food, then did a review in the paper. I may or may not have encouraged that line of thinking. Dad would probably have taken it better if I'd been over eighteen when I suggested it. He wanted to know how many male revues I'd been to.

"Counting this one?" was apparently not an appropriate reply.

Someone put a plate of food in front of me.

"Compliments of the chef."

I glanced up at Teri, my dad's best bartender. She knew I was working an infidelity case and probably guessed that I'd struck out, thus the comfort food. The heavenly aroma hit me so fast, I had to force myself not to drool.

"Thanks." I took a slice off the plate and sank my teeth into the best chicken quesadilla I'd ever had. "Wow," I said, sucking in cool air as I chewed, "Sammy really outdid himself."

"What?" she said over the crowd.

I waved her on and continued to eat, letting my eyes roll back in ecstasy. I'd been enjoying Sammy's concoctions for years, and while they were always mouthwateringly good, this was incredible. I scooped equal parts guacamole, salsa, and sour cream onto the next bite, then went in for another trip to heaven.

Duff watched me eat while standing wedged between the back of my bar stool and the guy standing next to it. His left half was inside Duff's right. The guy looked up, searched the ceiling for air vents, turned to his left, his right, then . . . three . . . two . . . one . . .

He shivered and stepped away.

Happened every time. The departed were cold and when

people stood inside one, the hairs on the backs of their necks rose, goose bumps shot across their skin, and a shiver ran down their spines.

But Duff wasn't paying attention to the guy. While he pretended to center his attention on me, he kept a weather eye on the door to the kitchen, glancing over every few seconds, chewing on a nail.

Maybe the door to the kitchen was really a portal to heaven and if he stepped through it, he would cross to the other side. No, wait.

As I sat there stuffing my face, I began to wonder about something. I'd checked out Mrs. Tidwell's Friendbook page while researching Mr. Tidwell for more pictures. I liked to take every precaution when approaching a mark to make certain I could recognize him or her when necessary. I got the wrong guy one time. It ended badly.

I dug my phone out of my jeans again, found Mrs. Tidwell's profile, and clicked through her photo history. Sure enough, when they got married a little over a year earlier, Mrs. Tidwell had been much heavier. She'd clearly lost a lot of weight, and she'd kept a log on her page with her progress, losing over one hundred pounds over the past year. While I cheered her dedication, I began to wonder if Mr. Tidwell would share my enthusiasm or if he'd liked his wife better before.

The concept kind of floored me. Most guys strayed when their wives gained weight. Tidwell seemed to be straying for the opposite reason. Maybe he felt threatened by her new look. She was a knockout.

I panicked when Tidwell stood to leave. He threw down a few bills, then started for the door, and I realized this night would be a complete bust. I was really hoping for a money shot to put this case to bed. With my optimism dwindling, I began contemplating my schedule to set up a second attempt when Tidwell stopped. His gaze locked on the front door. I looked past him and almost gasped at the raven-haired vixen walking through it. The moment our eyes met, Barry White started playing through the speakers overhead. The lights dimmed and a smoky, sultry kind of aura centered on the newcomer.

Coincidence? I think not.

Enter Cookie Kowalski. Loyal, stalwart, and just the right size. Cookie walked toward me, her expression a mixture of curiosity and hesitance. Surely she wasn't worried I'd get her into trouble.

And she was dressed to kill. She wore a dark pantsuit with a long sparkling frock and a silver scarf opened at the neck to reveal her voluptuous attributes.

"You saucy minx," I said when she sat beside me at the bar.

She grinned and scooted closer to me. "This is okay?"

I looked her over again. "It's fantastic. And it definitely did the job."

Tidwell sat back down at his table, interest evident in every move he made. I gestured toward him with the barest hint of a nod. She did a quick scan of the room and let her gaze pause a fraction of a second on Tidwell before refocusing on me.

But she still wasn't convinced. "So, if you were a guy, would you be into me?"

"Hon, if I were a guy, I'd be gay."

"Yeah, me, too. So, what do I do?"

"Just give it a sec. He'll probably—"

"The man at the table behind you would like to buy you a drink, darlin'," Teri said. Her brows rose as she waited for a response. Sobriety clearly came late in life for her, but she was what my father would call a handsome woman, with long dark hair and striking hazel eyes. Still, she'd seen too many illicit rendezvous, complicated hookups, and had one-night stands to be overly impressed. Experience had hardened her.

I could be hard. If I practiced. Gave it my all.

"Oh," Cookie said, caught off guard, "I'll take a whiskey sour."

Teri winked and began practicing her magic.

"A whiskey sour?" I asked Cook.

"Your f-friend seems nervous," Duff said, and I agreed with a nod.

Cookie stared ahead as though standing before a firing squad. "Liquid courage," she said. "It seemed like a good idea at the time."

"That's what they said about nuclear energy on Three Mile Island."

She cast me a horrified look.

I fought a grin and tucked a small mic into the folds of her scarf, pretending to adjust it. "Look, all you gotta do is open the lines of communication. I'll be able to hear everything he says." I tapped my ear to indicate the receiver I was wearing. "Just see how far he wants to take things. Unfortunately, him buying you a drink does not prove infidelity."

Her pallor turned a light shade of green. "I have to have sex with him?"

"What? No. Just, you know, see if he *wants* to have sex with you."

"Do I have to make out with him?"

Oh, wow. I never realized how uneducated Cookie was in the ways of extramarital investigations. She was more of a behind-the-scenes kind of gal. I just figured she'd know what to do.

Teri set the drink down. Cookie grabbed it and took a long draw.

"Don't do anything that makes you uncomfortable," I

said as she took another hearty swig. "Just try to get him to proposition you. Now, turn and offer him a salute. Let him know you're interested."

Before I could coach her further, she did exactly that. She turned to him, her back rigid, and saluted.

Jessica's table of airheads burst out laughing. I closed my eyes in mortification and said through gritted teeth, "I meant lift the glass."

"What?" she asked through equally gritted teeth. "You said to salute him." She was starting to panic. I could feel it radiating off her in waves. "I thought maybe he was in the military."

"It's okay, just calm down."

"Calm down?" She turned back around. "You calm down. I'm completely calm. I'm like deep water that's deep and still."

I wrapped a hand around her arm and squeezed to coax her back to me. She drew in a long breath and let it out slowly, forcing herself to calm.

"Better," I said, giving her another minute to recuperate. "Okay, if he hasn't penciled you in as a loony, go over there and strike up a conversation."

"What? Me? What?"

"Cook, you can do this. It's just like high school only without the socially crippling aftereffects of failure."

"Right. High school." She gathered up her courage, eased off her chair, and stepped to his table.

And she transformed. She became confident. A true mistress of her own destiny. I almost giggled in triumph while I took another bite and listened in.

"S-so, you're s-setting him up?" Duff asked.

I wiped my mouth, then checked the recorder in my pocket to make sure it was set to record. It would suck if we went to all this trouble and ended up with no proof.

"Not so much setting up as taking down. He's the one trolling the clubs with the intention of cheating on his wife. We're just giving him the opportunity and giving her the proof she needs to move on."

It wasn't until I heard Jessica snickering that I realized I was talking to Duff too openly.

"There she goes again," Jessica said loud enough for me to hear. "What did I tell you? Absolute freak."

The gossip girls burst out laughing again, but I could hear Jessica's high-pitched crow above the others. It was the one thing that drove me crazy when we were friends. She had a nasally, piercing laugh that reminded me of the stabbing scene from *Psycho*. But that could've been wishful thinking on my part.

I'd made the mistake of being honest with her when we were freshmen. She seemed to accept the fact that I could see ghosts. But once I told her exactly what I was, that I was the grim reaper and that the departed could cross through me, our friendship shattered like a house of glass, cut as the remnants showered down on me. It left some fairly deep scars. Had I known our friendship was so fragile, had I known it could be severed with a single truth, I wouldn't have thrown so much of myself into it.

Afterwards, all bets were off. She told the entire school what I'd said. What I was. Thankfully, no one, including herself, believed it. But the betrayal cut deep. Hurt and vindictive, I went after—and landed—the boy of her dreams, a senior basketball star named Freddy James. Naturally, that did nothing to reconcile our friendship. Her venomous spite multiplied tenfold after I started dating Freddy, but suddenly, I didn't care. I'd discovered boys on a whole new level.

My sister, Gemma, knew the moment it happened. She accused Freddy of stealing my virginity. But saying Freddy

James stole my virginity would be like saying Hiroshima stole a nuclear bomb from us. Theft didn't fit into the equation.

As Jessica and her friends snickered across the way, I ignored them, knowing indifference would bite more than anything I could say. Jessica hated to be ignored and it worked. My disinterest seemed to be eating her alive. The abrasive texture of anger and hatred raked over my skin like sharp nails. That girl had issues.

"Sorry about the salute," Cookie said to Tidwell.

He gestured for her to sit. "Not at all. I found it enchanting."

Despite everything, Tidwell was a good-looking man, and clearly articulate. Now I had to worry about another possible outcome altogether: Would Cookie fall for his charm?

"I'm Anastasia," she said, and I tried not to groan aloud. Normally noms de guerre were fine on a job, but we were in my dad's bar. We knew half the people here, which came to glaring light when someone called out to her.

"Hey, Cookie!" an off-duty officer said as he strolled in and took a seat at the bar. "Looking good, sweet cheeks."

Cookie blinked, taken aback, then smiled and said to Tidwell, "But everyone calls me Cookie."

A most excellent save.

"I'm Doug."

Oops, incriminating evidence number one. It would seem Marv liked noms de guerre, too. I'd turned so I could see them through my periphery and watched as they shook hands. Cook mumbled something about how nice it was to meet him. He said likewise. And I took another bite of quesadilla, fighting the urge to moan in ecstasy. Sammy had definitely outdone himself.

Still, I had to get over it. I had a job to do, damn it.

I turned toward them, my expression one of complete

boredom, and snapped a few shots with my phone. Phones made close-up surveillance so easy. I pretended to text while zeroing in on my target. When Tidwell leaned forward and put a hand over Cookie's, I almost became giddy. Not really a money shot, but pretty darned close.

But then I noticed something. A darkness in his gaze I hadn't seen before. The more I watched Tidwell, the less I liked him. Almost everything out of his mouth was a lie, but there was more to my discomfort than his deception. He reminded me of one of those guys who sweeps a girl off her feet, marries her after a whirlwind romance, then kills her for the insurance money. He was a bit too smooth. A bit too personal with the questions. I'd have to do a little more digging where Mr. Marv Tidwell was concerned.

"What is that?" Tidwell asked. His voice had hardened and the emotion that dumped out of him startled me.

"This?" Cookie asked, suddenly less certain.

He saw the mic I'd hidden in the folds of her scarf. Crap on a quesadilla. Before I could scramble out of my seat, he reached over and ripped it off her, dragging her forward in the process.

"What is this?" he demanded, shaking it in her face before curling it into his fist.

I rushed toward them. The investigator in me continued to take a couple of shots for good measure. They'd be blurry, but I had to take what I could get. Cookie sat stunned. Not because she was caught, I was certain, but because of his reaction. I would have been stunned, too. He went from charming admirer to raging bull in a matter of seconds.

His face reddened and his lips peeled back from his teeth in a vicious snarl. "Is this a game? Did Valerie put you up to this?"

Valerie Tidwell was Marvin's wife and my client, and

clearly he suspected that she suspected his extracurricular activities. The entire bar fell silent as I hurried forward, weaving around tables and chairs, snapping shots as I went, wondering why on earth Cookie was digging into her purse. I didn't have to wonder long. Just as I got to her, she pulled a gun, and all I could think was *holy freaking crap.*

"Cookie!" I said as I skidded into her.

But before I could do anything, Tidwell lunged across the table and grabbed Cookie's wrist. He knocked her back into me and we all three started to tumble to the ground the exact moment a sharp crack splintered the air.

Chapter Two

I intend to live forever.
So far, so good.
— T-SHIRT

The world slowed, as it had so many times before, the instant the sound of the gun going off reached me. I realized then that when Tidwell grabbed for it, he'd pushed it until it was pointed directly at my heart.

Naturally.

Because where else would it be pointed?

I had been charging forward, but when the world slowed, I decelerated and watched the bullet burst out of the barrel of Cookie's pistol, mere inches away from me, with a puff of fire behind it. It traveled straight toward my chest as I reared back.

But time was different here. Gravity didn't work quite the same. The laws of physics broke. As the bullet crept forward, I tried to shift my weight away from the projectile rocketing toward me, but it seemed like all I could do was stare at it.

From my periphery, I could see the beginnings of panic in many of the patrons' faces. Some were in the middle of raising an arm to duck and cover. Some were still oblivious, looking on with only mild concern. And some, cops mostly, jumped into action, their expressions calm as their training took over.

The bullet kept coming, centimeter by centimeter, the air behind it rippling with friction. I needed more time. To figure out what to do. To figure out how to dodge a bullet. Literally. Feeling as though I were swimming in cement, I made a minute amount of headway, falling back in the direction I'd come, pushing off Cookie's shoulder. But not fast enough. If the world came crashing back now, the round would enter the left side of my chest just under my collarbone. And unfortunately, I was never able to slow time for very long. It had a way of bouncing back, like a rubber band snapping into place, when I least expected it.

Just as I felt my hold slipping, as the bullet gained a precious inch too quickly for my eyes to track, as sound skipped forward like a scratched record jumping across grooves, a hand, large and masculine, wrapped around the slug and pulled it out of my path. A heat as familiar as the sun bathed me in its warmth. And another hand slid around the back of my neck as Reyes Alexander Farrow palmed the bullet and pulled me into his arms.

And what beautiful arms they were. Forearms corded with sinew and tendon. Biceps sculpted with the hills and valleys of well-defined muscle. Shoulders wide and powerful beneath a khaki T-shirt.

My gaze traveled up until I was looking into the face of an angel. Or a fallen angel. Or, well, a fallen angel's son. Reyes's dad just happened to be public enemy number one, the first and most beautiful angel to fall from heaven, Lucifer. And Reyes had been created in hell, literally forged in the fires of sin. Which would explain his allure.

His dark eyes glistened with humor as he asked, "This again?"

My knight in shining armor. Someday I was going to

he, able to save, my own ass. Then I wouldn't have, to owe, people. People like the son of Satan.

I fought past the primal urges that surged through my body every time Reyes was near and said as nonchalantly as I could manage, "I totally had this."

An evil grin, probably one he'd inherited from his evil father, spread across his face, and I found myself trying not to drool for the second time that night. He glanced at the chaos surrounding us. "Yeah, I can see that. What's she doing with her tongue?"

I tore my gaze off him and looked at Cookie. Her face was frozen in horror, her features contorted, her tongue poking out from between her teeth.

"Oh, my god. Will my camera phone work? I have *got* to capture this moment." I could blackmail her for years with a shot like that.

He laughed, a deep rich sound that sent shivers racing down my spine. "I don't think so."

"Damn, if ever there was a Kodak moment." I looked back at him and his ridiculously long lashes. "That bullet was traveling pretty fast," I said. "What's it going to do to your hand when time bounces back?"

He dropped his gaze to my mouth, let it linger there a long moment before saying, "Rip through it, most likely."

I hadn't expected such an honest answer.

A dimple appeared. "Don't worry, Dutch. I've had worse."

And he had. Much worse. But when would it be too much? Why should he have to endure any amount of pain for me? For a predicament I'd gotten myself into?

He raised his head. "Here it comes."

And come it did. Time bounced back like a freight train crashing through the bar. The sound ricocheted through me. The force, like a hurricane, knocked the air from my lungs, left me gasping.

Reyes held me to him as though we were caught in the center of a tornado until we joined the same time-space continuum as the rest of the world. Then he set me at arm's length, keeping hold of my shoulders until I gained my balance. Screams and shouts echoed through the room as people ducked and scrambled out of the way. Several patrons dived behind the bar while a couple of the off-duty cops tackled Tidwell and Cookie to the ground. Tidwell would not be a happy camper. Cookie would enjoy every moment of being groped by a hot cop. She was such a hussy.

When another cop had similar plans for me, Reyes jerked me out of the way, and in one smooth movement, he used the cop's own momentum to slam him to the ground. He did it so fast, no one could've said what really happened should it come to that, and since the cop was in plainclothes, I doubted they could charge Reyes with assaulting an officer of the law. But I'd recognized this particular cop, as I did most of the cops who came into the bar. This one was a semi-friend.

I grabbed his arms and said, "Reyes, wait," before he did any real damage. He stilled but kept Taft pinned to the ground with an arm twisted behind him and a knee on his back.

Taft groaned and, having no idea who had taken him down, tried to break the hold. With effortless ease, Reyes stayed as solid as a boulder as Taft squirmed beneath him. I kneeled next to the off-duty officer. He'd probably lunged in my direction more for my protection than anything since we were kind of, sort of, friends.

"It's okay," I said to Reyes. "He's a cop."

Reyes's expression was so unimpressed, I had to glare at him to get him to loosen his hold. Of course, I knew he wouldn't care that Taft was a cop, but I wanted Taft to believe that had Reyes known, he wouldn't have dropped him like a sack of potatoes on Sunday morning.

"You okay, Taft?" I asked, nudging Reyes with my shoulder. Finally, and with deliberate slowness, he let Taft up.

Once he gained a little wiggle room, Taft pushed Reyes off him and scrambled to his feet. Reyes straightened as well, his full mouth straining to keep a grin in check when Taft stepped nose to nose with him.

I jumped to get between them, but a scuffle caught my attention. Cookie kept still as one cop held her bent over a table, hands behind her back, but Tidwell was fighting the officers and continued to do so even after they identified themselves. His face glistened red with anger. Still, the officers took him down without too much fuss. Clearly Tidwell had an intellect rivaled only by kitchen utensils. And he had a temper to boot. He knew Mrs. Tidwell put us up to this. What would he do to her? Would she be in danger?

The room began to calm and suddenly all eyes focused on me. Like this was my fault. I raised my hands to assure everyone all was quiet on the Southwestern front.

"Don't worry," I said, patting the air to console it. "Cookie is an excellent shot. None of you were ever in any danger."

If there was a special place in hell for liars, I was so going there.

I looked back to make sure Reyes and Taft hadn't started World War III only to find my uncle Bob strolling in, his shirt collar unbuttoned, his tie loosened, and his brows drawn in mild curiosity.

He started toward me, then spotted the cop who had Cookie pinned to the table, the same cop who'd called her sweet cheeks earlier. "Christ in a Crock-Pot, Smith, let her up."

He did, brushing Cookie off apologetically, but said in his own defense, "She had a pistol. It discharged when that man lunged for her."

"Only because he attacked me," Cookie said, pointing at Tidwell, who was still struggling under the weight of one of the cops. "Jerk."

Uncle Bob was more than alarmed. Anger rushed through him like wildfire, and I could only imagine what he would think when he found out I'd used Cookie on a job that almost got her shot. Maybe I'd leave that part out.

"Was anyone hurt?" Uncle Bob asked, and everyone glanced around. A couple patrons patted themselves down to double-check. Then everyone shook their heads in unison.

Taft spoke behind me. "I'm going to let this little incident slide for now," he said to Reyes. Then he stepped even closer to him. "But if I ever—"

"Taft!"

Since we were a tad on edge as it was, every person in the bar jumped when Uncle Bob yelled at his colleague. Including Taft. Uncle Bob rounded a fallen chair and took Taft's arm to pull him away from Reyes. He didn't know what Reyes was exactly, but he knew enough to steer clear of him unless left with no other choice.

"Why don't you start asking around, see if we have any solid witnesses to the events?"

Reluctantly, Taft nodded and backed off to question a group huddled in a corner booth. I was glad. They looked terrified.

Sirens sounded outside and more cops entered the scene one by one. I scrubbed my face with my fingertips. My dad was going to kill me. This was so bad for business.

"And you!" Uncle Bob—or Ubie as he was known on certain X-rated forums thanks to yours truly—pointed directly at me, and said, "Don't even think about leaving."

I pointed to myself. "Me? I didn't do anything. Cookie started it."

Cookie gasped.

Ubie shot me a stormy glare.

Taft glanced over his shoulder and shook his head.

And Reyes leaned back against the bar, crossed his arms over his chest, and studied me from beneath those same ridiculously long lashes. Men and their freaking lashes. It was so unfair. Like the exorbitant cost of designer shoes. Or world hunger.

I stepped over to him, sulking like a kid who'd been sent to stand in the corner, and leaned against the bar, too. I wasn't about to try to get near Cookie. She was surrounded by veteran cops on an adrenaline rush. My face would eat floor before I could say, "Hey, Cook. So how'd it go?"

I pocketed the receiver I'd been wearing and noticed that Duff had disappeared, not that I could blame him. Still, it wasn't as though a stray bullet could hurt him. As nonchalantly as I could, I took Reyes's right hand and opened it. He let me, keeping a vigilant eye on my every move. An abrasion that was part incision and part blistering burn streaked across his palm and fingers. The bullet had kept going after time bounced back. It had to. That kind of energy didn't diffuse just because I'd wanted it to, and though Reyes healed fast, he wasn't bulletproof.

"Reyes, I'm so sorry," I said, ducking to hide my face. I'd caused him so much pain recently, not the least of which was a .50-caliber bullet ripping through his chest. A .50-caliber bullet that had been meant for me.

"How sorry?" he asked, his voice suddenly permeated with a husky awareness.

I dropped his hand and cleared my throat. Despite everything, Reyes was still my number one suspect in an arson case. I had to remember that. "What are you doing here anyway?"

He tucked his hand back over his chest. "I was just passing by. Saw the commotion. Figured you were involved."

"Hey, I was handling it."

"I can see that. You want me to leave?"

I did, but only because his presence caused every molecule in my body to quake. And I didn't, but only because having him near was like basking in the glow of the sun. A really sexy sun that wasn't so much yellow as a dark, sultry bronze. Still, I had work to do. And a lot of explaining.

"You can't leave now. There's an active investigation going on, in case you've forgotten."

"That's not what I asked."

I looked on as Uncle Bob helped Cookie to a chair. "Yes."

"Then say it."

I raised my chin, striking a defiant pose for him. "I want you to leave."

A slow grin spread across his face. He eased closer and bent toward me to whisper in my ear, "You have to mean it."

I closed my eyes, tried to stop the flood of lust that rushed between my legs. Our relationship was a lot like underwear in a dryer without a static control sheet. One minute we were floating through life, buoyant and carefree. The next we were attached at the crotch.

Rattled, I said, "You still owe me a million dollars." I'd presented him with a bill for proving his innocence and getting him freed from prison. He had yet to pay. Couldn't imagine why.

"Yeah, I was hoping we could work that out."

"The interest alone is going to kill you."

"What do you charge?"

"Three hundred eighty-seven percent."

"Is that ethical?"

"It's as ethical as my dating the son of Satan."

I took inventory of the patrons still in the bar, a little surprised to find that Jessica had stuck around. That was not her strong suit. Then I realized why. Her eyes were glued to Reyes's crotch. Her friends were only slightly less obvious as they took in every sultry shadow that dipped between Reyes's muscles, their expressions a cross between appreciation and raw lust.

Ruffled despite my every desire not to be, I said, "You have a fan club. I had no idea."

Completely uninterested, he ignored me and asked, "We're dating?"

I glanced at him in surprise. I hadn't meant it that way. He'd given me a key to his apartment when he moved in next door. I had yet to use it. I wasn't sure if I was scared or just plain terrified. He was still my number one suspect in an arson case. I had to remember that. And he was still healing from the gunshot he'd received thanks to me. And he'd grown up with a monster so abusive, it defied explanation. And he'd gone to prison for killing him—an act he didn't commit since Earl Walker was still alive—because I had failed him. My first vision of Reyes Farrow was of him being beaten senseless by Walker when he was nineteen. I had failed to call the police—at his behest, yes, but I should have done it anyway. At the very least, I should have told my dad, who was a cop at the time. How much would Reyes's life have changed? How much of the suffering would have been avoided?

Like me, Reyes could feel emotion. He could feel anger rolling off people. Fear. Doubt. And sympathy. He most certainly felt mine. I realized my mistake when his expression hardened.

He brushed a thumb across his mouth in annoyance. "Surely that's not pity in your eyes."

I heard someone call out before I could answer.

"You!" a male voice said.

We looked to our right and saw a uniformed officer motioning Reyes over, Taft standing beside him.

Reyes sighed and I felt his annoyance dwindle. He leaned close again, his mouth at my ear, his breath warm across my cheek. "Use the key, Dutch."

The thought of using the key, the key he'd given me to his apartment, caused an electrical charge to race up my spine.

He felt that, too. With a soft growl emanating from his throat, he turned and walked over to the officer. But I felt something, too. The heat of Jessica's glare as jealousy consumed her. Normally I would giggle like an insane schoolgirl in such a situation, but I couldn't quite manage it. That growl washed over me like cool water, caused another tingling in my abdomen, and I had to remind myself to fill my lungs with air before I turned blue. Blue was not my best color.

When a spot beside Cookie opened up, I hurried to get to her. In all the chaos, she'd somehow been elbowed in the face. I tried to feel bad, but I was still a little shell-shocked. Reyes did that to me. Still, Cookie would be sporting a shiner for days. I'd never hear the end of it.

"Are you okay, Cook?" I asked her as Uncle Bob sat in a chair beside her.

She was shaken and flustered. I put my hand on hers.

"How about I get you some water," Uncle Bob said to her, "and you two can tell me what happened."

"Thank you, Bob," she said, her voice quivering. When he left, she patted her cheeks and neck with a napkin, then asked me, "So, how was your day?"

There she was, the Cook I knew and loved. Taking the good with the bad and turning it into an opportunity to grow and, quite often, make fun of innocent bystanders.

I decided to play along. I dropped my head into my hands. "My day sucked. I failed again."

"This was not your fault," she said, rubbing my shoulder absently.

I bounced up. "Oh, no, not this. This was totally your fault. A gun?" I asked, astounded. "No, really. A gun?"

She gaped at me a solid minute before conceding with a long sigh. "It seemed like a good idea at the time."

"Three Mile Island, Cook."

"I know. Geez. I can't believe I didn't kill anyone."

If she only knew.

She waved it off, then asked, "So, what did you fail at?"

"I failed my cardiology test," I said, watching Reyes's interrogation, his every move pure perfection, his every feature stunning. Like he'd been Photoshopped. I suddenly felt gypped.

"Cardiology test?" Cookie asked. It was fun to watch her, with her face kind of lopsided from the swelling. "You went to see a cardiologist?"

"Yes. And he refuses to do open-heart surgery based on my insistence that something is wrong with it. According to Dr. Quack Head, the tests have all come back normal. I just think he needs a bird's-eye view, you know? A hands-on kind of thing."

She pressed her mouth together. "Damn it, Charley, you scared me. And there is nothing wrong with your heart."

"Yes, there is. It hurts." I poked myself in the chest several times for dramatic effect. "Having Reyes so near is painful. I think it has apoplexy."

"Do you even know what that means?"

"No, but it sounds serious. Like Ebola. Or hives."

"You're going to wish you had Ebola after I'm done with you."

"What? What the hell did I do?"

"I don't know, but all of this has to be your fault."

"You just said it wasn't."

"I was lying."

"You're the one who brought a gun to the party." When she refused to address that little elephant in the room, I took out my phone and dialed an old friend of the family's.

"Who are you calling?"

"Noni. You're taking his class. The next one starts tomorrow morning at eight o'clock, and you're going to be in it."

"What?" She grabbed for my phone, but I dodged her attempts like Mr. Miyagi dodges the punches of his enemy. "I don't need a concealed weapons permit."

"It's also about gun safety, Cook," I said, holding up an index finger to put her in pause. "And if you carry a gun in a concealed way, you need a permit. The class is eight hours tomorrow and seven on Sunday."

She lunged for the phone again. She missed. "That's my entire weekend. I had plans."

"A *Vampire Diaries* marathon is not plans."

She looked at me like I'd lost my mind. "Have you even seen the Salvatore brothers? Holy mother of ginger snaps. And I was going to make a pan of enchiladas for us to eat next week, too."

Gah! She knew that would hurt. I sighed in defeat. "Then clearly we are both making a huge sacrifice here."

Noni picked up, saying something grumpy about the time. It was weird. I charged forward, explained the situation to him as Cookie watched Uncle Bob's every move. Or, well, drank in Uncle Bob's every move. He was consulting with one of the off-duty officers, and Cookie seemed to find his actions mesmerizing.

That wasn't disturbing at all.

"Thanks, Noni."

"I hate you right now," he said.

"For gravy's sake, it's nine thirty. Who's asleep by nine thirty on a Friday night?" I hung up and said to Cook, "You're in."

"Fantastic." She said it, but I didn't think she meant it.

"Right? Okay, so he'll ask you a lot of questions to determine your mental stability. How good are you at lying?"

She scowled at me. "As good as you are at staying out of trouble."

"Crap. Well, just do the best you can. He'll also give you a handbook on all the gun laws in New Mexico. And Noni is—" How did I put this without making him sound like a fanatic? "Noni's enthusiastic. He takes his gun with him into the shower, but he's a good guy and you'll learn a lot. More important"—I took her shoulders to get her full attention; then I shook her a little for good measure—"everyone will be a lot safer."

She nodded, then shook her head, changing her mind mid-shake. "I don't know, Charley. I don't think I can shoot a gun in front of other people."

"What were you planning on doing with it tonight? Seeing if Tidwell was interested in buying one?"

"No, I just thought that showing it would get him to calm down."

"And how'd that work out?"

"Charley," she said, her voice sharp with warning.

"Okay, okay. But for future reference, never pull a gun unless you're willing to use it. Anyway, firing your sidearm is only a small part of the class. By the time you get to that point, you'll be comfortable enough with everyone to take off your bra. Don't. Trust me. It never ends well. Before that, he'll go over specific laws and give you real-life scenarios, self-defense situations to mull over. You know, everyday things." I scooted closer to her. "Cook, he's going to ask you if you're ready to kill someone."

"What? Like right now?"

"No, he'll probably give you a scenario and ask if you'd be willing to pull the trigger."

"Wonderful." Again, she said it but I questioned her sincerity.

"And then he'll teach you different techniques. How to enter a room when there's a terrorist raiding your refrigerator. What to do if someone breaks down your front door with an axe. It's all about staying alive and defending yourself and your family." When she only stared off into space, I added, "You'll do fine, Cook."

Oh yeah, that special place in hell was looking more and more likely by the minute.

Chapter Three

667: The neighbor of the beast.
—BUMPER STICKER

The moment I could feel my knees again, I decided to check on my old friend-ish type person-slash-associate of sorts, Garrett Swopes. He was always good for a laugh. On the way over, I pulled up one of my new, possibly pirated GPS apps my friend Pari told me about. So even though I could find his house with my eyes closed—a feat I was fairly certain I'd done one night during a bout with insomnia—I brought up the app on my phone, picked a voice, and plugged it into the auxiliary outlet. Heavy breathing, as though someone were on life support and breathing through a machine, flooded the car. It might not have been so creepy if it weren't dark out. I punched in my destination, i.e., Garrett's address, then hit Route.

"In three hundred feet, turn right," Darth Vader said. *The* Darth Vader. I felt like we were friends now. Like I could tell him anything.

"Thanks, Mr. Vader. Can I call you Darth?"

He didn't answer, but that was okay. As the non-favored child of a stepmother, I was used to being ignored. I headed that way.

The breathing sounded again. "In fifty feet, turn right."

"Okay, well, thanks again."

We did that the whole way. Him telling me what to do. Me thanking him. I suddenly felt dirty, like he was using me for his own amusement. This relationship seemed very one-sided.

When I was almost there, Darth spoke again. "In two hundred feet, your destination will be on the right. Your journey to the dark side is almost complete."

Why did I get the feeling he was related to Reyes?

"Your destination is on the right."

"Yeah, okay, got it. Had it before."

"Your journey to the—"

I exited the app before he could finish his sentence. It seemed wrong to cut him off prematurely, but I could take only so much heavy breathing before inappropriate thoughts involving whipped cream and a Ping-Pong paddle crept into my mind. And I was going to see Garrett Swopes. While not anywhere near the top of my to-do list, the guy's abs were to die for.

I hopped out of Misery, my beloved cherry red Jeep Wrangler, and strolled to his front door. He lived in a small bungalow-style house with lots of lush vegetation, which was kind of unusual for Albuquerque. We were more of a lush-free kind of state. Sparse was more our style. I knocked before realizing his truck wasn't out front like usual.

The door opened anyway and an exhausted-looking bond enforcement agent in dire need of a shave stood before me. Garrett Swopes was a lot like a hot gay friend only he wasn't gay, which was too bad because then I could tell him how hot he was without him getting the wrong idea. He had smooth mocha-colored skin that made the silvery gray of his eyes even more arresting. And again he had abs to die for as evidenced *not* by his lack of a shirt but his negligence in buttoning said shirt.

I drank in a hearty swig of Garrett-abs before addressing him. "How's it hanging, Swopes?" I asked, ducking past him.

He rubbed his eyes with a thumb and index finger. "Charles, it's late."

"It's always late when I come over. At least you weren't in bed this time."

After a lengthy sigh to let me know just how annoyed he was pretending to be, he closed the door and headed for the kitchen. For some reason, every time I came over, he felt the need to drink. It was weird. "To what do I owe the pleasure?" he asked.

"To my pleasure, duh. I get all kinds of joy annoying the ever-loving crap out of you."

"I meant, what's going on? Is the world ending? Is a mass murderer stalking you? Are you trying to stay up for days at a time to avoid alone time with your evil neighbor?"

Damn. He knew Reyes had moved in next door to me. I'd wanted to be the one to tell him, to break it to him gently. My relationship with Reyes was complicated and, at one point, involved me staying up for days to avoid summoning the guy into my dreams. Unfortunately, Garrett had become a victim of my circumstance. He'd helped me through a rough time and I should've been the one to tell him about Reyes's new pad.

"Who told you I had a new neighbor?" I heard him twist the top off a beer, the snap and hiss strangely comforting.

"I've been keeping tabs," he said.

That probably wasn't good.

"So what's going on?" he asked again.

"What? I need a reason to come see my oldest and dearest friend?"

When he walked back to the living room and handed me a Corona, he kind of glared at me before sinking into a recliner.

"Okay, well, my old-ish and most annoying friend anyway." I sat on the sofa opposite him, taking note of the chaos strewn about the room. Just like the last time I'd come to visit, the coffee table was littered with books and notes on the spiritual realm, heaven and hell, demons and angels. "I've been worried about you."

"Why?" he asked after taking a swig.

"I don't know. You just seem different now. Distant. Like you have PTSD."

I knew from where I spoke. My TSD got P'd when I was tortured by a monster named Earl. While attempting to execute my rescue, Swopes was shot and died as a result. The doctors were able to resuscitate him, but he'd recently told me that while in the jaws of death, he went to hell. That worried me. What worried me even more was the fact that, while in the fiery pit of eternal damnation, he had a heart-to-heart with Reyes's dad, an experience that had to be traumatic on all kinds of levels.

"I'm fine," he said, as he had the last seventeen times I'd asked. "I'm just working on something."

I scanned the area. "I can see that. Anything you want to share?"

"No."

He'd said it with such determination, no way was I going to argue. "Roger that," I said instead. Wait. Who was I kidding? "But you know you can tell me anything, right?"

He eased his head back, closed his eyes, and stretched out his legs in front of him, his foot sending a stack of notes sprawling across the floor. He didn't care. "Stop fishing, Charles. It's not going to happen."

"Roger that." I took a sip of beer, then added, "But this

stuff looks really interesting. I could help with the re search."

"I'm good," he said, his voice edged with a hard warning.

"Roger that." I picked up a page of scribbled notes and tried to decipher his handwriting. "Who is Dr. A. von Holstein? And is he related, by chance, to a race of cows?"

He bolted upright and snatched the page out of my hand. Oh, yeah, that wouldn't stimulate my curiosity. "I said no, Charles, and I meant it."

I sat back. "Geez, roger that."

After placing the paper back in the exact same spot from which I'd freed it, he leveled an exasperated stare on me. "Why do you keep saying 'roger that'? You don't get to say 'roger that' unless you've been in the military."

I regarded my beer, pausing a long moment for dramatic effect, then said in a quiet voice, "Roger that."

The sigh of annoyance he released was long and meaningful. I won. My journey to the dark side really was complete. And I owed it all to my bestie Darth. Where would I be without him? Without our friendship? I shuddered to think.

He polished off his beer, leaned forward to steal mine, then sat back to nurse it at a slower pace. "Who sent me there?" he asked, his voice suddenly distant, and I knew exactly what he meant. Who sent him to hell? "Why did I go?"

I folded my legs until they resembled a pretzel and settled back against the sofa cushions. "You saw me right after you died, right?"

He nodded, eyes closed, beer perched on a thigh while he rubbed the bottle absentmindedly with long fingers.

"And then your dad met you on your way to heaven to tell you that you had been brought back to life. That you had to go back."

His fingers stopped but he didn't answer.

"But before you went back into your body, you went to hell?"

That was pretty much all I knew about Garrett's vacay down under. He'd refused to go into detail when he told me and had shut me out every time I'd tried to talk about it since. While I was hungry to know every minute detail of what transpired, he was determined to let me starve.

"You said you were sent for a reason," I continued. "To understand. To learn more about Reyes. How he was raised. What he had done."

Without opening his eyes, he said, "And you only made excuses for him."

He was angry with me, but I'd surprised him at the time by knowing before he told me that Reyes was the son of Satan. By being okay with it, in his eyes.

"Like I said, he wasn't raised in the most nurturing environment."

"So you insist. And you take up for him every chance you get. A general from hell. A skilled assassin who rose through the ranks of a demon army, who lived for the taste of his kills, who became the most feared creation in their history." Then he did open his eyes and pinned me with a lethal stare. "An abomination who was sent to this plane for one reason and one reason only. You."

This would get us nowhere. I unfolded my legs and instead folded my arms across my chest in a defensive maneuver. "I told you, he was sent for a portal. Any portal. Not me specifically."

The way I understood it, Satan had sent Reyes to this plane to nab a grim reaper. Reyes was Satan's way out of hell and he supposedly wanted a way into heaven. With the two of us, he would have a direct door into the very realm he'd been kicked out of. But Garrett was dead set on the idea that Reyes had been sent for me specifically, which was ludicrous. There was no way for Satan to know that out of all the beings like me in the universe, I would be chosen to serve on this plane as the portal. I would be sent here. From what Reyes told me, there was an entire race of us, a fact I had yet to verify or explore. But he said I had a celestial family out there. I found the concept both intriguing and comforting.

"And I told you you're wrong," he said.

I would never win this. "Fine. So you sat around a fiery pit and swapped war stories with Reyes's dad." I picked lint off my shirt and asked, "What did he tell you?"

"It's not important."

I gaped at him. "You've got to be kidding me."

"No, I'm not. What's important is why I was sent there. I mean, who sent me? Who has that kind of power?"

He had a good point. Solid. Sharp. Pointy.

"One thing I did figure out while I was there is that they are all liars and manipulators. You can't believe anything they have to say."

"Is that a comment about Reyes?"

"If the fiery pit fits." When I got up to leave, he added, "I'm working on something. I promise, Charles, the minute I know more, you'll know more."

He groaned and got up from his seat to follow me to the door.

I opened it, then turned back to him. "Swopes, I know you don't like to talk about it, but you can't just go to hell and come away unscathed."

A humorless grin spread across his face. "Sure you can. What would you do if you were sent to hell?"

I stepped out. "Stop, drop, and roll? What I mean is, did anything bad happen? Did they, I don't know, hurt you?" I leveled a probing stare on him. "Did they torture you?"

His grin morphed into something that resembled pity. "No, Charles. They didn't torture me."

He closed the door before I could say anything else. I stood there a solid minute, stunned, unsure of what to do, what to say, how to help. The only thing I knew for certain was that he'd just lied to me.

Not really in the mood to deal with Darth, I decided to try a new voice on the way home. I plugged in my phone, brought up the app, then listened as KITT powered up all systems. I was a huge *Knight Rider* fan growing up, dreaming of a car that could talk to me, one that could warn me of impending doom like terrorists ahead or cops running radar. And when Misery transformed into a supercar with a turbo engine and an array of onboard weapons, I was sold. At last. I could finally nuke people who refused to get out of the left-hand lane. Life was good.

But Garrett had been tortured. In hell, no less. The concept was so foreign, even with everything that I knew, I couldn't quite wrap my mind around what he could have gone through.

What would they have done to him? I doubted that Chinese water torture came into play. But he was incorporeal at the time. Could the soul be tortured? Then I thought about all the people who supposedly went to hell, who supposedly spent an eternity burning in agony. Was that real? Could the soul burn? Could it be cut? Torn? Brutalized?

My mind reeled with all the potentialities bouncing through it. It was hard to imagine hell as a physical place, a real place, even though Reyes was created there. Grew up there. It was just so foreign. So otherworldly. So creepy.

KITT broke into my thoughts, suggesting we fire a missile before telling me to take the next exit. Alas, I did not bond with KITT as much as I'd hoped. His music kind of sucked and his weapons were useless against the power of ignorance. I'd voted him off the island before I even pulled into my parking space.

"What do you think?" I asked the elderly dead guy in my passenger seat. I'd picked him up somewhere around Lomas and Wyoming. He seemed nice. He was also as naked as the day he was born. Trying not to look at his penis was proving harder than I thought it would be. "Is it breezy in here to you?"

He didn't answer, so I left him to his thoughts and took the stairs up to my third-floor apartment, where I found a sticky note on my door. I'd been getting them a lot lately. Ever since my number one suspect in an arson case took the apartment I'd coveted for years and moved in down the hall. Two things led me to suspect the son of evil incarnate had taken up flamethrowing. First, he'd smelled like smoke a few nights ago, and I later learned that a condemned apartment building had been torched that very night. Second, the first time I saw Reyes Farrow was in that very apartment building being beaten by the monster who raised him, Earl Walker. After a little more digging, I discovered that at some point in his life, Reyes had lived at every address the arsonist was hitting. The realization caused a ribbon of dread to knot in my stomach, to twist it into a mass of raw nerve endings that pulsed with empathy and regret for what Reyes had gone through.

I looked down at the note. This one read: *What are you afraid of?*

What was I afraid of? The fact that he may be the very person burning down buildings left and right? The fact that I might have to have him arrested and sent back to the same prison in which he'd spent ten years doing time for a crime he didn't commit? The fact that arsonists have a unique psyche that leans toward either extreme arrogance or extreme sexual deviance? Reyes had neither as far as I knew, but did the idea of finding out otherwise scare me?

"Hey, Ch-Charley."

I looked over my shoulder and saw my new dead friend Duff standing beside me, shifting his weight from side to side with nervous energy. "Hey, you," I said, unlocking my door.

"I—I thought m-maybe you might need someone to talk to after wh-what happened."

And there went my heart. Damn it. Time to see the cardiologist again.

"I'm okay, but thank you."

"Oh, g-good. I'm glad."

Part of my job was to help people cross over when they were ready. Sometimes that included the role of shoulder. As in to cry on. I held the door ajar and offered him my full attention. "Do you know what I am, Duff?"

He stuffed his hands in his pockets and kicked a non-existent rock at his feet. "Y-yes."

"You know you can cross through me when you're ready."

"Y-yes, I know. I just thought m-maybe I'd keep an eye on you for a while."

I straightened. "An eye on me?"

He did it fast, but I saw it anyway. He glanced toward Reyes's apartment. "Y-yes, you know, in case y-you need help or s-something."

"Duff, I appreciate the offer, but—"

"I m-moved in down the hall if you n-need anything."

I followed his gesture toward Mrs. Allen's apartment. "Oh, okay. So, you're living with Mrs. Allen?"

A shy smile lifted the corners of his mouth. "Y-yes. She has a dog."

I put a hand on his frigid shoulder. "That's not a dog,

Duff. That's a demon named PP. I'm about ninety percent certain he's possessed."

Duff chuckled. "At least he doesn't have any teeth."

"Just be careful. I think he has one fang left and he knows how to use it."

After another quick glance toward the dragon's lair, Duff lifted a hand. "S-see you later, then."

"Sounds like a plan," I said with a wink. "Just remember, steer clear of that fang."

The smile that commandeered his features was contagious and charming. He took another step back, gave me a shy wave, then disappeared.

I started inside my apartment, then rethought that decision. If anyone would know what Garrett went through, what he had to endure in the fiery pits, Reyes would. He'd grown up in hell, after all, and then suffered a whole new version of the word here on Earth at the hands of Earl Walker, who had ended up with Reyes through nefarious means when he was very young, abused him mercilessly, then framed Reyes for his murder and had him sent to prison despite the fact that Earl Walker was alive and kicking.

Well, not kicking anymore, thanks to an expertly placed blade that Reyes himself had swung, but alive anyway.

I walked to his apartment and knocked. The fact that my hand shook a bit surprised me. It wasn't like I'd never been in his company. Lots. And in various states of undress. But I'd never been to his humble abode, to his lair. He'd never had the home court advantage, and the realization that the minute I stepped through that threshold we would be on his turf gave me butterflies. That and the fact that I owed him. Again. He had saved my life tonight. Not from Tidwell but from Cookie. That woman was a menace.

He cracked the door open just enough to give me a

partial view of him, and the butterflies swarmed. Especially when he cocked a brow in question.

"I thought we could talk," I said, keeping my exterior calm. Unassuming.

For a moment I thought he was going to brush me off, tell me he was tired or he had work to do, he hesitated so long. But he turned and busied himself while I tried to peek over his shoulders into his apartment. Then he faced me again. A wicked grin crinkled one corner of his mouth as he secured another sticky note on the door before shutting it in my face.

I blinked, then read the note.

Use the key.

Oh, for the love of gravy. I marched back to my apartment, grabbed the key from my bag, then went back and used the darned thing, trying to figure out what the big deal was. Though I had to admit, I liked having it. I liked having access to his place, his life. I'd been denied him so long, it was nice to have one small piece of him, one tiny token of confirmation. It slid easily into the lock. Turned like it had been recently oiled. And naturally my mind came up with all kinds of situations for which that could've been a metaphor. I was such a ho.

I walked through the apartment and spotted one Mr. Reyes Farrow busying himself in his kitchen. In a domestic capacity. The image was jarring and endearing at once and I had to tear my gaze away before he noticed. I couldn't let him get too used to the idea that I adored him. Best to keep him guessing.

I had yet to see his new digs. It wasn't at all what I'd expected. Of course, I really didn't know what to expect. Perhaps something in cool tones with lots of grays and chrome. What I got was warmth, very much like the man himself. It was nice. Lots of textures with earthy colors and a freestanding black marble fireplace separating two rooms. In the next was a pool table with dark wood and a cream-colored top. It was stunning. His apartment had a homey feel I hadn't expected.

I looked up as he walked back in, his swagger drawing attention to his hips, up his slim stomach to a set of wide shoulders that would make any man proud. I knew they made me proud. He wore a white button-down hanging loose over jeans. The sleeves were rolled up, allowing his tan forearms to show from underneath. That led me to his hands. He had the most incredible hands, and his arms were like steel. I should know. I'd been held captive in them before. It was a place I longed to return.

He handed me a glass of red wine. Another nicety I hadn't expected.

"A toast?" he asked, raising his glass.

"What are we toasting?" I clinked our glasses together, then brought mine to my lips.

"The fact that a girl I know named Charley survived another day."

He didn't call me Charley often, and it somehow seemed more intimate than when anyone else said it. It felt nice, the syllables falling from his mouth like honey.

When I didn't drink, he called me by the nickname he'd given me. "Dutch?" And that felt even more intimate. His voice, rich and velvety and smooth like butterscotch, thrummed a string somewhere deep inside me. "Are you okay?"

I nodded and finally took a sip. A fruity heat filled my mouth, warming my throat as I swallowed the crisp liquid. "I'm fine," I said. "Great, actually, thanks to you. Again."

One corner of his mouth tilted, the gesture charming. "I love what you've done with the place."

He smiled and looked at his own masterpiece.

"I'm still not sure how you convinced the owners to shell out the money," I said.

"I can be very persuasive when I want to be, and besides, they didn't shell out anything. I paid for the remodel."

"Oh. I didn't realize."

"I hear that the owner's a little crazy anyway. She's always getting into sticky situations. I was glad to help her out with this remodel."

I had never met the owner of the apartment building itself. The only contact I had was with the landlord, Mr. Zamora, and a light pang of jealousy spiked within me with his intimate use of the word *she*. It galled me. I was not a jealous person. Had never been jealous of anyone for any reason, but in walks Reyes Farrow and suddenly I'm that chick from *Fatal Attraction*. Next thing you know, I'll be boiling rabbits.

"Why haven't you come to see me?" he asked as he stepped to an overstuffed sofa and sank into it, stretching his legs out in front of him. Like it was something he did every day, had done his entire life. I wondered what prison had been like for him. With no sofas and no marble fireplaces and no refrigerators he could raid whenever he wanted to. And I wondered what all of that would have been like, that kind of restriction, that kind of punishment, for someone who didn't even commit the crime for which he had been sentenced. Would the lack of freedom be all the more difficult?

I shook out of my thoughts and followed him. "I don't know. The last time I saw you, you'd been shot with a fifty-caliber bullet because of me. I wasn't sure you'd want to see me."

"So all the notes on your door didn't clue you in?"

I sat on a chair that catty-cornered his seat. "Fine, but you'd still been shot."

"And?"

"And . . ." I wasn't sure how much to tell him about how I felt. About what had happened and how I was choosing not to deal with it in classic Charley fashion. I pressed my lips together, then said, "I killed a man, Reyes. A man is dead because of me."

"A man who was trying to kill you."

And that was the truth of it. A man I'd turned in as a bank robber had been hell-bent on making sure I didn't testify against him. Unfortunately, he'd been in training to be a sniper in the marines when he received a dishonorable discharge. The guy was a loon with a hair-trigger temper, so it was probably only a matter of time, but he'd learned enough to try to take me out from a rooftop a hundred yards away. His plan would have been successful had Reyes not stepped in front of me, let it rip through him before turning to catch it when it continued toward me on its path of destruction. He had literally taken a bullet for me. A huge one that should have ripped him apart.

It was probably the blood spreading across Reyes's torso that caused the spark of rage to burst within me. In an instant, I was in front of the guy. I reached inside his chest and stopped his heart before I took the time to consider the consequences. Then I looked back at myself, still standing beside Reyes, an expression of shock still evident on my features.

I had left my body. I had killed a man and I'd done it incorporeally, a fact I still had a difficult time wrapping my head around. Accepting as truth.

"I'm just not sure how much that should make a difference," I said. "I still feel guilty. I took his life. He could have reformed, you know? He could have been the next van Gogh or the next Shakespeare, but now we'll never know because I didn't give him the chance."

"Do you really think that a man like that would have been the next Shakespeare?"

"Probably not, but again, we'll never know. I'm not a judge and jury. I don't have the right to take lives." I studied him, then asked, "You've killed in self-defense in the past when you were in prison. How did that make you feel? What did it do to you?"

"It didn't do anything to me. They were coming at me. I fought back. In the end, they were dead and I was not. Don't ever underestimate the fundamental need to survive, Dutch. It drives us all. If we are going to play at being human, then we have a basic human right to defend ourselves, and you did what was necessary."

Play at being human? Who was playing? I was human as far as I was concerned, but it was an odd statement. The fire crackled and I looked over because, no matter how real it looked, it was electric. "It even has sound effects?"

He laughed softly. "They have everything nowadays. I had no idea."

The fact that he'd spent ten years in prison hit me again. And there I was, contemplating sending him back. Could I do it? Even if I were to discover he was the arsonist, could I send him back? *Would* they send him back? How would that work? Would he get a reduced sentence for time served?

"You're very serious tonight. Any particular reason?"

"What were you doing at the bar?" I asked, changing the subject.

"I told you, I was passing by."

"Oh, right. But you weren't following me or anything?"

He ran a fingertip along the top of his glass. It was the sexiest thing I'd ever seen. "Is that what you think? That I follow you around to keep your ass out of trouble?"

"If so, you're not very good at your job."

A huge smile spread across his face. "True enough. So what's eating you? Because, sadly, it's not me."

A sharp thrill spiked inside me with the thought of him doing that very thing, but I was there for a reason. Since I couldn't quite bring myself to ask him if he was burning the city to the ground one dump at a time, I veered toward the subject for which I'd originally sought him out. "What's hell like?"

His fingertip stilled. "What do you mean?"

"Hell," I said with a shrug. "You know, home sweet home. You grew up there. What's it like?"

He sat back and stared into the fire. "It's exactly like all the stories your mom told you when you were a kid."

"My *step*mom didn't tell me stories, so indulge me."

"The summers are hot. Winters are hot. Fall and spring are hot. Not a whole lot of climate change. We did get a scorching breeze every so often, though. It was almost refreshing."

Fine, he wasn't going to answer. I'd move on to more pressing questions. "What would it do to a human who was sent there, then escaped?"

His gaze darted toward me. "Escape is impossible. You know, in case you're planning a trip." Odd thing was, he seemed serious. Like a trip to the underbelly of the supernatural world was within the realm of possible vacation spots.

"I'm not. I thought I might write an article. Or a book. I've always wanted a Pulitzer. Or I could get really lucky and score a Nobel Peace Prize. I'd kill for a Nobel Peace Prize."

He'd gone back to staring into his wine, to running his finger along the rim of his glass. The movement mesmerized me. Without breaking his gaze, he said, "Come here."

The butterflies attacked again. His arm corded and released as his finger tested the edge of the glass. His mouth, full and sensual, parted as he concentrated on the burgundy liquid.

"I should probably go."

What if he were the arsonist? What would I do? On one hand, I had Uncle Bob to consider. He'd done so much for me, was always there for me, but so was Reyes. He could be an ass, but he'd saved my life more times than I could count. Could I really accuse him of arson and turn him over?

Maybe I should just ask him. Maybe he would be honest with me and we could figure out what to do, where to go from here, together. And maybe they would get air-conditioning in hell.

I set my glass on the coffee table and rose to leave. "Thank you for tonight, though. Thank you for everything."

"That sounds ominous," he said without rising. He arched a brow in question. "Planning on never coming back?"

"No, just . . . I don't know. I need to check on a few things." And get the image of him in a prison uniform out of my head. Earl Walker had done a number on him growing up. Torture. Abuse beyond imagining. Was he trying to erase his past? To remove any evidence that it had really happened by burning down the places in which he'd lived? My chest tightened.

I walked to the door and pulled it open. Then Reyes was there. Behind me. He didn't just close the door. He slammed it, the handle jerking out of my hand. Then he pressed in to me.

"What are you doing?" he asked, and he sounded hurt. Confused.

I laid my head against the door. "I'm just going to check on a few things. I have some research to do for a case."

"Why is every breath you release filled with pity? Why

in damnation would you feel sorry for me when you know what I am? What I've done?"

Of course he would be able to feel my compassion. My sympathy. I turned to face him even though he gave me no margin. His arms were braced on the door above my head. His crystalline gaze hard. But just as he felt my compassion, I felt the cut it left, the wound.

"I don't feel sorry for you," I said.

He scoffed and pushed off the door to head back to his kitchen. "And once again she lies."

Regret consumed me. I didn't want to fight with him. "I'm not so much lying as trying to keep the peace."

"Then you should probably walk away."

Chapter Four

I'm a virgin.
But this is an old shirt.
——T-SHIRT

I glanced over at a message board he had on the wall. It had dark cork on it and silver pushpins, but only one note had been tacked onto it. I walked closer and recognized the handwriting. It was the bill I'd presented him a couple of weeks ago. The one I'd written on a Macho Taco receipt. The one that stated one Mr. Reyes Farrow owed Davidson Investigations a cool million. With interest. He'd kept it. That ridiculous bill.

And a new realization dawned. We were fighting. Well, we always fought, but we were fighting like real couples did. In an apartment with him flesh and blood and me flesh and blood and him so adorably sexy, he could melt the polar ice caps.

We were almost kind of sort of like a real couple. And he'd kept my bill.

The noise level rose in the kitchen as Reyes banged dishes. Slammed doors. Quite possibly threw a pan. It was enough to make my heart burst with joy. Walk away from him now? I would rather swim through broken glass.

He stopped what he was doing and though I couldn't see him from my vantage point, he called out, "What?"

Could he feel my abrupt change of emotion? Did I give a crap? Not so much.

Whatever tomorrow brought, tonight he was mine. Sure he might be burning down half of Albuquerque, but he'd targeted condemned buildings and shoddily constructed cubbyholes that were eyesores anyway. Nobody missed the shacks he torched, and the owners were collecting a heap of nice coin from the insurance companies for their piles of rubble.

He was doing Albuquerque a favor.

He was a hero!

Okay, that might have been stretching it a bit, but still . . .

"Double or nothing!" I called out to him.

After a moment, he stepped around a wall, his forehead crinkled in mild interest.

"Double or nothing," I repeated.

He crossed his arms over his chest and leaned against the wall. "I'm listening."

"I'll make you a bet. You can win your money back. Every cent. But if you lose, I get double."

"And what money would that be?"

"The million you owe me."

"Ah." He thought for a minute, then asked, "And just how do I manage to do that?"

"Uh-uh-uh," I said, stepping closer. "You're going to owe me *two* million if you lose. Are you sure you don't want to think about it? Perhaps put it on the back burner, let it simmer?"

His gaze took a leisurely tour of my body, pausing on my girls, Danger and Will Robinson, before continuing. "I'm pretty sure I'm up for whatever you throw at me."

"It's your funeral, buddy." I looked around his apartment and found just the thing. After retrieving a tieback off his curtains, I walked back to him and explained the rules. "Okay, you have to trust me. Stand here and put your hands behind your back."

He pushed off the wall and walked over to me, his expression wary but intrigued. "Is this going to hurt?"

"Only your bank account."

He did as instructed, putting his hands behind his back.

"Do you trust me?" I asked.

"As far as I can throw you."

"Good enough." He was strong. He could probably toss me a goodly distance.

I tied his wrists together behind his back, and while I knew his history, knew all the horrible memories that could surface with that one act, I also hoped this would begin to form a bond of trust between us. A thread of peace. He had to know that I would not hurt him. True, I couldn't hurt him physically if I wanted to, but he had to know that sentiment applied to our emotional relationship as well.

He tilted his head. "Seems promising."

"If you can hold this position without moving for—" I looked toward the ceiling and thought about it. "—for five minutes, you win. But if you even so much as flinch," I added, shadowboxing to warm up, "then I win."

"I can't flinch?"

"No flinching. This is a flinchless game of concentration and control. I learned it in the air force."

"You were never in the air force."

"No, but the guys who taught it to me were." I danced around, showing off my mad skill, probably intimidating the holy macaroni out of him. Poor guy. "These are fists of fury. They will get close. You'll feel the air as they swoosh by you. You'll stand in awe of their speed and accuracy. But if you move, you lose. You still up for this? Speak now or forever hold your peace."

The lopsided grin he wore was a ploy, a ruse to get me

to lower my guard. He cleared his throat and nodded. "I'm good."

"Are you sure?" I threw a few punches in quick succession just to let him know what he was up against. He had to be at least a little nervous. "We're talking a lot of money here. No one would blame you if you begged off now."

"Have you ever boxed?"

"Took some lessons. Didn't want to be anybody's bitch in detention." He didn't look convinced, so I explained. "I went to a rough high school. Our mascot was a hit man named Vinnie."

"I thought you went to La Cueva."

"I did. I went to a subdivision of La Cueva called La Bettawatchyaass, Girlfriend. It was a portable building a little south of the main school. We didn't get invited to many events."

He acted as though he were fighting a grin, but I knew better. The only thing he was fighting was the paralyzing fear rushing through his body. He tried not to let it surface, to let it ruin this majestic image I had of him. Too late.

"In case you are unaware of this fact, my nickname in high school was Uppercut Davidson." I threw one in to demonstrate.

"I thought your nickname was Charley."

"Only to those who had nothing to fear from me." I totally needed a tattoo on my neck.

"Has the clock started?" he asked, a dimple appearing on his left cheek.

I let my arms fall to my sides, and gave him one last chance with a challenging quirk of my brow I saw in a movie once. When he held fast, I couldn't help but be just a little impressed.

"You are a worthy opponent, Reyes Farrow." I took a deep breath, raised my fists to first position as it was called in ballet, and said, "Time to pay the piper."

He watched, waiting for me to throw a punch to see if he would flinch. His eyes smiled behind his mask of concentration. I almost felt sorry for him. Especially when I dropped my arms again and gazed at him from beneath hooded lids.

"You are the most beautiful thing I've ever seen."

He sobered and regarded me a bit more warily now.

I stepped to him, leaving only inches between us. Without releasing his gaze, I said, "Ever since the first time I saw you, when Earl was hitting you that awful, unforgettable night, your image has been burned into my mind. You were so unimaginably beautiful. And noble. And strong."

He watched as I raised my hands and began unbuttoning his shirt. His mouth parted and he started to bend down to me, but I held up an index finger and wagged it.

"No moving, mister. Those are the rules."

He narrowed his lids and straightened.

I unfastened the last button and pushed his shirt over his shoulders. The tattoos that ran across his chest, back, and shoulders were darker than most. Then again, they weren't made of ink, but something supernatural, something otherworldly. Their lines interlocked like a maze with dead ends and traps that would keep a soul locked in the oblivion of space that existed between dimensions, lost for an eternity.

Scars from the abuse he'd endured growing up still marred his perfect skin, but only a bit. And then I found what I was looking for. The point of entry for the .50-caliber bullet that had torn through his body only days earlier. What would have ripped a normal man to shreds merely wounded Reyes. It entered through his rib cage and punctured a lung, exiting out his back. But all that remained as evidence of that night was a small scrape on his skin. I pushed his shirt down his arms farther and walked around to check his back. The scrape was better, but he healed even faster than I did.

"That's not pity I feel, is it?" he asked, his voice suddenly hard.

I walked around to face him and crossed my arms over my chest. "What if it is?"

"I wouldn't suggest it."

"You can't stop me from feeling sympathy for what you've been through, Reyes."

"Would you care to test that theory?"

"Yes." I raised my chin. "I would." I put my hand on his chest, his skin scorching against my palm. "You are everything to me. How can I not empathize with you for what you've endured?"

The heat in the room magnified with his anger. "Stop."

I shook my head and stepped closer. "No. I am in agony every time I think about what happened to you, and that's not something you can change just because it makes you mad."

And there it was. That blistering heat that burst from him when his temper got the better of him. "Would you like to know what true agony is?" he asked, his voice a husky shell, fragile, in danger of crumbling at any moment.

I stepped into the flames that engulfed him. Though I couldn't see a fire, I could feel it, blazing across my skin, lapping over my nerve endings. I wrapped an arm around his waist, his hands still behind his back, his expression murderous. Then I reached up and touched his face. "If it meant I would know more of what you went through, then yes. If it would bring me closer to you, to understanding how you think, how I can best help you, then a thousand times yes."

He bent his head, losing the game in the process, and whispered in my ear. "You got it."

His arms were free at once and around me. He moved in a different time, a different reality. I wasn't prepared. One second we were standing in the middle of his living room; the next I was against a wall, his body hard against mine, unforgiving. But if he meant to bring me agony, the only kind he brought was the anguish of longing for more. His mouth trailed hot kisses down my neck. His knee pushed my legs apart. His hand twisted into my hair while the other ripped my blouse and sought the weight of Danger and Will.

Then my pants were down and his blistering touch pushed inside me.

I gasped and took hold of his wrist as that familiar spark ignited in the core of my viscera. As molten lava spread through me, burning me from the inside out, I guided his fingers deeper and heard a growl a microsecond before I found myself on the ground. This was not the sensual being I had come to know. This was not an act of love but of punishment. Yet all he managed to do was drive me closer to the brink of ecstasy. It was as though he wanted to hurt me, to force me into not caring, not sympathizing, but that simply wouldn't happen. I felt his desire mount as quickly as mine. As much as anger led him, so did his raw sexual appetite, and in that area we were a perfect match.

He lay on top of me with a hand around my throat to hold me beneath him as he unfastened his pants. I plunged both my hands in his hair, twisted my fingers in a firm grip, then pulled his mouth down to mine the moment he entered me. And a jolt of pleasure bucked inside me with his entrance. I breathed in the air he breathed out. I tasted him on my tongue. I sank my fingernails into his back when he pushed too hard too fast. But he didn't stop. This wasn't about pleasure. This was about reprisal. Revenge. His mouth tasted of wine and fire and his kiss grew just as hard as his fucking had become. A piercing arousal rippled through me as his thrust went deeper. He had clamped me to him so he could punish me, and yet even with all his anger and all his indignation, he did not hurt me. Just the opposite. Stinging tendrils of ecstasy spread throughout my body, hot and hungry and carnivorous.

But was he solely punishing me or was he enjoying the act as well? I wrapped my arms around his head as he thrust into me, his breathing labored, his body molding into a marble-like hardness, and I did the unthinkable. I whispered into his ear the last thing he would ever want to hear. But I had to know where he was at.

"Is this what he did to you?"

He hesitated. Faltered. And my body cried out. It wanted that peak it sought. That prize at the top. But my heart wanted Reyes. With me. Not fighting me. Not punishing me. But riding this incredible wave together.

There was a wall above my head and he braced a hand against it, our bodies still entwined and locked together. His mouth sought my ear. "You would still feel pity for me?" He nipped at my earlobe. The small amount of pain caused a sharp spike of arousal. "I am a monster, Dutch. A demon. Unworthy of you."

I still had my arms wrapped around his head. "I don't pity you, my beautiful man." His hold tightened. "I have sympathy for what you've been through. And you are not a monster. If you want to punish me for the feelings I have—" I put one hand on a steely buttock and led him deeper. He hissed in a breath. Pressed harder. "—then I accept."

My body won. The heat swirling and bubbling inside me needed release, somewhere to go, and Reyes was just the one to set it free.

His mouth sought mine, the contact rough, raw, and he drank me in as though my kiss were the only thing keeping him alive. An exquisite pressure trembled throughout me as he buried himself over and over, urging me closer to the edge with each thrust, with each powerful stroke. The air disappeared from the room as his erection milked the tide swelling inside me, summoned the wave of lava, drew it closer and closer until it burst through and crashed against my bones, surging like a boiling sea throughout me.

He groaned in agony as he met his own climax with a shiver of ecstasy; then he lay on top of me, breathless and spent. When he went to push off me, I wrapped every available limb I had around him and kept him locked to me. He relaxed at last and I felt everything negative, every doubt, every grain of insecurity, every fragment of anxiety drain out of him. I kissed his brow and ran my fingertips over his back and if I didn't know better, I'd say he was happy. A ray of hope broke through. Maybe, just maybe, the lion could be tamed. Then again, did I want to tame such a wildly passionate beast? Such a stunningly feral being? I'd have to think on that one.

We eventually found a bed with a mattress that felt like clouds. I lay there curled in Reyes's arms. His warmth and steady breathing lulled me into a state of utter relaxation, but I couldn't quite sleep. Not because I wasn't at peace. Just the opposite. I'd never felt so at peace. So at ease. So at home. His presence was like a salve that soothed my frenzied thoughts, that calmed the roiling seas within me, and I didn't want to miss that feeling for a second, so I lay there and drank it in.

His room didn't have much yet. It didn't even have a clock, but it did have a bed, a couple of nightstands with lamps, a chest of drawers, and a chair in one corner with a copy of a Jack Williamson novel on it. Scattered on the floor was everything from George R. R. Martin and Tolkien to Ursula Le Guin and Asimov. He was a reader. And he liked fantasy and science fiction. It was like he was created for me and me alone. His taste, his temperament, his utter perfection. Admittedly lots of other women liked those things as well, but I chose to believe he really was created just for me. The only thing missing from his collection was *Sweet Savage Love*. I'd have to lend him a copy.

On the other side of his bedroom was mine. Our headboards butted against the same wall. Or they would butt against the same wall if I had a headboard. The one that came with my bed had an unfortunate incident one night when I'd mixed tequila and champagne with a rock band from Minnesota. In all honesty, I don't think I was even in the room when my headboard bit the dirt. Possibly not even in the apartment. I woke up in the stairwell with a new Blue Öyster Cult T-shirt and a slight case of internal bleeding. But I recovered quickly after crawling back to my apartment and kicking out the wayward souls who'd taken over my digs, including a guinea pig and an iguana named Sam.

Honestly, who brings an iguana to a party?

I lay there a long while, basking in the warmth of my man before easing out from under his arm and searching out a bathroom. I was just going to pee, then run back for round two of snuggle-palooza. Then I saw his shower. And I knew the true meaning of happiness. Two minutes later, I was thoroughly enjoying a massage beneath a waterfall made of stone and marble. Jets of water pulsated over my skin and kneaded my muscles. I named this ingenious invention George and decided to leave my own shower, Hector, for him. Some loves were just meant to be.

I turned to see Reyes standing at the shower entrance.

"It looks good on you," he said, his full mouth forming an appreciative grin. "The shower." His arms were crossed, his gaze sultry, and it took a moment for my eyes to adjust. He stood in all his naked glory. Long limbs and sinuous muscle molded into absolute perfection. Like he'd been sculpted onto this plane then airbrushed, the artist clearly fond of fluid lines and deep shadows.

"I thought it might be a bit much," he continued, "but I've changed my mind."

"This?" I asked, astounded that he would question George's worth. "This . . . this masterpiece?" I threw myself against his stone exterior. George's. Not Reyes's. "How could you ever doubt him?"

"Him?"

"George."

"His name is George?"

"Yes."

"How do you know?"

"Because I just named him." I tried to snap my fingers, but they were wet so I came away with more of a squishy thud than a snap. I'd take it. "Keep up, mister, or before you know it, life will pass—" I squeaked when he stepped inside and drew me against his chest—the airbrushed one—then bent down to nibble on my neck. An electric current shot down my spine before I came to my senses. "Hey, wait," I said, pulling back, "you *are* the son of Satan. Maybe we need a safe word."

His grin morphed into something wickedly charming. "Okay, how about, 'Oh, my god, it's so big.' "

Laughter burst out of me before I could stop it. Not that it wasn't. "That would be a safe *phrase,* but okay." I thought about it, then said, "How about 'Is that all you've got?' "

He nuzzled my neck again, causing a surge of pleasure to cascade over my skin. "That sounds more like a challenge."

"Good point. But it does get the adrenaline pumping."

He pushed between my legs. "Among other things."

An hour later, we were sprawled on a rug on his bathroom floor using towels as pillows. I lay staring at the ceiling, stewing in astonishment for several reasons. First, I had no idea a showerhead had so many creative uses. Second, Reyes's stamina was a thing of beauty. Third, I was beginning to feel him on a deeper level. In the same way I could glean emotion off him, off anyone, I was beginning to feel all the little intricacies of his physical reaction to stimuli. The same pleasures that raced across his skin, that bucked inside him, that burst as he reached orgasm, rushed through me with a supernatural intensity. I had never experienced anything like it.

"How are you?" he asked, regarding me from beneath an arm he'd thrown over his face.

"Pretty good, actually."

He took my chin and pulled my gaze to his. "No, really, how are you?"

"What do you mean?" I'd just been on a turbo-powered roller coaster ride and lived to tell the tale. How much peachier could a person be?

"You came here tonight for a reason, and as much as I'd love to believe otherwise, it was not for this." He glanced around, indicating our recent activities with a nod.

And his seriousness surprised me. "I had a few questions. But I didn't think you'd be into the touchy-feely stuff."

He ran a thumb over my bottom lip. "That depends entirely on who I'm touching and who I'm feeling."

"Oh, right. Well, I have to be honest, all of this was for nothing." I also indicated our recent activities with a glance and a nod.

"Really."

"Yeah, I got an email the other day. The ambassador to Nigeria said I inherited a million dollars from a Nigerian uncle. He's holding it in escrow for me. All I have to do is send him a money order for twenty-five hundred, and that million is all mine."

"You don't say."

"I had no idea I even had an uncle in Nigeria. Looks like I don't need your crappy million after all."

"The ambassador sounds like a really nice guy."

"Right? I'll have to send him a cheese ball to show my gratitude."

"But I lost the bet," he continued. "I owe you two now."

"That's true. I almost forgot. Can I get that in small, nonsequential bills? I like to hit the strip clubs occasionally."

He grinned, but then grew serious again. "Do you want to talk about what's really bothering you?"

"Something's bothering me? I had no idea."

"Your boyfriend."

I glanced toward his shower in surprise. "George? It's just a fling, Reyes. Nothing will come of it."

"Your other boyfriend."

"You know about Dead Duff?" That was fast. We'd only just started seeing each other. And we'd kept it so secretive. Meeting in a smoky bar, in a dark hallway.

"No, your other boyfriend."

I thought a moment. "Donovan, my biker dude?" I did miss him. Too bad so many of my boyfriends ended up in Mexico, running from the law. That could be a sign of something.

"No, your other— Fuck, how many boyfriends do you have?"

"Including Herman, the maintenance guy at the Jug-N-Chug who talks to celery?" If I didn't know better, I could've sworn Reyes ground his teeth. I couldn't blame him. I mean, who talks to celery in this day and age?

"Yes, including Herman."

"Oh, okay, then." I started naming all my menfolk under my breath and counting on my fingers. I knew he was talking about Garrett, but why give him the satisfaction? He was just so fun to rankle. After a minute, I ran out of fingers and had to raise my feet so I could use my toes as backup.

Reyes growled and rolled on top of me before sinking his teeth into my neck.

"Okay, I'm sorry!" I screamed, trying to talk past an inane attack of the giggles his nibbling caused. A combustible energy rushed over my skin when he removed his teeth and started suckling my neck instead. He curled me deeper into his arms. "Wait," I said, suddenly breathless, "you're not a vampire, are you? Living off my blood and compelling me to forget? I've seen the show."

After another growl, I laughed and tightened my hold, but my muscles protested. It surprised me. "I think I'm sore."

He stopped and raised his head. "You don't know?"

"No. I might be." I raised a leg to test it. "I'll have to think about it."

"Here, let me check."

He stood, pulling me with him, and threw me over a shoulder like I weighed nothing. Sadly, that just wasn't the case. I squeaked out a protest that was more giggle than complaint. "What are you doing?"

"I'm going to perform an exam."

"An exam?" I laughed as he carried me to a small area he'd set aside for a dining room table and laid me across it. A startled gasp escaped me when my back touched the cold wood. "Oh, my god," I said with a shiver.

"Stay here," he said, all business. "I have this covered."

"This is freezing," I cried, but he was gone.

Then I heard him rummaging around in his kitchen. I covered Danger and Will in an attempt to preserve their dignity. Also, it seemed like the right thing to do.

He walked out with a variety of sparkling new kitchen utensils. A whisk, a spoon, a spatula, and several other ominous-looking devices for which I had no name. He dumped them on the table beside me.

"And just what are you planning to do with those?"

"I'm going to give you an exam. Make sure everything is okay down there."

I kicked at him. "No, you aren't."

When I tried to rise, he pushed me back down with a hand on my chest. "Trust me. I took a correspondence course."

"From prison?" I asked, shocked.

"And I have a lot of experience in this area."

"You've been in lockdown for ten years. How much experience can you have?"

When I kicked out again, he took my ankle and placed my foot back on the table as he sought out the perfect tool for whatever dark machinations he had in mind. He picked something up. It was silver and shiny and foreboding. "I'm going to have to plug this one in."

"No!" I said, suddenly laughing so hard, my stomach hurt.

Holding my ankle with one hand, he tossed that appliance aside and picked up something else, keeping it low, hidden from my sight. Then he turned to me, growing even more serious. "You have to trust me." He leaned closer, watched me from underneath his lashes. "No flinching," he said, a soft warning reverberating in his tone. "This is a flinchless game of concentration and control."

"Reyes, you are not—!" I gasped aloud as something smooth and cool settled between my legs. I anchored a foot against his shoulder as insurance against whatever he was planning.

He nudged the utensil just inside, causing a sharp current to spike within me, then he knelt and feathered his tongue across the sensitive folds at my apex. A delicious warmth stirred with each touch, with every nudge, pooling deep in my abdomen, building and pulsating immediately.

He hadn't been lying. He clearly had experience. He knew exactly how much pressure to apply, when to go deeper, how long to stay there. I writhed under his expert touch, grabbed handfuls of hair, begged for release. He spread my legs farther apart with his shoulders, sucked softly as I became engulfed in liquid fire. I expected him to enter me, to take over, to pleasure himself as well, but he didn't. He lured me closer to the edge. Red hot embers spread through me once more, searing my flesh from the inside out. And then the tendrils that wound through me exited my body and entered his. I felt it the minute his pleasure met mine. I heard a soft gasp. Felt a cool rush of air as he breathed in.

He removed his toy and replaced it with his fingers. Just as I could feel his reactions, he could feel mine. He was riding the same wave I was. Absorbing the same blistering heat, the same energy. The contact of our essences caused a friction, a biting arousal as he churned and whipped me into a frenzy until the sweet sting of orgasm rocketed through me. I welded my teeth together, braced myself as the rush crashed against me and drowned every cell in my body in warm honey.

With a moan, Reyes reached underneath to finish what our connection had started. I grabbed hold of his hair and brought his mouth to mine, and with a soft groan, he wrapped his free arm around me, locking me to him as he spilled his seed onto my stomach. He trembled with the force of his climax, his breathing labored, his muscles like marble until slowly he relaxed against me.

"That was amazing," I said at last.

He nodded. "Told you. Correspondence course."

I laughed as he helped me off the table and led me to the bathroom. We visited George, chatted about everyday things like wine, cars, and the horrid taste of shampoo when I accidentally swallowed some; then we found his bed again and I lay with him until he fell asleep.

He was simply stunning. His lashes fanned across his cheeks, his lips slightly parted, his breathing deep and even. He looked like a little boy. Content and serene.

With a deep regret, I wiggled out from under him despite his sleepy protests and grabbed articles of clothing as I tiptoed to his door. What amazing willpower I had. What fantastic self-control. I'd come over for one reason, and everything but that reason seemed to be resolved. When I reached the door, I saw what looked like another note. But this was his door, not mine. I peeled it off, then angled it until I could read it by the light of the fire.

Is that all you've got?

With a smile spreading slowly across my face, I dropped everything I'd just picked up and went back for more.

Chapter Five

*I may not have any skeletons in my closet,
but I do have a little box of souls in my sock drawer.*
—T-SHIRT

I woke up to a very warm Reyes pressed against my backside and a very cold Artemis curled against my front. It wouldn't have been so bad if she were a smidgen warmer than the arctic circle. Artemis was a gorgeous Rottweiler who died a few months ago. She'd been protecting me ever since, and she had an incredible way of ripping demons to shreds and sending them back to hell, then rolling over for a belly rub.

Unfortunately, she snored. Why a departed Rottweiler who didn't actually need oxygen would snore was beyond me. I nuzzled her neck, then wiggled until I was out from under covers and arms and paws. Reyes lay there, his face the picture of innocence. True, it was a sexy, sensual kind of innocence, but it did magical things to my nether regions. I wanted to get one last kiss before the evening ended but didn't dare wake him again. I'd be sore enough as it was. He had an arm thrown over his forehead, his right palm open. The burns from the bullet were already healed.

The next time I gathered articles of clothing and headed for the door, I actually made it out of Reyes's apartment. The frigid air in the hallway startled me. I shivered and hurried to my own apartment about ten steps away. I hadn't locked it. I would never learn.

Unfortunately, my apartment was just as cold as the hallway. I changed into a pair of pajamas that said IN-STANT HUMAN. JUST ADD COFFEE. and scurried between my sheets. Figuring I'd never get any sleep, I contemplated for the thousandth time what it would mean if Reyes was setting fire to half of Albuquerque, albeit the seedy half.

And Garrett. What had he gone through? What had him so utterly obsessed with the dark underbelly of hell? Had he really been tortured? How was any of that even possible?

As I lay wondering about things I didn't want to wonder about, I heard a scratching sound under my bed. Had Artemis followed me? The sound started out as a faint scuffing but grew louder the longer I lay there. It wasn't like a dog pawing, but more like someone scratching on wood, as though trying to claw through it. Then again, that could just be my imagination getting the better of me.

Not much scared me, but someone scratching under my bed as I lay on it was way too urban legend for me. Next I would hear a drip only to discover it was the blood of my boyfriend hanging dead from a tree. Luckily, I had no trees in my apartment. Then I thought, *Hey, a tree would add a nice touch*.

No, I didn't need to think about things like that at the moment. Someone was definitely under my bed. Scratching.

I inched to the side, leaned over it slowly, and pulled up the bed skirt. A set of huge blue eyes stared back at me and it took every ounce of strength I had not to scream like someone being mauled by a wild animal. I bit down and met her gaze. She looked about seven, judging by the size of her eyes and the shape of her round cheeks. She was lying on her back, scratching the wood that held my mattress. Blond hair, tangled and matted, hung over her eyes, partially obstructing her view. Her childlike face was dirty, her hair completely covered in a slick, oily mud. I couldn't tell what she was wearing, but she looked absolutely frantic. She clawed at the wood with a panicked aggression. Her eyes wide, searching. She was terrified. Period. She wanted out of wherever she was.

"Hi," I said as softly as I could. She didn't miss a beat. She continued to claw and stare at me as though trying to escape, and my heart sank.

Just then I realized most of her fingernails were jagged and broken. They wouldn't have broken on my bed. The dearly departed come fully assembled. Or torn apart. If her fingernails were frayed and broken, it happened while she was still alive. But she kept clawing anyway, splintering the wood with her nails, trying frantically to get out of wherever it was she was trapped.

I climbed off my bed and lay flat on the floor beside her.

"Honey," I said, reaching out, hoping to ease her fears.

She paused, but only for a moment. She stared at me as though she couldn't quite figure out what I was or what I was doing there. Then she went back to clawing.

Angel, my departed thirteen-year-old investigator and partner in crime, once said that my touch, as the grim reaper, was healing. I reached under the bed and put my hand on her shoulder. She stared straight ahead, eyeing the boards under my bed, but she did seem to calm a bit. Then she slowly started to claw again, only with less of a frenzied panic. She clawed absently at the board in front of her face.

She had a pixie face with a bow-shaped mouth and huge eyes. I wouldn't have been surprised if she had wings. If pixies did exist, I was fairly certain they would look exactly like her.

Because I didn't know what to do for her, I stayed beside her the rest of the night with my hand on her shoulder. I fell asleep that way, on the floor. Sometime in the early morning hours, Artemis had joined me. I felt like Reyes and I had joint custody, taking turns with her. I didn't mind her sleeping with Reyes, though, because waking up with a ninety-pound dog on my back was not as fun as one might think. I liked air. I liked to breathe without my lungs being on fire. So when I woke up with Artemis literally taking up the length of me, her frigid body like ice, the fact that I was shivering should not have been surprising. Normally I was under the safety of covers when she slept with me. The floor did not conduct heat well.

Then I remembered why I was on the floor. I startled and glanced under the bed. The girl was still there, only she had scooted to the corner farthest away from me and lay curled into herself, her knees on the floor, her eyes peering out from underneath her dirty hair. And she was lovely. With the sun peeking over the horizon and casting a soft glow in the room, I was able to see her in a different light. I could see the departed in any light, but the darker the area, the grayer the departed became. Now I could see the blond hair beneath the mud more clearly. The crystal depths of her blue eyes.

My hand was still under the bed and there was something in it. I pulled it out and opened my palm. It was fragments of wood from where she'd scratched. I rolled over onto my side. This meant I had to kick Artemis off me. She'd been snoring, and moving her was like moving a small mountain.

"Oh, my god, Artemis, scooch over. Dogs," I said to the pixie. She didn't seem amused. It happened. Once I managed to settle on my side, I lay there a long while, hoping to coax her closer. To coax her to cross.

Then I heard breathing, panting, and not from Artemis. I rolled onto my knees and looked over my bed. There
in a far corner of my room between my nightstand and
leopard skin floor lamp, was another girl, only this one
was older. She looked about nineteen, but she was very
similar to the pixie. Matted blond hair, slick oily mud
from head to toe. She wore only a short gown. Her bare
feet were covered in scratches, as though she'd fought
back, kicking at someone, or she'd tried to run before dying. I wondered if the girls were related. Then I noticed
ligature marks on her neck. I hadn't seen them on the
pixie, but her hair and position had made it impossible to
be sure. I could get a probable cause of death of this one
at least. She had been strangled, and judging by the broken blood vessels in her eyes and the swollen face, that
was very likely the way she'd died.

Artemis woke up and began sniffing under the bed. I
was worried she would scare the pixie. Instead, the girl
seemed fascinated by her. Her features softened and she
almost smiled. Almost.

"You keep an eye on this one, okay?" I said to Artemis, and I went around the bed to try to talk to the
other one. Like the pixie when she first showed up, this
one was terrified, staring off into space with wide eyes.
She kept her hands up as though trying to defend herself. When I touched her arm, she curled into herself
even more. She ducked her head behind her arms and
whimpered.

Sometimes my job sucked. What had these girls gone
through? What made them scared of their own shadow?
Having recently gone through a bout of PTSD, I could
understand the "scared of your own shadow" thing, but
normally death brought with it a certain amount of healing. People didn't suffer their own ends for eternity. Yet
these girls seemed stuck in the moments they'd died.

I needed a plan. First coffee. Then Uncle Bob. Something must have happened. Surely these girls had been reported missing.

Cookie was going to be in class all day. For a second, I actually thought about postponing it, then realized the world would be a safer place with her in that class. I couldn't let the world down.

I visited the ladies' room and sat atop my porcelain throne. That's when I heard more whimpering coming from the living room. No way. Another one? Feeling better—there was nothing like ninety pounds resting on your bladder at dawn—I peeked into my living room. I didn't see anyone besides Mr. Wong at first. The sounds were coming from somewhere near him, but he wouldn't be making them. He was a permanent fixture, had been here since I rented the apartment, and was being his usual self, hovering in a corner, silent as the moon. Since he'd never said anything, had never even moved from that spot, I doubted he would be whimpering now.

I tiptoed to Sophie, my secondhand sofa, and saw a third woman. And while this one was blond as well, she was not a natural blonde. She looked Hispanic. Around twenty-five. But she had the same matted hair, only the blond in hers hung in uneven patches as though it had been bleached in a hurry or under duress. And she had the same terrified expression. Exhibited the same mindless behavior.

What the hell was going on? I would never figure it out without a caffeine fix. I turned to have my morning meeting of the minds with Mr. Coffee. We talked every morning about lots of different things. He mostly gurgled and let off steam while brewing the elixir of life. I mostly yawned and complained about mornings, the weather, men. Whatever struck my fancy.

Once he'd finished his rant, something about how I only loved him for his carafe, I realized I had run out of clean cups. And dish soap. After a quick trip to the bathroom and back, I washed a few cups with shampoo, then reached in the top cabinet for my hidden treasure of gold. Nondairy creamer. Some people would call me a sellout, a charlatan for using the fake stuff, but the fake stuff made me happy. Much like puppies did. And George. Reyes's shower.

But when I opened the cabinet, I found another woman holed up inside it. I jumped back, let out something that resembled a squeak on a rusty wheel, and clutched my heart. One would think that, since I was the grim reaper, I'd be used to the dead showing up unexpectedly. Nope. It still got me every time. On the bright side, the rush of adrenaline helped. Not a lot. I still needed a caffeine fix, but at least I was awake enough to realize I quite possibly had my underwear on inside out. Something didn't feel right down yonder.

I approached the woman with caution when another movement caught my attention. I had to look up. Up! And there on my wall was another woman. This one looked about thirty. She could've been a natural blonde. Wasn't sure. But she was crawling up my wall toward the ceiling. She scurried to a corner and curled into it.

I did a 360, turning to assess my surroundings, and counted no less that five more women in varying states of terror. They were all filthy, all covered in the same oil, and from what I could see, all strangled. My heart sank for them. They couldn't have all died recently. I would have heard something in the news. Then I realized their clothing and hairstyles were from different time periods. While one looked almost recent with a Faded Glory button-down, another actually looked from about twenty years ago, chunks of her hair pulled into a ponytail with a fluffy neon scrunchy. The terror in their eyes, the mindless fear that paralyzed them, ripped through my heart.

My front door opened.

"Good morning," Cookie said as she walked in, almost ready to face the world. She looked like she hadn't gotten much sleep, and she had a rather nasty shiner.

"Hey, you," I said, pretending not to notice. I poured her a cup and added all the fixings.

"What do you think?"

"What? Oh, you mean your black eye? I hardly noticed."

"Don't say that," she said with an indignant gasp before pointing at her eye. "I earned this puppy. I'm going to milk it for all it's worth. Amber made me breakfast."

"No way."

"Way. And it wasn't half bad once I picked out the shell fragments."

"Nice." I took a sip of my coffee. Smacked my lips. Took another sip, then handed it to Cookie. "Here, taste this."

She took a sip, then handed it back, smacking her lips, too. "What is that?"

"Not sure. Mr. Coffee has never let me down." I took another sip. "Maybe it's not him. I ran out of dish soap and had to use shampoo. I'm not entirely certain I rinsed well."

"You did your dishes with shampoo?"

"It was either that or my apricot body scrub."

"No, good call. A little shampoo won't hurt you."

"Right? I just don't know what my day would be like without coffee to give it a good kick start. Is it wrong that every time I run out of creamer, I become slightly suicidal?"

"Not at all. I became suicidal once when Jug-N-Chug ran out of French vanilla flavoring syrup."

"I hear ya." Coffee was that place where the sun comes up over the horizon and lights the heavens in a burst of vibrant colors. Shampoo remnants didn't change that fact.

"Is your aunt Lil here?" she asked.

Aunt Lillian had died in the sixties and was now a semi-permanent roommate. Thankfully, she traveled a lot. "I think she's still in Africa. She loves that place." Speaking of dead roommates, I perused the woman hanging—literally—in my space bubble. "When you get a break in class, I need you to do some research."

"Okay, on what?"

"I have an apartment full of departed women."

Cookie stopped. She looked around, suddenly wary. "Like, right now?"

"As we speak."

"How many are we talking?"

"Let me count."

I strolled into my bedroom, made a detour to count the one in the shower, then came back out and pointed my finger in every direction imaginable. Watching Cookie's expression go from slightly worried to horrified was also a lot like that place where the sun comes up over the horizon and lights the heavens. Only, you know, funnier.

I walked back into the kitchen and went through the cabinets. "Nine," I said, matter-of-factly. "Oh, wait." I went to the fridge and checked it, too. "Nope, just nine. All blond but not all natural. Caucasian, Hispanic, African American, and one Asian. Ages anywhere from around seven-ish to thirty, thirty-five."

She put her cup down, so I knew what she was about to relay was serious. "Charley, I need to stay home and help. This is serious."

Nailed it. "I know it is, but they aren't going anywhere and I am almost certain they didn't die recently. But why are they showing up now? And in droves?"

"Do you think this was the work of a serial killer?"

"Most likely. I can't imagine these deaths the result of more than one person's efforts. Two at the most. I tried to get them to chillax, but I don't think they know what that means."

"Okay, call me if you need anything." She started for the door, then stopped. "No, I can't go to this class. I need to help you with research and stuff. These poor women."

"No, you need to go learn how not to kill people unless you really, really, really want to. Like on purpose. And if I have to, I can get Garrett on this as well."

"Garrett," Cookie said, her voice low and sultry as she purred his name. I could have sworn her eyes rolled back into her head.

"Hmm, that's surprising."

She bounced back to me. "What?"

"It's just that last night you couldn't get enough of checking out Uncle Bob's ass. I thought maybe you had a thing for him."

"What? I was not checking out your uncle's ass." When I did that deadpan thing I was so fond of, she fessed up. "Okay, maybe a little. Is it just me or is he getting in shape?"

I had noticed. Uncle Bob was much more fit. And quite comely. I knew why, too. He had such a thing for Cookie, it was unreal. He was getting fit for her. It was sweet. And slightly disturbing. What if they dated? What if they dated, then broke up? Where would I be? I nudged her toward the door.

"Okay, I'm leaving Amber alone today. She's promised to stay in and do her homework."

"On a Saturday? All day?" I snorted. "I used to tell my parents the same thing."

"That's it. I'm taking her to her grandma's."

"That's too far. You'll be late for class. You don't want to sit in the back of the room, do you? Besides, I'm just kidding, she'll be fine. She's nothing like me. Now, off you go."

"Wait. What the heck is that?" I looked where she was pointing.

My newest painting sat propped against a bookcase. "I figured I would express my feelings through art. You know, for the new shrink." My sister, Gemma, had set me up with a psychologist to work on my PTSD. That painting should help move that right along.

"And you were feeling homicidal?"

"I felt macabre with a hint of beheading would do the trick. This stuff freaks the shit out of them."

"You know, Charley, they really are trying to help you."

"I know, I know. Now, off you go." I hated to do it, but I had to force Cookie out the door, then lock it behind her. She was being very uncooperative.

I turned toward the bathroom to shower and get dressed, but came face-to-face with another departed woman. Only this one was not at all like the others. She had long black hair and wore scrubs with an ID attached to a lanyard.

"Hi," I said, checking out her neck. She hadn't been strangled like the others either.

She blinked, surprised to be there. "Hi," she said back. "Can you see me?"

"Sure can." I stepped around her and headed that way. That way being the bathroom. "Are you here to cross?"

"Cross?" she asked, trying to gain her bearings. "I don't think so."

"Okay, well, there's coffee in the pot." When she frowned in confusion, I said, "Sorry, bad joke. How can I help you?" She followed me into the bathroom. I hated to turn on the shower with one of the departed women in there, but it had to be done.

"No one can find my body."

"Do you know where it is?"

"Yes, yes!" She grabbed my arm. "I do. It's under that

old bridge on 57, like the ones they make for trains. Metal and rusting."

I patted her hand. "Okay, an old bridge on Highway 57. Got it. Can you give me more?"

"My family can't find it. They have been searching and searching, and they can't find my body. My sister is— She's so upset."

"I'm sorry, hon. What's your na—?"

Before I could ask for her name, she disappeared. Darn it. All I got off her ID was Nic. Perhaps she was a Nicole or a Nicky. If she'd have crossed through me, I would have gleaned more info about her, but apparently this was going to be a game of cat and mouse. I could only pray I'd be the cat this time. I hated being the mouse.

After dressing in a cream-colored sweater, jeans, and my favorite boots, I started for my handy dandy office, which sat about fifty feet from my handy dandy apartment. I took another look at Reyes's door and felt an odd urge to use my key again. God, that man was talented. Still, honing my skills in self-control was good practice for later in life when dementia set in and I would try to take everyone's meds off the cart at the home.

I called Uncle Bob and got only a garbled hello for my efforts.

"Hey, mister. I need you to check something for me."

He cleared his throat and said, "It's Saturday."

"And?"

"I'm off."

He did sound a bit groggy. "Did I wake you?"

If I didn't know better, I'd have said he growled at me.

"So, has there been a rash of murders lately? Perhaps something in a blonde? Petite? Strangled?"

"What? Did you get something?"

Uncle Bob, always asking if I got something, like I

got messages from the great beyond. "No, but I do have an apartment full of women who were strangled to death."

I heard a rustling sound as though he were fighting sheets to get out of bed. I understood. Sheets were tricky. Losing the fight, he cursed. And dropped his phone. Twice. Ubie had never been a morning person. "Okay," he said at last, "give me the details."

I broke it down as I had for Cookie. "Okay, I have no less than nine women in my apartment ranging in age anywhere from seven to thirty-five, all blond but not all natural blondes. Caucasian, Hispanic, African American, and at least one Asian. Ring any bells?"

"Not offhand."

"I don't think these women died recently. And I think their deaths were spread out over an extended period of time, possibly with long gaps in between."

"Could be the killer did a stint in jail. Any names?"

"No, but they're scared, Uncle Bob. Terrified. I've never seen anything like it."

"I'll check around. How are you?"

"Okay, I just have no idea why they would show up now. Something had to trigger their appearance."

"I don't know either, pumpkin. But how are *you*?"

Uncle Bob. Always worried about me. Or, well, his ticket to solving case after case, thus his immaculate rep.

"I'm okay. A little weirded out, actually, and the departed never do that to me. They are just so terrified, Uncle Bob. It's like they're reliving their deaths. I need to solve this fast."

"We will, hon. I'll get on it today. Let me know if any new missing women show up or if you get any more information from them. Maybe another death is what triggered their appearance."

"Maybe."

"Oh, and I wanted you to know that our arsonist struck again."

I stopped halfway up the stairs to my office. "What? When?"

"Last night around midnight."

My free hand flew to my mouth. It wasn't him. It wasn't Reyes. He was with me at midnight. Unless . . . "Was it on a timer like the others?"

"Yes, but we have a witness."

Suddenly strangled with worry again, I asked, "Can the witness identify the arsonist?"

"No, but we did get a pretty good description. An odd one, actually. If I didn't know better, I'd say . . . Never mind. I'll tell you when I see you."

"No, what?" If he didn't know better, he'd say it was Reyes Farrow? Was that what he was going to say?

"Well, it's kind of crazy, but if I didn't know better, I'd say the arsonist was a woman."

I paused a moment, then asked, "A woman? That's kind of rare, right?"

"It happens, but yes, it's extremely rare."

Slowly, and with infinite precision, awareness crept over me. It couldn't be. "Can you describe her?" I asked, almost not wanting to hear.

"Tall, willowy, painfully thin. The witness said he, or she, was shaking, like she was scared."

I closed my eyes in regret. If anything would come between Reyes and me, it's the fact that I was about to put his only relative, his nonbiological sister, Kim Millar, in jail. Earl Walker had obtained Reyes through nefarious means. I didn't know the details, but I did know that Reyes had been kidnapped as a baby and later traded to Earl. Kim had been dropped on Earl's doorstep. Her mother, a habitual drug user and prostitute, was dying, so she left Kim with her biological father. The fact that her father was Earl Walker was a cruel twist of fate for Kim and a way to control Reyes for Earl.

I sat on a step and fought back the wave of sorrow I felt. Who else could it be? She'd grown up in the same houses as Reyes. She'd been subjected to the same horrors. Her abuse was different from Reyes's. Earl never touched her the way he did her brother, but he did other things. For one, he starved her to get what he wanted out of Reyes. Earl used them against each other their entire lives. What would that do to siblings? Reyes had stayed away from her when he was accused of killing Earl and made her promise not to go see him. He didn't want her hurt any more because of him and she didn't want anyone using her as a means to get what they wanted out of Reyes ever again, so they hadn't seen each other in years. Yet they had a fierce love for each other and would do just about anything to protect that love. Did that include arson?

"You there, pumpkin?"

I tried to snap out of the sadness that had overtaken me. "I'm here."

He must have sensed it anyway. "Who is it, hon?"

"What makes you think I know?"

"Have you ever heard the caveat about trying to con a con man? You know exactly who it is. You've suspected for a while, ever since that fire the other night."

He was talking about the night the condemned apartment building burned. "I might know," I admitted, my heart sinking. "I might not. I need to be certain, to check on a few things."

"Then tell me who you suspect."

"I can't."

"I thought we had an open line of communication."

"Come on, Uncle Bob. Don't pull the relative card on me. I'll do the right thing. You know I will."

"I know, hon, but—"

"Please give me some time."

After a long pause, he caved. "You have twenty-four hours. After that, I drag your ass in for aiding and abetting."

"Uncle Bob!" I yelped, completely appalled. "After everything we've been through?"

"Lives are at stake here, Charley. The next fire could kill someone. Could kill lots of someones, and I know how big that heart of yours is."

He was wrong. My heart wasn't big. It was just taken. "I'll do the right thing. I promise."

I hung up before he could make me feel worse. Damn it. Now what? Turn in Reyes's sister? He would never forgive me. And Uncle Bob would never forgive me if another building burned and I knew who the arsonist was. What if someone did get hurt next time? That would be on my shoulders as surely as my head was.

There had to be options. I knew people who knew people. I had connections. I nibbled on a hangnail as a fail-proof plan formed. Surely my plan would work. True, my plans tended to head south from the get-go, but sometimes they made a left turn just in the nick of time and veered onto an alternate course until they almost, if one squinted hard enough, ended up in the right place. Maybe a few feet off-kilter, but close enough to call them a win in my book. No matter that my book was titled *How to Call Even Your Most Dismal Failures a Win and Not Feel Guilty About It*.

No. I had to think positive. This could work. This could work. I chanted that mantra over and over while unlocking the customer entrance to Davidson Investigations. Not that I wanted a customer to enter, but business was business, no matter what day it arrived. I walked through Cookie's reception area, into my office, and straight toward the

Bunn. Coffee would take the edge off. Or put in on. Either way.

After starting a pot to get me through the morning, I powered up my computer and prepared to print out the pictures I'd taken of Tidwell fondling Cookie's right hand. They didn't really prove anything other than the fact that Tidwell had a fondling issue and a horrendous temper, but he was definitely there for nefarious reasons. Hopefully my shots would prove that at least, and hopefully Mrs. Tidwell would not be one of those women who made excuses for her husband. Of course, she'd hired a PI for a reason. People don't hire a PI to find out if their spouse is cheating. They hire a PI to prove it. They already know the truth, deep down inside.

I plugged in the USB cable to my phone and pulled up the shots. They weren't pretty. They could have been, however, had I used a wide lens with a softer focus and some strategically placed lighting. Sadly, as the evening progressed, they got a little worse until all I had was a shot of Cookie's eye and right nostril. In the upper left corner, one of Tidwell's fists was coming at me. He tried to hit me. How did I miss that?

My phone pinged. It was a text from Cookie.

I'm not that good at cocking guns.

Really? Did she not know me at all?
I texted her back.

You can do this. Learn the cock, Cookie.
Know the cock.
Be the cock.

Chapter Six

I'm not 100 percent certain,
but I think my cup of coffee just said, "You're my bitch."
—STATUS UPDATE

I walked Cookie through a quick lesson on how to cock a gun—or, since she was using a semiautomatic, how to chamber a round—without pinching the ever-loving crap out of herself. I'd been there. I knew the price. That steel sliding against steel was unforgiving, even on the smallest versions. She seemed to do okay once I gave her a few pointers, so I decided to do a quick search to see if I could get a hit on my new roommates. Surely there would be something about them in the news. But site after site yielded exactly squat. Nothing. Not a word about a group of murdered blond women.

"You need to go."

I jumped and turned to the departed thirteen-year-old gangbanger standing behind me. He looked at the door, his eyes wide with barely contained panic, then back at me.

"Really, you need to go. Somewhere else. Leave." He put his arms under mine and yanked, trying to lift me out of my chair, his hands alarmingly close to the girls, Danger and Will Robinson. My breasts were all I had. I had to maintain their integrity. Allowing a thirteen-year-old to grope them would be wrong on so many levels.

"But it's my office," I said, slapping at him. "You go." I kicked against my desk until he dropped me back into my ninety-nine-dollar office chair.

He knelt beside me. "Please, Charley, just go."

I grew wary. People had a tendency to try to kill me at the most inopportune times. But his pleading was much less "life-threatening situation" and much more "I screwed up."

"Angel Garza, did you steal all the toilet paper from the women's restroom again? We've talked about this."

"No, I promise. You just need to leave." The front door opened, and he dropped his head into his hands. Apparently, it was too late for me to escape. I was caught like a fly in a spider's web. I could only pray for survival.

I took a sip of coffee instead as a Hispanic woman walked into Cookie's office, a curious determination to her gait. I didn't recognize her, but I felt like I knew the face. She was in her late fifties with long black hair that hung in pretty waves over her shoulders. And she was dressed to kill. Hopefully not me, though. She wore skin-tight jeans, knee-high black leather boots, a soft gray sweater, and a D&G bag that hung from her shoulder like an Uzi. I liked her.

She spotted me and made a beeline to my desk.

"You can't tell her, Charley," Angel said, panic rounding his eyes again. And I suddenly knew who she was.

I looked up at her and tried to hide my utter shock as she came to a stop in front of my desk. "Are you Charley Davidson?" she asked, her Mexican accent soft, the sharpness in her tone anything but.

"I have no idea what you're talking about." I panicked right alongside Angel. It was the only thing I could think to say. "I don't know. What?"

She blinked at me, then realized I was panicking. Honestly, it was like admitting to murder before being interrogated.

"Ms. Davidson," she began, but I decided to trip her up, to throw her off the trail of blood I'd left like an injured animal.

"I don't speak English."

"I've asked around about you," she continued undeterred. "I know who you are. What you do. But what I can't figure out for the life of me is why you would be depositing money in my bank account every month. How do you know my account number? And why would anyone do such a thing?"

"What? Me?" I looked around, hoping she was talking to someone else.

"You can't tell her, Charley."

"I won't," I whispered through my teeth. Then again, his mother looked a tad hell-bent. "I have no idea what you're talking about."

"Yes, you do." She crossed her arms and tapped her toes on my carpeted floor.

"Can you just excuse me for one moment?"

"Look, I'm not accusing you of anything, but you've been putting money in my bank account. Five hundred dollars every month for almost three years now."

"Five hundred dollars a month?" Angel asked, appalled. "Is that all I'm worth to you?"

I grabbed his arm and held up an index finger to put his mother in pause mode as I herded him out the side door, the one that led to the interior stairs of Dad's bar. "Excuse me just one sec."

"Five hundred dollars a month? I could haunt a rich guy's ex for five hundred dollars a month."

When Mrs. Garza eyed me, her expression part leery and part suspicion, I smiled and closed the door between us. "Look—"

"Migrant workers make more than I do."

"Angel, you are part-time. *Part*-time. And that was all I could afford when I first opened up."

"Yeah, well screw you. I quit."

"Wait a minute," I said, eyeing him. "You know exactly how much you make. You've known the whole time. I told you."

"I know." He shrugged. "I was just hoping for a raise. My mother needs a new car."

"And I have to supply it?" I asked, taking my turn at being appalled.

"If you want to keep your best investigator, you do."

I poked his chest with an index finger. "This is extortion, buddy."

"It's business, *pendeja*. Pay up or shut up."

"And just who says you are my best investigator? You're my *only* investigator."

"Either way."

"This is wonderful. What am I supposed to tell her?"

"You're the one with all the answers. And you're a PI. Tell her an uncle died and left you in charge of doling out the money or something. Isn't that what rich people do?"

"That's a job for lawyers."

"Then I don't know. I can't think of everything."

"Angel," I said, placing a hand on his shoulder. His eyes were such a deep, rich brown and his face was so young, his chin sprinkled with the soft beginnings of facial hair. He died too young. Way too young. I often wondered what he would have done with his life if he'd had a chance. He was such a good kid. "Maybe we should tell her."

"Fuck that." His stormy eyes suddenly turned angry. "No."

"If I were your mother, I would want to know you were okay."

"If you were my mother, I'd need therapy. I've had

thoughts, you know." He gestured to Danger and Will with a nod, but I didn't let his confession—though it wasn't exactly news—deter me.

"I would want to know what an awesome kid you are."

One corner of his full mouth rose in a playful gesture. "You think I'm awesome?"

Uh-oh.

"Am I awesome enough to see you naked?"

Why did I bother? "Or I could just tell her what a perv you've become."

"Okay, never mind. But you didn't see her. She cried all the time, for months after I died. I can't do that to her."

Like I said, awesome. "Okay, sweetheart. I won't tell her. But your mother is sharp and stronger than you give her credit for."

"She's as tough as they come." Pride swelled across his chest. She was probably in her early thirties when he died. It had been at least twenty years.

I stepped back into my office. Mrs. Garza, who had also lost her husband after Angel died, was examining a painting on my wall. She turned to me, her expression still set on hell-bent.

"You're right," I said, defeat evident in my sagging shoulders. "I know who you are, Mrs. Garza. Would you like some coffee?"

I couldn't help but notice how close she was to the dark elixir. I liked to stand near it, too. It was like standing next to a fire in the middle of winter, warm and comforting.

She relaxed her shoulders, but just barely. "I guess."

I poured her a cup, then let her doctor it as she pleased while I sat back behind my desk.

After she sat down, I said, "I do put money into your account every month. A great-uncle of yours had me track you down a few years ago and he left provisions for you before he died."

"Great story," Angel said, his voice dripping with sarcasm. Smartass.

Her brows knitted in suspicion. "A great-uncle? Which great-uncle?"

"Um, the great one on your aunt's side."

"I'm Mexican American, Ms. Davidson. Catholic. We like to procreate. Do you know how many aunts I have?"

"Right . . ."

"And we are very close."

I was so going to that special hell. "This is a great-uncle that no one knew about. He was . . . a recluse."

"Does this have anything to do with Angel?" She pronounced his name in true Spanish fashion. *Ahn*-hell. But her voice wavered when she said it.

"No, Mrs. Garza. It doesn't."

She nodded and got up to leave. "Like I said, I checked around. When you want to tell me the truth, you obviously know where I'll be."

"That was the truth," I promised her.

She put her coffee cup down and left, completely unconvinced. And I was so good at lying.

I put an arm around Angel. "I'm so sorry, hon. I had no idea she knew about me."

"She's smart. She checked up on you. It's not your fault."

He walked back out the door and looked over the railing into the restaurant downstairs. "Why is he here anyway?"

"Who?" I walked over and looked down, too, but the place hadn't opened for business yet. Empty tables and chairs sat strategically positioned, ready for patrons.

"You have another visitor," he said, then vanished before I could say anything else. I was learning more about what I could and could not do, and I knew that I could've brought him back if I'd wanted to, but he needed some time to process what had just happened. With his mother so open and willing to know more, craving to know more, I was a little surprised that he still didn't want me to tell her. It made me more curious. Was there something in particular he didn't want her to know? Was he hiding something?

But sure enough, I had another visitor. I wasn't meeting Mrs. Tidwell for another half hour, so I was surprised the front door opened again. I looked over as Captain Eckert, my uncle's boss, stepped in, dressed impeccably as always. He wasn't like the captains in the movies, with their ties crooked and their jackets in dire need of an iron, though that pretty much described Ubie to a T. Captain Eckert was more like an older cover model for *GQ*. His clothes were always pressed, his tie always straight, his back always rigid. I could only imagine the anal jokes that floated around the precinct.

"Captain," I said, letting the surprise I felt filter into my voice. It was weird how every time I said the word *captain,* I wanted to tack on a *Jack Sparrow* at the end.

The last time we'd spoken was a few days ago when I'd basically solved three cases in one fell swoop. Possibly four. It was the wrong thing to do. He took note and had been curious about me, about my role at the station as a consultant, ever since. I wasn't sure what to make of his curiosity. He seemed suspicious, but unless he knew that there was a grim reaper roaming the lands solving his cases for him, what on earth could he be suspicious about? "What brings you to my neck of the woods?"

He analyzed my offices a full minute before answering. With his back to me as he took in the same painting Mrs. Garza had, he said, "I've decided to keep closer tabs on any and all consultants the APD has on payroll."

Crap. "Really? H how many are there?"

"Removing any experts we occasionally use, like psychologists and the like, CIs and any consultants who are not actually on the payroll, that pretty much leaves just one."

"Oh." I offered up my best Sunday smile. "Surely you don't mean little ole me?"

He executed a perfect heel-to-toe turn. "I do, in fact."

I tried not to be intimidated. It didn't work. "Well, okay, this is my office."

"I was a detective, Davidson."

"Right, I just meant that this is pretty much all there is. I'm not sure what kind of tabs you wanted to keep, but—"

"How do you do it?" He'd turned back to study the books on my bookshelf. I prayed he didn't pay too close attention. *Sweet Savage Love* was probably not the kind of material he wanted his consultants to read.

I sat back behind my desk and took a sip of coffee. Liquid courage. "I'm sorry?"

"You seem to be very adept at solving cases and I was just wondering what your methods were."

"Oh, well, you know. I'm a detective." I laughed, sounding slightly more insane than I'd intended. "I detect."

He strolled over and sat in the chair opposite me, laying his hat in his lap. "And what methods of *detection* do you use?"

"Just the everyday kind," I said, having no idea what to say to that. What was he trying to get from me? "I just think to myself, 'What would Sherlock do?'"

"Sherlock?"

"I even have a bracelet with the acronym WWSD on it. It's my favorite. It's plastic." I was losing it. Spurting out inconsequential facts. He was so going to bust me. But for what? Why was I so nervous? I had a difficult time with confrontations. Two in one morning was going to be my undoing.

"And when you were nine? What methods of detection did you use then?"

I coughed. "Nine?"

"And how about when you were five? How did you solve cases for your father when you were five years old?"

"M-my father?"

"I've been doing some research," he said, picking lint off his hat, "conducting a few interviews. It seems you helped your father for years and now you assist your uncle. Have been for some time now."

Holy cow, was this air-the-dirty-laundry day? I would've worn my good underwear instead of the ones that said ADMISSION BY INVITATION ONLY. "I'm not really sure what you mean. I just became a PI a little over two years ago."

"I mean, you've been helping your relatives advance their careers for quite some time now. I just want to know how."

"You know, some people would find that idea ludicrous."

"But not you."

"No, sir. Probably not me. But I do have to meet a client, if you don't mind."

"I'm fairly certain I do." He uncrossed his legs and sat forward. "I will get to the bottom of this, Davidson."

"I understand."

"Do you?"

I chose not to answer. Instead, I let my gaze wander to the left as he stared at me.

"I think there's something else going on here, something that perhaps can't be explained by normal means. And I'll find out what it is."

When he turned and left, I let out the breath I was holding. Bloody hell. Before I knew it, the entire world was going to know I was the grim reaper. Wait, maybe I could get a reality TV contract. We could call it *Grim in the City.*

By the time the captain—who was sadly no relation to Captain Jack—left, I was shaking. Literally. Not once, but twice today I'd been accused of underhandedness. This was insane. What was wrong with the world? Didn't they know that ghosts and supernatural powers where little girls helped their dads and uncles solve cases didn't exist?

It was books. It was television shows and movies. They had desensitized the world. Damn writers.

I took the interior stairs down to the restaurant and saw my father. He was a tall man with a stick-figure body and sandy hair forever in need of a trim. "You're back!" I said, caught off guard for the third time that day.

"I am. You seem surprised. Or, maybe, nervous?"

I laughed. Loud. It was awkward. "What? Me? Not at all."

"I know about the gun, Charley."

"That was totally not my fault."

"Mmm-hmmm," he said, giving me a quick hug.

Dad and I hadn't been on the best of terms lately. He'd wanted me out of the PI biz, and I'd wanted him out of mine. He went about it the wrong way, trying to force me out by getting me arrested, among other things. Then I found out he'd had cancer and wanted to see me safe before he passed. The fact that he magically healed was a conundrum. One for which he thought I had the answers. I didn't. I was pretty sure healing was not part of my gig. I was the grim reaper, for goodness' sake.

"Can we talk soon?" he asked.

Discomfort prickled over my skin. He wanted answers

that I didn't have. Since I was certain that's what he wanted to talk about, I deflected. "Is that a new shirt?"

"Soon, pumpkin," he said before heading back to his office. He was so demanding.

I glanced around the bar and was floored at how many women were in there once again. The place had just opened for lunch like twenty seconds earlier. What the hell?

Shaking my head, I sat at my usual corner booth and looked at a menu for some unknown reason. I had the thing memorized, but that quesadilla from last night had to be a new item. There was nothing about it on the menu. Maybe it was a special.

I spotted Mrs. Tidwell coming in and stood to wave her over.

"Wow," she said, unwrapping her stylish scarf. She was around my age and had been married to Marvin for just a little over a year. "This place is busy."

I frowned and looked around. "Right? It's never this busy this early. And there are so many women."

"That's unusual?" she asked as she settled in and asked for a water from our server.

"It is. This is kind of a cop hangout, and I've just never seen so many women in here. And once again, it is hotter than sin."

"I'm fine, but if you're hot—"

"No, it's okay."

Before we could get down to business, our server came back with our waters. I ordered a green chili stew, my usual, and Mrs. Tidwell ordered a taco salad. Maybe I should have ordered that. It sounded wonderful. Or maybe I should have ordered the chicken quesadilla from the night before. Now I was being indecisive. I hated the in-decisive me. I liked the decisive me, the one who ordered the usual, then longed for something else I saw as it passed on a platter after I was halfway finished with mine.

"Don't you think so?"

"I'm sorry." Had she been talking that whole time? I hated the ADD me, too. I much preferred—

"What do you think?"

Shit. Did it again. I called out to our server. "Can you bring me a coffee, too?" Coffee would help. Or not. Either way.

"So, what did you find out?"

I pulled out the pictures and told Valerie Tidwell everything I'd found out so far. "I know this seems damning, but I'd like to keep checking, if you don't mind."

She sniffled into her napkin. "I knew it. I could just tell. He's been pulling away from me, you know? He used to notice everything. If I styled my hair differently. If I raised the hem on a skirt. I thought it was so charming, but now, nothing. It's like I've become invisible."

"Hon, this isn't really evidence that he has been cheating on you. He invited my associate to a hotel, but that's as far as it got."

Through the tears, "And I suppose he just wanted to play canasta." Canasta was fun. Or it sounded fun. I'd never actually played, but it sounded kind of kinky for some reason.

"I know this is hard," I said, "but can I ask you about your weight?"

"My weight?"

"Yes, it's just, well, you weighed quite a bit more when you got married."

I'd embarrassed her. "Yes, I've had a weight problem my whole life. I had surgery so I could shed some pounds. It was beginning to affect my health. Why?"

"I just, it's just that I think that could be part of the problem. My associate is . . . well, bigger. And he wouldn't give me the time of day. I think he likes bigger women."

Her face morphed into disbelief. "He's cheating on me because I lost weight?"

"No, Mrs. Tidwell. If he's cheating on you, it's because he is not the man you thought he was. This is not your fault. It's his."

"I just can't believe it. I mean, I thought men left their wives when they gained weight, not the other way around."

"I was a little surprised as well. But again, your weight shouldn't matter. If he really loved you, he would love you for you, not your body. But I have to be honest. I'm a little worried about you."

"Me?" she said, her brows drawn.

"Yes. Your husband saw the recording device I'd put on my associate's scarf. He knows that he was set up."

"Yes, I got your messages. He spent the night in jail and is going to be arraigned this morning."

"I'm worried about you. He was pretty angry when he found that mic. I'm not sure what he'll do."

"Oh, no, he's a pussycat. He's never raised a hand to me, if that's what you're worried about. He knows better."

"Well, good. That makes me feel a little better, but just in case, do you have someone you can call?"

"I do. I can call my parents anytime. He reveres my father. He wouldn't risk making him angry."

I wasn't so sure about that.

"Just please call me if you need to."

"I will."

Our food came and we ate in relative silence. Partly because I wasn't sure what else to say, how else to console Mrs. Tidwell, but mostly because I was once again in heaven. The green chili stew, which was always delicious, seemed to melt on my tongue and cause each and every taste bud in my mouth to burst with joy. It was amazing.

Dad walked up. "How is it?"

"Incredible. Will you send my regards to Sammy? He has outdone himself again."

"Sammy's out, hon. Broke his leg trying to ski off his roof. I've warned him about mixing beer and ski equipment."

"Then who—?"

Dad's phone rang and he excused himself to answer it.

"Are you sure I can't do anything else?" I asked Valerie.

She stood to leave with her shoulders straight and her chin high. "No. I know exactly who I'm calling next."

"Who would that be?"

"My lawyer."

I smiled and got up to leave, too. Uncle Bob and I were meeting at the bridge to find a missing person. Just as I headed out the back door, Jessica walked in. Her expression was one of pity.

"What?" I asked her, suddenly self-conscious.

"I mean, really? Again?"

I looked around. "Hey, I was here first."

"And I'll be here last," she promised.

God, she was good at the comebacks. I had nothing. I felt like we were back in high school.

"Okay." I continued on my way.

I was still a little floored Sammy had broken his leg. And skiing, no less. That had to be painful.

I headed to the parking lot and searched out Misery. The Jeep, not the emotion. My days of being miserable were well behind me. But that didn't mean I couldn't wreak misery on others. I called Garrett.

"Hello, Charles."

He was so formal. "Hey, Swopes. I have a job for you."

"I'm not looking for a job."

"Pleeeeease."

"Okay. What?"

That was easy. "Can you run a name for me, see if he has any priors real quick? I want to make sure my client is safe before her husband gets out of jail."

"Name."

Honestly, he acted as though he didn't like me anymore. Wait, maybe he didn't. "Do you still like me?"

"I never liked you."

Oh, right. He had a point. "Marvin Tidwell."

"Got it. I'll call you back."

I climbed into Misery and called Uncle Bob. "We hooking up?"

"Why does everything out of your mouth make me sound incestuous?"

"Um, I wasn't aware that it did. Perhaps you have a guilty conscience."

"Charley."

"Is there something you need to get off your chest? Besides that skank I saw you with the other day?"

He cleared his throat. "You saw that?"

"It gave me nightmares."

"I was undercover."

"I stopped falling for that when I was five."

"Oh. Do you know where you're going?"

"Kind of. Are you already out there?"

"On the way now."

"Okay, I'll be there in a few."

I hung up just as Cookie texted me again.

Hurry, what would I do if someone grabbed me from behind with a knife?
Whatever he told you to do.

That's what I'd do, anyway. Knives were hard to send off. Mostly 'cause they freaking hurt when they sliced through your flesh.

On the way to the bridge to search for a body—a dead one—I decided to try another voice. I brought up the pirated app, punched in my destination, and listened as a being grunted and groaned. After a moment, he said, "In one thousand feet, turn right you will."

I loved Yoda. I thought about buying him and putting him on my mantel. I didn't, mostly because I didn't have a mantel, but during a recent addiction to a shop-at-home channel, I bought a tiny Yoda key ring that gave me comfort on long lonely nights. He didn't vibrate or anything. I just liked having someone tiny and powerful and oddly charming near me.

Sadly, I had no idea where this bridge was. I didn't get out this way often, and finding an old bridge in the middle of nowhere was harder than I'd expected. But two things were striking me as being just a bit harder. The fact that the dead naked man was back and the fact that a huge black SUV was so far up my ass, I could almost read his VIN from my rearview.

I slowed down. He slowed down. I thought about waving him past me, but if he'd wanted to pass, he would have. The interior of his vehicle was so dark, I couldn't see enough to get a description. All I could make out were dark glasses and a black baseball cap.

"Lost, you are. Make a U-turn, you will."

Shit. Did I miss a turn? I was losing my bond with Yoda. He was mocking me, I could tell. I scanned the area. I couldn't have missed a turn. There wasn't one to miss.

SUV Guy slowed down until he was about twenty feet

back. Just when I started to breathe easier, he gunned his engine and darted forward.

Damn. "Hold on," I said to Dead Naked Man, "he's going to hit us." If I veered off the road to evade him, he could broadside me, so I stayed the course, dialing Uncle Bob while trying to keep Misery on the road.

"In two hundred feet, bear right, you will."

Bear right? There was no bearing right. There was no bearing at all. Clearly Yoda was going to get someone killed.

Just as the SUV was about to crash into me, he slammed on his brakes, losing just enough traction to swerve into the other lane. But he regained control quickly and started the game all over again.

"Where are you?" Uncle Bob asked.

"In five hundred feet, find your destination you will."

Oh, awesome. I'd made it. "I'm close, I think. But someone—" I squeaked when the SUV pulled the same maneuver, rocketing forward, a microsecond away from driving up my ass before slamming on his brakes.

I let go of the breath I was holding. "Black SUV, GMC with chrome grille and moldings, tinted windows, male driver under the age of fifty, dark glasses and black baseball cap."

"Got it. What's going on?"

"He just tried to give me a GMC enema. Twice."

"I'm on my way," he said. It sounded like he was running to his own SUV.

I cursed New Mexico's lack of requirement for front license plates. The guy backed way off before turning around and heading in the other direction, too far for me to get his numbers. And no way was I turning around to try to get them.

"That's okay. He backed off."

I'm not sure why I didn't just have Ubie swing by to

get me. It would have been much less traumatic. Not to mention the fact that it just isn't as easy *not* to look at genitals as one might think. Uncle Bob was standing by the open door of his gray SUV, hands on hips, looking very worried.

The bridge was one of those old railroad bridges, all rusted metal bracings and rivets. I had no idea it was even out here. It was gorgeous against the stark landscape of New Mexico.

"Did you get anything else?" he asked when I climbed out, trying not to crumple to the ground.

"Besides lost? Freaking Yoda." Blaming Yoda seemed like the right thing to do. "That guy could've killed me. And there's a naked man in my car. He's elderly."

I tried to play it cool, but Ubie saw right through my bravado. I decided to name my bravado Saran Wrap. Then again, my uncontrollable shaking could've given me away. He pulled me into his arms.

"No one has driven by here since the faded red Pinto with a chicken coop strapped to the top."

"What is my stepmother doing out here? Her and her chickens."

Uncle Bob tried not to grin. He failed.

"No, the guy turned around and headed back to town."

"Nothing," a voice from beyond said.

I peeked over an incline into the dry ravine. Ubie had brought Taft, the cop who gave Reyes such a hard time the night before.

"Hey," I said to him when he looked up. He'd climbed down and was scouting the area.

He nodded in greeting. "I haven't found anything."

Taft was kind of good to have around. Because of his little sister who died when he was a kid, he knew about my ability to see the departed. Thankfully he didn't ask questions beyond that. It took him a while to swallow the small amount of what he did know. I couldn't imagine what he'd do if he were to find out the whole truth. I didn't figure him for a grim reaper advocate.

"Any tracks or disturbances in the area down there?" Ubie asked.

"Nope, not a single one that I can find."

"I don't know, hon, are you sure this is the place?"

"It's the place she told me about. She was Hispanic, dressed in nurse's scrubs."

"And she said her body was here?"

"Yes, did you find any missing women matching her description?"

"There was one from a couple of years ago, but that's about it. You said she came to you this morning?"

"The very one."

He went back to his SUV and took out a file. "Is this her?"

I took a quick look. "No, this girl is much more Asian than my visitor. Who was Hispanic," I reminded him. He never listened.

"Okay, look through these and let me know. I'm going to call in the SUV. We might get lucky and find another officer on this road."

"Sounds good."

He called the station while I perused. After a few minutes, he strolled back to me. "Anything?"

"No. And no missing Nicoles or Nickys today?" I asked him as I thumbed through the pictures of missing women. I had also hoped to recognize one of the women in my apartment, but nothing popped out at me. Of course, it was hard to make out their faces from beneath the tangled masses of hair and mud.

"Not that I found, but she may not be from here."

"Can you widen the search?"

"I can try now that I have a description."

Taft climbed back to the top, his breathing only slightly labored from the effort. "Not a thing, boss."

"I love it when you call me boss," I said.

He frowned.

"I was really hoping to find her," I said. "She was so worried about her family."

"Did you get anything else that might lead us to her identity?" Taft asked.

"She was wearing scrubs and a name tag on a lanyard. I saw the letters *N-i-c*. I'm really just guessing on the name Nicole."

He dusted off his uniform and squinted as he surveyed the area again. "What hospital?"

"Presbyterian, I think. I'll go there and see what I can dig up later today."

When Uncle Bob went to answer a call, Taft stepped closer to me. He stuffed his hands into his pockets and looked out over the desert. "Have you seen my sister?"

I closed the file folder. "Not in a few days. She's still hanging at the old asylum."

"But she has friends now?" he asked.

"Yeah, she has friends." Taft was an okay guy. He almost died trying to save his sister and still looked out for her. But he needed to know the truth about her. "And she's still as psychotic as ever, in case you're wondering. Did she have a fondness for scissors when she was little?"

He chuckled. "She cut the hair off all her dolls, if that's what you mean."

"I knew it. I would have left that place completely bald if she'd gotten a hold of me. I'll have to remember that in the future."

"Okay, I guess I'm heading back."

"Follow Charley back into town," Ubie said.

"Uncle Bob!" I said, my voice a nasally whine, the kind I knew he hated. "Wait, that's a great idea. SUV Guy could come back." I looked at Taft. "Just shoot any black SUV you see coming our way."

"I'll do that," he said. But he was lying. I could tell.

"I'm sorry I dragged you out here," I said to Ubie. "She has to show up eventually. She said her family couldn't find her body. That she had been there for days. Someone had to report her missing."

"We'll look into it," Ubie said. "In the meantime, I have a date with a golf club and a little ball."

"You and your little balls." I shook my head in disappointment. How could I get any work done without slaves? Speaking of slaves, I called Garrett on the way back to town.

"A guy in an SUV tried to kill me."

"That's strange."

"Why?"

"Because the guy I hired doesn't drive an SUV."

"That is strange." Swopes. Always the kidder. "Wait. If someone else kills me, do you still have to pay him?"

"I think I should at least get a discount."

"Right? There's also a naked elderly man in my passenger seat."

"TMI, Charles."

Poor dead naked man. No one wanted to know about him. "Well? Does Marv have any priors?"

"Nothing. His record's spotless, but how old did you say he was?"

"I don't know, around thirty-five?"

"Then I have the wrong Marvin Tidwell. This guy is fifty-four. And dead."

"Really, yeah, this one didn't look that dead."

"Probably not, but it could be you're dealing with a case of identity theft."

"Seriously?" I asked, straightening. "I hadn't thought of that."

"Again, it's doubtful, but I can look into it if you want."

"I want. Thanks a gazillion."

I knew I tolerated him for a reason. I hung up and contemplated what he'd said. Identity theft. Now, that would be incriminating. I knew the odds were against it, as my dead naked man was well beyond fifty-four, but just in case, I looked over and asked him, "Your name doesn't happen to be Marv, does it?"

Chapter Seven

I am currently unsupervised.
It freaks me out, too, but the possibilities are endless.
—T-SHIRT

Unfortunately, I had an appointment with a psychologist. I'd remembered my paintings, the ones that involved several counts of death and dismemberment. I wanted to impress her, to start our relationship off on the right foot. Albeit a severed one. On the way over to her office, I brought up another voice. There was one guy I could listen to all day and still not understand a word coming out of his mouth. Ozzy. Who could resist a Brit with a slurry accent?

"Um, okay, yeah, so in aboot three hundred feet, beah right." Poor guy always sounded drunk. This app had to be pirated and altered in some way. Surely the real app would make Ozzy sound a little more coherent.

"All right, then in two hundred feet, tahn left."

The funny thing about GPS was it didn't always send you in the right direction.

I knew that if I took a right and took Twelfth instead, I'd get there faster, so I turned right. Ozzy did not approve.

"Wut the foock?"

Did he just say the F-word?

"Ya not even foocking listening."

"Ha! This is great," I said to the dead naked guy. He ignored me. Ozzy was so entertaining, though, I had a hard time cutting him off. He got really mad when I missed the right on Central, so I started missing turns on purpose just to listen to him rail at me. I was almost late for my head shrinking.

But I finally found the office of one Dr. Romero, the shrink my sister, Gemma, set me up with, despite Ozzy's nagging. Gemma was so determined for me to deal with my PTSD, but I thought I was doing pretty well with it. We were friends now. I had my incontinence under control and Chihuahuas rarely frightened me anymore. Besides, I was certain the one that did was rabid. He had foam around his mouth and a crazy eye that looked off into the distance. The fact that he gave me nightmares was hardly my fault.

I stepped inside a nice office with the usual Southwestern decor of so many professional offices in Alb. Sadly, this was the cheesy Southwestern decor. The kind that was popular in the nineties, complete with plaster cactus plants and a howling coyote. Okay, I had a thing for the howling coyotes, especially the kind with bandannas around their necks, but I wasn't going to let Dr. Romero know that.

"You must be Charley," she said, and I could smell the New Age coming off her in waves. She was going to be one of those. This shouldn't take long.

"I am," I said, and forced a smile.

"Come on in."

She led me into another room with two chairs and a small sofa. "I'm feeling much better," I said to her before sitting on the sofa. It was the farthest I could get from her without being rude.

"I hope it's okay, your sister filled me in on what happened to you."

"Isn't that breaking some code of confidentiality?"

"Not technically, but does it bother you that she told me?"

"Not at all. I was just wondering."

"Well, I'm sorry we had to meet on a Saturday. Your sister's a good friend and I'm going out of town next week. She wanted me to get you in before—" She noticed the portfolio I was carrying. "What is this?"

"Art therapy. I thought I'd impress you with my rehabilitation. I painted this one last week." I lifted the painting of dead birds with a brown-haired girl eating them. "And I painted this one last night." I showed her the one of the birds flying past a bright sun with a rainbow and unicorn in the background. If this didn't prove my sanity, I didn't know what would.

She smiled. "Your sister has filled me in. I know all your little tricks."

"Really? Did she tell you about the one where I say, 'Pick a card. Any card.' And then I say, 'Now put it anywhere in the deck. Don't show me!' And then—"

"This is called deflecting."

"That's weird. I was just told yesterday that I *re*flect. Like the sun off a chrome bumper." When a sly smile spread across her face, I knew I would not win this round. "So, she told you about all of my little tricks, huh?"

"Yes, she did."

"Did she mention the big ones? Because I have some doozies."

"Why don't you tell me about them," she said, her expression one of absolute understanding and infinite patience.

I leaned forward, regarded her from underneath my lashes, and added an evil tilt to my smirk. "I can make the earth quake beneath your feet."

"Really?" she asked, as though fascinated.

What was I doing? Begging for a bed in a psych ward? She was just so smug, I felt I needed to put her in her place. But she was also Gemma's friend. If I screwed her up, I'd never hear the end of it.

She leaned onto her elbows as well. "Why don't you show me?"

It wasn't so much a question as a challenge. That did it. I let the power inside me gather near my heart, let it swirl and coil together until it collided in my center. I let it slide out of me, let it grab hold of the earth beneath us and the air around us. I let it take charge and build energy, and then I nudged it.

The world quaked beneath our feet. The objects on her desk shook and a lamp fell over before I reined in the energy I'd let out.

She paled, but fought her fear. "Like I said, your sister told me about you."

Well, crap. I reached for my phone. "Can you excuse me for just a minute?"

She sat back and waited as I rang Gemma.

"Hel—"

"Gemma, what the hell?"

"What? What'd I do now?" She seemed winded.

"What were you doing?" I asked suspiciously. She'd been very secretive the last few days. She was totally doing someone.

"Nothing. Why are you cursing at me?"

"Who's there?"

"No one. Did you miss your appointment?"

"Oh, you mean the one where you told a complete stranger all about me? That one?"

"Yes."

"Gemma! What the hell?"

"Couldn't scare her off, could you?" she asked, satisfaction sparkling in her voice.

"No. What did you say?"

"Ask her. I'm busy."

"Who's there?"

"No one. Stop asking me that. And it's none of your business."

"Fine." I hung up and went back into Dr. Romero's office, preparing myself for an hour of hell on Earth.

While Dr. Romero wasn't as bad as I'd originally suspected—she had courage, stepping up to the plate after the curveball I'd thrown her—I really didn't see our relationship going anywhere. After my session, I headed straight toward Presbyterian Hospital to see if I could get any information on a missing woman named Nic-something-or-other. I walked into the hospital and went straight to the information desk. Since it was information I needed.

"Hi," I said to the lady sitting behind it. "I was just wondering if you could help me. I had an amazing nurse named Nicole the other day, and I hoped you could tell me what ward she worked in."

The woman stared at me, then asked, "Well, what ward were you admitted into?"

She had a good point. "Oh, well, that's the thing. I don't remember, exactly. I was, um, inebriated."

"What's your name, and I'll look it up."

"Well, I didn't check in under my real name."

After a long sigh, she said, "I can't just give out information on a whim." Her mouth did that schoolmarm grim line thing. I was being chastised and chastised good.

"Look, all I need to know is if you have a nurse or anyone else who would wear scrubs named Nicole. Or possibly Nicki. Or, well, anything that starts with an *N-i-c*." I flashed my PI card. It made me look official. "I'm working on a case for APD. We would really appreciate your help."

"And what case would that be?"

I jumped at the sound of a male voice behind me and turned to see the captain there. Was he following me? "Captain Eckert, what are you doing here?"

"Wondering the same thing about you. I just checked your status this morning and I don't recall you being on a case for us presently."

"Oh, well, I'm working with my uncle on something."

"And what would that be?"

Holy cow, this man was going to get annoying. Why was he so determined to figure any of this out? "It's a missing persons case."

"I don't recall Bob being on any missing persons case at the moment."

"It's more like a potential missing persons."

"Fine, I'll do anything I can to help."

"Oh, no, I couldn't bother you."

He ignored me, flashed his badge to the receptionist, and said, "Employees named Nicole, if you don't mind."

"All right." She clicked a few keys and gave me the names of two Nicoles. One worked in diagnostics and one was a charge nurse in the neonatal unit.

As bad as I hated to do it—I didn't want to give him any more clues than I had to—I asked, "Does your screen bring up pictures?"

"Yes, it does." She swung the screen around to me. "This is Nicole Foster."

Nicole Foster was a tall redhead with a lot of miles on her. "No, that's not her."

"Okay." She tapped a few more keys. "This is Nicole Schwab."

This one was younger, but she was a blonde with freckles and glasses. "Darn. That's not her, either."

"You know, we do have a Nicolette." She turned the screen back toward her and tapped again. "What about her?"

When she turned it around again, I nodded. "That's her."

"Okay, well, Nicolette Lemay works in post-op. Third floor." She flashed a smile at the captain. "I'm glad I could be of help."

"Thank you," I said, and looked over my shoulder at the captain. I had never realized it, but he was an alarmingly handsome man. Okay, I'd buy her interest as genuine. Many women were attracted to the uniform and little else.

I took off toward the elevators. Captain Eckert followed. "I can take it from here," I said to him, then gestured toward the receptionist. "You know, if you want to get her number."

He raised his brows in surprise. "I'm good, thanks."

The captain was a widower. His wife had died of cancer a couple of years earlier, and I felt like that was one reason my approval for a consultant position with APD went through so seamlessly. He was mourning his wife. I doubt he would have noticed if Uncle Bob asked for an elephant in the break room. I stayed as far away from the man as I possibly could back then. His grief was suffocating. It enveloped me and pushed the oxygen from my lungs and I could hardly look at him without feeling an overwhelming sense of loss. Even now I associated him with that feeling of extreme discomfort. It made him genuine and honorable, but my knee-jerk reaction to him was to run in the other direction.

Still, I'd had a soft spot for him ever since I met him. A soft spot that was full of wary reverence. The guy was sharp, and now that he was on my trail, I'd have to be careful. He'd just never paid much attention to the goings-on of Ubie and me. We solved cases and that was good enough for him. But after my last fiasco, which involved me solving four cases in one day, including one of a serial killer . . . well, okay, I could understand his sudden interest.

We walked to the elevator and I pressed the third floor. Nothing screamed awkward like being in an elevator with someone who sucked the oxygen from the room.

"So, how's crime been treating you?" I asked to get my mind off the lack of ventilation. My red blood cells were screaming for air.

He only looked at me.

Okay. I rocked back onto my heels and found a fascinating panel of buttons to look at. After a thousand years of agony, the doors opened. I tried not to gasp for air aloud.

We stepped out onto the third floor and I walked to the nurses' station, pretending like the cap'n wasn't stalking me. I flashed my PI license. "Hi, I was wondering if I could ask you a few questions about Nicole Lemay."

Of the three nurses who sat behind it, only one didn't look up right away, clearly too busy to answer any questions.

"Nicole?" one asked me. She had wiry brown hair and gold-rimmed glasses.

"Yes, I was wondering when you last saw her."

The nurse stared at me, her expression blank. She checked her watch. "I guess about five minutes ago."

"No," I said, shifting on my feet. "Nicole Lemay. I'm sorry, Nicolette?"

The other nurse spoke up then, a pretty blonde with an affinity for carbs. "You're right," she said, checking the clock on the wall. "We haven't seen Nicolette in about twenty minutes."

The first nurse laughed. "Right. Time flies when you're having fun."

"I told you not to get near Mrs. Watson. She likes her bubble."

"I had to get her vitals."

"Oh, there she is." One of them pointed.

"I'm Nicolette."

I turned around and came face-to-face with my departed woman. Only she wasn't departed anymore. She was alive. And, well, breathing. It was a miracle!

"Um, Nicolette Lemay?"

"My whole life." She was busy cleaning out her pockets, relieving them of syringe wrappers and stray wads of tape. "Sadly," she added. "If I don't get a marriage proposal soon, my mother is going to take out an ad."

"Oh, well, I was just—"

"You look familiar," she said. She paused and looked me over, then focused on my sidekick.

"Right, sorry. I'm Charley and this is Captain Eckert of the Albuquerque Police Department."

She straightened, growing alarmed. "Did something happen?"

"No, no, not at all," I jumped to assure her. "It's just that— Um—" I stood there completely tongue-tied. I'd never had a departed woman show up, tell me where to find her body, then show up later completely alive. She was just so corporeal. Not a hair out of place. No wonder we couldn't find her body. She'd moved it.

"Have you ever been to the old railroad bridge on 57?"

"I have no idea where that is."

"Oh. Do you, by chance, have an identical twin?" I asked her, realizing how inane I probably sounded.

"Nnnnno. What's this about?"

"Nothing. Never mind. My mistake. I think I have the wrong Nicolette."

"Oh." That seemed to calm her a bit. "But you really do look familiar. Did you ever date my brother?"

"It's quite possible. I tend to date. Or, well, I used to. So, like where?"

"I'm sorry?"

"Where would your mother take out an ad?"

"Oh, well, she's talked about taking out an ad in the personals but has also threatened to list me as an escort. You know, to get dates."

I could understand that. Captain Eckert tensed, not used to having to listen to the idle chitchat of us womenfolk. "But we'll let you go for now. So sorry about the mistake."

I turned to leave, but the captain just stood there as though confused. Left with little choice, I took hold of his arm and led him away with me, a maneuver he did not appreciate at all.

"That's it?" he asked.

"That's it."

"What was that about?"

"Nothing. I was mistaken."

"You recognized her, so clearly—"

"No, I'm not sure what happened. That wasn't the girl."

"What girl?"

"The girl who might or might not be missing."

"What makes you think there's a missing woman? Did someone file a report?"

"I got an anonymous tip. Someone must be playing a joke."

"Do you always go to such extremes for anonymous tips?"

"No. Sometimes." He was trying to trip me up. He suspected something; he just had no idea what. I got that a lot. "It seemed legit at the time."

Once I stuffed him into the elevator, I let go of his jacket sleeve. "Sorry," I said, smoothing it.

He took a step in the opposite direction and gazed

straight ahead when he spoke to me. "You solve cases, Davidson. A lot of them. I want to know how."

Crap. This was not going to end well for anyone. "You know, it's really all Uncle Bob. He's great at his job."

"I know he is, and yet I can't help but wonder how good he would be if he didn't have you at his beck and call." He turned to me then. "Or is it him at your beck and call?"

The elevator doors opened. "I should probably be offended, Captain. My uncle is a fantastic detective. He's helped me a lot over the years."

"I'm sure he has. You scratch his back. He scratches yours."

I backed off the elevator. "I have skin allergies. I'm itchy." Before he could ask me anything else, I practically ran for the glass doors of the hospital.

The minute I got to Misery, I called Ubie. "So, I found our missing girl, but so did your captain."

"What?" he asked, alarmed. "Captain Eckert was there? Did he see the body? Has he called in a team?"

"Not exactly. There's no body. She's alive. It's a miracle!"

He let out a lengthy sigh, and I could see him scrubbing his face with his fingers. "Charley, you told me she came to you."

"She did. Trust me, Uncle Bob, I am just as lost as you are. But we need to deal with your captain. He's acting really strange. Like he knows something, or thinks he knows something. I'm not sure what to say around him. He wants to know how I am solving so many cases."

"Damn. He said that?"

"Yes, and he knows that I've basically been helping both you and Dad since I was five. He went back and checked! How is that possible?"

"I have no idea, pumpkin. But everyone knows you help

me with cases, thus the consultant position. Hell, he approved it."

"Yeah, but now he's getting curious. He's digging. I totally shouldn't have solved murder, missing child, bank robber, and serial killer cases all in one day. It drew too much attention. I'm going to have to spread out my cases better. Solve them at regular intervals."

"That might be a good idea."

I tried three more voices on my way to Rocket's, and while I'd never considered Bela Lugosi particularly creepy, his telling me to turn right here and take a left there made me think he was leading me to my death. Especially since the guy had died before I was born and I doubted they had navigation back then. Either these voices were done by impersonators or Bela really was immortal. I ultimately decided to stick with Ozzy. I may get completely lost for lack of understanding, but at least he was entertaining.

I was excited to see the Rocket Man. Rocket, a giant version of the Pillsbury Doughboy, was a departed savant who knew every name of every person who had ever lived and died on Earth. And he was a great resource. I could give him a name, and he could tell me where that person stood in the cosmic scheme of things. Alive. Dead. Not dead yet but well on his way. But trying to get any other information out of Rocket was like pulling teeth with tweezers.

The abandoned asylum where Rocket lived was owned by the Bandits, a motorcycle club whose leaders were now wanted and on the run for bank robbery. One of those leaders, a scruffy rascal who went by the name of Donovan, held a special place in my heart. Actually, they all did, but Donovan and I had shared something special. Thankfully, not herpes. Our relationship had never gone that far, but he was such a gentleman. I realized how much

I missed him when I drove past their house next to the asylum. Well, I would have driven past their house if it had still been there.

I screeched to a stop in front of an empty lot. Where the Bandit headquarters—aka Donovan's house—had been now sat a single tree that had been in their backyard and a bald patch of land where the house had once stood. Even the detached garage had vanished, along with all the tools and motorcycle parts therein. I could've sworn that's where I'd left it. Donovan was going to be pissed when he got back. If he ever came back.

Thankfully, the asylum was still there, but my key to the front door, which I'd never even had the chance to use, would do me no good. In place of the old chain-link fence that had surrounded the asylum was a new chain-link fence, shining and sparkling in the sun, and it bordered the entire block, not just the asylum itself. Normally this would not be a big deal. I could just scale the fence and sneak in through a window out back that led to the basement of the abandoned hospital if they'd changed the locks. But this new fence, with its crisply installed posts and tight weaving, had been topped off with razor wire. Razor wire! Who did that?

I sat in Misery and contemplated my odds of getting over the razor wire unscathed. I'd seen it done in film. All I needed was a prison uniform, a pair of gloves, and a few sheets tied together.

I coasted forward until I could see the new billboard-like sign in front of the asylum. It simply read PRIVATE PROPERTY in huge black and blue letters. And below that, THIS PROPERTY IS OWNED BY C&R INDUSTRIES. ALL TRES-PASSERS WILL BE PROSECUTED.

Sounded ominous. How was I going to get to Rocket now? I'd just have to come back tonight and try to find a way in.

Fortunately, it would be dark soon. I could go grab a bite and make a plan. As I headed that way, the super-duper downside of some big business buying this land hit me. Rocket. If they tore down the asylum, where would he go? Where would his sister go? I would invite him to live with me, but he had a habit of carving names into walls. My walls were drywall. They wouldn't last long, and the landlord would probably have a cow. Or at least a small game hen.

I dragged out my phone and called Ubie. Not having Cookie at my constant beck and call was turning out to be a pain in the ass. No more classes for her.

"Did that guy try to kill you again?"

"No."

"Then it's still Saturday and I haven't finished my game yet."

"I need you to check something for me. Can you find out who bought a building downtown?"

"Don't you have an assistant for these things?"

"I do, but I sent her off to a concealed weapons class."

"Why?" he asked, becoming alarmed. "Is someone harassing her?"

"Besides me?"

"When is she getting back?"

"Tonight, but she has class all day tomorrow, too."

"Well, we'll all be safer for it."

"Can you find out who owns C and R Industries? They bought the old abandoned mental asylum downtown."

"That old thing? What are they going to do with it?"

"I don't know. I was hoping their overcompensating sign would say, but it just says 'private property' and shouts lots of threats in capital letters, all of which I plan to completely ignore later. I need to find out if they are going to tear it down, build apartments, create a sand garden, what."

After a long sigh, he said, "Okay, I'll put someone on it. But you know, the Albuquerque Police Department wasn't really created to find things out for you."

"Really? That's weird."

Before he could get too snippy, I hung up and took one last look at the asylum. Then a plan formed. I didn't need a prison uniform—sadly, because I was rather looking forward to the visit. I was on the outside. I had access to things those guys in the movie didn't. Of course, I'd have to come back at night, but come nightfall, I would be reunited with Rocket. Hopefully I'd come out of there alive. With the merry band of ghosts inside, that outcome was always questionable. Especially since Officer Taft's little sister, Strawberry Shortcake, had joined the gang. Either way, I made a mental note to put my hair up in a hat before going in.

I got another text from Cookie on my way home.

Almost home. Learned a lot.

Well, good. If I had to do without her for two whole days for nothing, Noni, the instructor, was getting an earful.

I stepped to my door and for the first time in several days there was no sticky note on it. I looked over at Reyes's door. Was that it? Was he already tired of me?

It would figure.

Being extra careful, I opened my door slowly, not really knowing what to expect. Would the departed women still be in there? I found out quickly the answer to that would be a resounding yes. And yes. Where I'd left probably nine or ten women, my apartment was now populated with at least twenty dirty blond women in varying states of trauma. I stopped just inside my threshold and looked on as women crawled across my carpet, scurried up my walls, and clung to my ceiling like a spider. One was huddled in a corner where two walls met the ceiling. It was the same woman from this morning. She hadn't moved.

While the average person would walk through this carnage none the wiser—besides being a little chilly perhaps—I could not walk through the departed. They were as solid to me as anyone else on the planet. So I ended up having to maneuver around my houseguests, trying not to step on fingers or toes. It made for an interesting walk. If anyone were to see me, they'd think I'd had one too many margaritas.

After finally making it to the breakfast bar, I put down my bag and hurdled the counter to get to the kitchen. Mr. Coffee was waiting for his usual greeting, and I couldn't let him down just because we'd been invaded. And I came up with a plan. I seemed to be full of plans lately. Maybe it was my new outlook on life. Don't invite certain death without a backup plan. Maybe I could plan other things. Like a wedding shower for Cookie and Uncle Bob. Or a bar mitzvah.

While Mr. Coffee gurgled and sputtered, I summoned Angel with the power of my reaper mind. Okay, I just thought about him and sort of wished him beside me.

Annnnnd . . . *Poof!*

"What the fuck, *pendeja*? Didn't I tell you not to do that anymore?"

I gestured to the women surrounding us. "Can you talk to them?"

"What do I look like, the ghost whisperer? They're loony. I'd have better luck talking to my cousin Alfonso's Chihuahua. At least Tía Juana knows Spanish."

"Your cousin's Chihuahua is named Tía Juana?" When he shrugged an affirmation, I said, "Just try. If anyone can talk to them, it's you."

"Why is that?"

"Because you're dead. You're one of them. You can do this."

"Not for five hundred dollars a month, I can't."

"Seriously?"

"It's a dog-eat-dog world, *mijita*. And my mom needs a new car."

"This is so wrong."

"I need at least—" He counted on his fingers "—seven hundred fifty dollars a month or I ain't risking my life again for no one's ass. Even yours." He bent to get a better look. "Fine as it is."

"Seven hundred fifty dollars a month?" I balked, gurgled, and sputtered like Mr. C. But in the back of my mind, I considered how much a real—as in living—detective would cost me, and it wasn't no $750 a month. Then again, I couldn't use any of his investigating in court. I couldn't turn it in to APD as evidence of dick. So there was that to take into consideration. Still, he had saved my life a couple of times. That was worth something. "You drive a hard bargain, Mr. Garza."

"Damn." He shook his head. "You would have gone higher, huh?"

I winked. "You'll never know. But what happens the next time your mom comes demanding answers? What then?"

He leaned against the counter and ran his fingers along the horrid chrome molding. "I don't know. I think she bought the whole great-uncle thing."

I lifted my hand to his cool cheek, ran my thumb along the fuzz over his top lip. "No, *mijito,* she didn't."

Angel and I had been together for over ten years, ever since I found him at an abandoned school, scared and alone. He meant so much to me.

Unfortunately, he'd died mid-puberty, and his hormones

were the worse for it. He stepped closer and put his hands on the counter, one at each side, blocking me in. I rolled my eyes, but he just closed the distance between us and ran his mouth along my jaw, not kissing it. As though taking in the warmth, testing the texture.

"We could make this work, you know."

"I will knee you in the groin."

"I could give you a night you will never forget."

"Because you will be writhing in agony all night and I will laugh unmercifully. It will be unforgettable."

"You know what they say. Once you go dead—"

"Reyes lives next door."

That did it. He stepped back and crossed his arms over his chest. "I told you not to let that *pendejo* into your life. We're all going to pay for this."

"What do you know about it?"

"Well, that's pretty much it. We're all going to pay if you two get together."

"So I've been told, but if that's all anybody has, then you can all bite me."

"It's wrong. It's against nature," he railed as I took my coffee and stepped over the woman in my kitchen archway. "You two can't be together. It's like milk and pretzels."

"Look, Romeo, we came to an agreement with the pay, so can you talk to these women or not?"

"I already tried. They ain't talking."

I pressed my lips together, chastising. "You could have mentioned that."

"You don't understand. They're here with you now. Just being around you will be healing to them. It's like if you took the sun and shrank it down to the size of a basketball. It would still be the sun. It would still shine all bright and shit and burn just as hot. It would still be soothing. Healing. That's you. Your light. It's soothing like that menthol crap my mom used to rub on my chest. Your presence is like a salve."

"I always thought my presence was more of an irritant. You know. Like paint thinner. Or napalm."

Chapter Eight

It's all fun and games until someone loses a testicle.
—T-SHIRT

Since Angel the pickup artist was no help whatsoever, I decided to see if Gemma could help. I tried calling her, but she didn't answer. Did she not know me at all? That wouldn't deter a grim reaper. Maybe a glum reaper or a bleak one, but never a grim.

I put down my coffee, grabbed my jacket, and wound through the throngs, dodging one who scurried between my legs and ducking under another hanging from the ceiling. My apartment would never be the same.

I opened the door only to find another gorgeous boy on my doorstep, only this one was still alive. He had blond hair and blue eyes and had stolen my heart the moment I first met him a couple of weeks back.

"Quentin," I said aloud for no one's benefit but my own. Quentin was Deaf. "Hey, sweetheart," I signed. "How are you?"

Fortunately, as the grim reaper, I'd been born knowing every language ever spoken on Earth. That included the vast and beautiful array of signed languages.

A shy smile spread across his handsome face. He nodded a greeting and I threw my arms around him for a hug.

He buried his face in the crook of my neck and held me to him a long minute. When he let go, he drew in his shoulders. Something was bothering him.

"What's wrong?" I asked in alarm.

He shrugged and looked down, seeming embarrassed. "Everything is different now."

My chest muscles tightened. He had been possessed by a demon hell-bent on killing me and ended up here in Albuquerque as a result. Artemis killed the demon that had possessed him, and Quentin basically woke up out of a catatonic state in a strange place with no family and no friends. But later I found out he had no family and no one to go back to in D.C., either, so I asked if he wanted to stay here. While he lived at the School for the Deaf in Santa Fe on the weekdays, we decided he'd spend his weekends at the convent with the sisters for now, at least until someone found them out and told the sisters they couldn't have a sixteen-year-old boy living at a convent full of nuns. But the Mother Superior had fallen a little in love with him, like pretty much everyone else, and was breaking all kinds of rules to have him there.

Still, he'd been possessed. As in a demon had taken up residence inside his body and kicked him out for a while. I didn't know how much of that time he would remember. How much it would affect him.

The reason the demon had possessed him in the first place, the reason they had possessed anyone, was because he could see into the supernatural world. Just barely. Just enough to make him a target. He could see a grayness where a ghost might be standing, but those who could do that could also see my light. In other words, they could pick me out of a lineup. They could lead the demons to me. Reyes's dad wanted me, the portal into heaven, and he apparently wanted me bad enough to ruin the lives of other people. Some who had been possessed had died as a result.

"Why don't you come inside?"

I opened my door farther. He started to go in, then stopped midstride. He surveyed my apartment, then took a wary step back.

Surprised, I asked, "Can you see them?" I figured even if he could, he could see only a fine gray mist where the women would be. But he was looking directly at them, his expression guarded, his stance almost hostile.

"I see them now," he said, his signs sharp, frustrated. "Not like I did before. I see dead people everywhere." He looked at me then, his brows drawn in anger. "Did you know the school in Santa Fe was built right by a cemetery?"

I sighed aloud. I did know that.

"So you can see them now? Not just their essence?"

He wrapped his arms around himself and nodded, refusing to take his eyes off the woman clinging to my ceiling. I had to admit, that had taken me by surprise, too.

I took a hand and put it on his face to gently bring him back to me; then I signed, "I'm so sorry, Quentin." Seeing dead people walking around would put anyone on edge. While I had been born with the ability, I did try to see it from another's point of view and I could understand how that fact would put a crimp in one's outlook.

His eyes watered and his mouth formed a grim line.

"Why don't we go in here?" I pointed behind him to Cookie's apartment.

He nodded.

After closing my door, I knocked on Cookie's, knowing her daughter, Amber, was home. Even then, I didn't normally knock, but I had company. I didn't want to catch Amber off guard. She was a twelve-year-old girl. She was probably prancing about to the latest pop song in her underwear. Or maybe that was just me.

Amber answered with her usual bounciness; then she

spotted Quentin. I figured he would stun her a little. He did. He'd stunned me a little when I first saw him, too.

"Hey, hon, can we use your living room for a minute?"

"Sure," she said. She seemed to be overcome with shyness all of a sudden. Amber wasn't exactly the shy type, but I got it. Quentin was arresting.

I signed as I spoke. "Awesome, thank you. This is Quentin. And Quentin, this is Amber." They both smiled a greeting and we stepped inside.

"Can I get you something to drink?" she asked him.

I quickly interpreted and Quentin waved a hand in negation. "No, thank you," he signed.

And Amber melted. I could see it in her eyes. Her forlorn expression. Her hand over her heart. Subtlety was not her strong suit.

"Thanks, Amber," I said, hoping to herd her out of the room. "We just needed a place to talk for a few. I'll let you know if we need anything."

"Okay," she said, her voice breathy with newfound love.

Yep, I'd so been there.

We sat on Cookie's earth-toned sofa, and Quentin took out his sunglasses. I almost forgot. He saw me as a spotlight shining in his face. That couldn't be pleasant.

"So, what's going on?" I asked him when he sat on the edge of the sofa. "How's Sister Mary Elizabeth?"

Sister Mary Elizabeth was a mutual friend with a similar unique ability, only she could hear the angels as they chatted amongst themselves. And, according to the sister, they were very chatty.

"She's good," he said. His jacket sleeves were almost too long for his arms. The cuffs covered half his hands as he signed, but his hands were masculine already with hard angles and long fingers. "She said to say hi."

"Oh, how nice. Tell her hi back. And now that we're done with the pleasantries, what's going on?"

He drew in a deep breath. "I used to see only ghosts, like shadows in the air. But now I see everything. I see people. I see their clothes. I see the dirt on their feet. I see the blood in their hair."

I put a palm on his knee in support as he vented about everything he'd been seeing. I was a little surprised Sister Mary Elizabeth hadn't called me about this. Then again, maybe he didn't tell her. When he was finished ranting, he blinked back at me, wanting answers, wanting a solution. A solution I would not have.

"You see what I see," I said, my face showing the empathy I felt. "You see the departed who are left on Earth, who haven't crossed over. It's not like in the movies. They aren't here to scare you or hurt you."

He kept his eyes focused on mine, hoping I had better news.

"They just want answers like you do. They want to finish something that was left undone."

"Like unfinished business?" he asked.

"Yes. Who told you that?"

"My friends at school. They think it's cool I see dead people." He almost seemed proud of that fact. That was one thing about the Deaf community I always admired beyond belief—they were the most accepting lot I'd ever come across. It didn't matter what else you had to deal with, blindness, mental challenges, fetal alcohol syndrome, autism, whatever else you were dealing with, if you were culturally Deaf, they accepted you as one of their own. Even, apparently, if you had supernatural sight.

"I think it's pretty cool, too," I said.

He looked down. "It's okay, I guess."

"But it can be scary."

"Yes."

"Just remember, they are exactly like us. They were us, they've just crossed to another level of existence."

He furrowed his brows. "So it's like they're still alive?"

"Yes, very much so. They just don't have their physical bodies anymore. And they could probably use a friend."

His gaze slid past me. "I didn't think of it that way." I let him absorb that information a minute before he blinked back to me. "Maybe they want to go to heaven but they can't find you."

I shook my head. "The way I understand it, they can see me from anywhere in the world."

His eyes rounded. "Even if they're in China?"

"Even if they're in China," I said.

"How? There's a whole planet between you and them. Can they see through things like we can see through them?"

"I have no idea. It's strange. I can't see my own light, so I have no idea how they do."

That caught his attention. "You can't see it? Your own light? Because it's crazy bright."

"Nope."

"You can see them, but you can't see your light?"

"Right."

"That's weird." His mouth tilted into a mischievous grin. "Maybe you need help with your brain."

"People keep telling me that. No idea why."

He nodded, agreeing with those people, so naturally I had to tickle his ribs. And lo and behold, the kid was more ticklish than a newborn babe. He laughed and pushed at my hands. When I didn't give up my quest, he curled into a fetal position, his laugh husky and endearing.

"Are you mauling that poor kid?"

I looked over as Cookie walked in carrying take-out bags. "Only a little. He thinks I need mental help."

"Well, if I have to take sides . . ."

His laugh grew louder when I found a particularly sensitive rib. "Peeeeese!" he said with his soft voice muffled from his jacket.

"Please?" I asked aloud. "You'll get no quarter from me, mister."

He wasn't looking and I wasn't signing, so I was speaking only for my own benefit.

And Cookie's. "I brought a pan each of chicken Alfredo and spaghetti and an order of garlic bread."

"Yum," I said, letting Quentin up so he could apologize accordingly. His sunglasses were somewhere in the sofa and he blocked my light with a hand as he searched for them, a huge grin on his face.

"Is that who I think it is?" she asked.

"It's Quentin," Amber said, bounding in like a northern wind. "Isn't he beautiful? And he has no idea what I'm saying. I can talk about him and he won't know."

Quentin chuckled and looked over at her.

She paused, her joy turning to mortification, then asked, "Aunt Charley, did you tell him what I said?"

"Yes, I did. And it's rude to talk about people behind their backs."

Her face turned a bright shade of scarlet. I almost felt sorry for her.

"You didn't have to tell him."

My expression softened in sympathy. "Do you think that's fair? For you to take advantage of his hearing loss like that?"

"Well, if you put it that way." She bowed her head and rubbed her fist in a circle on her chest. "I'm sorry, Quentin."

I was impressed that she knew the sign.

Having finally found his sunglasses, Quentin propped them on top of his head and stepped over to her. "It's okay."

His smile disarmed her completely. She forgot all about

her mortification. "Can you stay and eat with us?" she asked aloud.

I jumped over the back of the sofa, regretted it when I landed and almost took out a rubber tree plant, and interpreted what Amber had said.

Quentin shrugged and nodded. "Sure, thanks."

And Amber was lost.

"Hi," he said to Cookie.

She took his hand in hers. "It's so nice to see you again, and you are welcome here anytime, Quentin."

I interpreted, then added, "But only if Cookie and I are here as well."

He gave me a thumbs-up, understanding my meaning completely. I didn't miss the interest in his eyes when Amber opened the door. This had trouble written all over it. In permanent marker.

Amber took Quentin's arm and led him over to the table, where she took out a pen and paper for them to write notes. I was soon demoted to third wheel. Since I'd been summarily dismissed without so much as a severance check, I went to help Cookie in the kitchen, which—very much like my own apartment—was about five inches from where we just stood.

"Oh, heavens, Charley, I just can't get over him. He is an absolute doll."

"Yeah," I said, keeping a close watch on the rascal, "that's my worry. So how'd it go today?"

"Oh, my gosh, I learned so much."

"Yeah, that's great. But seriously, I have to figure out what's going on with these women. I can hardly get through my apartment. And Nicolette? She's alive? What's up with that? They never come back to life."

For some reason, Cookie poured the pasta into her own bowls.

"You realize you're not fooling anyone."

She ignored me. "Is Nicolette, you know, like a zombie?"

I curled a string of spaghetti onto a fork and slid it into my mouth. "She didn't really look like the walking dead," I said, talking with my mouth full. "You look more like the walking dead than she did. You know, in the mornings anyway."

"That was uncalled for."

"Do you know me at all?"

After Quentin and I crashed the Kowalski dinner, we sat around the table drinking tea and telling embarrassing stories about Amber. She was so in love, she didn't notice when I told the one about where she'd tried to dye her hair with Kool-Aid and it turned gray for a solid week.

"I know sign language, too," she chimed in after a bit.

"You signed 'sorry' earlier," I said. "I was impressed."

She blushed. "Yeah, I learned some in the second grade. My teacher taught us. She took a class in college."

"A whole class?" I asked, trying not to sound facetious, even though I was. "That's great."

"Yeah."

"And you still remember what she taught you?" Cookie asked her.

She nodded.

Quentin raised his brows, waiting for her to show him something. There were few things Deaf people found more amusing than hearing people who knew just enough sign to be dangerous. But he seemed genuinely interested.

"But it's dumb," she said, deflating a little now that the spotlight was on her.

"No." I encouraged her to stand. "I bet it's great."

"Okay, well, I can sign 'I am very special.'"

"Perfect," I said. I had interpreted for Quentin so he would know what to expect, just in case what she signed was nowhere near what she was trying to say.

Since she had the room, Amber stood and cleared her throat. No idea why. She lifted her hands and produced three signs for us that were supposed to be *I, very,* and *special.* I was thrilled she didn't throw in the *am.* There was no such word in American Sign Language. The *am* that did exist was thanks to any number of English sign systems that had very little to do with the actual language. *Very* was bad enough, but I could forgive her that one.

Still, there is a certain nuance to any language, a certain gradation, and shifting that nuance can change the meaning of a message entirely. One misplaced hand shape or one wrong movement, and the sign switches from a noun to a verb, or from one adjective to another. It would be like replacing the *p* in *puck* with an *f.* It may be one small sound away from the same word, but it was one giant step away from carrying the same meaning.

So when Amber did the movement in the English word *very* backwards, and extended the movement in the word *special,* using all the fingers on her right hand instead of the two allotted, I found myself more than a little taken aback.

I blinked.

Quentin blinked.

And believing we hadn't understood her, Amber signed her sentence again, to my utter horror. I lunged forward and grabbed her hands before glancing back at Quentin. He now wore a smile that expressed just how much he appreciated Amber's forthrightness.

I slammed my hands over his eyes. He giggled and tugged them down.

"What?" Amber said in dismay, clamping her hands behind her back. "What did I say?"

"She— She didn't mean that," I said to Quentin.

"I didn't mean what?"

"I'm pretty sure she did," he said.

"Nothing, sweetheart." I pulled Quentin out of his chair. "We need to be going anyway. Thanks for dinner."

Cookie sat with her mouth open, trying to figure out what had just happened.

"I think we should stay," Quentin said, the smile on his face gleaming. "See what else she knows."

"Absolutely not." I dragged him out the door.

Just as I closed it, Amber called out to me. "What'd I say?"

I leaned against the door and repeated my earlier sentiment. "She didn't mean that."

He rolled his eyes with a soft laugh. "I know what she was trying to say. I'm not a moron."

"Right. Sorry. But wipe that smirk off your face."

"What smirk?"

I pointed to it. "That one."

He tried to wipe it away with a swipe of his hand, to no avail.

"And just for the record, Amber does *not*—" I leaned in and whispered the next signs to him. "—fuck or give head."

He cracked up again, doubling over before sobering and asking, "Do you think that's how her teacher really taught her to say 'I am very special'?"

I hadn't considered that. "Probably not. Unless, of course, she worked her way through college as a call girl."

His shoulders shook; then he paused, sobered, and looked to the side. I felt it, too. A heat wafting toward us. We both watched as Reyes topped the stairs, his gait like that of a panther. Every move full of purpose, every motion made with the dangerous grace of a predator.

His gaze virtually sparkled when it landed on me.

"Mr. Farrow," I said as he passed.

He remembered Quentin. I could see recognition in his eyes. "Ms. Davidson," he said before nodding at Quentin as he strode past. He went to his apartment, closed the door slowly.

"I can see him, too," Quentin said, his signs guarded, his expression wary. "I can see who he is. What he's made of.

"Made of?" I asked.

"He's dark," he said, suspicion permeating every word. "It surrounds him like a shroud of black mist. I've never seen anything like it."

Just like I couldn't see my own light, I couldn't see this perpetual darkness that surrounded Reyes unless he de-materialized and came to me incorporeally. But I'd been told about it before. Angel had mentioned it to me once. I thought he'd been exaggerating.

"Yeah, well," I said, wrapping an arm into his, "he's had a hard life."

He couldn't seem to tear his gaze off Reyes's door. "What is he?"

After the conversation we'd just had, I wasn't sure I wanted him to know. He had been traumatized enough. But I didn't want to lie to him, either. "I'm not sure I want to tell you," I said, ushering him down the stairs.

He thought for a moment, then said, "I'm not sure I want to know."

Chapter Nine

*Whoever is in charge of making sure I don't do
stupid shit is fired.*
—T-SHIRT

I dropped Quentin off at the convent, said hello to all the
sisters, played a quick game of Yahtzee, got my ass kicked,
then headed back to Rocket's place with a new piece of
equipment lying across my backseat. If I couldn't climb
over the fence, I'd go through it.

I brought out the bolt cutters, which were much harder
to use than I thought they would be. And they were heavy
and bulky. What the hell? It looked so easy in the movies.
Like pruning an azalea bush. But this was work. I should've
bought gloves. My hands were so wimpy.

After finally making an opening big enough for me to
squeeze through, I forced my head through first and realized I'd left several clumps of hair in the links and lots of
DNA on the sharp edges I'd just cut. This was so not going as planned. I finally crammed my body through the
fence, comparing the unpleasant experience to my birth,
and found the basement window I always kept unlocked.
I wanted to use the key I had, but all the locks had been
changed. Whoever C&R Industries were, they would pay
dearly for my blood loss.

I took out a flashlight and navigated the staircases of questionable worth.

Strawberry Shortcake appeared in the glow of my light. Strawberry, aka Becky Taft, aka Officer David Taft's little sister who died when he was eleven, was a nine-year-old ball of fire who could teach Reyes's dad a thing or two as far as I was concerned. I called her Strawberry because she was still wearing the Strawberry Shortcake pajamas she'd passed in. She stood with her fists on her hips, her long dark-blond hair hanging in tangles down her back, and I always thought if I actually liked kids, I might have liked her. Probably not, but it was a thought.

"Hey, pumpkin," I said. "Where's Rocket?"

"He's hiding."

"God, he loves that game."

"No, he's hiding because of you. He has to show you something." She glowered at me accusingly.

I tried not to giggle. "Show me what?"

"Someone on the wall. He's scared you'll get mad at him."

"Really? Well, now I'm totally curious." Then I thought a moment. What if it was my name? What if the bolt cutter slipped and I'd accidentally cut my own throat and bled to death but I didn't know it? That would suck.

"Can I brush your hair?" she asked as she led the way, her disposition doing a 180 on a dime. Kids. Can't live with 'em. Can't eat 'em for lunch.

Then I realized what she was asking. "No!" I shouted before reining in the surge of fear that overcame me to say in a nicer voice, "No, pumpkin, maybe next time."

But it was too late. She stopped, crossed her little arms over her little chest, and whimpered like a puppy. Crap. That was all I needed. The SS following me around, tormenting me because I'd hurt her feelings. "Fine, okay, you can brush my hair when we find Rocket. But no scissors. I know what you did to your dolls."

She gasped, utterly appalled. "Only the bad dolls."

Oh, yeah, she was completely sane.

We found Rocket in one of the rooms in the medical ward. Which was by far the creepiest ward of them all.

"Hey, Rocket Man," I said, easing up to him. He sat in a corner, curled into a ball. I seemed to be sending a lot of people into the fetal position lately. I knelt beside him and placed a gentle hand on his shoulder. "What's wrong?"

He shook his head and curled further inside himself. I'd never seen him like this.

"Yeah, what's wrong?" Strawberry said right before she poked him with a stick.

He slapped at it.

"Strawberry!" I said. "Don't poke Rocket. Holy cow. Where's his sister?"

Rocket's sister went by the name of Blue Bell. No idea why. I'd met her only once. A tiny angelic thing with a short bob and overalls.

Strawberry shrugged and went to poke him again.

I took the stick from her. "I thought you wanted to brush my hair."

"Oh, I do! I do!" She took off back down the hall, I could only assume to get a hairbrush.

"Okay, Rocket Man, what's bothering you?" When he shook his head again, I enticed him with, "I'll bring you a soda next time."

He bit his bottom lip.

"A grape one."

"With an umbrella?" he asked.

The last time I had to bribe him with a soda, I'd put a little umbrella in it, a leftover from Hawaiian night at Calamity's.

"With an umbrella," I promised.

He wiggled until he was sitting with his back against the wall, his arms folded on bent knees. "Okay, but you're going to be mad."

The SS showed up then with a brush she'd retrieved from God only knew where.

"Sit on your bottom," she ordered. "And be still. I have a lot of work ahead of me."

I sat down and frowned at her while pulling out my hair band. "There is nothing wrong with my hair."

"I know," she said, suddenly defensive. "It's not really ugly. It's just dumb."

Well, that cleared that up. Next time I went to the hairdresser, I'd tell her what Strawberry thought of my hair. Maybe she could explain why it was dumb.

I gave her my back and let her take my hair into her fingers. She raked the brush through it, beginning at my scalp and ripping through it to the very tips of my tips. Hopefully I'd have a few locks left when she was finished.

I was always a little impressed with what Strawberry could do. Not all departed could move objects, much less carry them around and use them. I think the only reason she could was because no one had mentioned otherwise and the contrary had never occurred to her.

After another good scraping of my roots, I noticed a tiny hand sticking out from the wall beside Rocket. It was Blue's. She was holding on to her brother's arm like she was scared of me or scared for him.

"Rocket, why do you think I'll be mad at you?"

"Because."

"Do I ever get mad at you?"

"No, Miss Charlotte, but one time you got upset."

"Okay, I'll try not to become upset." By that point, my scalp was on fire. Strawberry scraped and ripped and tugged until my scalp bled. "What's wrong?"

"I'll have to show you, Miss Charlotte."

Blue tugged at his arm, trying to pull him through the wall with her.

"It's okay, Blue. She's gonna bring us a grape soda with an umbrella."

Rocket pointed behind my head. When I turned to look, Strawberry took a handful of hair and jerked.

"Ouch!" I grabbed my hair and pulled it out of her grasp. "Holy crap, Strawberry."

"You moved," she said, gazing at me as though I were an idiot.

I finally got a good look at the brush in her hand. "Where'd you get that?" It was oddly shaped with dirty bristles all the way around a broken plastic handle.

"The supply closet."

There was only one kind of brush that I knew of that had bristles all the way around.

"Oh. My God." I jumped up and screeched at her. "That's a toilet brush!"

She lifted her tiny shoulders. "Okay."

"Strawberry! That's disgusting." I swiped at my hair, trying to clean it. Maybe I had some Lysol in Misery. Or some hand sanitizer.

"Whatever," she said, and I had to remind myself that she'd died sometime in the nineties, at the height of the *whatever* revolution. Her vocabulary was so different from Rocket's, who'd died in the fifties.

I finally calmed down enough to look where Rocket was pointing. I walked over to the wall, swallowing back dry heaves. I would never live this down. I tried to find the name he pointed to, but just like always, name upon name had been scratched into the wall's surface. It was hard to know where one name ended and another began.

"A little more," he said, pointing past me.

I took another step and saw a cleared space with a name

set apart from the others. I saw a *W* and an *O*. I inched closer until I could read the last name of three. FARROW. I wavered, dived into a calming state of denial, then took another step. ALEXANDER. I stopped. My lungs seized as I stood there. My eyes tracked across the letters until they zeroed in on the first name. The only name I knew him by for over a decade. The name that meant so many things to me.

Beautiful.

Feral.

Dangerous.

Untamable.

"Are you mad, Miss Charlotte?"

The name blurred but I said it to myself over and over. Let the sounds caress my mouth, slide over my tongue, slip through my lips. Reyes. Reyes. Reyes.

"Are you upset?"

Blue had come through the wall. I could see her in my periphery. She tugged at his arm, tried to pull him through the wall with her.

"I don't understand," I said, my disbelief so utterly complete. "I just saw him." I turned to Rocket, anger rushing through me like a wildfire. "He's not dead. I just saw him."

Rocket's eyes widened as he watched me. He pushed into a standing position.

"Charley," Strawberry said, her tone scolding, "you need to stop that. You're scaring Blue."

"He's not dead," I said to Rocket.

"Not yet." He shook his head. "Not yet, Miss Charlotte."

I was in front of him at once, had the dirty collar of his shirt wrapped into my fist before I even thought to do it. To make sure he didn't disappear on me like he was so fond of doing. "When?" I asked, knowing exactly what his answer would be.

He tried to talk, his mouth opening and closing like a goldfish, but I'd scared him.

I pulled him closer until our noses touched. "When?" I repeated.

"Not when. Not how. Only who. N-no breaking rules."

I steadied my voice, pronounced each syllable carefully so he would understand every word that left my mouth. "I will rip your sister in two."

"Days," Rocket said as a tear fell over his lashes. He shook uncontrollably. "H-he only has a few days."

"Why? What happens?" When he hesitated, I reached down without taking my eyes off him and curled my fingers into his sister's overalls. She didn't fight me. She kept her arms wrapped around her brother's leg. But my point was taken.

"He gets sick," he said, his lids fluttering as he left this realm and peeked into the supernatural world. "But it's not real. It's not human. You have no choice."

"What? What do you mean I have no choice?"

"You— You have to kill him. It's not your fault."

Why would I kill Reyes? I wouldn't. Period. But clearly something would set me on that path. "How do I stop it?" I asked, the words hissing through my teeth.

He came back to me, his gaze sharp and clear. "You don't, Miss Charlotte. That's breaking the rules." When I dipped my head to regard him from underneath my lashes, he added, "No breaking rules."

"Charley, I'm telling my brother," Strawberry said. She was standing beside me, hands on hips, a comical glare on her face.

"Can it be done?" I asked him.

"It can be done, but you would have to break the rules. Something bad will happen."

"Works for me."

I shoved him against the wall, unable to control the

fury that had taken hold of me, and stormed out. Back outside the gate, I climbed into Misery, gasping for air, my cheeks wet from emotion and regret. What had I done?

I swiped angrily at my cheeks and left Rocket's with a thousand more questions than when I'd entered. I couldn't lose him. I couldn't lose Reyes. And I had absolutely no intention of killing him, so that pretty much settled that. But still, what could warrant such an extreme action?

I wasn't sure I could face the plethora of women in my apartment just then. I had lost control. With Rocket. The gentlest soul I'd ever known. I threatened his little sister, a five-year-old who hid in dark corners and cowered in shadows to avoid people like me. Threatening her took some kind of balls. I should be proud of myself, bullying a mentally challenged man and five-year-old girl.

And according to Rocket, I was about to lose the only man I'd ever loved.

The best place for me, the only place where I could clear my thoughts and find answers I still needed, was in my office, so I headed that way.

I walked in to find the restaurant and bar teeming with patrons. Again. Not horridly unusual for a Saturday night, but just like the last couple of days, the room was filled to the brim with women, and there were a lot more off-duty cops than normal. No doubt the sudden influx of feminine mystique lured the hunters. Officer Taft was there, Strawberry's big brother, and the last thing I wanted to tell him was that I'd just threatened two of the dearest people ever to exist right in front of his little sister. Strawberry may seem all that and then some, but my behavior was inexcusable. And worse, I had no idea what came over me. I'd become livid in seconds flat.

In trying to duck Taft, I walked right by a table with a familiar face. Jessica was there. Again. What the hell? It was too late to veer off my path now. She would know I was trying to avoid her. I had no choice but to walk by her table.

Jessica spotted me and smirked as I hurried past. This was so the wrong day to fuck with me. I paused mid-stride and backstepped until we were face-to-face.

"Oh, hey, Jess," I said, plastering on a huge smile and sprinkling so much fake sugar in my voice, I'd have to change my name to Splenda.

She blinked in surprise, then regarded me with enough distaste to warrant a bitch-slap, but I refrained. "What do you want?" she asked, and her friends snickered right on cue. It was inspiring, really.

"I've just been so worried about you, what with the chlamydia you got in high school on top of the herpes. I wanted to make sure you were practicing safe sex."

Her jaw fell open long enough for her friends to realize I wasn't lying. It was thoughtful of her really, to confirm everything I'd just said like that. I'd have to send her a thank-you card later.

"Are you okay?" I asked her when her face turned a lovely shade of scarlet.

"I do not have herpes," she said from between clenched teeth. Her gaze bounced among her friends self-consciously. "And I know why you're here. You may as well give up."

Okay, that threw me. Why was I here? Oh, right. "I work here. My dad owns this bar. My office is right up there." I pointed to the balcony that overlooked the restaurant. "Why are you here?"

She scoffed. "Like you don't know."

Damn. She threw me again. What the hell was I missing? I scanned the room, searching for clues, 'cause that's how PIs rolled.

Nothing. But I could hardly let her know that.

"Okay, well, it's been fun. Keep it in your pants, ladies."
I smiled and wiggled my fingers, walking away with as
much dignity as I could muster. I hated being out of the
loop. Being out of the loop was like being the only kid on
the playground without an Xbox.

I took the stairs two at a time and locked my office
door behind me, my mind still reeling at what I'd just done.
Not with Jessica, but with Rocket and Blue. I sat behind
my desk, still shaking, and covered my face with my
hands, trying to force myself to calm.

How would I fix this? How would I fix my relationship
with Rocket and Blue? I'd only just met Blue, and now she
saw me as a bully, a monster. And just why the hell was
Jess here anyway? It galled me. As immature as that was,
it galled me to no end.

I powered on my iMac and checked the Bunn for coffee. There was just enough left for one cup, so I popped it
in the microwave, added all the fixings, then went to work.
I needed answers. First off, who owned that building? If
it weren't a Saturday night, I could prance down to the
courthouse and find out, but maybe there would be something online about it. I did search after search. Nothing,
though I did find a couple of very cool sites that talked
about how haunted the asylum was. It talked about how
people had seen a glowing light in their cameras or found
an object in a different spot than where they'd left it. If
they only knew.

My main worry where Rocket was concerned was what
if the company that bought it demolished the asylum as
well? Where would Rocket go? My walls wouldn't hold
up to the abuse that was Rocket Man and all his knowledge. I needed to find out what their plans were. If demo-
lition was in Rocket's foreseeable future, I'd have to figure
out where to move him to. But I'd cross that suspension
bridge when I came to it.

When I came up with nothing, I sat there sipping coffee and wondering about everything. Nicolette the undead. The departed women in my apartment. The fact that Kim Millar was most likely an arsonist and the additional fact that Reyes Farrow would not be happy when I turned in his sister. There had to be another way.

In the back of my mind, one other fact poked and prodded. Trying to worry about other things besides the fact that Reyes had only days to live was like trying not to look at the elephant in the room. He could die. He was slated to die. I took a deep breath and made a decision. When the time came, I would do whatever it took to stop that from happening. He was not going to die. Not on my watch.

Since there was nothing I could do about the Reyes thing for now, having no idea whom I would ask about such a thing, I focused on Kim. Her situation was the only one I had a snowball's chance of improving. But how?

After two full hours of commiserating, I exited my offices through the front door and took the outside stairs. Knowing my luck, Jessica and her cohorts would still be in there. In the loop. Exactly where I wasn't. Nor was I in the mood to be reminded of that fact.

I walked around the bar to my apartment building behind it and trudged up the two flights of stairs there. Dead Duff headed me off at the top. His round glasses and backwards baseball cap made me smile despite everything.

"Hey, Ch-Charley."

"Hey, you. How's PP?" I asked, inquiring about Mrs. Allen's psychotic poodle, Prince Phillip.

He scowled, then caught himself. "PP's fine. He's not the p-problem."

"Really? Who is?"

"It's Mrs. Allen. I'm not sure she's very s-stable."

"Ya think? She believes her poodle is royalty. Seriously. How stable can she be?"

"That's true. I decided to m-move."

The sticky note on my door read *Ready for round two?* I pulled my lower lip in through my teeth, took the note down, and held it to my mouth. After a quick glance at Reyes's door, I said, "That sounds logical."

"I might move here," he said, pointing to Cookie's apartment.

"Oh." That surprised me. "Well, okay, but only if you'll spy on Cook for me."

"Cook? Cookie? Your f-friend from the other night?"

"The very one. I've been a little worried about her. What do you know about women's fashion?"

"Not much, but I g-guess I could take a look. Unless, you know, unless you have a spare room or s-something."

Oh, my god. Was he asking to move in with me? Figures the first guy who wants to move in with me ever would be dead. "Actually, I'm full up for the moment." I opened the door and did a Vanna to demonstrate just how full up I was. He winced when he saw the horde. I was just grateful they were staying put in my apartment and not venturing out all over God's green earth. I'd never be able to round them all up.

And there were more than before. Maybe I'd stay the night with Cookie, too.

No, I needed to stop running and try to get some information from these women. Surely one of them out of the baker's dozen could clue me in to what was going on. I was out of the loop even in my own abode.

"I s-see that. M-maybe I'll just go out for a while."

"Hey, could you talk to them?" I asked. "Figure out what's going on?"

But his gaze had landed on Mr. Wong. His brows snapped together a microsecond before recognition sank in.

"Um, n-no, I don't th-think I c-can."

I couldn't help but notice his stutter had gotten worse.

"Do you know him?" I asked, surprised.

"W-what? Him? N-no. I-I have n-no idea who th-that is."

I took hold of his arm. "Duff, who is he?"

"I—I have to g-go."

Was he scared? Surprised?

"Duff, wait." I dropped my bag and bent to get it.

But I'd let go. He vanished. To my chagrin.

I stepped into my apartment, closed the door behind me, and gave Mr. Wong the once-over. "Okay, mister, who are you really?"

He didn't move. He never moved. But how would Duff know him? Mr. Wong didn't get out much.

I thought about paying my comely neighbor a visit. Reyes, not Cookie. Though Cookie was comely, too, in her own special way. But knowing about Kim and what I had to do, I wasn't sure what to say to him. And he was going to die soon? I would figure out a way to break the rules, whatever they were, when the time came, but until then, having Reyes so near was wonderful.

It seemed I would be sharing a bed with a beautiful Asian woman. She sat on the far corner facing the wall. Her feet on the ground. Her palms in her lap. Her gaze distant. It seemed wrong to try to get some sleep with all these women mulling about, but I just didn't know what to do for them. I got on my knees and checked under the bed. The pixie was still under there. Her huge blue eyes stared out at me, and I realized she was the only one who made eye contact. Who saw me.

Out of all the women, she was the youngest by far. It seemed odd to me that a serial killer would kill a child in the midst of older women. Maybe she was an accident. Or

maybe he started killing them younger and younger as he
went. There was just no telling.

"Hey, hon," I said.

She scurried back, her movements haunting, her limbs
working like a bug's in the meager space.

"Sweet dreams."

I finally lay down, my mind racing with the events of
the day, and put my hand against the wall that separated
my and Reyes's apartments. Our bedrooms. His heat,
scalding and soothing at the same time, leached into the
wall. A comforting warmth penetrated my palm, worked
its way up my arm, and spread through my entire body.

I fell asleep with only one thought on my mind: Reyes
Farrow.

"I want you to know, I'm missing a *Supernatural* marathon," Cookie said the next morning when she came over
for coffee.

"It's for the greater good, Cook. Four out of five experts agree: Gun safety trumps an eye candy fix."

"Have they even seen the Winchester boys? Sammy
and Dean's existence proves there is a god and she is a
woman."

I laughed out loud. But she had a good point.

"It's true," she said, raising a saucy brow. "I read it on
a poster."

"Then it must be true. What are you doing in class
today?"

"We're going to the range this morning, then back to
the classroom later. You were right. Noni's great. And he
has some great stories."

I felt I should warn her. "You'll hit some harder stuff
this afternoon. Just think about his questions and answer
honestly. Noni's refused to sign off on only two students

before because they were a bit too . . . eager. I think you'll be fine."

"Let's get back to the harder stuff. What's he going to ask?"

"He's going to ask you to be honest with yourself. He'll talk about things like regret. If you do ever have to pull your sidearm, if you ever have to kill someone, how do you think you'll feel afterwards?"

"I don't know. I've never thought about it. The odds have just been so against me actually hitting anything."

"It's pretty simple, really. If you fire your sidearm to protect someone you love, you won't regret it. But if you fire it only to protect yourself, as crazy as this sounds, you'll probably harbor a lot of guilt."

"Why would I feel guilty protecting myself?"

"It's something about our psyche or our genetic code. I don't know, I think there's a chromosome in our DNA that prevents us from using violence to protect ourselves if we have another choice. Sadly, as humans are wont to do, we are always second-guessing ourselves. As a result, we end up feeling bad about killing the guy who was going to murder us with an axe." I shrugged. "You think we'd be okay with that."

"Are you still being invaded?"

"Yes. How'd you guess?"

"It's freezing in here."

"Sorry. Dead people are so impolite."

Amber popped her head in the door. "Can Quentin come over?"

"No!" we said simultaneously.

"Why? He doesn't have to be back at school until tonight."

Cookie did her mommy face. "No boys at the apartment when I'm not there, Amber."

She rolled her eyes as only a twelve-year-old can and closed the door.

"So, what did she sign last night?" Cookie asked.

"You so very much don't want to know."

She cringed. "That bad?"

"Worse. Let's just say we might should get her on the pill soon."

"Wow."

"Either that or we need to have her second-grade teacher investigated for solicitation. Wait, how does she know he doesn't have to be at school until tonight?"

"Apparently, they're texting."

"Oh." I could hardly blame Quentin, but he was sixteen to Amber's twelve. True, she was a tall, exotic-looking twelve, but a twelve nonetheless. I'd have to be careful there. Offer a few well-timed death threats should he decide to take things further than just texting. "I guess that's okay as long as there's a *T* in front of that word and not an *S*."

Chapter Ten

*My goal in life is to have a psychiatric
disorder named after me.*
—T-SHIRT

I tried calling Gemma a couple of times, then gave up and
tracked her phone. Illegally. According to the app, she was
at her office, which would explain why she wasn't answering. Still, she never saw clients on a Sunday. Maybe she
was in trouble. That would be my excuse when she inevi-
tably got mad for my illegally tracking her phone.

Sure enough, when I got to her office, her Beamer was
parked out back. I parked in front beside a white GMC
pickup, noted the take-out bags thrown haphazardly about
its interior, then let myself in with a key I had also illegally
obtained. She should've never lent me her keys when she
got pneumonia that one time. Did she not know I'd make
a copy? I could hardly be held responsible for my actions
when everyone around me gave me every opportunity to
sink to their low expectations.

The door to her secret lab where she shrank heads was
closed, so I picked up a magazine and waited. A few minutes later, she walked out the door and started when she
saw me.

"Charley," she said, closing the door behind her, "what
are you doing here?"

"I came to ask you a few questions." I looked past her. "What are you doing here?"

"It's my office." She blocked my view. "How did you know I was here?"

"GPS. I tracked your phone. PIs can do shit like that. That's how we roll."

"That's so wrong."

"And yet it feels so right. Why are you here on a Sunday?"

"I'm seeing a clie—"

Before she could finish, the door opened again. A tall man, broad with sandy hair, stepped through. He was a cop if his uniform was any indication.

"Charley, this is Officer Pierce."

He held out his hand, and I immediately noticed three scars on his face. They were how I remembered him. He became a cop about the same time I became a college graduate. There was a case I was helping my uncle with, and he'd been a rookie back then.

"Charley," he said, his mannerisms congenial. "It's nice to meet you."

"We've met, actually." I shook his hand and immediately noticed something shady about him. He seemed agitated underneath his cool exterior.

One corner of his mouth tilted up, puckering the scars that ran across his cheek, two right below his left eye and one along his jaw, like he'd been scratched by an animal, and scratched deeply enough for the scars to be permanent. "I didn't think you'd remember."

"I do. You were a rookie when we met."

"Yes, ma'am. That was some case."

Uncle Bob had called me to the crime scene of a family who had been murdered. "It was tragic."

He lowered his head as he thought back, then looked at Gemma. "I'll see you next week?"

"Absolutely. Next week."

Gemma seemed nervous. Did he scare her?

He headed toward the door.

"And," Gemma added, "think about what we talked about."

He looked at me as though worried I would hear something I shouldn't. "I will, Doctor."

After he left, Gemma led me into her secret lab. I took the couch, making myself completely comfortable.

"Do you want some coffee?" she asked.

"Seriously?"

"Right." She walked over to her small kitchenette. "What are you doing here? Is everything okay with Dr. Romero?"

"Sure." I straightened and leveled a death stare on her. "Why wouldn't it be?"

"What?" she asked, becoming defensive. She handed me a cup of coffee. I took it without breaking the spell of my gaze.

"What did you tell her?"

She turned suddenly, stirring her coffee. "Nothing. Why?"

"Because she seems to know an awful lot about me."

Her shoulders tensed.

When she turned back, I was in the middle of a sip, so I had to lock my laser glare on her from behind my cup and pray I didn't look silly.

"I told her only what she needed to know to treat you."

I put my cup down. "Which was?"

She chewed her bottom lip a moment, then said, "I told her you were a supernatural being with special powers and that you'd try to use them to deter her treatment." When my jaw fell open, she rushed to add, "Don't worry. I didn't tell her you were the grim reaper."

"Gemma," I said, adding a singsong whine to my voice,

"now I can't scare her. You can't go around telling people about me."

She sat beside me. "No, this is perfect. She is bound by confidentiality. She can't tell anyone."

"Unless she thinks I'm a threat."

"That's true. But she doesn't. I told her that you help people and would never intentionally hurt an innocent person."

"That makes me feel so much better. Why are you here on a Sunday?"

"Sometimes I see city employees and I try to work with their schedules."

She was totally hiding something. I felt the air around her wobble.

"And I figured I could get some paperwork done, too," she added.

"Are you scared of him?"

She turned back to me. "Officer Pierce? No. Why?"

That got me nowhere fast. "Fine. Who are you seeing?"

"What? No one."

"Gem," I said, rolling my eyes so far back, I almost seized, "you can't lie to me."

She put her cup down and pointed at me. "That is so unfair. Even when we were kids, you cheated."

"Cheated?"

"Yes. You shouldn't get to use your powers on just anyone."

"I didn't. You have an infinity symbol drawn on the inside of your wrist."

"Oh." She blushed.

"You only do that when you're seeing someone." She'd picked up the habit in grade school, and I quickly learned that when she started drawing infinity symbols, she was secretly in love. I couldn't believe she still did it. She was like thirty or something. Who did crap like that? I nonchalantly covered the letters *R-E-Y-E-S* I'd drawn on my knuckles.

"I do not only do this when I'm seeing someone. I'm thinking about getting some ink. Making this permanent." When I thinned my mouth, she caved. "Damn it. I'm not seeing him. I just would like to."

"Bummer. Unrequited love sucks ass. So, who is this mystery idiot who clearly has no taste if he hasn't asked you out yet?"

"No one. And you're not meeting him. Ever."

I placed a hand over my heart. "Are you ashamed of me?"

"Yes."

"No." I held up my palm. "Don't hold back. I can take the truth."

"I'm ashamed of you," she said, sitting behind her desk and shuffling through papers.

"Give it to me straight."

"I'm embarrassed to have you as a sister."

I slammed my eyes shut. "Just be honest with me, for the love of applesauce, Gemma."

"I'm mortified that we came from the same womb."

"So, who's the cop?" I asked, taking another swig of the good stuff.

She put down the paper she was studying. "I thought you knew him."

"I met him once. On a rainy night. Our love was all-consuming for about five minutes. Then it kind of dwindled. Much like my bank account."

She hitched one corner of her mouth. "Didn't give you the time of day?"

"Not even when I asked nice. And I was serious. I'd forgotten my watch. What can you tell me about him?"

"Absolutely nothing."

"How did he get those scars?"

She finally gave me her full attention. "Charley, I can't talk about my clients."

"Just making small talk. Holy cow. Besides, I thought he moved to Montana or something."

She gave me her best glower. If I'd had cards to hold up, I'd give it an 8.5 with higher marks for a crisp execution.

"What's he need a shrink for?"

After releasing a long breath, she said, "Since this is nothing you can't get off the Internet, he had to return fire at a crime scene and an innocent man was killed in the cross fire."

"Oh, I remember that. How'd he get the scars?"

"I don't know."

She was lying. Whatever. "So I have a problem."

"Just one?" she asked. "Aren't we being a bit unrealistic?"

"My apartment has been invaded by a plethora of departed women who seem to have been strangled by a serial killer."

She stopped.

"They are all blond but different ethnicities and ages and such." She wasn't a profiler, so I didn't go into the details much. "But they are absolutely terrified. I need to know how to get through to them. I can't get any information from them like they are. They won't talk to me."

"What behaviors are they exhibiting?"

"Think the psych ward from that horror movie we snuck into in grade school."

"Holy sh— Really?" Despite her best efforts, her face showed the horror she felt at the memory. She'd never been the same after that movie, which luckily for me made scaring the bejesus out of her all the easier. She cleared her throat and began again. "How many did you say there are?"

"About twenty. I don't know for certain. There are more every time I look. They are completely despondent, frantic, and/or catatonic. But there is one, a young girl around seven—"

"Seven?" she asked, her face the picture of heartbreak.

"Right? Serial killers are ass-hats. Anyway, she made eye contact. Other than her, however, none of them have made any kind of connection at all. Besides the one who kept her hand on my foot all night. I nigh froze to death."

I couldn't miss the shiver that rushed over her. "Okay, so you need information on what happened to them?"

"Yes. I mean, why are they in my apartment?"

"Well, you are the grim reaper."

"But none of them seem particularly interested in crossing."

"I think your best bet is to focus on the girl who made eye contact. A child's mind is more pliable than an adult's. Their brains can heal in ways ours can't. Maybe you can get through to her."

"Okay, focus on the kid. So what do I do? She's like a little bug, scurrying around, making scratching sounds. They all are, really."

"What?"

A wave of fear hit me. "Well, they're everywhere. Climbing up my walls. Clinging to the ceiling. One has discovered my shower. Do you know how difficult it is to shower with a departed woman trying to dig through a porcelain tub? It ain't gonna happen. I tried to tell her that." I stopped when I noticed Gemma's face go white. I was freaking her out, but someone had to do it, damn it. "This doesn't bother you, does it?"

"You are evil."

"Me?"

"Wait. Are you kidding about all of this?"

"About the women? Why would I kid about something

like that?" When she pressed her lips together, I said, "Oh, right, I would, but I'm not. I need to find out what happened to them so they can move on. You know, far away, out of my apartment."

"It sounds kind of awful, Charley."

"It is. For them. Can you imagine?"

"Does Uncle Bob have anything?"

"I heard he has an STD."

"I mean, on the women."

"Oh, I have no idea if they have any STDs."

"You're still evil. I'll never get to sleep tonight."

"Dude, you take industrial-strength sleeping aids."

"And whose fault is that?" she asked, coming out of her seat and slamming a palm on her desk. Unglued would be an accurate term for her condition. It was fun to watch.

I stood, too, and pretended to get huffy. "You're always blaming me for your inability to sleep just because I introduced you to a few departed people when we were kids. If I'd known that describing their head wounds as they stood over your bed at night would be so traumatic, I wouldn't have done it." When she cast me a look of doubt, I recanted my testimony. "Okay, I would have. Either way, I think you'll be fine." I sat back down and crossed my legs. "It's not like knowing there were really departed people out there stunted your emotional growth or anything."

Gemma went back to work while I pondered our sisterhood. Growing up, everyone thought I was the evil sister. I never fell for that story myself. True, I spent my days in school promising not to incite rebellion and to never again bring plastique to school—it wasn't even real—while she was busy being her perfect little self.

Maybe a little too perfect, if you know what I mean.

After harassing Gemma for another half hour or so, I headed to Misery with several options for my Sunday. I could watch the *Supernatural* marathon and torture Cookie about it later. I could try Gemma's methods on the kid under my bed. I could try to figure out how to save Reyes, but from what? From whom? I could go talk to Kim about her habit of setting fire to the world, but it was still early. I didn't want to wake her, to put her on the defensive before I even had a chance to tell her my plan. Or I could try to figure out why Nicolette, the possible zombie, wasn't dead.

Since I had a soft spot for zombies and my curiosity was killing me, I opted for plan Z.

I got a text from Cookie. Misery purred to life as I checked my phone.

> We're at the firing range. Everyone is doing a drop and roll then shooting the target.

I texted her back.

> Well, if all the cool kids are doing it.
> Do you think I can do it?
> I see dead people. Anything is possible.
> Okay, I'll give it a try.

Then reality sank in. This was Cookie. The last time she did a Dirty Harry impersonation, she came away with a strange bra and a broken ankle.

But for the love of marinara, I typed, *don't shoot anyone.*

> Thanks. That helps.

Aw, she was so nice. But Nicolette's state of aliveness was still eating at me. Maybe she was in danger and would die soon. Rocket could predict someone's death.

He knew exactly when it would happen. Maybe Nicolette had predicted her own demise and decided to visit me, the grim reaper, in advance? To what end? This was just so weird.

I started for the hospital again. Left with no other choice, I would just have to talk to her, to figure out if perhaps she had some kind of supernatural condition.

I got another text from Cookie as I pulled into the hospital parking lot.

> I did it. I hate you with every fiber of my being.
> Really? With every fiber of your being? R u sure there's not a little fiber left in u, perhaps compacted in your digestive tract, that still likes me?
> I'm positive.

Well, she seemed certain.

> Is anything broken?
> Besides my spirit?
> Does anything have a hole in it that shouldn't?
> Besides my pride?

She was fine. Or she would be. And thankfully, so was everyone around her. Dodged a bullet there. Literally.

> Chin up, hon. At least u know never to try that again. There's always a bright side to these things.
> Every. Fiber.

She was really into the fiber thing. Maybe she had a bran muffin on the way to class.

Nicolette was just getting off work. I spotted her coming my direction as I headed to the elevator. She pulled on her jacket and took off her lanyard, growling when it got caught up in her hair.

"Nicolette, right?"

She stopped and gave me a once-over. "Oh, right, from yesterday afternoon." She finally pulled her hair free and checked her phone, looking exhausted.

"I was wondering if we could get a cup of coffee or something."

"Now?" She looked devastated that I would even ask. "I just pulled a double shift. Can we set something up for tomorrow?"

"I'd rather not. It's just— You came to me yesterday morning. You said you were dead."

Surprise rushed through. She hesitated before her curiosity got the better of her. "There's a coffee shop about two blocks down. I was planning on getting breakfast there anyway, if you want to tag along."

"I'm all for tagging. Can I drive you?"

Her expression screamed possible abduction.

"Or we could just meet there."

I followed Nicolette's red Volvo to the Frontier, which was only a couple of blocks from my apartment building.

We ordered, then sat at a table in the back.

"So, you said I came to you? How?"

"Well, first let me say that I can see things others can't."

She shifted in her seat. "Okay."

"And you showed up at my apartment yesterday morning and told me that you were dead. That your body was under a bridge out in the middle of nowhere."

"That's strange." She ducked her head as though hiding something.

"Nicolette, you can tell me anything. I'll believe you, I promise."

She shrugged a shoulder. "No, it's just, that's strange.

I have these dreams, but I don't tell people about them, so I don't know how you could possibly know that."

"Because you showed up in my apartment and told me you were dead. That's how."

"That's impossible," she said, biting her lower lip.

"I don't think you believe that any more than I do. Can you tell me what happened?"

"Happens. What happens."

"This has happened before?"

She finally straightened and took a deep breath. "I have these seizure kind of things. It's weird. And when I come out of them, I remember incidents about other people. I remember how they died. Only I was that person. I was the one who died."

"So, you are actually seeing someone else's death through their eyes?" That was new.

"No, you don't understand. The deaths have never actually occurred. I used to check the papers the next day, but there wouldn't be anything about a death in the way that I saw it. I've never found a true connection between what I see and what really happens."

"You're certain?"

"One hundred percent. I used to check. I used to scour the Internet, do all kinds of searches, check all the news programs and papers. Nothing."

This was seriously odd.

"That's our number."

"I'll get it." I jumped up and grabbed our order, then went back to our table with my mouth watering at the scent of Nicolette's breakfast burrito. I knew I should have ordered one. I handed it over reluctantly. "How about you describe a few of these events," I said, pouring two pink packages and some creamer into my coffee. "Give me a couple of examples."

"Okay." She spooned salsa onto her burrito. "Well, a couple of weeks ago, I was an elderly man in a hospital and everyone thought I died of natural causes, but my grandson actually killed me. Right there in my hospital bed. He couldn't wait for his inheritance. Even though I didn't have that much longer to live, he couldn't wait."

I tore my eyes off her burrito and took out my memo pad and pen. "Do you get names when this happens?"

She took a bite and shook her head. "Only sometimes. Wait, that time I did get one. Something like Richard or Richardson. But I don't know if it was the name of the man or the grandson, first name or last. It could have been the name of his nurse, for all I know."

"No, that's great. I can work with that." I could check this out with Uncle Bob or have Cookie work her magic. If what she described had really happened, I'd find out. "Okay, give me one more."

She took a sip of orange juice. "All right, well, a few months ago I had a really bad incident with a woman. It was so weird. I was trying to get out of my apartment, and yet I kept reminding myself to leave the stew I was making boiling on the stove. That was really important. Then I forgot something. I'd left a blanket at the apartment, so I went back after it. And when I tried to leave, my husband came home and caught me." Her voice softened and a quake of sadness reverberated out of her. "He beat me to death."

Cold chills washed over me as I sat there and listened to that story, recognizing every minute of it. Every second. I wasn't sure what to tell her. How she would take it. Finally, I decided she needed to know. And I needed to know how this was happening.

"Her name was Rosie," I said, and watched as Nicolette cast a suspicious gaze at me. "And she was one of my clients. I was trying to help her get out of an abusive relationship and I failed."

Worried I was somehow trying to scam her, she hardened. Shrank away from me. "I don't think I believe you."

"The blanket was blue. She was going to have a son, but her husband had beat her and she lost it."

Her eyes watered with emotion, but she didn't want to believe me. "Anyone could have guessed that."

"She had dark curly hair and—"

"I don't see their faces. I *am* these people. I see everything else."

"Okay, her husband was tall, heavyset with wide shoulders and light hair. He had a birthmark on his jaw and still wore his class ring. It was huge with a ruby in the center."

Recognition dawned on her face.

"When did you have that vision?"

It took her a moment to shake out of her thoughts. When she did, she took out her phone. "I used to keep a journal on here. I stopped when I realized nothing was coming of them even though they'd always seemed so real." She thumbed through a couple of pages. "Okay, that was on October fifteenth."

I thought back. "You had that vision about four days before it actually happened."

"This is not what I want to hear," she said, shaking her head. "These aren't real. They're not real people I'm seeing."

I put a hand over hers to calm her. "When did these visions start?"

"I was nine. I'd drowned in my neighbor's pool and the paramedics resuscitated me. I started having the seizures soon after."

"That seems to be a common catalyst for extrasensory

perception of any kind." I thought about my friend Pari, who began seeing the departed after her near-death experience when she was twelve.

"Is that what happened to you?" Nicolette asked me.

"No." I took another sip, then said, "I'm something else."

Thankfully, she didn't seem interested in knowing what that something else was. "It's so weird," she said, "because with every death, I get almost the exact same feeling. It's not what you think."

"What feeling do you get?"

"Relief." She leaned forward as though telling me a guarded secret. "A release of all burden. With Rosie, her last thought was freedom at last."

That realization caused a schism to tear through me. I felt like a piece of paper that someone had ripped down the center, turned over, and ripped again. I'd failed her, and yet she was still free. I didn't know how to feel about that.

I cleared my throat and fought for control over my emotions. "Can you tell me about this latest vision?"

She thought back. "I just remember that bridge. It had metal bracings like an old railroad bridge. I think I could see the metal beams as I died. And I remember blond hair and the number eight. Like a tattoo or a mark of some kind. And I could smell an oil of some kind. Or a gas."

My Spidey sense tingled. Maybe the cases were connected. All the women in my apartment had blond hair. It was thin, but I'd done more with less. "Did you get a name?"

"No. Sorry. I'm channeling these people. How often do you think to yourself, 'My name is Charley Davidson'?"

"Well, I do that a lot, but don't use me as a measuring stick."

Nicolette Lemay could see into the future. I'd never met anyone who could do that, though I did meet a guy once who said he could see in the dark because he had secret wolf eyes. I bought it at the time. I was four.

Chapter Eleven

To save time, let's assume I know everything.
—T-SHIRT

Cookie called as I headed back to the office.

"Are you skipping class?" I asked. "You can't let one humiliating incident—"

"I'm not skipping. We get breaks."

"Oh. Sorry," I said, snacking on some Twizzlers I'd found in my backseat. They were a little brittle, but I had strong teeth. "Just so you know, I think I'm in love with the person who decided to sell Twizzlers in a two-pound bag. What mad genius came up with that idea?"

"Right? So, what did you find out about Zombie Chick?"

"She's totally not dead. I'll explain later. It's a little bizarre."

"This coming from the grim reaper. I just wanted to let you know that Noni told us a construction crew found what is looking like a mass grave on a ranch in southern New Mexico. They've found the remains of three bodies that he knows of. All female. And, Charley, they're all three blond."

I sat back, feeling like the wind had just been knocked out of me. "That would explain a lot. I'm not sure why the discovery of the grave would have them all running to me, but it had to be the catalyst somehow. Maybe they didn't like others on their turf. Do you think ghosts have turf wars?"

"I think ghosts have all kinds of pent-up angst. So, is Noni married?"

"Cookie!" I said, pretending to be appalled. "Focus on your instructor's words, not his ass."

"Have you seen his ass?"

I groaned inwardly and made a mental note to get Cookie laid. "Get back to class, and thanks for this. I'll call Ubie and ask him what he knows."

"No problem. But, really, is he?"

"Do you still hate me with every fiber of your being?"

She hesitated, then conceded. "No, I guess not."

"Yes, he's married, and his wife is a champion markswoman."

"Damn. Another one slips through my fingers."

"I am not touching that." I hung up with a chuckle and called Ubie.

"Hey, pumpkin," he said.

"You didn't think to mention the mass grave?"

"What mass grave? How did you know about that? They just found it late Friday afternoon. It was being kept quiet for the time being."

"You didn't happen to tell Noni Bachicha, did you?"

"Son of a— I may have. I had a few beers at his house last night."

"He grilled you for info and you caved like an unstable salt mine."

"Thanks for the visual."

"You're welcome. Mass grave?"

"I'm at the bar about to head out there, not that we have jurisdiction or anything, but we've joined forces with the state ME, the FBI, and local law enforcement to get this under control. I volunteered to assign a task force from APD to assist with the efforts."

"That explains your working on a Sunday."

"Yeah."

"With a hangover."

"How do you always know?"

"Because you always sound like you have a cold."

"It's about a three-hour drive, if you're interested."

"I'm interested," I said, trying not to sound desperate.

"Why don't you meet me here?"

I drove to Calamity's and parked in my usual spot. The spot where I'd put up a sign saying NO PARKING: VIOLATORS WILL SUFFER FROM SEVERAL EXOTIC STD'S FOR WHICH THERE IS NO CURE. It seemed to do the trick. My landlord didn't especially like my tactics, but everyone was a lot happier when I had a parking space. I walked over to the bar and ducked in the back door.

The place was packed. On a Sunday. At lunch. On a Sunday. And once again, women seemed to be the main enthusiasts.

"What'll you have?" Ubie asked when I walked to the table he'd snagged. I couldn't believe it. Jessica was there again. What the freaking hell? Had she moved in?

Emaciated from watching Nicolette eat her breakfast burrito, I said, "I'll have my usual breakfast fare."

"You got it, pumpkin." He waved over our server. She was new, so I didn't know her name. Because of this, I was forced to call her Sylvia. "She'll have huevos rancheros with scrambled eggs, and I'll have a *carne udovada* burrito smothered in red."

"So, we're going to the actual site, yes?" I asked him as Sylvia wrote down our order.

"Yes, and I know how you are with dead bodies."

Sylvia paused then restarted, pretending not to hear us.

"How am I with dead bodies?" I asked.

"Squeamish."

"Oh, right." Dead people I could handle. Dead bodies not so much.

"It amazes me that you deal with dead people all day every day, but toss a dead body at you, and you turn into a girl."

"I am a girl," I said, utterly offended. "And I happen to know plenty of men who would rather eat fried worms than come face-to-face with a dead body."

"Okay, sorry. That was sexist."

He best be sorry. "So what's up with this new cook, Sylvia?"

"Um, it's Clair."

That was disappointing. Now I knew her name, but she'd always be Sylvia to me. "That's too bad. And the new guy?"

She grinned and ducked her head shyly. If I didn't know better, I'd say Sylvia had a little crush on him. Or her. Either way. "He's a really good cook."

He it was. And she had a point. "Okay, well, thanks." That was about as useful as a chocolate teapot.

She headed for the order station when a large man in dire need of anger control therapy stormed into the place with fire in his eyes. He took hold of her shirt collar, and she was too startled to do much about it. Poor thing.

"Doesn't anyone know this is a freaking cop hangout?" I asked aloud. "Why do they do these things?" I jumped up, hurried over, and flashed my PI license. "APD," I said, illegally impersonating an officer in a room full of off-duty officers, but no one else was jumping to Sylvia's rescue. I looked over at Uncle Bob. He crossed his arms over his chest and leaned back to watch the show.

"What seems to be the problem?" I continued.

"This man is the problem. Look at this." He jabbed a phone in my face with a picture. Then he scrolled for me.

It took a moment for me to focus, but it took only a microsecond for me to recognize the man in the images. Reyes. Shot after shot, photos of Reyes scrolled past me. What the fuck?

"This is my wife's phone," he said, his voice screeching until the entire room quieted and a familiar heat rose around me.

Uh-oh.

"I want to talk to this asshole immediately."

I looked over as Reyes walked up beside us wearing Sammy's apron and wiping his hands on a towel.

"What are you doing here?" But he didn't have to answer. Suddenly it all made sense. The women. The heat. The food. "You're the new cook?" I asked him, stunned.

"You," the man with questionable intelligence said. "My wife comes in here every day to eat because of you. And she takes pictures!" He shoved the phone toward Reyes, but Reyes had no intention of entertaining the guy's accusations. He kept a deadpan expression on him, refusing to look at the phone, until I thought the man would explode.

I decided to intervene. "Oh, my god!" I said to Reyes, my eyes radiating accusations at him. "She took your picture? Just what kind of game are you playing? You're under arrest, mister."

His mouth tilted and a dimple emerged on one cheek as I took his wrist and threw him against a wall. Or, well, urged him toward it. I held him against the cool wood with one hand and frisked him with the other. Slowly. Deliberately caressing parts of him I had no right to caress in public. I ran my hand over his buttocks, caressed first one pocket, then the other. Then I slid my hand under the apron and did the same to his front pockets. He tensed when my fingers brushed across his crotch. Feeling the heat surrounding him magnify, I ran my palms down his thighs, front and back, then up over his stomach and ribs. I had no idea frisking could be so fun. Thankfully, we were partially hidden by a rubber tree plant.

Though I wasn't doing it to make anyone jealous, the lethal glares coming from half the women in the place told me they were not as amused as I was. Or Reyes. At least he got my sense of humor. And he didn't mind my groping him in public. Welcomed it, if the sultry look in his eyes was any indication.

The man stood back, not sure what to think. That was my secret weapon. Confuse 'em and keep 'em guessing long enough to run away.

I brought out the most powerful tool I had in my arsenal. "If you resist," I said into Reyes's ear, "I'll be forced to Taser you."

He looked at what I had in my hand. "That's a phone."

"I have an app. You'll probably experience nerve damage. Slight memory loss."

His grin widened. He reached back, took hold of a belt loop, and pulled my hips into his.

Finally deciding to join in, Uncle Bob walked over, his gait unhurried, his expression bored. "What's the problem?"

I held up a hand. "I have this, Detective."

Just then I got another text from Cookie.

Apparently my situational awareness sucks.

Oh, my god. I was busy groping my man. I texted her back.

Apparently, so does your timing.

I looked back at Reyes. "Have you learned your lesson, sir?"

I could feel a wave of jealousy swirl around me like a hot wind. After all, he was the reason the place was drowning in women. If looks could kill, I would have been writhing in agony, well on my way to the afterlife, clutching my throat and fighting for air with one eye slightly larger than the other.

Another woman said, "You can't arrest Reyes because this bee-yoch is obsessed with him." They knew his name even? I was always the last to know.

"Oh, right," I said, letting him go. "She has a point."

Reyes leaned into me. "No, she doesn't."

The man decided to take his life into his own hands and grab my arm. "Do you think this is funny?"

"Is that a trick question?"

But I realized Reyes had stilled. He stepped closer and pulled me out of the man's grip. "You don't want to do that."

"Look, sir," I said, now trying to appease two angry men, "this is clearly a conversation you need to be having with your wife. And just so you know, half the people in this place are cops."

Surprised, he turned to scan the area.

But Reyes was still simmering. He stepped even closer to the man so only we could hear him. "I'm not a cop. And I just got out of prison for killing a man. If you want to go outside, I can explain exactly how I did it."

The color drained from his face.

"Zimmerman," Uncle Bob said, calling out to one of the uniformed officers, "why don't you take this gentleman outside and convince him that what he just did was wrong."

"But I'm eating," Zimmerman said. When Ubie cast him one of his death stares, Zimmerman cursed. Now he

was mad and he was going to take it out on the guy. I
hoped he gave him a ticket. A bad one that required community service or anger management classes.

"Thanks, Uncle Bob."

"I had to stop you. I think half the women in here were
plotting your death."

"You're probably right." I turned to Reyes and took his
arm in mine to steer him back toward the kitchen. "Okay,
I'm fine. No harm, no foul. And look at you. I can't believe you're filling in for Sammy."

He shook out of his anger. "I was having lunch. Your
dad needed a cook. I offered."

"Wait, you didn't . . . break Sammy's leg?"

After rewarding me with a soft, deep laugh, he said,
"No, I'm pretty sure Sammy broke Sammy's leg."

"You realize you have a fan club?" I indicated the room
with a nod.

"Yeah, that tends to happen."

"Must be a bitch," I said, teasing him.

"You didn't come over last night."

"Right, um, I had to get some paperwork done."

"You realize you can't lie to me."

"I know. I'm not lying so much as stretching the truth."
We were at his stop. I leaned against the bar.

Reyes looked past me. "Your uncle is watching us."

"He does that. We're grabbing lunch, then heading out
to a crime scene down south."

"Okay, if you have to go. I'm not sure what I'll do with
all these women around."

Jealousy spiked in me so fast and so sharp, Reyes
sucked in a breath, the air hissing through his teeth. He
closed his eyes, leaned his head back, let my emotion roll
over him.

I bit down, embarrassed. "Are you enjoying that?"

"No," he said, panting. "A little. It's like being hit with

a hundred razor blades at once, each leaving a tiny cut as it passes."

"Ouch. That sounds horridly unpleasant."

He lowered his head, regarded me from underneath his lashes. "Someday you'll figure out I'm not like other guys."

"Actually, I figured that out a while back."

"Nothing and no one interests me besides you. But what's the deal with the redhead?"

My stomach clenched at the thought of him even noticing Jessica's red hair. He sucked in another sharp breath.

"Sorry," I said, trying to get ahold of my sudden streak of jealousy. "We were friends in high school. It did not end well."

The recognition on his face surprised me. "That's her?" he asked, his expression hardening.

"Her? You know about her?"

He looked down at me, regarded me as though wondering how much he should say. "I could feel your emotions even back then. I didn't even know you were real, but I could feel everything you went through growing up. Your stepmother was a constant source of pain. I considered breaking her neck several times."

Horrified, I said, "I'm glad you didn't."

"I'm not. But that one." He looked over at Jessica again. "I've never felt such pain from you. Such absolute devastation."

I crossed my arms over my chest. "Great. I would hate for you to be unaware of how gullible I am. How easily I can be duped."

His features softened and he lifted my chin. "You trusted her. You believed you could tell her anything. That doesn't make you gullible."

I scoffed. "Kids, right? And besides, I have Cookie now."

"Want me to sever her spine?"

"Cookie's?" When he only smiled at me patiently, I

shook my head even though his offer was so much more tempting than he could've imagined. Oddly enough, however, I didn't hate Jessica. I hated what she did, who she'd become, but I hated worse the fact that even to this day, I wanted her friendship. Her acceptance. Her approval. She was like a redheaded version of my stepmother, and I was forever seeking that unconditional love that had been denied me. Pathetic as that sounded.

Except with Jessica, I'd had it. For a little while anyway. She was like the sun. We laughed and cried together. We cuddled and watched scary movies. We made pancakes and pizza and drank Kool-Aid from wine-glasses. And we told each other our deepest and most guarded secrets. So at a sleepover one night, after she'd shared her belief that she once saw her grandmother's ghost in her hallway, I shared with her as well. I told her I could see ghosts. She'd seemed fascinated. Intrigued. So I continued.

I hadn't known at the time that I was, in fact, the grim reaper, but I told her about my abilities. How I helped my dad and uncle with cases by talking to the victims. How the departed could cross through me if they wanted to, a fact that boggled even my own malleable mind.

I'd gone too far. I'd scared her.

No, I'd lost her.

She seemed frightened at first, then repulsed. Revolted that I could be so inane as to believe I had superpowers. Her reaction surprised me so much, I didn't argue when she called her parents in the middle of the night to come get her. When she refused to answer my calls the rest of the weekend. When she crusaded the next week at school to single-handedly have me branded a crazy witch wannabe. As sacrilegious and sanctimonious. I didn't even know what *sanctimonious* meant at the time. If I had, I would've known where the true recipient of such an accusation stood. Oceans apart from me. In the blink of an eye, our friendship was over.

The second half of my freshman year was the hardest thing I'd ever gone through. The only bright spot I remembered was Reyes. I'd met Reyes. True, he was being beaten unconscious at the time, but it was still a pivotal moment for me. I thought back to the first time I'd touched him. He was doubled over, clinging to a Dumpster for support, dry heaving and coughing up blood. His muscles constricted with pain, corded around his arms, and I saw the smooth, crisp lines of his tattoos. A little higher, thick, dark hair curled over an ear.

Gemma had been with me. She'd raised a camera from around her neck to illuminate our surroundings, and Reyes, squinting against the light, lifted a dirty hand to shade his eyes. And his eyes were amazing. A magnificent brown, deep and rich, with flecks of gold and green glistening in the light. Dark red blood streaked down one side of his face. He stole my heart and I'd wanted him from that moment on.

"Where's your head?" Reyes asked me.

I snapped back to him. "Sorry. Where were we? Right, no spine severing for you, mister."

"You sure? She's staring at me." He hissed in another breath. Damn it. I had to get that shit under control.

"What do you want for lunch?" he asked.

"I ordered off the menu, actually. Sammy always made me huevos rancheros whenever I asked. They rocked. No pressure."

He quirked a brow. "How would you like your eggs?"

I tried. I really did. But I glanced at his crotch and it came out anyway. "Fertilized?"

A wicked grin spread across his face. "It'll be right out, ma'am." He tipped an invisible hat and started for the kitchen.

"And if that man comes back to kill you, do *not* kill him back."

"I can't make any promises."

"I mean it, Reyes," I called out to him.

He winked right before the door swung shut behind him.

Five minutes after I sat down with Uncle Bob, Reyes brought out our food personally. The room quieted to a whisper, and several women actually raised their phones to snap pictures of him. This was ridiculous. This was beyond ridiculous.

Of course, he was kind of famous now. He'd done ten years in prison for a crime he didn't commit. Everyone wanted his story. Reporters begged for an interview. And once the public got an eyeful of Reyes being released and escorted to a waiting car outside the courthouse, that same public clamored to know more about him. So, in a way, he was a celebrity.

But still, Jessica?

"Detective," Reyes said to Ubie as he set down his plate.

"Farrow, it's good to see you getting out. Working."

"You mean it's good to see me become a productive member of society?"

I winced. Uncle Bob had sent him to prison all those years ago, but in his defense, Earl Walker's setup was almost perfect. The evidence was too overwhelming despite Ubie's gut, which told him Reyes didn't do it.

Uncle Bob's mouth thinned into a forced smile. "This isn't poisoned, is it?"

Without taking his eyes off Uncle Bob, Reyes took his fork, cut into the burrito, scooped up a bite, and held it out to me. Then his gaze, still sultry and electrifying, locked with mine. I opened my mouth and wrapped my lips around his offering; then I closed my lids and moaned.

"Delicious." When I looked back at him, his features had darkened. He watched me eat, his gaze hooded, his jaw hard. I swallowed, then said, "You're really good at that."

"I know." He put the fork down and nodded a good-bye to us both before heading back to the kitchen. All eyes were on his ass, including mine.

"So," Ubie said, "you two seem to be getting along well."

"Don't even think about it," I said, staring at the door Reyes just went through.

"What?"

"Judging who I date." Then I glared at him. "Like you're any better with the trash you bring home."

"Charley," he said, offended.

But I was only preparing him, tenderizing him for my next statement. I leaned toward him and said, "I know you like her, Uncle Bob. Just ask her out."

"Who?" he asked, suddenly fascinated with his burrito.

"You know who."

He took a bite and nodded. "This is amazing."

That was my cue. I rounded my eyes in horror, grabbed my throat, and did my best impersonation of a silent screen actress's death scene. "No, he . . . he couldn't have." Only I talked. I choked out the words between gasps. "It's . . . it's poisoned."

"Okay, I'll ask her out."

"Seriously?" I asked, straightening. "When?"

He took another bite. "Soon. Eat up. We have to get out of here."

Good enough for now. I could torment him until he followed through with his promise. Cookie wasn't going to wait around forever. She was gorgeous, albeit challenged in many ways, like coordinately, but that just made her all the more interesting in my book. Which was a bestseller called *Charley's Book*. That gave me an idea.

"Hey," I said, cutting a bite and stabbing it mercilessly, "I should write a book."

"About me?" Ubie asked.

"I want it to be interesting, Uncle Bob. It would be about what it's like to see dead people."

"I think that's been done already. There's a movie, too."

Darn it. Always late to the game. I slid my fork into my mouth and smiled as my taste buds broke into a rousing chorus of "I'm So Excited." My god, that man was talented.

I left without saying good-bye to Reyes. The place was jam-packed. I didn't want to disturb him. I still couldn't believe he was working for my dad. I was stewing in that bit of news when Ubie broke into my thoughts.

"By the way, it's been twenty-four hours," he said as we headed toward I-25.

I knew he would ask about the arsonist. "I was going to take care of that little situation this afternoon, but since you insisted I come to this crime scene with you—"

"I didn't insist. And at the moment, the arson case trumps this one. These bodies aren't going anywhere. We can turn around right now and close the case." He spun an index finger in the air.

"I don't know for certain that we can. I promise, Uncle Bob, I'll let you know the minute I'm positive."

"Charley, if this person is innocent, we'll figure it out."

"It doesn't always work that way, and you know it." I hated to throw Reyes's case in his face, but this was important. I needed to be sure.

He stiffened but didn't argue. "I at least need to know who you suspect. What if something happens to you between now and then?"

"What could happen?" When his expression dead panned, I shrugged. "Fine. I'll text who I think it is to Cookie with explicit instructions not to tell you unless something dire happens. Like if I have a fatal allergic reaction to your cheap cologne."

He didn't like it, but he nodded in agreement. "Now, if you don't mind."

"Geez. Okay." I took out my phone and texted Cookie. "And my cologne's not cheap."

I snorted and typed.

> Kim Millar Save this name and don't give it to Uncle Bob unless I die some time in the next day or two. Or if I go into anaphylactic shock and the prognosis looks bad. He will beg. Be strong.

I didn't trust the guy. He'd be bugging Cookie the first chance he got, and I knew it.

> And make a note to buy Ubie a bottle of Acqua di Gio.
> Okay. Is there something I should know?
> Yes, his taste in cologne sucks.

I started to put my phone back in my bag when Ozzy yelled out, his accent so thick, I was only half certain he said, "Where the foock are ya goin'?"

Uncle Bob jumped. I must've turned on my GPS.

"You have to tahn the foock around. You're in the middle of foockin' nowhere."

"What the hell is that?" Uncle Bob asked, almost swerving off the road.

"Sorry, it's Ozzy." I grabbed my phone and turned down the volume. "He's so demanding." I pushed a few buttons to turn off the app, then put the phone to my ear. "Sweet buttermilk pancakes, Ozzy, you have to stop calling me.

You're a married man!" I pretended to hang up, then rolled my eyes. "Rock stars."

Uncle Bob blinked and stared ahead, not sure what to think, a moment I would cherish forever. Or as long as my ADD allowed me to.

Chapter Twelve

Life is short. Buy the shoes.
—INSPIRATIONAL POSTER

We pulled onto a private road and drove another half hour, easing through gates and over cattle guards until we came to the burial site. Uncle Bob parked beside a bulldozer, then handed me his handkerchief.

"This could be bad, pumpkin."

"The bodies?"

He shook his head, his expression one of sympathy. "No, the remains they've found so far are at the morgue. The smell."

"Oh, right."

I jumped out of his SUV filled with a sense of dread. The site itself had been taped off. There were a dozen official vehicles including several state cars, a couple of local law enforcement, and one with federal plates. I recognized it. Looking around for Special Agent Carson, I spotted her and her partner talking to the sheriff. She waved me over.

"Hey," I said, surprised at how normal the area smelled. Then the air shifted, and I gulped and bit down, trying not to gag.

"Good to see you," she said, struggling through a

similar reaction. She held a kerchief to her nose and mouth as well. But the smell wasn't what I'd expected. It was gaseous and oily, not so much of death as just an odd, heavy smell.

The entire site was covered in slick oil, thick and dirty. I bent and rubbed some between my fingers. "This is it," I told Uncle Bob under my breath. "This is where the women are from."

He nodded an acknowledgment. "They've found the remains of five possible bodies so far, but they aren't intact. They brought out an archaeologist from the university, and a forensics expert from New York is on his way to assist the investigators as well."

I stood and looked out over the area. It went on for miles, a gorgeous display of New Mexican desert with earthy colors punctuated with splashes of violet. "There are more. Many more. Is this oil coming from underground?"

"We don't think so," a sheriff's deputy said. He walked up and handed the sheriff some kind of report. "It looks like it's been dumped here. Hundreds if not thousands of gallons of oil."

"Why would anyone do that?" I asked, frowning. "Where would they get that much oil from?"

"We're checking into it. We've sent samples to the state lab to determine exactly what kind of oil it is."

"What about the land?" I asked. "Who owns it?"

"First thing we checked," Agent Carson said. "This is the Knight Ranch. Mrs. Knight, an elderly woman, actually owns it now. Her husband died a couple of years ago and she's been in a nursing home ever since, but she ran the ranch for years by herself."

"Could it have been the couple? Perhaps the woman's husband?"

"Not likely," the sheriff said. "Doyle had an accident

while branding cattle and used a wheelchair the last thirty years of this life, which is why Alice, Mrs. Knight, took over the daily operations. There's just no way he could have dug those graves. It could have been anyone from relatives to ranch hands to a random stranger using their land as a dump."

I shook my head. "It just doesn't seem random to me. There were too many obstacles to get to this point. Too many locked gates. And it happened over too long a period of time. If I had to guess, I'd say our killer was at it for more than twenty years."

"Can I ask how you know that?" Agent Carson asked.

She was much too savvy to lie to, so I evaded the question. "You certainly can. In the meantime, I would love a peek at your case file as well as a list of all of the Knights' relatives, ranch hands, anyone else who had access to this land."

Since we'd worked together on a couple of other cases, Agent Carson knew to trust me. So where another agent would balk at such a demand, she just shrugged. "That's a pretty long list."

"I'm a fast reader. What was a construction crew doing out here anyway?" I asked, surveying the cleared land. "Of all the places on this two-thousand-acre ranch, why here?"

"The Knights' son retired from the rodeo circuit a few years ago and took over operations. He decided to build a new house out here."

"Can't say as I blame him," Uncle Bob said. "The view is incredible."

I wondered if the view was why the killer chose that spot. I also wondered if the son found it as incredible as Ubie did. But if the son was doing the killing, why would he send a construction crew to this very site? Maybe he wanted his victims found. Maybe he wanted to be captured.

Or chased. Serial killers loved the chase. Maybe no one was paying attention, so he decided to make them.

"Your timing is spot-on," Agent Carson said, gesturing toward a huge silver pickup as it pulled up to us.

She seemed to be getting the fact that when I talked to people face-to-face, I could siphon information she was not privy to. I loved how much she trusted me. Her partner, on the other hand, was not so impressed. A crisp dresser, he kept looking over at Carson as though she were crazy on toasted rye for even talking to me.

She gestured toward the truck. "That's the son."

"Oh, perfect. I'll let you know if he's guilty in a few."

She smiled. "Appreciate it."

But it didn't even take that long. The minute he stepped out of his truck, I felt grief combined with a strange sense of outrage pouring out of him. He was angry at whoever did this, whoever dumped these unfortunate women on his land, buried them in his dirt.

"Never mind," I said to her as she and Uncle Bob followed me over. "He's as innocent as my great-aunt Lillian."

"Figured as much."

She was a smart one.

"Mr. Knight," Agent Carson said as we approached him.

Slightly bowlegged from years atop an animal of one sort or another, Knight walked with a straight back and a stiff gait, but he was strong, still in his prime. Probably in his late thirties, he had a tall, thin frame and a tan face underneath hair the color of a desert at dusk. But what was even more striking than his handsome features were his startlingly green eyes.

"This is Detective Davidson," she continued, "from the Albuquerque Police Department and his consultant Charley."

"It's just Kenny, Detective," he said, holding out his hand. Uncle Bob took it. "Charley," he said in turn.

I scrutinized him as we shook. Kenny Knight. I'd heard of him. A champion bull rider who'd competed all over the world.

"Kenny," I said, and figuring there was no time like the present, I charged forward with, "any idea how these women ended up on your land?"

A defensive reflex bucked inside him, but he calmed himself instantly. Scanned the area. Worked his jaw in annoyance. "No, ma'am."

"What about this oil?"

"What oil?" he asked, examining the killer's dump site.

Agent Carson explained. "There's oil in the ground here, but it's not a derivative of this area. In other words, it's not the kind that will make you rich. Do you know anything about that?"

"What the hell?" He shook his head, baffled. "Why would there be oil here?"

"That's what we would like to know."

As they questioned Kenny on the oil thing, I walked to the overlook. Underneath was a sheer cliff about twenty feet high, the sparse beauty that was New Mexico stretched as far as the eye could see. I took in its vastness and waited for the departed woman who'd been hanging around since I got there to talk.

"Thought I'd never get him out here."

I looked to my right. She stood beside me dressed in a hospital gown and wearing a head wrap, the kind that cancer patients wore. And she had been beautiful. Even painfully thin with her cheeks sunken and her eyes dulled from illness, she had a glow that radiated strength and elegance. I glanced around and gestured for Uncle Bob. He walked over, his brows raised in curiosity. I raised an index finger, then nodded to my side. He nodded in understanding. I could talk to her in front of him and make it look like he and I were having a conversation.

"So, this was your idea?" I asked her.

"It was. I always wanted a house out here, but it seemed like Kenny didn't have it in him to settle down long enough to build one." She looked out over the landscape. "He didn't want this ranch. Didn't want anything to do with running it. His spirit's wild. Always has been. I thought kids would quiet the rider in him, but they just weren't in the cards for us." She laced her fingers together, her eyes brimming with sadness. "He's still young. He can still have kids if he'll give it another go."

"I'm sorry," I said to her, "about the kids." For me, the thought of having kids caused hives and a slight wheezing sound to emit from my chest. But I understood that most women wanted them. "You said you were trying to get Kenny out here?"

She nodded. "Someone had to find these women."

Surprised, I asked, "You knew about them? You knew they had been buried out here?"

Uncle Bob perked up, but kept quiet, waiting for information from a one-sided conversation from his point of view.

"Not like you think," she said, shaking her head. "I heard them one day when Kenny brought me out here. I wanted to see this place one more time. I guess I was so close to death, I could hear them."

My chest tightened at the image. "What did you hear?"

"Their crying. Their wails of agony. I didn't tell Kenny. I thought I was going crazy, so I didn't mention it. Then it was too late." She breathed deep, then leveled a determined stare on me. "I couldn't cross, knowing these women were out here. I had to get someone to come. To set them free."

"I don't understand. How were they trapped here? The

departed are incorporeal They can pretty much pass through anything. And how did they get set free?"

"I'm not certain. The minute the construction crew started clearing the land—" She stopped and thought back. "No. No, the man running the bulldozer thought he saw something. He jumped out and lifted a hand out of the dirt. And that did it. That set them free."

The workings of the supernatural realm still surprised me. How could a departed be trapped? How could the touch of a human set them free? I would never fully understand. "How did you get Kenny out here?"

"I haunted him," she said, a mischievous smile emerging from behind the sadness. "I moved books and shook glasses until he paid attention. I couldn't do much, but when I finally got his attention, I tried to get him to come out here. I left clues for him to come out to the land. A saltshaker on a map. A pencil on a sketching I'd done of our house. He knew I was haunting him, for lack of a better phrase, but he thought I wanted him to build our dream house." She shrugged. "Whatever works. It got him out here. But it took longer than I thought. He had to 'make plans.'" She used air quotes to emphasize the last bit. "You know, for a champion bull rider, that man can move slower than molasses in January."

I laughed. "I think that's an impediment for most men."

"What?" Uncle Bob whispered. "What's she saying?"

I patted his cheek, then asked, "Do you know who did this? There have to be at least twenty women buried here."

"Twenty-seven," she said, bowing her head. "There are twenty-seven."

After allowing myself to absorb that bit of knowledge, I asked, "Do you know their names? Where they're from? Who did this?"

She looked down in regret. "Nothing. I know exactly

how many there are, what they look like, but none of them talk."

Disappointment gripped me. "I'm having that same problem."

She glanced at me in surprise. "What are you anyway?"

I lifted one corner of my mouth. "I'm the portal, whenever you're ready."

She took in another superfluous breath and surprised me again by saying, "Somehow I knew that. I'm ready, I suppose. I've done what I needed to do. And the longer I stay, the longer Kenny will put off the rest of his life. I'm afraid in my haste to get him to come out here, he promised to wait for me, to never marry again."

"Uh-oh," I said.

"Can you give him a message for me?"

"Absolutely."

"Can you tell him to build our house over there instead?" She pointed to a spot about fifty yards back. "And to put a garden here? In honor of these women? When he can, anyway. I'm not sure how long the state will keep the land tied up."

"I'll tell him."

She looked back at her husband. His eyes were redrimmed, his shoulders drawn as he regarded a wildflower he twirled in his hand.

"He is such a rascal," she said. Then she stepped through.

Salient images of her life flashed before me as her essence soaked into my body, rushed through my veins. She'd taken ballet as a child but preferred saddles and cowboy boots to tutus and slippers. She had a horse named Cinnamon and a dog named Toast. They were buried on her parents' farm outside of El Paso.

The first time she saw Kenny, he was getting ready to

ride at the state fair. She was nineteen and enthralled with the way his leather chaps left one of his best features exposed. She told him so. They'd been together ever since except for a few weeks he'd gone on a drunken binge in Mexico after a white bull named Hurricane crushed two vertebrae in his back. She hunted him down and found him passed out in a hotel room with another woman asleep beside him. With her heart almost shattered, she sent the woman away, packed up his clothes, and brought him home to the ranch. She never told him she knew about the other woman, and he never mentioned it. It was likely he didn't even remember her. That's what she told herself.

But she loved him as fiercely as he rode bulls. His face was the last thing she saw before she passed, and it was her most prized memory.

I breathed deep as she crossed, and clasped Uncle Bob's arm to steady myself.

He took hold of my elbows. "What just happened?" he asked as I caught my breath.

I wiped at the wetness under my eyes. "She crossed."

"What? What does that mean?"

Uncle Bob didn't know about that part. He knew I could communicate with the departed, but that was about it.

"She crossed to the other side," I explained.

"You mean, you can't talk to her anymore?"

"No. But she had no idea who did this."

Noticing my distress, Agent Carson walked over to us. "Everything okay here?"

I straightened and let go of Uncle Bob. "There are twenty-seven." Having seen enough, I started for Ubie's SUV. "Don't let them stop until they find all twenty-seven."

After a rather quiet ride back, Uncle Bob dropped me off at Misery. He had questions. He wanted to know more about me. About what I did. But I set my mood to somber and didn't give him a chance for idle chat.

I wondered if Reyes was still at work, then decided to check on Cookie instead. The class would almost be over and I wanted to make sure she'd passed it before heading over to Kim Millar's apartment. If my plan was going to work, I would need Kim's full cooperation. I hoped to get it, because I didn't have a backup plan of any kind. Besides prayer.

Would Reyes talk to me afterwards? The late Mrs. Knight's love for Kenny echoed my own for Reyes. I understood the fierceness of it. The absolute need. His pull was like a gravitational force on my heart.

"Are you okay, pumpkin?" Ubie asked me before I got out.

"I'm good. Thanks for not asking me anything."

"Oh, that was just a reprieve. I have many questions, you can count on it."

"Mm-kay." I closed the door and sneaked in the back of the Crosshair Gun Shop, which was probably not my finest moment, considering it was a gun shop and everyone in the place could kill me from a hundred yards without so much as blinking an eye. But the classroom in the back of the store was where Noni held his concealed carry workshops.

The door to the classroom was open, and I found myself relieved he'd let Cookie in on such short notice. The class was full up with about twenty-five students. Normally, he didn't allow more than fifteen or so.

"I understand," Cookie said to Noni. "I do. But I just don't know if it would be that easy, no matter the circumstances."

I sneaked in the door and stood against the back wall. Noni nodded at her. He had a medium build with thick black hair and olive skin. He owned a local body shop, but was also a gun expert and had taught gun safety for more than two decades. "Then you've taken everything from this class that I hoped you would. It's not easy. No matter what the circumstances are, pointing your sidearm at someone, pulling the trigger is not nor should it ever be easy."

Cookie stared absently, a thousand miles away. Something Noni said before I got there had her thinking, and that was always dangerous. I'd have to warn him next time.

"What if," she said, her voice faltering before she caught it, "what if your best friend is being tortured in the apartment next door by a man who'd just put a gun to your daughter's head?"

My lungs seized. I didn't tell Cookie that part, the part about Earl Walker putting a gun to Amber's head, until a few days ago. I hadn't known how to tell her, and I didn't deal as well with the whole torture thing as I'd wanted. How could I have expected any more from Cookie?

Clearly Uncle Bob had told Noni about that night. He didn't seem surprised in the least. He leaned forward and locked gazes with her. "Then you aim straight."

"What if, even if I'd been there, I couldn't have pulled the trigger?" Her voice broke and I felt the weight of her sorrow from where I stood. It was almost more than I could bear.

"Cookie, that's a decision you have to make before pulling your sidearm. I have a feeling you could've done it, given the circumstances."

I started to step out of the room. Pain consumed me. Stole my breath. Watered my eyes. Not at the memory, but at the knowledge of how deeply that night had affected my best friend.

"And would you look at what the cat dragged in." Noni had spotted me the moment I stepped into the room, but made it sound like I'd just arrived. I was grateful.

I smiled as everyone turned, offered a hesitant wave. "Just checking on my employee. You know, making sure she didn't skip class. Or kill anyone. She's been known to do that." Cookie looked back at me, surprised at first, then self-conscious. She had absolutely no reason to be. "Oh, not kill anyone," I corrected. "She's never done that. But she's a pro at skipping. She has a ribbon."

"This is one of my former students, a PI who moonlights as a consultant for APD." Noni waved me to the front. "I bet she has some stories to tell."

I pulled my mouth into a grim line as I walked up for a hug. He knew darned well I had stories. Uncle Bob told him everything. Then I let my left dimple show through and turned to the class. "Actually, I do have a story about an incident that happened during my class with Noni. We were all out at the firing range and this woman walked up wearing a skintight sweater, and Noni almost shot off his—"

"Oh, you," Noni said, interrupting. He wrapped an arm around my neck and put me in a headlock. Then he scrubbed his knuckles on my scalp. "This one likes to fib," he said, laughing off my whimpers of dismay. "I'd like to thank you all for being here, and I'll get all this paperwork in. You should have your permits in a couple of months." Everyone got up to leave, but Noni didn't dare let go of my head. He really didn't want that story getting out. It's not like he actually hit anything. Thank god, because if he had, he would have had a lot of explaining to do to his wife.

"Coming to check on me?" Cookie asked, averting her gaze.

"Yes," I said from between my scrunched cheeks. Noni

was shaking hands and answering a few last-minute ques
tions. "I was worried you'd run after the drop-and-roll
incident."

She laughed softly and picked up her bag. "This was a
good class. You were right."

"Told you."

"And I have no idea what you were talking about," she
said, turning to leave. "Noni's not a complete fanatic."

Oh, crap. Noni's grip tightened, and I felt the knuckles
of death on my head again. Everyone was right. I'd never
paid attention, but they were absolutely right: Payback was
a bitch.

Chapter Thirteen

If it weren't for physics and law enforcement,
I'd be unstoppable.
—T-SHIRT

Outside the gun shop, I explained my text about Kim Millar to Cookie. Flabbergasted would be my best descriptor of her reaction. But I told her my plan, and she agreed with me. It was worth a shot. So, twenty minutes later, I found myself knocking on Kim's turquoise door. And knocking. And knocking. I could feel her inside, but she didn't want to answer. Her guilt thickened the air, gave it an oppressive texture.

After my third knock, the one where I added, "I'm not leaving, Kim," she opened the door. She'd always looked fragile, and nothing had changed. She was like fine porcelain—so delicate, I feared one wrong word would shatter her.

"Sorry," she said, gesturing me inside. "I was washing dishes."

She didn't look like she'd eaten a bite since I saw her last. "I was wondering if we could talk."

"Sure." She didn't seem happy about the prospect but didn't argue, either.

We sat in her tiny living room. Since the sun had set, a

single lamp was the only light afforded us. It made the sharp angles of her face stand out.

"Have you seen him?" she asked, her voice small and unsure.

It angered me. "Yes, I have seen him, and he should've come to see you the minute he got out."

She shook her head, defending him as always. "No, no, I understand. He doesn't want anyone to know about me."

"That was before, when he was being charged for murder. He has no reason not to visit you, Kim."

Her eyes watered instantly. "He has every reason," she said, almost begging me to understand. "You don't know what he endured for me."

"I do, actually." When she offered me a questioning gaze, I said, "I have a picture from that time."

"A picture?" Dread flooded her central nervous system.

"Yes, of Reyes being—" I didn't know how to put it mildly, because there was nothing mild about the picture. "You told me a while back that Earl Walker had kept pictures in the walls. Is that what you meant? Pictures of Reyes being tortured?"

A slender hand covered her mouth as tears pushed past her lashes.

"Is that why you've been burning down all the places you lived growing up? Because Earl hid the pictures in the walls?"

Her surprise was palpable. Her grief even more so. She rose and went to the kitchen for two glasses of sweet tea and a tissue, then sat back down, her resolve solidifying. "Yes," she said, closing her eyes in shame. "I've been burning down the buildings, the houses, the filth-infested garages. . . . Everywhere we lived, every place Earl defiled my brother. They're all soiled, stained with decay and degradation." She handed me a glass of tea and took a drink herself.

I took a sip, giving her a moment, then asked, "Kim, I know we've talked about this, but did Earl ever . . . did he—?"

"No," she said, swallowing. "Not me. Not ever." A savage disgust fueled the next look she gave me. "He liked boys. He liked Reyes. He took women only when he had to, as a means to an end." She cast me a puzzled gaze. "Why would any woman give that pile of sewage a second look?"

I shook my head, seeing a strength in her I had never seen before. A fierce determination to protect Reyes. She would do anything for him, and he didn't even have the decency to visit after he got out. I was furious with him at that moment, but I could deal with that later. Now was about Kim. About getting her help. I took a sip as I watched her, giving her a moment to vent.

"Reyes did everything to protect me. He still does. With this apartment. With the money."

I knew about the money. She'd told me, and it did play a big part in my plan. Fifty million dollars went a long way to appease insurance companies, especially when almost every place they'd lived, every place she'd burned to the ground, was little more than squalor. I placed a hand over hers to get her complete attention. "Kim, I think I can get you a deal."

"A deal?"

"With the police. With the DA."

"Oh." She looked down, embarrassed. "Of course. I'll be arrested. But I made sure no one was in those buildings. I would never have hurt anyone."

"I know, and I'll make sure they know it, too. I think that if we paid back the insurance companies and offered any other restitution, considering the unusual circumstances—"

"No!" She stood and backed away from me. "You have to leave Reyes out of this. No one knows he was ever a part of my life, and I will not drag him down for this. If anyone found out—"

I put my glass down and stood, too. "Kim, if it means—"

"No. Charley, he went to prison without anyone the wiser about what Earl did to him. You don't understand the kind of scars he has, the kind of weight they carry."

She was right. I didn't understand. But if I was going to get her the deal of the century, I would need to bring him into it. Reyes may not have been willing to let the government know he had a pseudo-sister to save his own ass, but surely he would to keep his sister out of prison. I was scared to death she wouldn't survive prison, and since I was going to be the one to turn her in, if she did go and she didn't make it, whom would Reyes blame? He would have no choice but to blame me.

Kim sat again and took another sip to calm down. I did the same, giving her a moment to gather herself and me a moment to decide how clean I should come. If I went to Uncle Bob and the DA and explained everything, if I had evidence . . . A thought hit me. I wouldn't need her statement. I had the picture. I had a piece of the very thing she was trying to burn down.

"Can you excuse me?" she asked.

I nodded as she rose to go to the bathroom, giving me time to think through my plan. I had no idea if it would really work or if the DA would have her in shackles the minute we stepped through the door. I needed some kind of guarantee. I checked the clock on my phone. Almost eight. Surely if I called Uncle Bob, he'd have time to call the DA and set something up for tomorrow morning. And if I had to, I'd confide completely in Ubie. He could tell me how to go about this while guaranteeing Kim's rights and safety. Maybe I would even call Gemma, see if she could be at the meeting as backup. And I might should have a lawyer on standby in case things went south.

Kim came out after a few minutes and had clearly been crying. She'd pulled her hair into a hair band and changed her clothes. She went from fragile schoolmarm to international spy, covered in black from head to toe.

I raised my brows at her as she sat on the sofa again, but when she sat down, a wave of dizziness overtook me. A warmth started at the back of my neck and spread throughout my body, and I realized I hadn't eaten since lunch several hours earlier. My blood sugar was dropping fast. Maybe I'd force Reyes to cook me something when I got back. Then again, if he knew what I was planning, he might poison it for real.

Poison.

I blinked down at my tea. It blurred and tipped to the side, spilling over my hand and onto the carpet. Then Kim's arms were around me. She pulled me onto the couch, laid me across it the best she could. I still felt crooked as she looked down at me.

"I'm so sorry, Charley. There's one left." Her brows knitted in thought. "And this one will be tricky."

"You . . . you drugged me?"

"There's just one left and then this will all be over. I've arranged everything. The money is in Reyes's name. If he wants to pay back the insurance companies, fine. That will be up to him."

My lids drifted shut.

"Wait," she said, patting my cheek.

I blinked back to her.

"All the papers are in my desk in the kitchen. And here is a note for Reyes." She held up a note. It blurred across my line of sight. "I don't want the cops getting it," she said, stuffing it into the pocket of my jeans. "Please, just tell him I've loved him since the first time I saw him."

I knew the feeling.

"And, and tell him—" She thought a moment, then grinned. "Tell him I'll see him on the flip side."

Her voice blurred, too, and faded as I fell into a warm, fuzzy darkness.

"Unle Blob," I said, fighting my tongue's refusal to work right.

"I know you're upset, Charley, but that's no reason to call me names."

"No, lou lon lullerland." What the hell did I just say?

"What the hell did you just say?"

It sounded like *You don't understand* when I thought it in my head. I gritted my teeth and fought harder. "Le larson." Wonderful, now I was French. "The. The arson . . . ist."

"The arsonist?" he asked, suddenly very interested in what I had to say.

Sadly, "Lelally," was what he got. No idea. I swallowed and stumbled out the door. Putting one foot in front of the other and trying to talk at the same time became quite the challenge. The cool air seemed to help. I shook my head. "The arsonist. I want to make a leal. A deal. Only, I don't have a lot of time."

"Why not?"

Crap. Kim was so going to ruin my plans for her. "Another building or house or something is about to go up in lames. Just alert the flyer department," I said. "I'll try to find the arsonist before lat happens."

"Who, Charley?" he asked, his voice hard, brooking no argument.

Then again, I could brook with a fence post. "I'll meet you and the DA first ling in the morning. I promise. Everything will be explained."

"Tell me now or I swear I will have you picked up on aiding and abetting."

"Uncle Bob, lat is so unflair."

"Let me at least put a BOLO on the car."

That was an excellent idea. Unfortunately, I didn't know if Kim even owned a car. There wasn't one registered to her. I'd looked.

"Just call me the minute you hear anything about a flyer." Hopefully Ubie could translate.

"Charley, you are placing innocent people in danger."

He was disappointed in me. "She won't hurt anyone. You know she won't."

"She?"

"Just call me."

"I don't need to. There's been another fire. Same MO." Already? How long had I been out? "Where?"

"Tell you what. I'll share when you do."

Before I could brook more arguments, he hung up. In my face. I rolled my eyes, almost ate the sidewalk as a result. I called Cookie to find out where the flyer . . . fire was. Who *thought* in slurs?

"There's a grass fire," she said after listening to the emergency band thanks to the wonders of the Internet. "That's all the chatter for now."

"A grass fire?" That was strange.

"Oh, wait, yes, there's a grass fire but some kind of underground structure burned."

"Like a bunker?" I asked.

"Possibly. They're trying to put it out. That's what started the grass fire."

Did Earl have them living in a bunker at some point? I wouldn't have put it past him. And Kim had been right. That would've been tricky. How did one burn down an underground building? Clearly, she was getting good at the whole arson thing. Maybe that would give her street cred if my plan failed miserably—which my plans tended to do—and she ended up in the big house.

I started to back out of the parking space when Kim appeared in my headlights. I threw Misery into park and got out, a bizarre sense of indignity sparking my own fire.

"You drugged me!" I said, incensed.

A lady walking her dog paused to listen, then ducked her head when we looked at her and kept walking. She had the decency to look ashamed. Kim, not the woman.

"Only a little."

"A little? From what I understand, you set fire to the world while I was out."

"Just one tiny corner of it." She held up her thumb and index finger to show me just how tiny.

"And I sounded stupid when I tried to talk to Uncle Bob."

She wrung her hands. "Sorry. I didn't mean for you to sound stupid."

I folded my arms at my chest. "So, are you finished? Can we discuss my ingenious plan to keep you out of prison now? Or were you still planning on killing yourself?"

The surprised look on her face told me . . . well, that I'd surprised her. That was pretty much it, but I knew the signs of suicide. She'd gotten her affairs in order and had every intention of killing herself tonight. I couldn't help but wonder what stopped her. Or if a trip to the morgue was still in order.

"No, I—" She pressed her mouth together and let a tear slide down her cheek.

"Nice try, sweet cheeks," I said, taking her arm and leading her back inside. "But I'm not falling for that act again. You're stronger than I ever imagined."

"No, I'm not. I'm meek and fragile."

"Tell it to the judge, sister. Right now, we have to synchronize our watches."

"I don't actually wear—"

"Figure of speech." I pushed her into her apartment,

then closed the door. "And if you think you can make some coffee without doping it, can I get a cup?"

"Okay."

She headed toward the kitchen. I followed. Watched her every move. Meek and fragile, my ass.

Kim didn't buy my plan 100 percent. She had every intention of walking into a police station and turning herself in, confessing to everything. While that was an integral part of my plan as well, there were steps to be taken to guarantee her fair treatment. Once I convinced her of that, and stopped threatening to press charges for the roofie, she came around.

But would Uncle Bob? Would the captain or the DA? Kim refused to bring that part of her life into our negotiations, but her entire stint as a pyromaniac was based on that part of her life. She was burning those memories. Trying to protect Reyes, to get rid of the pictures in the walls. To sterilize her past. If she didn't want to talk about it, I would respect that, but I still had one bit of evidence in my arsenal. The picture itself. The one I had of Reyes. If I showed it to the DA first, then negotiated a deal for Kim if she were to confess and pay back the insurance companies, surely they would agree. If anything, she did the city a favor. Every place she burned down, everywhere they'd lived, was an eyesore.

I ran up both flights of stairs and barreled through my door before remembering I had company. I stopped short, surveyed the room, and though I didn't take an actual head count, I would guess there to be exactly twenty-seven departed women in my apartment, which was twenty-seven too many.

One clawed at my carpet, desperately trying to get out. And another pulled at her hair, ripping it out by the handfuls. I couldn't take any more. I hurried over to her, knelt down, and took her hands into my own. She continued to rock but calmed a bit. I drew her into my arms and watched as women scurried over my cabinets, up my walls, under my desk.

We found the mass grave, but now what? What did these women need? If they were waiting for their killer to be found, it could be a long wait. I might have to camp out on my fire escape.

When the woman in my arms calmed enough for me to leave her, I wound through the masses, careful not to step on fingers or toes, and went to the dresser drawer where I kept the picture. I started to get worried when I didn't find it. I tore through the other drawers, a little thrilled when I found my boxers with ENJOY RESPONSIBLY across the ass, then searched through my socks and sweaters and scarfs. No picture. By the time my room looked like it'd been carpet bombed, I realized the picture had disappeared.

Then understanding dawned. Reyes. He'd been upset when he found it. He must've taken it.

I grabbed my key to his apartment and marched over there. It was a short march.

"Where is my picture?" I asked after finding him. In his bedroom. In a towel. Still dripping wet. Holy mother of—

"When were you going to tell me your plans for my sister?"

That brought me up short. His eyes glittered with anger. He hadn't talked to her in years. How the hell did he always know every time I went to talk to her?

"Do you know what she's been up to, your sister?"

He busied himself with putting on a watch with a thick leather band. "I thought we had an agreement. You stay away from her, and I don't slice you in two."

"No," I said, walking up to him. I jabbed an index finger at his chest. "You don't get to threaten me."

"Who said it was a threat?" The guy liked to talk big.

I stepped closer. His scent, like a lightning storm in the desert, enveloped me. His heat, radiating off him in waves, seemed to grow hotter by the second. "If you ever threaten me again—"

"What?" he asked, crossing his arms as he examined me from behind hooded lids.

After clearing my throat, I said, "If you ever threaten me again, I'll bind you." I had bound him once, tied his incorporeal body to his corporeal one so that he couldn't leave it. He was stuck. It was not a place he liked to be.

His brows shot up and the room got even hotter. He closed the distance between us. "And just how do you propose to do that," he asked, his irises shimmering, "if you cannot speak?"

A rush of fury shot through me. My gaze darted to the towel. The shadows in the valleys at his hips caught my attention. They shifted as he took another step, forcing me back. His abs rippled with the movement. He kept advancing until I could go no farther. Backed against a wall, I put one hand on his chest. He braced his hands on the wall behind me.

"I thought we were over your petty threats," I said.

His gaze dropped to my mouth. "My threats are never petty." He ran his tongue over his bottom lip, then pulled it into his mouth as he pondered our situation.

"And neither are mine. Don't threaten me again and we can be lifelong friends."

His head tilted to the side. "You think to tame me?" he asked. Without taking his eyes off me, he reached for the top of a chest of drawers, retrieved the Polaroid, and handed it to me. "You think to tame that?"

I didn't look at it. The image had been branded into my mind from the moment I first saw it. Reyes bound and blindfolded, tied to a chair, rope biting into his flesh, re-opening wounds that appeared to have been healing. I'd recognized him instantly, his mussed dark hair; the fluid, mechanical tattoos along his shoulders and arms; his full mouth. He looked about sixteen in the picture, his face turned away, his lips pressed together in humiliation. Huge patches of black bruises marred his neck and ribs. Long garish cuts, some fresh, some half healed, streaked along his arms and torso.

I swore I would never look at it again, but I wasn't an idiot. I would also never let it go. If nothing else, it was evidence of what Reyes went through, of what both he and Kim had endured, and now it would serve to help with his sister's case.

Without looking at it, I stuffed it into my back pocket.

"Don't you want to see what I am?" he asked.

"That's not what you are, Reyes. That's what was done to you."

The smile that spread across his face held little humor. "And you think to fix me like a bird with a broken wing."

My hands slid to the towel. "I think you're a big boy and you know that I'm here for you no matter what." I teased him, brushed my fingertips along the top of the towel, down the front until they slid along his erection. Clearly, he wasn't that mad.

He tensed. "No matter what?"

"No matter what," I said, nudging him back. "And when you can stop threatening me every time I stand my ground, you can have me. Until then, we can be neighbors." I started to duck under his arm, but he lowered it, blocked my escape.

"You're kidding, right?"

I looked up at him. "Not at all. If you don't mind." I indicated his arm with a glance.

Instead of moving aside, he closed the distance between us until we were only centimeters apart. "Neighbors?"

The fire that consumed him licked over my skin, soaked into my sweater and jeans. I rested my head against the wall and gazed up at him. Waiting. He would either move and make this easy on both of us or he would *make* a move, rendering my ability to walk away very, very difficult. He did neither. He stood there, watching me carefully, and at first I didn't understand why. Then I felt it. I felt him. Reaching inside me with a hot, probing energy.

"If I thought for a moment you took my threats seriously, Dutch, I would hold my tongue."

I could think of other things he could do with his tongue. "That's no excuse," I said instead, my voice a soft whisper.

"At least when I threaten you, you stop feeling sorry for me."

"Empathy," I corrected.

"It's just— I can take the anger much easier than I can the pity."

"Empathy," I said again.

"And you can use any euphemism you want, it's pity."

"It's compassion."

"It's piteous consolation."

"It's appreciation for what you've gone through. It's understanding and it's heartfelt. If that's too much for you to bear, then you can bite my ass."

"Is that an invitation?"

"It's a fact."

He lowered his head. "I want you to trust me."

"Oddly enough, I do. No matter what you say, I do trust you."

He moved his hands to either side of my head and ran his thumbs along my temples. "How much?"

I instantly began to relax. His touch was amazing. "Right now, a lot. But you still don't get to have me until you can behave."

He leaned in, put his forehead on the wall next to my ear, not quite touching me but so close I could feel his breath on my neck, and said softly, "Then make me."

His words combined with the deep timbre of his voice were my undoing. He knew they would be, damn it. My restraint system failed and I reached out, ran my hands over the hard rungs of his stomach. It clenched with every movement as my fingertips slid down to the top of his towel again. One tug and he was free. His heartbeat quickened. His blood rushed through his veins a little faster. Or maybe that was mine. Either way, the room warmed even more.

"Keep your hands on the wall," I said, my tone resolute. Then I ducked under his arm and pushed him until he was almost flat against it.

What a beautiful position to be in. Reyes Farrow at my beck and call, forced to behave, to follow my orders explicitly. I could get used to it. And I could really get used to seeing him naked anytime I wanted. He looked over at me as I took him in. His dark eyes shimmering from behind his damp hair. His long limbs shaped to exquisite perfection. His steely buttocks with divots on either side tightening when my gaze landed there.

I stepped forward and ran my fingertips down his spine. His back flexed. When I kept going, brushing over his sculpted ass, continuing down and under until I cupped the base of his erection from underneath, he lowered his head. Curled his hands into fists on the wall. Fought for control.

A liquid warmth pooled between my legs as I fondled him from behind. I stepped closer, molded myself to the curve of his back, and reached around to take him into my other hand.

"Fuck," he said, his voice a harsh whisper.

Blood pumped beneath my grip as I stroked, my fingers

unable to encompass his erection completely. It stood
rock hard, throbbing beneath my touch, a fact that gave
me a heady sense of power. To have him so responsive
to my every embrace, my every caress. I raked my fingernails over the length of him. He groaned through
clenched teeth, his voice a husky shell of the original. It
was suddenly a fragile thing. Brittle. Breakable.

I began to stroke more rhythmically, kneading the base
with my other hand, reveling in his reaction.

"Dutch," he said. The hoarseness of his voice was almost as sexy as the man himself. "Wait."

But I didn't. I pushed him to the edge, to the brink of
orgasm, because I could feel it, too. As though I were being seduced, I felt the rush of heat in my loins, the sting of
ecstasy spread through my body. Wanting more, I knelt,
turned his hips, and took hold of him from the front,
readying him for my mouth, but he gripped my arms and
jerked me up, locking me against his chest.

"This is not behaving!" I cried out in protest.

He ignored me, buried his face in the crook of my neck,
and walked me back until we found the bed. Then he pulled
me up and crawled onto it, laying me down and pressing
into me. He immediately went to work on my jeans, unbuttoning them and pushing them off my hips, down my legs
as he trailed tiny kisses along my neck. I kicked off my
boots and managed the removal of my pants as he lifted
my sweater over my head. Then, with the deftness of a
seasoned rake, he unfastened my bra in record time and
freed Danger and Will. Cool air hit them, hardening their
peaks, but it was immediately replaced with the heat radiating off my disobedient neighbor. He took them into his
hands and covered Danger's peak with his scorching
mouth. I almost cried out as his blistering tongue circled
and coaxed. He sucked softly and a sharp spike of arousal
shot through me, like a string tugging from there to my

stomach had been tightened and strummed. He gave Will the same attention and I wrapped my arms around his head, writhing in the sensations pulsating through me.

Then he stopped. I opened my eyes as he lifted his head and gazed down at me.

"Do you trust me?" he asked.

"You're not minding very well." I drew my brows together, chastising him, not that I really cared at that point.

His lips parted, his breathing still labored. "But do you trust me?"

I caved. "Yes. Fine. I do." I wanted to add words like *implicitly* and *inexorably* and *for the love of god please make me come,* but I kept them at bay.

He lay propped on his elbows, his face a picture of seriousness as he studied me. Then he cradled my head in his hands and started the stroking thing again. The one where he rubbed my temples with his thumbs and I relaxed straightaway, just as before.

"Close your eyes," he whispered.

I did so hesitantly.

"Relax and let me in," he said.

His touch was mesmerizing, his thumbs circling softly until I melted, giving myself over to him completely. Then I felt it. A gentle nudge in my mind. A parting in the folds of reality. An inaudible voice came to me, spoke to me in a foreign language. It took me a moment to identify it. Ancient Aramaic.

"May I enter you?" it asked, and I recognized Reyes's voice, the soft accent, the deep timbre reverberating in my mind. He was speaking to me on another level, on a visceral, psychic level. And he wanted in.

I was so fascinated with what he was doing, how he was speaking to me, I didn't answer him at first.

"Dutch," he said, the voice growing clearer, the nudge growing more insistent, "may I enter you?"

I responded in kind, mentally and in Ancient Aramaic. "Yes."

In an instant, he sent his essence inside me, penetrating not only my mind but every molecule in my body. I felt soft tendrils of pleasure lace down my spine, curl into my abdomen, settle around my heart. As though a sensual smoke had entered me, my skin began to respond. It tingled and tightened until it felt too small for my body. My blood began to boil. The crests of Danger and Will hardened as a prickling hunger spiraled and nipped. My muscles contracted and released with sensuality. Hot ribbons of ecstasy spread through me.

The probing grew harder, more demanding, as it pooled at the apex between my legs and swelled inside me. Then it moved, pulsated, bucked, and milked me closer to the edge. Scorching, pulsing waves rocked inside me, bathed me in sweet, unimaginable heat. Reyes locked me in his arms, then nudged with his mind again, sending the sensations deeper, harder, faster. Anticipation throbbed between my legs until I could take no more. I needed his flesh inside mine.

"Rey'aziel," I said from between clenched teeth, writhing beneath him. I sank my fingernails into his back. "I order you."

He buried his fingers in my hair, spread my legs with his hips, and entered me in one long thrust. I gasped aloud as the swell of orgasm crested and rushed over me like a whirlwind of liquid fire. That was all it took. One thrust. One piercing impalement to unleash the storm.

I cried out but Reyes's mouth came down on mine as he embedded himself farther inside me. Then he pulled out, trailing kisses to my ear, clutching the inside of a thigh to hold me wide, and plunged into me again and again until the crest reappeared. I clawed at him, urged him deeper, reveled in his pleasure.

"Dutch," he said into my ear, his hold so tight, I should have screamed in agony, but I relished the feel, the strength of his orgasm as it crashed into me. He tensed, his breathing labored as it shuddered through him in sweet, astonishing waves.

When he came down off his high, he rolled over and took me with him until I was on top. Then he locked his arms around me, refusing to let go. Not that I wanted him to. He sought the comfort of my neck, burying his face in the crook before saying with a muffled voice, "We should date."

I laughed, curled him into my arms, and kissed the soft spot underneath his earlobe. "You're going to have to go to obedience school for that to happen. You have authority issues."

"Never mind. We should have sex again and then date."

"Since you put it that way, okay." I squeaked out a protest when he rolled me back over with a growl and started the whole thing again.

It was a pretty weak protest.

Chapter Fourteen

If god is watching us,
the least we can do is be entertaining.
—BUMPER STICKER

Someone was knocking. Pounding. And as I fought the lids that wanted to stay closed and the body that wanted to stay horizontal, I swore by all things holy someone was going down. Whether that someone ended up being the intruder or me remained to be seen, but come morning, one of us would be lying on the ground, moaning in agony.

"What the bloody hell?" Reyes asked, fighting lethargy as well.

I tried to answer, but my voice came out sounding more like a rabid moose with a head cold, so I shut up and wiggled out from under his arm and Artemis's hind legs. Then I fell off the bed, which wasn't that unusual.

"You okay?" Reyes asked, his face buried in a thick down pillow. The guy had taste.

"Mmm," was all I could manage as I navigated the room in search of underwear and a bra. I just had them. How far could they have gotten?

The knock sounded again. Then voices. Then footsteps followed by a lighter tapping on Reyes's door, and I realized the earlier knocking had not been on his door but either Cookie's or mine. Artemis raised her head, but only for a moment before sleep won out.

I found the towel Reyes had been wearing and wrapped myself into it. If people were going to knock on doors in the middle of the night, they needed to be prepared for the consequences. After dodging a coffee table and narrowly missing a planter, I found the door and opened it. Then I saw the front door, so I closed the pantry door and headed in that direction.

Another soft knock sounded. More voices.

"What?" I asked, tearing open the door. I could almost see at that point, though everything was a blur of grays and blues. Until I saw Cookie.

"Oh, Charley," she said, wearing a fuchsia robe and lime green slippers. My pupils constricted in horror. "Mr. Swopes was looking for you."

"Call me Garrett," he said to Cookie.

She smiled bashfully. Darn it. Uncle Bob had better get a move on.

Then Garrett turned to me. "Charles. Late night?"

"What the fuck, Swopes?" I still sounded like I had a head cold. "Do you know how rude it is to knock on someone's door at—" I had no idea what time it was. "—early in the morning?"

"I thought that was your favorite pastime." He wore a heavy tan jacket and had a backpack thrown over his shoulder.

Reyes walked up behind me in a pair of long pajama bottoms, his hair mussed, his jaw shadowed, his lashes tangled. Tangled! Freaking men. Sexy just didn't get any sexier. Cookie sucked in a soft breath when she saw him. Garrett stiffened.

"It is," I continued, rubbing my left eye with a fist, "but I'm privileged. You have no excuse."

"Can I sever his spine?" Reyes asked. He put his arms

on the doorjambs on either side of me and stepped forward until his body molded to mine.

Garrett straightened further, accepting the challenge. They were almost the same height, same build, same blinding good looks. I had such a hard life.

"Don't even think about it," I said under my breath. I looked up and chastised Reyes with my infamous death stare, then led Garrett to my apartment, opened the door, and shoved him inside. "Wait here," I said, adding a warning edge to my voice before going back for my clothes. "Sorry he woke you, Cook."

"Can I make some coffee?" she asked, the hope in her voice so endearing, I couldn't possibly refuse her. "Sure. Though I think Swopes is more of a beer guy."

"Coffee's fine," he said from inside my abode.

I grinned at her. "Coffee it is."

Garrett called out again. "And bring your boyfriend with you."

After tearing her eyes off Reyes, Cookie headed into my apartment while I herded the son of evil back into his and hurried to find my clothes. How my socks ended up in the kitchen sink was beyond me, but I found everything else with relative ease and began getting dressed in the stylish contemporary bathroom. My bathroom was contemporary, too. Or it would be if we were living in the late seventies.

Reyes stood with his arms crossed, leaning against the door frame, watching me with a particular interest as I jumped to get my pants up faster. "I didn't realize you two were so close," he said.

The sensation radiating off him raked over me, left tiny slits in my skin as though someone had thrown a box of razor blades at me. I sucked air in through my teeth, suddenly understanding what he went through earlier at the bar. This was jealousy.

No, I'd felt jealousy. This was jealousy from a super-natural being. From Reyes Farrow.

"Yes, you did," I said, playing it off. "And we aren't close. We're colleagues. Kind of. Have you seen my other boot?"

He gestured toward the receiver under his flat screen, where one leather boot sat perilously close to toppling off.

"Oh, thanks. So, are you going over?" I asked him.

He shrugged an indifferent affirmation.

"Thinking about getting dressed anytime soon?"

"Not really."

"Oh, no, you don't," I said, wagging an index finger.

"What?" he asked, all innocence and myrrh. He knew exactly what I was referring to.

"You put on a shirt or you stay home. You'll give that poor woman a heart attack." Cookie would have enough to deal with having both Garrett and Reyes in the same room together. If one of them were shirtless . . . I shuddered to think.

He grinned and went to his closet, looking just as good going as coming.

By the time we got there, the coffee was brewed and Cookie had brought over a basket of muffins. Muffins! She was such a great hostess. I only brought an open pack of gum with pocket lint on it. Both Reyes and I had to navigate around the throngs of departed women. Our actions had to look odd to the two nonsupernatural beings in the room, but they didn't say anything.

We sat in my living room, Reyes and I on Sophie and Garrett and Cookie on lesser chairs who were apparently unworthy of names. The guilt of my negligence tried to get a foothold. I didn't let it, assuring it that I'd just been busy. The chairs would get names first chance I got.

Garrett busied himself by taking books and materials

out of the backpack he was carrying. From the looks of things, I was about to get some answers. Sweeeeet.

"Do you want to take off your jacket?" I asked him.

"No, I'm good. I just wanted to explain a few things, what's been happening and what I've figured out."

"Sounds ominous," I said, settling deeper into the sofa. Reyes threw a possessive arm across the back, almost touching my shoulders.

Cookie noticed, her expression full of longing before she caught herself.

Garrett's gaze darted toward the movement as well, then back at me. "You have no idea how ominous. But first, you might want to know something about how I got started in the bond enforcement business."

Not the direction I thought the conversation would take, but okay. "You were in the military."

He took a stack of notes and sat back. "Right, and that training definitely comes in handy. But you know how I told you my dad was an engineer working in Colombia?"

"Yes," Cookie said, chiming in. "He was kidnapped and you never heard from him again."

"Exactly. What I didn't tell you is why I'm so good at my job. I have a talent for reading people. I see the world through a different lens than most."

Sounded legit.

"My father was the first person in my family to go to college, to really do something with his life. But his ancestors were a little less academically inclined. Basically, I come from a very long and very well established line of con artists."

"Con artists," I said in disbelief. "Like real con artists?"

"Yep. Grifters of every size, shape, and color. And that's probably why it took me so long to believe in what you could do. In who you are. We don't harbor an overabundance of trust, especially when we use the same tactics for a con. We know every trick in the book."

"Wait, for real?" Cookie asked, still trying to wrap her head around it.

I was right there with her. "Like genuine con artists?"

"All the way back to a great-great-grandfather of questionable morals who claimed to be a Romani prince and an enslaved grandmother who used voodoo to raise the dead."

"Wow," Cookie said, "that's so cool."

"Yeah. My dad put himself through college by setting up cons and selling moonshine. He was a pretty famous moonshiner, actually."

"My dad's pretty famous, too." We all turned to stare at Reyes.

"Wait," Cookie said, recovering first, "could your grandmother really raise the dead?"

"No, hon. Thus the term *con artist*."

"Oh, right. But that does explain why you didn't believe Charley for so long."

Garrett continued. "Exactly. Even after I saw cold, hard evidence, it took a bit of convincing." He raised the notes he had in his hands. "And what if this whole thing, everything that happened when I died, the story, the setup, the trip to hell and back, what if it was all just an elaborate con? Smoke and mirrors to get me to do Lucifer's bidding? I'm kind of like you, Charles. I can tell when someone is lying, and Lucifer was lying to me about how Reyes is going to destroy the world."

Finally! Someone with some common sense.

"How do you know?" Cookie asked.

"Because he spent a lot of time, too much time, trying to convince me of that, of how bad Rey'aziel is, of how he is going to kill you, Charles, everyone—" He seemed to fight for the right words. "—everyone . . . close to me, then destroy the world in a fit of rage."

"And you think he was lying?" I asked.

"I know he was. He creates a way out of hell, a portal like you named Rey'aziel, then sends him away? Why would Lucifer send the portal, his *only* way out of hell, to Earth to get you? There has to be a pretty fucking good reason to risk his only way out of that hellhole he lives in. But Junior's been bad." He shook his head at Reyes. Reyes ignored him. "And so now, instead of fixing the problem, Roger Ramjet has increased it sevenfold. And Daddy's thinking, 'Well, shit.' " He glanced at me. "Let's just say he's really upset about the whole 'Reyes was born on Earth to be with you' thing."

"You know about that?" I asked.

"I know about everything. Lucifer supposedly sent Reyes to get you, to take you back to hell with him so he would have a key into heaven, but Romeo changed his mind and decided to stay on this plane to be with you? To be with the very being he was sent to bring back? Why would he wait an eternity for you, risk so much by sending his only escape route onto this plane, to then turn around and send his army to try to kill you?"

I shrugged. None of it had ever made any sense to me, but who was I to judge? My plans often went awry. Much like my thoughts. Hold the phones. Maybe Satan had ADD, too. It would explain a lot.

"Think about it," Garrett continued.

I was. How could I not?

"They've been trying to kill both of you since you were born. Earl Walker was supposed to kill you, Reyes, but he became obsessed instead. Some pedophile was supposed to kill you, Charles, but Reyes saved you. Again and again. A bond, an otherworldly connection, was formed before you were even born, and it's strong. It's kept both of you alive. If that connection is ever severed, you'll each be much more vulnerable. And I think that's what they wanted. To sever that connection. To keep you apart until one of you could be killed. But they've failed time and time again."

He was right in at least one aspect: Reyes and I were supposed to grow up together, but he was kidnapped and everything that he'd planned went up in flames.

"Why else would he send hundreds of thousands of his troops to their deaths just to try to navigate the void of oblivion? God made it very difficult to get out of hell. There's a void, like a moat around a castle, and it's almost impossible to navigate. That's why he created Reyes. He is a key, a map through the void. And he wanted to make sure at least one being made it onto this plane who could send you to your grave."

I crossed my arms. He had me on some points, but lost me on others. He didn't send Reyes to kill me but to get a portal. Any portal.

Garrett scrutinized the notes, deep in thought. "But then that pesky connection crept in. It's kept you alive decades longer than most reapers."

"Hey," I protested, suddenly offended. "I'm not that old. I'm twenty-seven. Holy cow."

"But most reapers die young, right? Because most reapers don't have a lovesick supernatural assassin guarding their asses."

Reyes had told me that very thing. Most reapers' physical bodies pass young and then they do their duty for hundreds of years incorporeally.

"But this still begs the question, why would he want you dead, Reyes? You? The only being in existence that could navigate the void? Because you're going to destroy the world? That's what's been keeping him up at nights? He cares that much about humans?" Garrett scoffed. "He cares nothing about us. We're points in a game, and Earth is the ultimate playing field, but the only one keeping score is him."

Cookie's brows drew together in concentration as she absorbed Garrett's story.

"And he wants a portal to heaven?" he continued. "Why? So he can get his ass handed to him on a silver platter? Again? Why would he want back in there? What's that old saying? It's better to rule in hell than to serve in heaven? And he's the ultimate ruler with hundreds of thousands, possibly millions of beings to serve him. To worship at his feet."

"So if getting ahold of the portal, aka me," I said, indicating myself with a sweep of my hand, "isn't his motivation, then what is?"

"Fear."

"Fear?"

"Think about it. He created a son to do his dirty work, and like any pigheaded teenager, the son rebelled. Refused to do his father's bidding. It was never about a war. It was never about Lucifer getting back into heaven. It's about something else, something that only he would fear."

I was sitting on the edge of my seat, chewing on my nails. I totally should have made popcorn. "Okay, so what? What's he so scared of?"

Garrett pressed his mouth together, then said softly, "You."

I straightened. "Wh-what? Why would he be afraid of me?"

"No idea, but I have to tell you, I'm more than a little impressed."

"Me, too. I rock," I said, pretending to go along with it. He'd lost it. He'd gone over the edge of a waterfall and landed on a sharp, pointy boulder.

Before I could give him my professional opinion of his

mental state, he pinned Reyes with a stormy gaze. "You weren't sent to get her, to bring her back, were you?" When Reyes didn't answer, he continued. "You were sent to kill her, just in case all the elements that seem to work naturally against a reaper fail. Just in case she lived through all the evil beings on Earth who were attracted to her light, who were drawn to her essence. You were insurance, sent to make sure she was put in the ground before she had a chance to breathe." He leaned forward, spoke directly to Reyes. "You were created to assassinate her. She would still have been the reaper. She just wouldn't have had a life as a human. So for some reason, it is Charley in human form that is a threat to him. And you exist for one reason and one reason only. To kill the only being in the universe who was prophesied to bring Daddy down."

This was great. I wiggled farther into my seat and clasped my hands. It was like being told a very cool bedtime story that had no truth to it whatsoever.

"You're going to do something," he said to me, his expression severe. "I'm just not sure what. You're going to gain some kind of power, or make some big decision that is going to change the course of human history. You are going to bring an army against the ruler of hell and put him down once and for all. And he is doing everything in his power to stop you."

Oh, yeah, Garrett needed to be on medication. "But why would I want to do all of this? And how would I raise an army? I'm just not that good at organization. Will they expect to be fed?"

"I don't know how you're going to do it or what part you'll actually play. I was shown only bits and pieces, and with all the information I got from the underworld, trying to separate fact from fiction, reality from dream, it was hard to sift through it. Thus all the research." He lifted the notes for me to see.

"Where on Earth did you find all of this?"

"Like I said, I have interesting relatives. eBay helped, too. All I know is that grim reapers—by the way, they aren't actually called that down there—are extremely powerful. Not like the angelic beings or the demons from the dimensions we know of. They have souls and can exist in this realm either in human form or as spirits. They are a completely different species. They're like butterflies in a world of moths.

"But you," he said, staring pointedly, "you are even more powerful than most of your kind. You were born with the ability to draw energy from anything around you, animate or inanimate. Your powers are like liquid, ever changing, forming and molding to the situation. They called you a word from their language that meant 'malleable,' 'adaptive.' From what I could tell, you were very special even in your world. And you were royalty of some kind."

"Wow, you guys had quite the talk." Reyes had told me about the royalty thing. The rest was new, though, and interesting enough. Still, I couldn't help but question his sources. Maybe it *was* all a big con, but not the way Garrett thought. Maybe Satan *wanted* Garrett to believe he was lying.

"Like I said, it's different there. It's like you internalize the contents of a thirty-five-volume encyclopedia in the span of a few seconds."

"I so could have used that in college."

"Do you remember that letter you found in my apartment the other night?"

"Yes," I said, ignoring the pang of jealousy that rushed out of Reyes. "The one you ripped out of my hand."

"Yeah, sorry about that."

He wasn't. He really wasn't.

"It was from a Dr. von Holstein from Harvard Universtiy. He's been working on some translations for me."

"Translations of what?" Cookie asked.

"And how did you find him?"

"He's published quite a bit. I came across his name during a search for dead languages. And translated from some very old documents I found on an antiquarian book site. And, again, a couple were on eBay. Unfortunately, no one could read them, so I contacted Dr. von Holstein for help."

"The cow guy can read ancient texts?"

"A hell of a lot better than I can. And once I told him my story, he helped me gather information and told me what to look for. What really interested us were the works that were reportedly written by a Byzantine prophet named Cleosarius."

Cookie tsked. "That's an unfortunate name."

"Yeah, well, it's probably really old," I told her. "Though I knew a Cleo once. His wife killed him with a meat cleaver."

She shuddered. "Was it still in his head when he came to you?"

"No, thank god. How creepy would that be?"

Garrett cleared his throat.

"Sorry," we said in unison. Then I whispered to Cookie. "I'll tell you more later. That woman was psychotic."

"'Kay," she whispered back.

Garrett waited to make sure he had the floor.

I blinked. Surveyed my toenails. Chewed on my lips.

"Unfortunately," he continued after a millennium, "we can't find much on *Cleo.* But historically, prophets couldn't just go around spouting prophecies. They would be marked as heretics and executed. So many wrote their visions down in verse. Nostradamus wrote in quatrains. A monk from Tibet named Ajahn Sao Chah recorded his visions in poems even though he would never have been condemned for them. He said he got his visions from magical amulets. But this guy Cleosarius wrote in code."

"Like a secret code?" I asked.

"Exactly. At first Dr. von Holstein thought the documents were written in Illyrian. No idea what that is, but they weren't. The code threw him. Once we figured out the guy was Byzantine, the doctor knew what language he was using and could go from there. But take the fact that this Cleo guy wrote in both a dead language and code . . . Let's just say Dr. von Holstein had his work cut out for him."

Cookie sat fascinated. "So, he deciphered the code and translated the texts?"

"He's gotten only bits and pieces so far."

"And he did all of this in—" I raised my gaze in thought. "—in two months?"

"He's been a little obsessed since I contacted him. He said it's like finding the Holy Grail. It was always there in different historical texts, but no one ever made the connection between a dead language, prophecy, and code. The way I understand it, everyone just figured the guy was a lunatic and called it good."

"Okay, what did he find out?"

"Just that all of Cleosarius's prophecies revolve around one person. You."

"Me?" I asked, suddenly super-duper interested.

Garrett nodded and tore through his notes. "I realized it when Lucifer referred to you as the royal daughter and once he called you the royal daughter of light. That's what I based all of my searches on. The royal daughter of light. There are several texts that refer to you as either the royal daughter or as the daughter of light. But in his later writings, there are a couple that refer to you as just the daughter, and that's where things get really interesting."

I scooted to the edge of my seat. "Okay. I'm hooked. Why?"

"Those are the ones that refer to your unimaginable power and your army."

"Okay, power's good. I'm still not sure about the army thing, though."

"Not just power," Garrett said, growing excited. "Unimaginable power. According to his prophecies, you will recruit a warrior, a scholar, a prophet, gatekeeper, a warden, and a couple of other figures Dr. von Holstein is still working on." He read from a letter. "Okay, here's the part I was looking for. The ruler, or king, of evil will take the daughter's father captive to lure her into a trap—"

"Wait. What would Satan want with my dad?"

"Maybe it's not your father here on Earth, but your other dad."

"Oh, right. The king from that other realm?" I asked Reyes, but Mr. Farrow was busy stewing in his own thoughts.

"And with the daughter's army protecting her," Garrett continued reading, "she will take on the ruler. There will be a great and terrible battle, but she will defeat him and peace will settle on the Earth for a thousand years."

Reyes stood and walked to gaze out the window. I had no idea where his thoughts were. But I knew exactly where mine were. "Um, I don't think that's how it happens in the Bible," I said, suddenly skeptical again. "And I don't really want to fight Reyes's dad. Can I just hand in my resignation now? Cross that off my to-do list?"

"But isn't it amazing that this guy wrote hundreds of prophecies about you hundreds of years before you were even born?"

"So you believe. And there's just one problem with your theory. Reyes wasn't sent to kill me. He was sent to kidnap me, to take me back to hell with him. Right?" I looked at Reyes. He stood looking out over our illustrious parking lot. He was so not cooperating.

A microsecond before I was going to continue my rant, Reyes spoke at last. "And how do you think I was supposed to manage that, Dutch?"

I crossed my legs. "What do you mean?"

He turned to me, his expression severe. "How do you think I was going to get you into another dimension?"

Garrett looked at me sadly. "He was sent to kill you, Charles. There was no other way."

The oxygen evaporated from the room as the realization that Garrett was actually on to something dawned. I brought my knees to my chin.

Cookie's fingertips rested on her mouth in a mixture of astonishment and regret.

Reyes turned back to the window. "My father gave me the same line of shit he gave Swopes. And like him, I doubted my father's motives. Swopes is right. Why would he want back into heaven? It never made sense. Every word out of my father's mouth is full of ulterior motives, but that was different. I always got the feeling he was hiding something. He created me for a reason. He needed to make sure I would make it through the void and onto this plane. And he had me wait. For centuries I waited in the dark until you were chosen."

"But you saw me," I said, my feelings hurt. I felt like a silly schoolgirl. "You saw me in another form and you fell in love."

He bit down and lowered his head as though embarrassed. "I did."

"Still," I continued, memorizing the pattern on my sofa, "if you hadn't, you would have killed me?"

After a moment, he leveled a hard gaze on me. "Most likely, yes. But I also didn't trust my father. He wanted your physical body destroyed, and I didn't know why. I cannot say what I would have done. Either way, you would still have been you. You would still have been the reaper incorporeally."

I nodded, trying to swallow his admission. "So, all that crap about the key inserted into the lock—"

Garrett's head snapped up. "You know about that?"

"Yes," I said, suddenly tired, "one of the demons told me. Said that if Reyes and I got together in the flesh—if the key was inserted into the lock, so to speak—it would start a war or destroy the world or something else equally as horrid. You know, the usual doom and gloom. But let me tell you, the key has been inserted into the lock, and while the earth moved, as far as I know, we did not start a supernatural war."

He looked down at his books in thought. "I can't figure that one out, either. I remember hearing that same caveat. I think it's part of the prophecy I was told about, but I just don't know what it means."

"And who told you about this prophecy?" I asked. "Lucifer wouldn't have done that, not if it meant you would figure out he was lying to you."

"The only one who could have. The only being with enough power to both send me to hell, then rip me back out again. And the way I see it, only one being has the power, the know-how, and the inclination to send me to hell and back." He cast a hard stare at Reyes. "The son of Satan."

I blinked in surprise, then scoffed. "Reyes? Swopes, that's ridiculous. Why would Reyes do such a thing? More importantly, *how* would he do such a thing?" After a few seconds defending my man, I realized I was the only one in the immediate vicinity who was doing so. I turned to Reyes, to the frigid glimmer in his eyes as he fixed a steady gaze on Garrett.

"You're smarter than you look," he said.

Garrett's expression turned deadly. "What the hell were you thinking?"

"I saw an opportunity and I took it," Reyes said. He was the picture of tranquillity on the outside, but his insides were churning, boiling with aggression and unspent emotion. "There is an instant," he continued, "when a person dies and is brought back to life where his soul is caught between two dimensions. In that instant, I decided I could use you as a spy."

While I sat dumbfounded, Garrett's anger swelled. "Only I wasn't in on the plan, jackass," he said, his voice harsh with barely contained fury. He leaned forward, his teeth welded together. "You sent me to hell."

"For all the good it did me. You didn't learn anything I didn't already know."

Garrett's fists were in Reyes's shirt before I knew it. He lifted Reyes off his feet and attempted to throw him against the wall, but naturally Reyes got the upper hand in a matter of seconds. He turned the tables, threw Garrett back, shoved him against the wall, and jammed his forearm in Garrett's throat.

Cookie jumped back as I had the opposite reaction. I rushed into the melee.

"Reyes, let him go!" I shouted, pulling on his arm.

But Reyes wanted Garrett to know how much effort he was *not* expending. He smiled as Garrett grunted and fought. I was worried he would actually crush his larynx.

"We get it," I said to Reyes. "You win. Now, let him go."

Cookie recoiled, her face ashen, her eyes wide.

Reyes released his hold and threw him to the floor. Garrett coughed and gasped for air, holding his throat. I bent to help him up and while I half expected him to shrug off my offer, but he put a hand on my shoulder and tried to stand. But he was heavier than I remembered and

I struggled to get him to his feet. Reyes had no choice but to help me. Together we got him up, but Garrett started to stumble into me. Reyes caught him and in the next instant, Garrett proved just how good a con artist he was. He shoved Reyes back, pretending to be falling, drew a long dagger with a razor-sharp point, and buried it in Reyes's chest.

A startled shock of electricity dumped adrenaline down my spine. I covered my mouth with both hands in utter disbelief as Garrett smiled and leaned into the man he'd just stabbed. It was Reyes's turn to suffer. He tossed his head back and tried to breathe as Garrett buried the blade deeper, impaling him to the wall.

"I did learn a few things about how to bring your ass down."

When Reyes grabbed the knife, Garrett pushed again and Reyes groaned in agony.

I didn't understand. It was just a knife. It had a long thin blade, almost like a small sword, and it wasn't in his heart but just under his right collarbone. He'd been shot with a .50-caliber bullet, something that would rip a normal man to shreds, and walked away. Why would such a slim blade paralyze him?

I ran to them and tried to pull the blade out, but Garrett pushed me back. I tripped and fell to the ground.

He locked his jaw, his expression full of hate, his anger palpable. "Do you have any idea what they did to me?"

Reyes couldn't answer. His eyes rolled back, his hands braced on the wall beside him. Then he reached up and ripped at his shirt like it was burning him. He clawed at it, but once he tore it to shreds, I realized he wasn't clawing at the shirt, but at himself. His tattoos, the crisp lines and patterns of the map through the gates of hell, began to crack. A bright orange light, like molten lava, began to seep through them.

I sat on the floor, transfixed. Why didn't he just pull out the dagger? I didn't understand.

Garrett braced both hands on the tip of the handle, one on top of the other, and pushed again. Reyes groaned through clenched teeth as the blade slid in even farther. As the fissures widened and a roiling fire began to leach out of them. And I knew what was about to happen. Reyes was about to die.

Was this it? Was this Rocket's premonition?

It couldn't be. I stood and prepared to charge forward. If I could just get Garrett off him, I could pull out the dagger. But how? He was tall and strong and—

A sharp thud sounded and we all stood there a stunned moment before Garrett looked back at me and crumpled to the ground. I glanced at Cookie. At the frying pan she had in both hands like a baseball bat.

Another grunt from Reyes had me lunging forward. I took hold of the dagger, braced a foot on the wall beside him, and pulled. The blade slid out easier than I thought it would, and I fell back with it.

"No killing friends in the house," Cookie said, terrified and shaking. "I am so glad I didn't have a son. Boys are so destructive and violent."

Reyes gulped huge rations of air. The fissures that covered his torso darkened and closed until he was back. Garrett stumbled to his feet at the same time I gained my own balance, and the murderous glare on Reyes's face was like a jump start to my nervous system. Before I could shout a warning, he took hold of Garrett's head and twisted.

Time slowed as I watched Garrett's head spin to the side, farther than it should. Then I was in front of them. I broke Reyes's hold with my arms and caught Garrett to me, stopping the momentum of the motion by cradling his head to my chest.

Then I closed my eyes and let time snap back into place. It hit like a freight train crashing against my bones. Garrett and I tumbled to the ground with me holding his head so tight, I was afraid I would break his neck with the fall. Fortunately, he seemed okay. Just dazed, unsure of what had happened.

But Reyes's anger still raged. He came back for more. Bound and determined to end Garrett's life, he charged forward. I straddled Garrett and turned on him like an angry bear protecting her cub. And Cookie was right beside me, frying pan in hand, jaw set in determination.

"Stop," I said to him, my tone low, even. "Now. This is not going to happen."

He fought for control, then growled and turned away from us, shaking off the pain that had consumed him. I helped Garrett up.

He tested his neck and jaw before addressing Reyes again. "This knife will kill you. Not just your physical body. You. All of you. Your essence. Your incorporeal being. Your spirit. Everything."

The fact that he'd come very close to dying just then struck me hard. I looked at Reyes, confused. "Why didn't you just pull it out? What stopped you?"

"The dagger," Garrett said.

He tossed it to Reyes, who caught it, then just as quickly dropped it with a hiss of pain. He shook his hand, then glowered at Garrett again.

Garrett was ballsy. I'd give him that.

He smiled. "Romeo can't touch it. That dagger was Daddy's insurance should Junior betray him."

"His father told you about it?" I asked.

"No, he didn't." A calculating smile spread across Garrett's face. "Romeo did."

While I stood perplexed, Garrett took a brave step closer to him.

"You knew I'd figure it out," he said. "All your clues. All your hints. You knew I'd find it."

Reyes glowered at him. "I didn't think you'd be stupid enough to use it. When I couldn't find it, I hoped that someone with your connections could."

Garrett scoffed and shook his head. "And to think, I never even believed in those connections. I thought my entire family was crazy."

"Who says they aren't?"

He shrugged, unable to argue. "But why take the risk? Why put such a powerful weapon in my hands?"

"Because it works on any supernatural being, ass-hat." Reyes rubbed his shoulder and flexed it, still trying to shake off the pain. "Demons. Poltergeists. Hounds of hell."

Wait, there were really hounds of hell?

"Charley can use it to defend herself against them."

"See," Garrett said with a smile, "I knew I liked you for a reason."

Chapter Fifteen

I'd rather be in Virginia.
—T-SHIRT WORN OFTEN BY REYES FARROW

I saw Cookie and Reyes out as Garrett gathered his books and notes. He stopped to massage his neck every so often, and I couldn't believe how close he'd come to death. Again.

"You're going to be sore for a few days," I said, bending to help him. "That wasn't very smart."

"I had to know if the dagger would work."

I looked over at it. It sat on an end table. "How exactly did you know about it?"

He drew in a breath and sat back to zip his backpack. "Like I said before, it all happened so fast. It's like I was in hell for an eternity and yet here it was only a few minutes. The time I spent in hell I remember with a crystalline clarity. It's the other parts that took me a while to figure out."

"The other parts?"

"The trip back. Whoever dragged me out of hell had a few things to say to me. When I woke up in the hospital, I could only remember bits and pieces, but I started to remember more and more. And at odd times. I'd be standing in my kitchen and another memory would materialize in my mind." He shook it off and stood to leave. "It took a while, but I slowly began to realize those particular memories had been planted somehow. They were clues." He gestured toward the dagger. "Whoever planted them wanted me to find that."

After I sidestepped past a few women, we stopped at my door. "And you figured out it was Reyes? He planted those memories?"

"He was the only one who could have. The only one who wanted it found. And I had a little help."

"Help?"

"I have a few relatives who claim they can see into the supernatural world."

"Right, but I thought it was all a con."

"So did I. According to my aunt, it's about fifty-fifty. Some of my relatives really are sensitive to otherworldly occurrences. They use that to their advantage. My aunt said I had a darkness following me. It wanted me to find something. Between her sight and my research, we found the dagger."

"Where was it?"

He smiled and shook his head. "I'm still investigating the area. I think there's more to be found there and I don't need you snooping around."

Though I pretended to drop it, it was so on. I would find out. It may take me a while, but I'd get there. "Fine, whatever, but why would you use it on him? Why would you risk your life like that?"

"Like I said, I had to know. There's more at stake now."

"You mean more because of this supposed war, not between heaven and hell but between *me* and hell?" The idea was almost laughable. No, wait, it was entirely laughable.

"Yes, and no. I—" He hesitated, unable to make eye contact. "I may have a son."

Astonishment shot through me. I choked on air, then

gaped at him. "You may have a son? You mean you don't know if you have a child or not?"

"She had a child. Marika. And I'm about ninety percent positive he's mine."

I set aside my shock over the fact that Garrett could actually be with someone long enough to get her pregtastic he was a man, after all—and zeroed in on his emotions. Sadness came at me in waves. And determination. "Have you asked her if he's yours?"

He put his hand on the door handle, clearly uncomfortable and ready to dart. "I saw her at a store a while back. At first she smiled, then she looked down at a kid in a stroller. She got scared. She had the kind of fear someone gets when they're trying to hide something. Like I said, I'm very good at reading people. She didn't want me to look at her son."

"What did you do?"

"I looked." He opened the door.

"And?"

"And I saw my eyes."

"Holy cow, Swopes. Have you done any digging? Pulled up his birth certificate?"

"Unknown." He laughed humorlessly. "She listed his father as unknown. She was scared to death I'd figure it out. It was all over her face."

"Why wouldn't she want you to know?" I narrowed my eyes suspiciously. "Is she afraid of you?"

"No. Why the hell would she be afraid of me?"

"I don't know. You just said—"

"We dated only a couple of times." He grew agitated. "All she wanted was sex, actually. It was kind of nice. She'd show up. We'd do it. She'd leave. Then she just stopped. I never saw her again. Figured she'd moved on."

I took a long, leisurely look at the man standing before me. At the lean, muscular limbs, the wide shoulders, the perfect mocha-colored skin, and the shimmering silvery gray eyes. "Maybe she wanted to get pregtastic. If I were looking for a baby daddy, you'd definitely be on the list."

His gaze slid past me. "Are you serious? She wanted to get pregnant?"

"Pregtastic," I corrected. I put a hand on his. "And I don't know, Swopes, I'm just saying. That could have been her motive all along. Do you want me to look into it?"

"Not just yet. I have an idea, and since you owe me—"

"What?" I said, cutting him off right then and there. "I don't owe you. Since when do I owe you?" When he did that deadpan thing, I said, "Okay, I owe you. Let me know what I can do."

He nodded and started out the door before turning back to me. "I still don't trust him."

"Your own son?" I asked, appalled.

Unruffled, Garrett looked toward Reyes's door, then back at me. "Just be careful. I won't hesitate to bury that dagger in him for real."

"That looked pretty real to me, Swopes."

"Yeah, but next time I'll make sure it stays buried."

Exasperated, I nudged him out the door and closed it. Freaking men. It didn't matter what the problem was, they saw only three solutions to it: food, sex, war.

Since dawn waited just around the corner and my mind raced too fast to sleep, I decided a shower wasn't out of the question, especially since I had my annual appointment with the girl-parts doctor. One couldn't be too clean for these things. Thankfully, the woman who'd taken up residence in my shower had moved. I figured with the recent vacancy, Artemis would be chasing water droplets as I washed, but she must've still been napping. Why would a departed dog need sleep? I added that to the twenty million other questions I was saving for when I finally met someone in the know. Like Santa. Or, no, God! Yeah, probably God.

The world had gone mad. That was the gist of what I figured out as a blast of scorching water eased the tension from my neck and steam rose around me. The world had gone berserk. There was a knife that could kill Reyes. Lucifer wanted me dead. Garrett might or might not have a son. Kim Millar was an arsonist. Nicolette was not a zombie, sadly, but some kind of prophet, which was almost as cool. A serial killer was running loose on the streets of—well, I had no idea where, but somewhere. And I had a house full of departed women I didn't know what to do with. I should probably have gone back to bed, but I had a big day ahead of me.

After I rinsed, I stood in the shower a bit longer to let the heat pulsate on my neck and down my spine, and ran down my to-do list. Girl-parts doctor. Work magic for Kim. And find a serial killer. Another one. I'd just found one a few days prior. Surely there was someone out there better equipped to hunt down serial killers.

Oh, and try not to obsess too much over Reyes. I needed to stay frosty. Alert. And figure out why I suddenly had blond hair mixed in with my brown. My gaze traveled up until it landed on the girl, the pixie from under my bed, hanging from the ceiling, staring down at me. Her dirty-blond hair hung in matted strips, her huge eyes peering out from behind them. Before I could say anything, she lashed out at me. Her nails raked across my face with the speed of a cobra.

"Son of a bitch," I said, falling back out of the girl's reach. The sting spread instantly and blood dripped in the water to become tiny red clouds swirling around the drain. I turned off the shower and stumbled to the mirror to inspect the damage. Three lines of blood streaked across my face. I grabbed a towel and held it to them.

Then the girl appeared behind me. I tensed, waiting to see what she would do next. With her eyes barely visible as she peered around me, she reached up, pulled down the towel, and pointed to my cheek. I tried not to react, to cringe away from her or push her back. I stood there, realizing she was trying to send me a message. She held up three fingers in the mirror and waited until I nodded.

"Got it," I said. "Three. Are you trying to tell me—?"

She disappeared before I could question her further, but she couldn't have gone far. And even if her message wasn't quite sinking in, she gave me a pretty vital clue. She held up the number three, but not like most people do, not like hearing people do. She held up the number three the way Deaf people do, a thumb, an index and a middle finger. Could she have been Deaf? Or perhaps she had a parent or sibling who was Deaf?

After applying ointment to my already-healing cheek, I hurried to the phone to call Uncle Bob.

"It's early."

"One of the girls may have been Deaf. The young one."

"How do you know that?"

"I don't. It's just a hunch. Can you check if there have been any missing girls from the School for the Deaf in Santa Fe? Like, ever?"

"Sure. What time will you be in?" He was in short supply of patience when it came to the whole arson thing.

"Around ten."

"Can't you come in sooner? The DA is going to be here at nine."

"Can't. I'm getting checked under the hood."

"Okay, but if Captain Eckert finds out you've known who the arsonist is for days, he's not going to be your biggest fan anymore."

"I knew he liked me."

"Charley, you're putting me in a very awkward position."

"Then paint polka dots on me and call me Twister, but I think you can sweet-talk your boss. Or, well, lie. Yeah, lying is probably best. And besides, I told you I didn't actually know *for sure, for sure* until last night."

"Right after that bunker burned."

"Pretty much."

"Well, if you do a little time for conspiracy, I'll *for sure, for sure* bring you something to read."

"Aw, that's so sweet. Thanks, Ubie." He always had my back.

I found the pixie again when I stepped out of my room fully clothed and ready for action. Or, well, a vaginal exam. The girl was sitting on the floor by Mr. Wong, picking at the hem of his pants, which hung above his bare feet, trying to pull a stray thread off him. At least she was occupied and not attacking me. Always a plus.

I sank to my knees beside her, hoping she didn't think I was there to pick a fight. My moves were innocuous, unhurried as I examined her hands. I had three scratches on my face, two under my left eye and one along my jawline. But why not four? Why not four scratches? I watched as she plucked at the string absently. She had a small mouth, round cheeks, and thin nose. She would have been beautiful, given the chance. I looked at her hands and even as filthy as they were, I could tell she was missing a fingernail. The nail on her ring finger had been broken past the quick. I winced at the thought. She fought her attacker and hopefully he paid some small price for his actions. But it would never be enough.

I reached over and took her hand into mine. She let me. She didn't look at me but stared off to the side, well aware of my presence. Then, as though afraid to do so, she removed her hand and touched my jeans. The knee had a small rip. She ran a tiny finger along it, then examined her own clothes. Sadly, there wasn't much to look at. She'd been wearing a nightgown when she died and nothing else.

I reached out, tentatively touching her forearm and, just in case, I used my voice and signed as I asked, "Can you tell me who did this to you, pumpkin? Do you remember who it was?"

She withdrew back inside herself, crossing her arms at her chest and rocking.

I tucked a lock of hair behind her ear. "It's okay, honey. We'll figure it out."

In a movement almost too subtle to notice, she lifted a finger over her crossed arms. Then another. And another. Until she held up three fingers once again.

Sadly, that could mean a million things, but just in case, I texted Ubie.

Can you see if any convicted felons have only three fingers on either hand?

Sure, will have Taft do a search, he texted back.

It would take a miracle to solve this case. Luckily, I believed in miracles. No, wait, that was testicles. I believed in testicles.

We were so screwed.

I opened Cookie's door and yelled into her apartment. "I'm taking Virginia to the doctor!"

"Got it," she said from her bedroom. "I'll be at the office in fifteen. Let me know what's on the agenda for the day."

"Okay, but I might be hard to pin down. I have a lot of crap to stir. People to annoy. Lives to ruin."

"Sounds like a plan." I started to close the door when she called out again. "Wait, who's Virginia?"

She'd figure it out later. Or sooner if I complained ad nauseam, as I tended to do after offering a doctor a free glimpse of paradise. And two hours later, I was on the phone with her.

Complaining.

Ad nauseam.

There was nothing like a trip to the gynecologist to make one feel just a little violated.

"But it's important," Cookie said, defending my gynecologist's overzealousness.

"I get that. I really do. But why use enough to lubricate the Panama Canal? I went through an entire box of tissues." My phone beeped. "Oh, got another call. It's Ubie. He has the hots for you."

"Does not," she said.

"I'll call you right back. Unless I get arrested. Then it could be a while. And costly. How much cash do you have on you?"

"No, really? He has the hots for me?"

I'd lost her. I hung up with an evil grin and accepted Ubie's call. "Charley's House of Tiny Tomatoes."

"I have an arson case just begging to be solved that, oddly enough, is still sitting on my desk," he said.

"I'm sorry, sir, but what does this have to do with tiny tomatoes?"

"It's almost ten."

"That's old. Aren't those unsolved mysteries called cold cases?"

"The time. It's almost ten o'clock."

"Oh, thanks! I hadn't checked in a while. Is this part of the new initiative to better serve the public? You call and tell random people the time before they can wonder about it?"

"You have five minutes."

"You're so testy. Are you getting enough tiny tomatoes in your diet?"

"I checked, by the way," he said, his voice softening. "There has never been a missing girl matching the description you gave me from the New Mexico School for the Deaf."

Disappointed, I asked, "Can you check other schools for the Deaf? It's honestly the only lead I have at this point. I'm getting nothing."

"Will do. Sorry, pumpkin."

"Thanks for playing my hunch."

"Well, you were right. They were not all natural blondes, and some had their hair bleached postmortem."

How did they know such things? "At least we're kind of getting somewhere with the case."

"Small steps. We'll get him, pumpkin. And you have five minutes."

After a long sigh, I said, "I'm on my way."

This would either work or not. I would either ruin Kim's life, who could probably have gotten away with the whole thing squeaky clean if she really were to stop like she promised, or get her the help she so richly deserved.

Uncle Bob met me at the front doors of the station. He seemed agitated, ready to get this over with.

"Okay, we have the DA, the ADA, the fire marshal, Captain Eckert, and a couple of other detectives who were working on the case. Would you mind telling me who this mystery arsonist is before we go in there? I don't want to be blindsided."

"To be honest, Uncle Bob, I don't plan on telling you who it is at all."

He pulled me to a stop. "Charley, what the hell?"

I'd expected his face to turn purple with anger, but he seemed more stunned than livid.

"I want my client to have the opportunity to turn herself in. I'm just here to negotiate the terms of her surrender."

"Hon, are you sure you don't want a lawyer for her first?"

"What? A cop suggesting a lawyer? Besides, I have one." I winked to the lawyer I'd *hired* as he walked up.

Uncle Bob looked around, rolled his eyes, then asked, "You mean the lawyer you got for your client is dead?"

"He's departed, yes. And you've met him."

I reached out and shook Sussman's hand. He, along with his two partners, had been murdered a few months back. I'd worked on the case with Uncle Bob.

"It's Patrick Sussman from that case a while back. The one with the three lawyers?"

"Right, right," he said, becoming more nervous by the second.

"Hey, Charley," Sussman said. Like the newest dead guy in my life, Sussman wore round-rimmed glasses, but unlike Duff, Sussman wore a suit and tie, mussed as they both were. The only thing missing was a centuries-old briefcase.

"How's the wife and kids?" I asked him. He'd stayed behind for them despite my encouragement to cross.

"They're better. I think they'll be fine."

"I'm glad. Shall we do this?"

He beckoned me forward. "Absolutely."

Uncle Bob leaned into me. "You're not going to talk to him in there, are you?"

"Since I'd like to avoid a stint in a padded room, no."

Sussman chuckled and pushed his glasses up his nose with an index finger. "I think you're on the right track with this one, Charley. Your plan is solid. I can't imagine they won't take it, but if they look like they are going to back out, call that other lawyer I told you about immediately.

Your attorney–client privilege will get you only so far. They could have you in handcuffs in minutes."

"Got it. Thanks. Oh, and Ubie, can you send a patrol car to Gemma's house and her office? I really need to make sure she's okay."

"Why?" he asked in alarm. "What's going on?"

"I'll explain inside," I said as we walked into a room full of suits. It was a small room. Everyone stood when we entered, and Uncle Bob introduced me to the ADA and the fire marshal. I'd met the DA, a fashion-centric man who I thought was entirely too young for such a stressful position. Why nobody asked me these things beforehand, I never knew.

The ADA was actually a little older than the hotshot DA, but not much. Our legal institution was being run by kids. That was scary. Oh, well—half the staff that sent the first men to the moon were kids.

The captain eyed me in that austere and slightly curious way of his. I had no idea why he made me so uncomfortable, but he did. He could have me sacked from the department. That could be one reason, but I didn't rely on my consultant position to pay the bills. However, I did rely on it to keep me knee-deep in mocha lattes. That explained it. If I lost this gig, no more mocha lattes at whim. A cold shiver ran down my spine. I had to make this good. Both Kim's and my mocha lattes' futures were at stake.

The captain spoke first. "Davidson, is there something you'd like to share?"

I could have shared the reason I didn't get to the station until ten, but I figured that would fall solidly under the label of oversharing. So I just nodded as we sat at a long wood veneer table.

"I want to make sure my client is given every opportunity for a reduced sentence and to make restitution for what she's done."

That knocked the wind out of everyone. Did they think I was kidding when I said I knew who did it?

"So, you really know who the arsonist is?" the ADA asked.

"I know exactly who it is, though I just recently found out."

With Sussman whispering what to say in my ear, I repeated his instructions word for word. "I want immunity from prosecution and I want my client to get a reduced sentence in a private psychiatric ward which she will pay for."

The men balked. A couple scoffed out loud.

"Ms. Davidson," the DA said, "surely you realize you're tap dancing on some very thin ice. We could charge you with—"

"Now, hold on there, Michael," Uncle Bob said. "I told you how this was going to play out. You promised to listen to everything she has to say and charge her with absolutely nothing."

The DA glared at him. "*I* know that and *you* know that, but until about fifteen seconds ago, *she* did not."

"Charley came here of her own accord, and she's worked miracles for this department. We aren't playing games with her."

So proud I could burst, I took his hand under the table and squeezed. He squeezed back, and Sussman leaned over again, whispered something about how having Ubie in our corner was going to be very beneficial. I had yet to figure out why he was whispering.

"If you'll just hear me out," I said, "I think you will be pleased with the outcome."

After a moment of contemplation, the DA smoothed his tie, then sat back down. "Fine. What are your terms?"

"First, my client has agreed to pay back everything. Every penny of damage she caused."

"That will take a long time and a lot of payments she won't be making if she's soaking in the tubs at the state nuthouse."

"No, no, no, a private nuthouse that she will pay for."

"Yeah, right, do you have any idea how much—?"

"Will fifty million cover it?" I asked, shutting him up before he could dig himself in too deep.

That got their attention.

"My client has fifty million to play with, although I've seen those properties. We will not accept inflated prices the insurance companies want to throw at us. I've seen the properties she's destroyed. The value of everything combined couldn't possibly be more than four million, but that will be between my client and her lawyer to negotiate. And while we're on the subject, I also wanted to discuss why she did this, if that's okay. You'll understand more once you understand what she's been through, and perhaps leniency won't be such a hard pill to swallow."

"I'm not sure we're up for hearing a sob story, Davidson," the DA said.

I was kind of impressed with the captain. He had yet to say anything. He just sat back and watched me, his gaze unwavering, like a hawk's right before it swooped in for the kill. I shifted away from him, just in case.

"No, you have no idea. Everything the arsonist did was to protect her brother. They had both been horribly abused growing up, and when I say horribly—" I took out my picture of Reyes. "And no, you can't keep that." If they looked at it long enough, they would be able to identify Reyes by his tattoos quite easily. I needed to make sure that didn't happen, as promised. "I know that doesn't excuse what she did, but if it helps you acquiesce to my terms, then so be it. This is her brother."

Uncle Bob knew the moment his gaze landed on the picture. He knew exactly whom he was looking at. I furrowed my brows and shook my head to silence him as the others took in the brutality of what they were seeing. It worked. They were stunned. Sickened. Heartbroken.

"She has been through so much. The man who raised her and her brother would starve her to get her brother to comply with his demands. I'll let your imaginations fill in the demands part. Just conjure the most vile, heinous acts you can imagine and multiply by ten. That should get you somewhere in the ballpark."

Uncle Bob stood abruptly and walked to the window as the men deliberated. He once told me he'd known, deep down inside, that Reyes was innocent, but the evidence was too overwhelming. He had no choice but to do exactly what he did—turn over his findings of Reyes's guilt. And now, ten years after the fact, that knowledge was eating him alive. We'd have to talk later. I worried about him over this. It bugged him more than I thought it would.

Sussman leaned over to me again. "I think now would be the perfect time for your trump."

I grinned and nodded. "But wait," I said to the table, brightening, "there's more."

The department liked to look good. They liked to solve cases, and what would look better than solving the mystery of a mass grave outside of Las Cruces? "I'm still negotiating here, and I can sweeten the pot if what I've brought to the table isn't enough, though why it wouldn't be is beyond me."

"What else do you have?" the captain asked, chiming into the conversation at last.

"I am almost positive I know who killed those women in the mass grave they just found."

The captain's face went blank. The DA looked at me skeptically, and the ADA's mouth fell open, but just a little.

"I need a couple of days to get the proof, but I have a very good idea who it is."

"Charley," Uncle Bob said, stunned, "if you know who—"

"Really, Uncle Bob?" I asked, giving him my best incredulous expression. "I'm using this as leverage." Then I looked at the DA. "Do we have a deal? All my client will get is twenty-four months in the private institution of her choice."

"Twenty-four months?" the DA asked, appalled.

"Twenty-four months."

He let my terms simmer, spoke softly with the other officials in the room, then leveled a hard stare at me. "She'll pay back everything?"

"Every penny."

"And you'll hand over a shiny new serial killer," the captain said matter-of-factly. "You seem to be doing that a lot lately."

My discomfort mounted. Not a horse or anything. Maybe something small like a donkey or a goat. The man was a shark. He knew something. But what on earth could he know? It wasn't like consorting with departed people was a crime.

"Yeah, well, I get lucky a lot."

"I have no doubt that your success rate has nothing to do with luck."

Deciding not to comment on his use of a double negative, I cleared my throat and looked at the DA askance. "Well? My client needs help, not a prison sentence."

"Fine. She won't see the inside of a jail cell. You deliver her and I'll have accounting sort out the restitution details before we sign anything."

Sussman whispered to me again and I nodded, then said, "Can I get that in writing?"

With their mouths drawn in grim lines, the DA and ADA set down to write out a legally binding document stating the terms of my client's surrender.

I stood and went to Uncle Bob. "Are you okay?" I asked. I could feel a pang of regret filter out of him.

"I failed him so completely." I knew he was talking about Reyes. That picture affected him more than I'd imagined. "He was just a boy, Charley."

"Uncle Bob, everyone failed him. Every single person in his life, including me."

"You?" he asked.

"From that first night, the first time I saw him being beaten by Earl Walker. I did nothing."

"Pumpkin, he told you not to. He threatened you, if I recall."

"But still, I should have at least filed a report so it was on record. I didn't even do that, and I had two cops in the family."

"This is all contingent on your arsonist turning herself in by five P.M. today," the DA said.

Taking in a deep breath, I looked back at him and nodded. "I'll go get her now."

"I'm going, too," Uncle Bob said.

"I'm not sure that's a good idea," I said, worried she'd change her mind if she saw him.

"I'm not sure I care."

"You're not playing me, are you, pumpkin?"

"What?"

"Farrow. He doesn't have a sister."

"Not a biological one, no, but he was raised with a girl he thinks of very much as his sister."

"Was she . . . Were they—?"

"Yes, they were really abused in the way that I described."

"How did we not know that?"

"She has a different last name. They look nothing alike. They rarely ever attended school. They were ghosts, Uncle Bob. Earl Walker made sure of it."

"And her name?" he asked, dying to know.

"Kim. Kim Millar."

I pointed the way to Kim's apartment. She knew to expect me. I'd told her about what time I'd be showing up and she was going to have her affairs in order and be ready to surrender. I had Cookie looking into private psychiatric institutions. She should be getting back to me soon.

We walked up the path and I noticed a cup on the lawn outside her door. There were also bits of trash here and there, which was unusual for this complex. "This is her," I said, knocking on Kim's turquoise door. When I got no answer, Uncle Bob went to the window and looked in.

He turned to me, startled. "Is this a joke?"

"What?" I asked, completely perplexed. Then the fact that Kim had been suicidal the night before sank in. I hurried over and looked in. "No. No, no, no, no, no. We had an agreement."

I rushed back to the door. It was unlocked. I practically stumbled into something that resembled a clean room at a software corporation. The apartment was completely and utterly empty. I rushed from room to room, looking for evidence of Kim's existence. Nothing. Absolutely nothing.

"Charley," Uncle Bob said from the living room.

I hurried back and nodded toward the wall. An envelope had been taped there. My name had been written in black marker across the front. I tore it off the wall and opened it. There was nothing but a cashier's check to the city of Albuquerque for ten million dollars. No other name on the check. No other indication of whom it had come from. I suddenly knew how Angel's mom felt when she got anonymous check after anonymous check, month after month. Only I knew exactly who had purchased this one.

I stood stunned.

"How soon do you need a place?"

I turned to a man standing in the doorway. "I'm sorry?"

"I assume, since you're in the apartment, you're looking for one."

Uncle Bob pulled out his badge and flashed it. "We need to know where the occupant of this apartment went."

I patted my pockets and realized I'd left my PI license at home, so I dug through my bag and flashed my driver's license instead. "And we want to know how." I was just here last night. The place was immaculate, neat and orderly like Kim herself. But there was no sign of her leaving anywhere.

He blinked a moment, then said, "Well, hopefully he went to heaven, and he did that by way of heart attack, I'm told."

It was my turn to blink. "He?" I asked, walking toward him. "Kim Millar has been living in this apartment for years. Tall. Dark auburn hair. Painfully thin."

He rubbed his mouth in thought. "Well, she sounds great, but she never lived here. This has been Old Man Johnson's place for almost ten years."

"And your workmen just happened to clean this place out in twelve hours?"

"No, ma'am," he said, chuckling. "Mr. Johnson died about two weeks ago. His family moved everything out last week."

Uncle Bob took out his memo pad. "I need a name and address for his family."

He rubbed his mouth again. "Not sure I have one, but I can look."

"You do that."

The manager nodded and headed back outside.

"I assume he's lying?"

"Through his teeth, and happily so. There's no telling what Reyes paid him."

"You think he's behind this?"

"I know he is. These are the most connected siblings I've ever met. Who can get an apartment stripped and re-finished in the middle of the night like that? And I was with him." Then it hit me. Reyes's BFF Amador Sanchez, that's who. I didn't dare mention his name to Ubie. There was no need to drag him into the station. He'd only deny everything and have a rock-solid alibi.

"Well, I can send around a couple of uniforms to inter-view the other tenants. Get a few eyewitness reports and possibly a couple of descriptions of whoever did this."

"Not sure what good that will do besides prove to the DA that I'm not crazy and I wasn't lying. But she's gone, Ubie. If Reyes wants her gone, she's gone."

After the manager couldn't turn up an address for Mr. Johnson anywhere, we went back to Ubie's SUV with our tails between our legs and started back to the station.

"This is going to negate my little contract with the DA."

He fluttered the check. "I think this will help, pump-kin. And the fact that you have a strong suspicion on who our serial killer is. He wouldn't give up that lead for any-thing."

"You don't think they'll have me arrested for aiding and abetting?"

"I think they have better things to do with their time than prosecute one of their best and most successful con-sultants."

That made me feel a little better, like a balloon with just enough air in it to be pear-shaped. "Would you really have had me arrested if I hadn't told you?"

"In a heartbeat."

The air in my balloon rushed out, making a disturbing flatulence sound as it went.

"But don't let it bother you. I would arrest my own mother if it meant a collar."

"You would arrest Grandma?" Okay, I was better again, even though I had never met my grandmother. Both sets of grandparents had passed before I was born, actually. All I had was my stepmother's father, and even he died when I was four.

This time we went straight to the DA's office. He had meetings all afternoon, and we were hoping to catch him before he headed to lunch. We did, and the circus began anew. He ranted and railed until Uncle Bob handed him the check. It was strange how fast that cooled his overheated jets.

He called in the captain and the ADA, and I gave them Kim's name, but not her connection to Reyes. He could be held liable for all this. Then again, Kim had proved herself mighty resourceful. Who can burn down two buildings, seven houses, a ramshackle garage, and a bunker and leave the cops scratching their heads? I admired her for her conviction, for her fierce desire to protect Reyes, more than I cared to acknowledge.

Chapter Sixteen

I don't expect everything to be handed to me.
Just set it down wherever.
—T-SHIRT

The first thing I did when I got back to Misery was to call Gemma again. Now that the whole arson thing was out of the way, I could concentrate on the other issues at hand. Namely the identity of the possible serial killer. When she didn't answer either her cell or her office, I tried the GPS thing. No signal. She was probably with a client and had turned off her phone. But I was beginning to get worried. If the serial killer was whom I suspected, she could be in trouble for the mere fact that she was blond. I left her another message. Thankfully, Gemma was savvy and resourceful. And she didn't have any tattoos. Nicolette said the victim had a tattoo of the number eight. Which, oddly enough, resembled an infinity symbol on its side.

My heart leapt into my throat. She was next. Gemma was the serial killer's next victim.

I tore out of the station parking lot amidst glares from a couple of cops walking in and called Uncle Bob.

"Did you find her?" I asked him. "Did you find Gemma?"

"No, according to her secretary, she canceled all her appointments this morning and she's not at her house."

"Bloody hell." Okay, no more playing games. "Uncle Bob, I think the serial killer is a client of hers. He's a cop."

"A cop?" That stole the wind from his sails. "Okay, explain."

"The girl that scratched me left the exact same marks on my face that he has on his."

"Charley, that's really thin."

"I know. I know how it sounds, but she was trying to tell me something, to give me a clue."

"Well, I can't accuse a cop of something like this without some solid evidence."

"And I'll get it, but first we have to get Gemma to a safe house. I think she's next."

"Holy shit, Charley. You definitely should have led with that." I heard him snapping his fingers as though getting another officer's attention.

"Sorry, can you put out a BOLO on her car?"

"Just did. I'm looking up the license plate now. Where are you?"

"I'm headed to the bridge."

"What bridge? The one that woman told you about?"

"Yes, she said she saw a body, blond hair, and a tattoo or a mark with the number eight on it."

"And?"

"And, Gemma drew an infinity symbol on her wrist."

"Are you saying you think this woman predicted your sister's death?"

"Let's just say she's good. Someone is going to die under that bridge, Uncle Bob."

"Okay, okay, I'll send a car out. You need to get back here."

"I'm already headed that way."

"Charley, damn it."

"I'm not stupid. Just send a car. I won't do anything until your patrolman gets there."

"Christ on a cracker, Charley, I will not survive you."

"And call me the second you find anything. Check for her car at that nail salon. She's such a girl. And there's that macaroni place she likes."

"I'm on it."

I hauled booty toward the bridge, going 110 in a 55, hoping a cop would chase me. I could use the backup. On the way, I called Reyes.

I spoke the minute he picked up. "Reyes, I need you to find my sister."

"How'd the meeting go?"

"Reyes Farrow, there is no time. I need you to find Gemma and protect her."

"Okay, so what's in it for me?"

"What? What do you mean, what's in it for you?"

"I mean, what do I get if I find your sister and protect her from all the evil in the world?"

"Reyes, this isn't a game."

"And I'm not playing one. I'm asking a question."

"Oh, my god, I don't know. What do you want?"

"You," he said, his voice lowering an octave. "I want you, Dutch, body and soul. I want you in my bed every night. I want you there when I wake up in the morning. I want your clothes strung across my apartment and your scent on my skin."

Was he asking for a commitment? Now was not the time to be negotiating for drawer space. "Fine. I'm yours. Body and soul." I swerved to pass a Pinto with a chicken coop on top. Uncle Bob wasn't kidding.

"I mean it."

"So do I." I took in a deep breath. No matter how he was getting it, he was getting it. If he wanted a commitment, then I'd give him one. I'd have given him my left ovary if it meant him dematerializing and finding my sister. "I mean it. I'm yours." The words caused a sharp tingling in the pit of my belly. "I've always been yours." When he didn't answer, I asked, "Are you there?"

"I'm here. I was just worried. After what happened with Swopes—"

"What? You didn't think I would still want you? I assumed last night would have proved that I did. Thank you for the picture, by the way."

"Did it help your case?"

"Yes. Or, well, it did until I showed up to pick up my client and she had morphed into an elderly man with a bad ticker and then vanished into thin air."

"Weird how those things happen."

"Reyes," I said, pleading with him to understand, "the things she's done are not exactly nickel-and-dime. Kim needs help."

"And she's getting it." His tone brooked no argument. The topic was not open to debate. While those were precisely the kinds of topics I liked to debate, I dropped it in lieu of more pressing issues.

"Fine, but right now, my sister could be gasping for air beneath the hands of a murderer with an affinity for blondes."

"I don't think so."

"You can't know— Wait, why don't you think so?"

"She looks happy to me."

I slammed on Misery's brakes and pulled over to the side of the road. "What? You already found her?"

"I'm not sure she was ever lost, but yeah."

I could have kissed him. I could have kissed the ground he walked on. I could have kissed the phone he spoke through.

"Hold it. I don't understand. How are you talking to me?" If he had gone into ghost mode, how was he still on the phone with me in corporeal mode? Then again, the last time he ghosted himself, his corporeal self still fought a demon.

"Well, I put the phone to my mouth and—"

"Seriously, Reyes, where are you? Where's Gemma?"

"I'm at work, and Gemma's eating the Monte Cristo I just made for her."

"Holy shit, she's there? She's at Calamity's?"

"Every ounce of her."

"Is she alone?"

"If you don't count the guy she's with, she is."

I pulled a Uey and headed back to town. "What guy? She's with a guy?"

"Yeah, a cop. He's must be on his lunch break or something. He's still in uniform."

A thick dread tightened around my chest. "Does he have three scars on his left cheek?"

"Yes, but enough about him. What are you wearing?"

"This is not the time, Reyes. Whatever you do, do not let Gemma leave with that cop."

"And how would you suggest I stop them?"

"You're the son of Satan. You can't come up with something?"

"For a price."

"You already have me. I'm paid up, buddy."

"You have to strip for me."

"Now?"

"Tonight."

"What is it with guys and lap dances?"

"I can't imagine," he said, his voice deadpan.

"Okay, I'll strip. I'll tap dance. I'll sing 'La Cucaracha' in C minor."

"They aren't going anywhere. You have my word."

A relief so cool I shivered washed over me. "I'll call Uncle Bob and get him over there ay-sap. Thank you."

"Thank me tonight."

A different kind of shiver flitted over my skin like a caress at the sound of his voice.

Letting the deliciousness linger, I hung up and called Uncle Bob.

"Well?" he asked, waiting for word.

"Found her. She's at the bar. Reyes is watching her, but Uncle Bob, she's with the guy I suspect, the cop."

"You've got to be kidding me."

"See, Gemma gets in trouble, too. It's not all me."

"Mm-hmm." He didn't sound totally convinced.

"I'm going to get Cookie down there to help make sure they don't leave together."

"I'll be there in ten. How far out are you?"

"Well, I was going pretty fast. I made good time. I can be back to town in about fifteen."

"Got it. Hurry."

The second I hung up with Uncle Bob, Cookie called. God, that girl had good timing.

"Hey, where are you?"

"At the office. Did you know that women actually take Reyes's picture with their phones when he walks past?"

"I know."

"It's disturbing."

"Yes, it is."

"But I got some really good shots."

"Seriously? Text them to me," I said, excited; then reality sank in. "Wait, first you have to go down to the restaurant and help Reyes stall Gemma from leaving."

"Oh, okay." I heard her walking, a door opening. "What's going on with Gemma?"

"I think she's dating our serial killer. So, you know, don't make eye contact unless you have to."

"O-okay. Should I go back and get my gun?"

"Because Dad's bar needs another hole in it?"

"But what if she tries to leave?"

"And you're going to pull a gun on her?" I dodged a roadrunner and almost flipped Misery, a fact she did not appreciate. "Reyes can handle it, but just in case, you be his backup. Uncle Bob is on the way."

"Wait, no, it's okay. I can see her. She's with a cop."

"Aka the serial killer."

"No," she said, whispering into the phone. "The serial killer is a cop?"

"He's my lead suspect, so just keep your distance."

The minute I parked, I jumped out of Misery and ran into Calamity's through the back door. I'd sped even worse on the return trip, trying to get there before Gemma could leave, and I arrived just as Uncle Bob was barreling in the front. Good thing we hurried. Officer Pierce had Reyes against the bar, about to cuff him. An off-duty cop named Rodriguez was holding Gemma back as another cop whom I didn't know was assisting a dramatically distraught Cookie.

"What's going on?" Uncle Bob asked.

Cookie pointed at Reyes. "This, this monster attacked me."

I stood transfixed, trying to reconcile that bit of knowledge, when Reyes glanced over his shoulder and winked.

Dad was there, too, leaning against the wall with his arms crossed at his chest, not buying it for a minute. Luckily, the only one who needed to buy it was Officer Pierce, and he did. Paid full price, too. With tax. But that was nothing compared to the price he would pay when I sent him to prison for five thousand years.

Dad waved me over. "Hey, can you tend bar a couple of nights this week? Teri'll be out."

"Sure. This is entertaining, at least."

He smiled. "It sure is."

"Okay, Wyatt," Ubie said to Officer Pierce, "you can let him up now."

"But, sir, he assaulted this lady, then shoved me when I tried to intervene."

I gasped. "You didn't," I said to him, unable to keep a grin from sliding into place. He totally needed to be frisked again.

Uncle Bob patted Pierce's shoulder. "And he was just following orders."

Pierce straightened in surprise, and without waiting, Reyes twisted out of his grasp. He'd let them take him, let them get the upper hand, thank goodness, but even he could play the victim for only so long.

"You okay?" I asked him, my heart bursting with gratitude.

Reyes's smile said it all.

"Charley, what is going on?" Gemma asked.

I turned on her. "What are you doing here with him? I thought he was your patient."

Guilt flooded her body. It hit me like a London fog, thick and murky. She bowed her head in embarrassment. "He was my patient, yes, but now I'm seeing him. He has a new therapist, so—"

"Gemma," I said, shocked and dismayed. Not a lot—she was only human—but enough to push the limits of her discomfort to an all-new high.

With emotions set on full alert, now was the perfect time to find out if Officer Pierce was my serial killer. I loved my internal guilt-o-meter. Everyone should have one of these babies. It would eliminate a lot of problems. Or, on the flip side, it could cause a lot more. Maybe I'd keep mine to myself. And cancel that patent I'd applied for.

"Sir," Pierce said to Uncle Bob, "what is this about?"

I stepped over to him, got a reading of his emotions, then hit him hard. "We found the mass grave," I said, hardening my features and my voice. "We know what you did, and you, my friend, are under arrest for the murder of twenty-seven women."

Uncle Bob's emotions bucked when I said that, but he kept his apprehension to himself. For now.

The befuddled look on Officer Pierce's face would have been comical in any other situation. "Murder?" he asked, questioning Uncle Bob. "What are you talking about?"

"Charley!" Gemma gaped at me. "Have you gone insane?"

"He's a serial killer, Gemma, and you were about to be his next victim."

There it was at last. That bristling of indignity. That spark of injustice that proclaimed his innocence. No one, not even the best liars in the world, could control their own gut reaction to that degree. He was innocent. Not the verdict I'd expected, but at least I had an answer. My shoulders wilted, and I sat on a bar stool beside my man. He moved closer to me, the movement almost imperceptible.

"Never mind," I said, waving to Uncle Bob, my innards deflating. "It's not him."

The appearance of a half smile on his face was enough to tell me he was relieved. Gemma rushed over to Pierce, put her arm on his in support.

"Your assistant is quite the actress," Reyes said.

Cookie grinned as she walked over. "I have to admit, it was fun pretending like Reyes was assaulting me. Me!" she said, indicating the women at one particular table. Thankfully, none of them was Jessica. For once, she seemed to be elsewhere, but the entire table bristled when Cookie said that. It was fantastic.

As Uncle Bob tried to calm Officer Pierce and Gemma, Reyes leaned forward, wrapped Cookie in his arms, and kissed her full on the mouth. I plastered a hand over my mouth as she clutched on to him like a cat hanging from a tree limb.

He released her slowly; then he spoke in a voice loud enough for the table of women to hear. "If life were fair, Cookie Kowalski, you would be mine."

Her jaw dropped open, and the knowing grin he offered her accompanied by a conspiratorial wink had her shoulders shaking with mirth.

Uncle Bob couldn't take any more. He stepped in between them. "But life isn't fair," he said. "You of all people should know that." He took Cookie's arm and led her away. Hopefully to a chair because I wasn't sure how much longer she could stand.

Reyes watched them leave, then raised his brows at me. "I think I ruffled your uncle's feathers."

"That was pretty amazing," I said to him when he reached past me for his towel. "Thank you."

He paused just long enough to put his mouth to my ear and say, "Thank me tonight." Then, before the women at the table next to us realized he was coming on to me, he walked back into the kitchen.

Gemma turned on me like a wildcat protecting her young. "Charley, what is this about?"

Uh-oh. Fess-up time. "It's about the fact that I thought Officer Pierce was a serial killer."

He stared at me aghast. Gemma stared at me aghast. Officer Rodriguez stared at me aghast. The only one who wasn't staring at me aghast was Uncle Bob. He was too busy trying to recover the ground he'd lost with Cookie. He'd have a hard time, considering the Adonis with whom she'd just sucked face, but I had faith in him.

"Ubie," I said, interrupting, "I could really use some backup here."

"You honestly think I killed someone?" Officer Pierce

asked, astounded. "Why would you even—? I mean, I can't even comprehend—"

"I get that a lot. But look." I pointed to my face and then to his. "See?"

"My scars? You think that means I killed someone?"

"That's what I thought initially, yes." I could've sworn on a stack of Bibles the pixie under my bed was pointing me to him. His scars were exactly like my scratches. And then with Nicolette predicting the blond hair and the number eight tattoo . . .

"Charley," Gemma said, her tone edged with warning, "he had an incident when he was nine."

"Yeah, it's called— Wait, nine?" I ogled him. "You got those scars when you were nine?"

"Yes, he saw a young girl fall to her death, but by the time the police got to them, she was gone."

Could it have been the same girl? "Did she scratch you?"

He frowned at me. "How did you know that?"

"How old was she? This girl?"

"I don't know. It was dark and she was dirty. She had on a nightgown."

"If you had to guess."

"Six. Maybe seven. I'm just not sure."

"You tried to save her," I said as realization dawned.

His gaze dropped to the floor. "Yeah, well, I failed."

I saw an empty table and herded our group toward it. Quickly because someone else was making a run at it as well. I beat them and pulled out a chair. "Sit," I said to Officer Pierce. "And explain."

Chapter Seventeen

By reading this,
you have given me brief control over your mind.
—T-SHIRT

"I was in the Boy Scouts," Wyatt explained, "staying the summer with my grandparents in Elida, and my troop had gone on a camping trip to Billy the Kid Springs."

"I've never heard of it," I said, pulling out my phone to look it up.

"Don't bother. I've looked on every map out there, trying to find it. I'm not sure it was an official name or anything. That's just what everyone from the area called it. It was this little cove out in the middle of nowhere with a pond inside. I remember the water glowed a lime green color."

"Lime green? Is it near Roswell? They have a lot of alien stuff down there."

"Yes, it is, but I don't think aliens had anything to do with the water there. Anyway, we were out there camping and I woke up in the middle of the night. I had to take a leak, so I put on my shoes and walked over to the top of the cliff above the cove. The water was glowing. It was amazing. I sat there and watched it, looked at the stars, the full moon, all that nature crap. Then I thought I heard something. Like scraping and whimpering. I called out but no one answered. So I lay on my stomach and looked into the cove from up top. There was a girl."

"She was in the cove?" I asked.

"No, she was trying to climb up the side of the cliff, kind of around the cove part." He bowed his head in thought. "Looking back, I think she may have seen our campfires, been trying to get to them. Anyway, I reached down to give her a hand. I kept telling her to take it, but she didn't even know I was there until my hand touched her. She jumped, looked up at me, her eyes huge. She was terrified."

I felt a wave of anguish surge through him. Even after all these years, it affected him deeply.

"I kept trying to get her to take my hand, but she wouldn't at first. I thought she was going to climb back down, but then she must've realized I wasn't a threat to her. She put her hand in mine and I pulled. But she slipped and swung to the side." He took a sip of water before continuing.

Gemma put a hand on his arm. "This is what you couldn't talk about with me," she said. "This part."

He nodded. "She was hanging over the cove and pulling me with her. She tried to get her footing again, but then she cried out. She was falling or being pulled. I couldn't be sure. I lunged for her and she put out her other arm to me, but she missed." He bit down. "I missed. Her fingernails scraped across my face and she fell."

"I'm sorry, Wyatt," Gemma said.

But he had succumbed to his memories. He stared into the water as they resurfaced and took hold. "There was no sound," he said. "The cliff wasn't that high. Maybe twenty or so feet. I should have heard her fall." He withdrew inside himself and I realized this wasn't just a painful memory but a traumatic one. "I realized someone else was there. In the dark. I heard breaths echoing in the cove and I was scared to death it was a mountain lion or something."

"What did you do?" I asked, knowing full well it wasn't a mountain lion or something. But he knew it, too. Even then, he could tell the difference.

"I ran for help," he said, an agonizing pain evident in his expression. The wounds he had inside were much deeper than any scar he carried as a reminder of that night. "I left her there."

Gemma squeezed his arm as Uncle Bob got up to answer a call.

"Officer Pierce—," I started, but he interrupted.

"Please, just Wyatt."

"Wyatt, this may sound really weird and I can't explain how I know this, but I am absolutely certain that there is a connection to this girl and the mass graves that have been found down south."

He blinked at me in disbelief. "How can that be?"

"You say you were nine?"

"Yes."

"And you're thirty-one now?"

"Yes, that's right."

God, I hated math. "Okay, that means that dump site is at least twenty-two years old. I'm wondering if the girl you saw wasn't the first of the killer's victims."

"Why would you even make that connection? The springs are over two hundred miles east of here. And hundreds from the mass grave site south."

Uh-oh. The sticky part. I looked at Gemma, then at Uncle Bob, who didn't care because he was still on the phone, but it was Cookie who set him straight. "Look," she said, throwing down some attitude, "you just have to trust her. She solves a lot of cases based on her hunches because they are never wrong."

That was a bit of an overstatement, as Wyatt pointed out. "She was wrong about me," he said.

"Almost never," she corrected.

Gemma nodded. "Cookie's right, Wyatt. Charley just kind of knows things. It's weird. Like supernatural or something." She snorted. "Not that she's supernatural. That's absurd. It's not like she sees ghosts or talks to dead people or anything."

She never quite got the concept of stopping while she was ahead.

"And she has issues. Like she's always in trouble."

I gasped. "I am not. And besides, you're dating a guy who could have been a serial killer. What were you thinking?"

She gaped at me, then sputtered, then threw her hands up, utterly frustrated.

"Use your words."

"He's not a serial killer."

"Yeah, but you didn't know that," I said, totally winning.

"Oh . . . my god." She was annoyed. "Why do I turn into a fourteen-year-old every time I'm near you?"

"I do that to a lot of people."

"The lab just called," Uncle Bob said, totally interrupting. "The oil at the grave site is used oil of all types, motor oil, cooking oil, industrial lubricants. . . . They think it was slated for a recycling plant and the truck driver dumped it on that land instead."

"Okay, then why that land in particular?"

"I don't know, pumpkin. We're still working on it."

He went back to talking on the phone.

"Why are you in therapy?" I asked Wyatt.

"Charley," Gemma said, scolding me once again.

"It's okay, Gem." He refocused on me. "According to my supervisor, I have anger issues."

"And why would he think that?"

Gemma's mouth thinned, chastising me. "You don't have to talk about this, Wyatt, if you aren't comfortable."

"No, it doesn't matter anyway. Anyone with a laptop can find out. According to the department, I have a problem with men who use violence against women. I used excessive force to bring a man to the ground who was hitting his wife with a nine iron."

After a startled gasp, I said, "Well, good for you."

"Yeah, well, he has money and connections. I almost lost my job. But if I hadn't been ordered to do six months of therapy, I would never have met Gemma."

I liked him.

"You know, I have everything back at my place. All of my notes. I've been investigating the girl kind of obsessively since I became a cop. I have to get back on duty, but—"

"This takes precedence," Uncle Bob said. "I'll call your sergeant and let him know you're helping with an ongoing investigation."

"Perfect," I said, clasping my hands together. "Then that's where we'll start. After we eat, of course."

Reyes brought out green chili stew and a couple of quesadillas for us to share. I batted my lashes and promised to tip him later. It was no wonder he kept brushing across me as he helped the server set down our plates. The guy was such a rake.

"So what did you do next?" I asked Wyatt after taking a bite of hot stew.

"I woke up the counselors," he said, dipping his quesadilla. "They called the sheriff's office. A deputy came out. One." He wiped his mouth on a napkin. "That was it. I kept trying to tell them there was a little girl lost in the area, but no one believed me. The deputy actually implied that I'd been scratched by a raccoon or a coyote or something."

"In their defense," I said, "those scratches had to be pretty deep for fingernails, considering your scars."

"Not really. After everything that had happened, the scratches got infected. My parents had to come get me from my grandparents' house early that summer to take me to a doctor in Albuquerque, and I had to go through a round of rabies shots, because the deputy on the night shift couldn't tell the difference between a coyote's track and a human's."

"Oh," I said. "That sucks."

"Still, he did find tire impressions that didn't belong to our bus."

"What did they belong to?"

"A few of the other kids thought we saw a pickup the next morning, but the deputy said it was probably just a ranch hand."

"A ranch hand?" I asked, taking a sip of iced tea. "You guys were on a ranch?"

"Yeah. But I've been investigating. I can't find any links to a missing girl and a ranch hand."

"Who owned it? The land you were on?"

"A family by the name of Knight."

I tensed in alarm. Mostly to keep myself from falling over.

Uncle Bob was just as shocked as I was. "The mass grave site is on a ranch owned by a Knight family."

"No shit? Wait, I remember something about that." He closed his eyes and thought back. "Yes, that ranch was owned by a Carl Knight, and I remember discovering that he had a brother who owned a ranch in southern New Mexico."

"Brothers?" I asked, thrilled that we were getting places. Maybe not anywhere near a solid conviction, but places. "I'd say we have a pretty strong connection now."

Uncle Bob nodded and started looking up a contact on

his phone. He stood to call in our findings. No idea to whom. Cookie wiggled in her seat and clapped, exhilarated to be in on the conquest, especially one so heartbreaking. We were still miles away from a suspect, but every inch brought us closer to the truth, and the women in my apartment deserved at least that.

"So," I said to Wyatt, "you said you've been obsessed? Have you found anything out about the girl?"

"Um, a little, yes."

My hopes soared like a kite in the wind. "Do you have a name?"

"No."

And crash landing.

"But I have tons of research materials at my place. You're welcome to go through it."

"I have to admit, Officer Pierce, I'm a little in love with you right now."

Gemma smiled, knowing my seal of approval when she saw it.

I offered him my best Sunday smile. "So, now? Would now be a good time to hang at your crib?"

He chuckled. "Sure, if it's okay with you, sir."

Uncle Bob hung up and nodded wholeheartedly. "It's more than okay. I'll meet you there."

He left to make yet another call. That man loved his phone.

We went en masse to the house of Officer Wyatt Pierce. He was renting a small two-bedroom in Nob Hill. It was a nice neighborhood, old and well established. Uncle Bob walked in still on the phone. He hung up as we went inside.

"Okay, I have Taft following up on our leads right now, and I've contacted Special Agent Carson to fill her in as well."

"Awesome," I said. "She'll like me even more."

"I just want to prepare you," Wyatt said to Gemma as we stepped toward the back bedroom.

"For what?" Gemma asked.

"Remember when you asked me if I'd been able to put that night behind me and I said yes?"

"I do," she said, wary.

"Well, I may have exaggerated."

He unlocked and opened the door. Hundreds of papers littered every available surface. The window was covered in old news clippings and pictures. There were dozens of drawings of huge eyes hidden behind a mass of blond hair. He was quite the artist, and he had been searching for years. That girl never left him. He clearly felt responsible for her disappearance, which couldn't be further from the truth.

"You realize that none of that was your fault," I said.

"I know." He added a completely unconvinced shrug for my benefit. He had no intention of shirking the responsibility he felt. I admired him for his conviction, but I could see worry flash in Gemma's eyes.

We walked in and perused his research material. He had collected evidence on every missing girl in that time period from all over the United States.

"I don't know if this will help, but I suspect the girl was Deaf."

"How can you possibly know that?"

"It's a hunch. I suspected it anyway, but when you said you'd tried to call to her and she didn't look up at first, it made me realize she probably was."

"Wait." He held up a finger in thought, then tore through some files he had on an old trunk. "There was a girl missing from the Oklahoma School for the Deaf." He found the file he was looking for and took out a picture. "This is her."

He handed it over and a jolt of recognition spiked within me. Same pixie face. Same bow-shaped mouth and huge eyes, only she was smiling in the picture and her bangs were crooked. I ran my fingertips over her image. "It's her eyes," I said, and then I showed the picture to Cookie and Uncle Bob. "This is the girl." I turned the picture over. Her name was Faith Ingalls.

"It was so dark out there," Wyatt said, "and she was covered in dirt and blood, almost like she'd been buried and dug back up. I just didn't recognize her from this picture."

"Did they ever solve this case?" Uncle Bob asked.

He read through the file. "Not when I was looking into it, but that was a few years ago. She'd been missing for over a decade. They suspected a maintenance man by the name of Saul Ussery but could never prove it."

I read over his shoulder. "Did you get anything else on him?"

"No, but we can run the name," he said. "Something might come up now."

Uncle Bob put down the file he was reading. "I can do that." He called in to the station while I had other plans.

The girl was probably the serial killer's first victim. His trial run. He wanted her but couldn't have her, so he tried to take her by force perhaps. He may even have killed her accidentally, though I doubted it. He seemed to enjoy the act even then. The power. And it only fueled his thirst for blood. His obsession for blond women.

I tried Agent Carson first, but couldn't get through. If she was at the mass grave site, she could have been out of bars. So I called Kenny Knight instead.

"Mr. Knight," I said when he picked up. "This is Charley Davidson, a consultant for APD. We met yesterday."

"Yes, I remember." He didn't seem particularly happy to hear from me. I could hardly blame him.

"I was wondering if I could run a name by you. See if you recognize it."

"Sure." He was spent and tired of all the media that had surely hit that morning. The sheriff's department had no choice but to announce the discovery of a mass grave, and every news crew in the state had to be there, vying for a story.

"Do you know or do you remember your parents ever hiring a man named Saul Ussery?"

"Saul? No, he never worked here. My parents couldn't stand him."

Adrenaline flooded my system. "Wait, they knew him?"

"Knew him? He was their nephew. My cousin. He only showed up when he needed money or a place to sleep. Wait, the oil—"

I snapped to get Uncle Bob's attention. Both he and Wyatt rushed over to listen in as I switched on the speakerphone. "What about the oil?" I asked.

"It just didn't occur to me. Saul drove a truck for several years. He worked for some company that recycled plastics and used oil. Part of his job was to truck the oil they collected from mechanic shops and restaurants to a processing company in Cruces every few weeks."

"But why would he dump it on your land instead?" I asked.

"Because he was a lowlife son of a bitch. I'm sure the company he worked for in Albuquerque had to pay the people in Las Cruces to take it. He could've pocketed that money every so often and dumped the oil here where no one would know."

Uncle Bob was taking notes in a memo pad while Wyatt, Gemma, and Cookie stood speechless. "Kenny, I don't want to upset you, but I think your cousin might have had something to do with the deaths of those women."

"Ms. Davidson, that wouldn't surprise me in the least He was a piece of shit. Threatened my parents one time when they wouldn't give him money for some harebrained scheme of his. He was always joining one pyramid scam after another."

"Was?"

"Well, is, only now he's not doing much of anything. He's in a nursing home. Had a stroke or something a while back."

I took down the information, then asked, "Can you have Agent Carson call me if you happen to see her? I can't get through."

"It's the cell service out there. How about I take a drive and let her know." He seemed so relieved to know who the killer most likely was, and I was relieved for him.

"Thank you so much," I said.

"No, ma'am, thank you. I got your note."

I cleared my throat. "Um, my note?"

"It's okay. I know she was here and I know she's gone." His breath caught in his chest and he began again. "I'll put a garden there for those girls. Something she would have been proud of."

Damn. He must have seen me put the note in his pickup. "Thank you," I said.

"It will be my pleasure."

I hung up as Uncle Bob gaped at me. "Did we just solve this?"

I smiled at the gang. "I think we did."

Gemma beamed. "I can see the allure, sis." She offered me a quick hug. "It's kind of intoxicating."

"Yes, it is. And it's even more so when you solve cases actually intoxicated."

"You have to sully everything."

"I do," I said as she hugged me again. "I really do."

* * *

The nursing home smelled like a fermented combination of bleach and urine. The scent stung my nose as I went up to the nurses' station. We didn't want to converge on the home, so only Wyatt, Uncle Bob, and I went in. The nurse behind the desk was busy with paperwork, but looked up when she saw Wyatt's uniform.

"Can I help you?" she asked.

I spoke up first. "We're looking for Saul Ussery."

"Oh, are you family?"

"We're here on official business," Uncle Bob said, his tone too sharp for her to argue with.

"He's in room 204. Down the hall, second door on the right."

"Thank you," he said.

We walked in just as a young nurse was putting him back to bed. Saul was about my height with a wide brow and tiny eyes. His pudgy face probably didn't show his age as much as it would have had he been thinner. He looked like a character from a J. R. R. Tolkien novel.

The nurse winked at us. "You here to see this rascal?" she asked, tucking his sheets around him.

"We sure are," I said, trying to keep the distaste from leaching into my voice.

"Mr. Ussery's a hoot. He's always cracking jokes. And he likes the blondes, if you know what I mean."

I did, sadly. "You aren't missing any, are you?"

"Any what?"

"Blondes?"

She giggled. "Not that I know of. If we ever do, I'll know where to look, won't I, Saul?"

She had no idea.

I couldn't help but notice how the rascal's eyes had

zeroed in on Wyatt's badge. He seemed worried. I couldn't imagine why.

"Okay, well, I'll leave you alone," she said. "Don't give them any trouble."

A killer smile lit across her face as she pranced out. Even with a job like hers, she was able to keep her spirits up and enjoy her day. Either that or she was on something really good.

"Hey, Saul," I said, stepping beside his bed.

"Oh, my god," Wyatt said, surprised, "I interviewed him in 2004. I didn't make the connection. He was a maintenance man at UNM when a student went missing."

"You mean he worked there when another girl disappeared?"

"He sure did."

"She didn't happen to be blond, did she?"

He nodded.

"Uh-oh," I said to him. "Strike two. I hear you like to kill little girls."

"Nope, nope," he said, shaking his head and rocking back and forth, playing the feebleminded bit to the fullest extent of the law. I felt deception roll off him in waves. Then why was he here? A roof over his head? Food in his belly? Was it all a charade?

Uncle Bob was on the phone with the captain. "Yes, we have some pretty solid evidence, but we'll have to build a strong case if we want this closed." He looked back at Saul. "He'll never see the inside of a jail cell, but at least those women's families will have some closure."

I bent down to Saul, waited until his gaze met mine, and said, "You're going to burn in hell."

Not very poetic, but most likely true.

Chapter Eighteen

What the world needs is more geniuses with humility.
There are so few of us.
——T-SHIRT

Cookie went back to man the phones at the office. Gemma had clients to see, poor suckers. And Wyatt, Uncle Bob, and I headed to the station to report our findings and start the paperwork. Unfortunately, I had a statement to write. Paperwork wouldn't be so bad if it weren't for all the paper. And the work. On the way back to the station, Ubie called the DA, the captain, and several other important people so that, by the time we arrived, we had a small mob waiting for us.

"What do you mean you have a strong lead on the Knight Ranch killer?" the DA asked as we marched inside.

Oh, man, was that what they were calling him? Kenny Knight would not appreciate that at all. I would have to suggest something else, like the Scumbag Serial Murderer or the Lowlife Oil Dumper Guy. No, that didn't really have a good ring to it, but giving serial killers cool names was such a bad pastime. Why glorify their horrific deeds? It never made sense to me.

We converged in the same conference room from that morning, and Uncle Bob went over the case. He even drew a diagram on a whiteboard to connect the dots. He used lots of colors. It was very pretty. Wyatt explained his part, how he'd been trying to solve a two-decades-old cold case and how it all tied together. And I sat back and offered my opinion every so often. Mostly when they got things wrong. I realized I could have a bright future as a corrections officer, going around and correcting people when they got things wrong. I wondered what that paid.

No less than three agonizing hours later, we broke. After all that, I still had to submit my report, but that would have to wait until mañana. I did my best to blend into the background so I could sneak out unnoticed. The gang was still talking about the case. The DA was having a field day. Two huge cases kind of sort of solved in one day. And the captain—

"You did it again."

I turned to see the captain standing just outside the conference room. Staring at me with perfect posture. Like a killer robot from an Isaac Asimov story.

"And you did it when I wasn't looking." He walked forward.

I thought about running but realized that would only make me look guilty. Of something. No idea what.

"I'll have to try harder next time," he said, stopping short in front of me.

"That was all Uncle Bob and Officer Pierce," I said, trying to stand my ground. But looking up at him from so close a distance was like looking up at a skyscraper.

He nodded and surveyed the room. Every officer in the place was talking about our case, their movements exaggerated, their excitement infectious. Clearly the captain had been inoculated against such shenanigans. His expression exhibited only one thing: annoyance. He'd missed the boat on this one.

"Another time, then," he said. He turned, his movements sharp, his execution crisp, and headed back to his office.

I couldn't help it. It came out of me before I could stop it. I had recently been to a nursing home. Maybe I'd caught dementia. I clicked my heels together and did the Heil Hitler salute.

Just as he was turning to say something else.

When his gaze landed on me—busted beyond belief—I stood transfixed. Then I folded all my fingers down except the index. "Look," I said, pointing to the wall behind him, "there is no camera there. But you have one there." I swept my arm, elbow locked, fingers rigid, a foot to the right. "See, there is a camera. However, that camera cannot record all the events in this—" I indicated the opposite side of the room with my left hand. "—side of the room." I dropped my arm at last. "I feel like your security measures are not what they should be, Captain." *Don't say Jack. Don't say Jack. Don't say Jack.*

His mouth formed a grim line across his face. He turned and left without relaying what he was going to say. Wonderful. Now I was going to be curious all day. Not terribly, but still.

My old frenemy, David Taft, laughed behind my back. Literally. "I swear, Davidson, you sure know how to make friends and influence people."

I turned to him as he sat at his desk. "If you aren't careful, I'll tell your sister you're dating that call girl from Poughkeepsie again."

He sobered and cast a worried glance over his shoulder. "I am not. How did you know that?"

With a smile drenched in saccharine, I winked and said, "I didn't."

He closed his eyes and hung his head in shame.

I tsked at him. "You fall for that every time."

Gemma walked into the station as I was leaving, probably to see her man. The thought made me happy. She didn't date much, as gorgeous as she was. She needed the distraction from her miserable, lonely life before she started collecting stray cats.

Wyatt saw her and headed our way. Seeing his scars made me wonder about my little pixie, Faith Ingalls. She'd sent me straight to him. How could she possibly have known he'd been investigating the case? Or maybe she didn't. Maybe there was another reason. He was probably the last person she saw before she died who tried to help her. Who risked his life to help her. And I still had to wonder why the women were still in my apartment. What did they want, need?

"I need to ask a favor of you," I said to Wyatt as he walked up and gave Gemma a sweet smile. He probably didn't want to make a big deal in front of the guys, so he kept his greeting G-rated.

"Shoot," he said.

Gemma raised her brows in suspicion. What'd I say?

Wait, what would I say? I couldn't really ask him to come over to meet the ghost of the girl he'd tried to save. So I improvised. "I need you to check something at my place. I have a leaky faucet." Oh, my god, I was so good at improvisation.

His posture said, *I'm confused,* but his eyes said, *What?* "I don't really fix leaky faucets."

"Please. I won't ever ask you for anything again."

"Oh, no," Gemma said in warning, "don't ever believe that. She'll have you painting or moving boxes or burying her neighbor before you know it."

It was like she didn't know me at all. I would never ask him to paint.

We met at my place, and I led Wyatt into my living room. Gemma knew about Faith being in my apartment, but making the introductions between Faith and Wyatt could prove tricky. Then again, I had to find her first. She wasn't under Mr. Wong. "Hmmm," I said, looking around, "that leaky pipe doesn't seem to be in here. Let's try the bedroom."

Wyatt cast Gemma a questioning gaze, then followed me. "You know, everyone says you're crazy."

"Really? That's weird. But how about we go with that and call it good?"

"Works for me."

I got on all fours and checked under the bed. Sure enough, Little Miss Sunshine lay scrunched under my bed, her huge blue eyes staring out at me. I bounded up. "Found it!" Then I got on my stomach and offered her my best Sunday smile. "Hey precious," I said, holding out a hand. "I brought someone to see you."

She backed away from me, eyed me as though I were an axe murderer. Crap. And I thought we were friends.

At least Artemis was happy to see me. And even happier that I was on the floor. She pawed at me, her tiny tail practically vibrating with enthusiasm. I rubbed her ears and nuzzled her neck before popping up over the bed again. "You're just going to have to look for yourself."

When Artemis went in for the kill, tackling me to the floor, I called out, "It's okay. I'm okay." Wyatt walked around the bed and saw what could only look like a seizure of some kind. I had Artemis in a headlock and was gnawing on her ear, but I stopped instantly when I saw him, tried to push her off me as nonchalantly as I could.

"It's down here," I said.

Hopefully he would dismiss my behavior as a side effect of lunacy. I smiled and turned back onto my stomach, but Artemis pounced. Ninety pounds of airborne Rottweiler landed on my back. The air rushed out of my lungs and I groaned in agony.

Then I heard a giggle. Soft. Lyrical. I looked under the

bed and said with strained words, "You think this is funny, do you?"

The beginnings of a smile widened her mouth. Sadly, however, I had to push Artemis off me before I lost consciousness. I wrapped an arm around her head and made her lie beside me. "Stay," I whispered into her ear. She whined, wanting so very much to pretend to rip out my jugular. Dogs loved that shit. Having no other choice, she chewed on my hair instead. That would keep her busy for a few.

With a great and powerful sense of doubt, Wyatt got onto his knees, I took his hand and pulled him down to the floor with me. Gemma laughed and got onto her knees as well, curious.

"This," I said to him, pointing underneath an empty bed, "is a little hurricane who goes by the name of Faith."

He stilled, and his emotions flatlined. It was a lot to take in. I probably should have warned him about the whole dead-people thing. Trying to imagine it from Wyatt's point of view, I looked under the bed. The only thing he would see was the red thong I'd lost a couple of weeks back and a Butterfinger wrapper.

"Sorry," I said to him. "I forgot to mention that I see dead people."

He nodded. Since his adrenaline didn't spike in surprise, he'd heard the rumors. Not the ones where I saw dead people, but the ones where I was a crazy-ass psychic wannabe who *thought* she saw dead people. At least it wasn't a complete surprise.

The real surprise would come next. Faith saw him. She saw the scars on his face. She looked into his eyes. An instant later, she was in front of us.

I eased back and encouraged Wyatt to sit with a hand on his shoulder. Faith balanced on her toes, hunched down in front of us, but at least she'd come out from under the bed.

"She led me to you, Wyatt," I said as his gaze tracked every shadow, every speck of dust in the air, trying to see what his eyes simply couldn't perceive.

Faith duckwalked forward, inch by inch until she could reach out and touch his face.

I signed to her. "His name is Wyatt."

She didn't look at me directly, but she nodded an acknowledgment. It was the first glimpse of actual communication I'd gotten from her. Now we were getting somewhere. She reached up and touched his face.

"She recognizes you."

When her fingers brushed across his face, he bucked back.

"Just stay still," I said, encouraging him with a steady hand. "She's touching your face. Your scars."

He bit down and held fast as she brushed her fingers across his jaw, over his chin and mouth. His was the last kind face she'd seen.

"I think she wants to see you, to know that you are okay."

I signed again, but I used my voice so the other two would know what I said. She could hear now. That wasn't the problem. The problem would lie in the fact that she didn't know spoken English. "Your name is Faith?" I asked.

She lifted a shoulder to her cheek in shyness and nodded. Then she lifted her index finger, just barely, and pointed to Wyatt. "My friend," she said, her signs a mere whisper on her hands.

Tears sprang to my eyes so fast, I couldn't stop them. "Yes," I said, patting Wyatt's shoulder. "He's your friend."

And the dam broke. Wyatt's shoulders shook as he tried to dam the flood of emotion. He wrapped his fingers over his eyes, and Gemma fell to her knees beside him.

"It's okay, hon," she said, rubbing his back.

Without removing his hand, Wyatt said, "Can you tell her how sorry I am that I failed her?"

I disagreed but nodded and relayed his message to her.

"Failed?" she asked, her tiny fingers sliding across her palm. "He tried to save me."

"I know, but he feels like he failed you. Like you died because of him."

She patted his cheek with her left hand and signed with her right. "He's wrong. I died because of Mr. U."

Finally, I got a name. Or an initial that stood for the name of Ussery. And we were right. Not that I had any doubt, but verification was always nice.

"I thought of his face," she continued. "His face makes me feel happy."

"She said you're wrong," I told Wyatt. "You didn't fail her. And your face makes her happy."

He nodded. It was all he could do.

"Do you remember what happened?"

But I'd lost her. Artemis had army-crawled past me and laid her nose on Faith's foot. She laughed and bent to pet her. "I like dogs," she said.

Artemis soaked up the attention like a dry sponge thrown into a swimming pool. Her little tail wagged and she rolled onto her stomach, pushing me out of the way with her butt. That was the thanks I got.

We'd made leaps today. Giant leaps. Hopefully I could talk to her more, convince her to cross, to be with her family.

The women hadn't gone anywhere, but they had changed. They had calmed, were less erratic, less frantic. But they still stared off into space, their gazes vacant as though lost. I didn't know how to help them. And I really wanted to help them. It would still be a while before Reyes got off work. Even thinking that felt foreign. Reyes working. Making a living. Surviving in my world. Keeping it real.

First I had to fix things with Rocket and Blue. Only then could I probe Rocket for suggestions on how to help the women in my apartment and for answers about Reyes, why my man's name was on his wall of doom.

As I drove to the asylum, another thought struck. It happened. But I realized I'd solved a case without almost dying. Without being beaten senseless or dragged through broken glass. That shit sucked. But I'd done it. Things were looking up.

I straightened my shoulders and let pride swell for almost seven seconds before another thought popped into my head. I'd just tempted fate. By thinking the first thought, I'd quite possibly jinxed myself. I'd thrown caution to the wind, damn my pride.

But I'd done it. No doubt about it. So when a large vehicle slammed into Misery's driver-side door—the sound of metal colliding and crumbling in on itself deafening—my last thought as darkness crept in was, *Honestly, it's like I don't know myself at all.*

Chapter Nineteen

Never underestimate the power of a woman
on a double espresso with a mocha latte chaser high.
—T-SHIRT

I awoke in total darkness to the hum of an engine. Then I realized there were lights ahead in the distance. I figured I should walk toward them. It seemed like the right thing to do. But my legs wouldn't move. Neither would my hands.

I was paralyzed!

Or tied up.

Probably tied up.

A truck hit me!

Memories flooded back. A huge truck, no, an SUV, came barreling toward me, then a grille, then the emblem on that grille proclaiming it as a GMC as it got closer and closer—so fast, I didn't have time to think. To put up my guard. To slow time. I so very much needed to get control over my powers. Seriously, could I slow time or not? It seemed like I could defend myself only when my senses were already on high alert. With Cookie's gun in the bar. With Reyes's anger at Garrett in the apartment. I'd been aware, I'd known something bad was about to happen. But being blindsided was like, well, being blindsided. That truck came out of nowhere, thus the term.

The world spun and my head throbbed, letting me know it did not appreciate the collision one tiny bit. It was probably concussed. I'd had more concussions than an NFL defensive lineman. Permanent brain damage was looking more and more likely. Poor Barbara. I didn't deserve her. She deserved to be in someone else's skull. Someone with half a brain who didn't dangle a carrot in front of danger and say *nah-nah-nah-nah-naaaah-nah.*

Slowly, feeling crept into my limbs. My hands were bound behind my back, my ankles tied together. Other than that, I was quite comfortable. The backseat in this thing went on for days. I realized the lights I'd seen were from my abductor's dash. We were driving, and since I saw no streetlights overhead, we were probably not in the city anymore.

I tried to make out the driver through the haze. Caucasian with short blond hair. His sleeves were rolled up, and I saw a tattoo of an eight ball on his forearm. Blond hair and the number eight. Son of a bitch, I was going to die under that bridge. Nicolette had seen me.

"She filed for divorce."

My abductor knew I was awake. I tried so hard to pull out of the fog, but my vision just would not clear. The world kept tilting to the right. I felt drunk and was beginning to wonder if he'd drugged me as Kim had.

"Now all my planning, all my hard work, means nothing. I can't kill the bitch now. I'd be the main suspect. Everyone will know."

Yes! I'd nailed it! I was an expert at nailing things. Ideas, two-by-fours, men with low self-esteem. If it could be nailed, I could nail it. I should probably change my name to the Nailer. I knew he was that kind of man, out for the insurance money. Maybe I really was psychic. Stranger things had happened.

"You had no proof that I'd ever slept with another woman."

"And I told her that," I said. My words slurred together, and I realized my jaw wasn't working right. It hurt like the dickens. And my shoulder. Holy cow. "I said we had no real proof of you cheating."

"Oh, I'm sure you fought for me."

I tried to roll off my side and onto my back. My left shoulder felt dislocated. Though the world flip-flopped with the movement and my stomach lurched, I did manage to ease the pain a little. A warmth ran down my temple and cheek, and I realized I was bleeding. Ha! I was getting blood all over Marv's SUV. No getting that stuff out. At least there would be forensic evidence.

"So I figured if I couldn't kill her, I'd kill you. No one would make *that* connection."

They would when they brought out the luminol. And he was clearly forgetting the part where he attacked my assistant in a room full of off-duty cops. Why did no one remember that?

I squeezed my eyes shut to stop the spinning and concentrated, but Angel didn't pop in. He always popped in when I needed him. I just couldn't focus, couldn't assemble my thoughts. They were coming at me too fast and they were fractured, broken and in pieces.

"Why were you at this bridge?" he asked. "How did you know about it?"

He looked back at me, but he was shrouded in darkness. I was seeing his aura. I'd caught glimpses of people's auras before, but this was different. Marv's was cloudy. Evil. Plain and simple, his aura was evil. It surrounded him, consumed him. He felt no remorse for anything he did to get what he wanted.

If nothing else came of this, at least I had saved a woman's life. He had every intention of killing his wife for the insurance money. It took a special kind of asshole to do something like that. To be able to convince a woman that he loved her, to convince her family that he loved her, that he was a loving and devoted husband, and the entire time he plotted her death in the back of his mind. If only he could have kept it in his pants, Valerie Tidwell would never have called me.

"A dead girl told me," I said, answering his question at last, "only she wasn't dead."

"You're about to be. That's all that matters."

I couldn't take the spinning anymore. The pain shooting through my shoulder, ribs, and hip, and I had a horrible feeling my leg was broken. If it wasn't, it had a lot of explaining to do. Pulverizing me with that much pain for nothing was not acceptable. But the spinning was the worst.

Marv pulled onto a rough patch and threw his SUV into park, giving my dislocated shoulder a nice little jerk.

"What did you give me?" I asked him.

"A GMC sandwich." He turned back and glared at me. "How dare you interfere with something that is none of your business."

"That's kind of my job," I said, but he didn't hear me. He got out, opened my door, and yanked my legs until I fell onto the dirt. My head hit the frame on the way down, and Barbara screamed in protest. I was right there with her.

I tried to concentrate on the surroundings, but it was difficult when those surroundings were part of a merry-go-round carnival ride. The one thing that did catch my eye was the bridge. The old, dilapidated bridge for a railroad track that was no longer used.

"You are about to have a nasty fall," he said, trying hard to sound clever. "But cause of death will probably be strangulation."

He clasped my arm—the non-dislocated one, thank god—and dragged me up the side of the incline. Then he shoved me over one track and across the wood slats of the bridge until we stood above the highway. It wasn't that high. The fall probably wouldn't kill me. It would just hurt really bad. He was such an idiot. I lost all respect for him.

"Don't worry," he said, "you won't be my first."

He'd killed before. That was so not comforting.

"My best friend died on this bridge. Everyone thought it was an accident. It's amazing what people will believe. He just happened to fall when a truck was approaching? Idiots."

His best friend. He had a strange idea of friendship.

He pushed me onto my stomach and straddled me. The next thing I heard was a rip. He tore the back of my shirt open, and the crisp night air swept across my skin. Then he reached around my front and unbuttoned my jeans. Unzipped them. Yanked them and my underwear down to my ankles.

When I heard his belt coming off, I slammed my eyes shut and tried to concentrate again. Tried to summon Angel. But before I thought too hard, a crack split the air as leather and metal whipped across my back. I gasped at the sting. Gasped again when the belt lashed across my buttocks and thighs. He was whipping me with the buckle, the sharp metal slicing into my skin. Over and over. I couldn't help it. I cried out, but that only seemed to increase his fervor. His zest for cruelty. My one saving grace was that every point of contact left forensic evidence. But that didn't help when the metal ripped through my skin. My body seized with every lash. A spasm bolted through me every time the metal struck. I ground my teeth together, tried to breathe through the pain.

The world spun.

The pain crippled.

And the thrashing continued.

Just when I thought I would lose consciousness, it stopped. He pulled me from the fetal position I'd curled into and straddled my back again, his mouth at my neck, his groin on my ass.

"You think you're so much better than me. You have no idea what I'm capable of."

He flipped me onto my back, the rough wood cutting into my fresh wounds, and started to undo his pants. Disbelief struck so hard, a wave of dizziness washed over me.

No. I shook my head. *No way. Not rape. Not rape.* I had been stabbed. I had been sliced so deep, the knife scored bone. I had been dragged by my hair and had my neck broken. But in all my years getting into every bad situation imaginable, I had never been raped.

And I wouldn't be. I couldn't be. I was the grim reaper, for Christ's sake, yet I couldn't clear my head long enough to summon Angel or Reyes. They had no idea I was in trouble. Maybe it was the head injury blocking me somehow. So I did the next best thing. I used my girl powers. With a fierce determination, I knocked him off balance. He fell next to me, and I leaned over as fast as I could and buried my teeth in his neck. With adrenaline rushing through my veins, I clamped down hard and refused to let go. I was going for the nose, but that was out of reach, so the neck would have to do.

He howled in pain and pushed until I flew off him. Fortunately, the bottom half of the bridge had a lattice barricade also made of metal. I hit it and fell face forward, but I twisted until I was on my back again.

"Son of a bitch," he said, anger filling him so completely, his aura roiled with a murky darkness. Clutching his neck, he scrambled onto his feet and charged forward. I kicked with both legs, a shrill pain shooting through me with the contact. He flew back and tripped on the wooden slats of the bridge, hitting his head on a bolt in the bracing. "Fuck!" He clasped his head, pressed his fingers to his neck, and rocked a moment, doubled over from pain. "You fucking whore." He glared at me then, with jaw set, he staggered back down the bridge to his SUV.

I lay between the barrier and a train track, gasping, pants down to my ankles and barely able to move. The world spun at warp speed as I waited to see what he would do next. Would he just throw me off the bridge? Strangle me as promised? Stab me or beat me with his tire iron next? I felt like the bridge was tilting and I was going to fall off it with my pants down and my shirt ripped almost completely off.

I rolled slightly, trying to get my own weight off my back, but everything hurt, so I gave up and rolled back against the rough wood. The metal bracings overhead were beautiful, intricate, like a spider's web glistening in the night, spinning with the stars, blurring. A movement captured my attention, and I saw Faith. Little Faith, out from under my bed and about to watch me die. She was on one of the metal bracings above, looking down at me, her expression one of mild curiosity. I heard nothing for a long time. That probably meant I was in for a whole lot more trouble, but I was just glad to be rid of him for a minute. I wished I could have signed to Faith.

Marv walked up until he was standing over me. He could have been swaying, but most likely, I just couldn't see straight. He had patched up his neck with a rag, like the kind mechanics used.

"You shouldn't have done that."

Like I'd never heard that before.

Then he brought around a handheld torch. Like the kind mechanics used. And I knew my life was about to get a whole lot worse.

"Let's see how you like this," he said, pulling the trigger on the small torch until the tip emitted a blue glow. It made an airy sound like the low hum of a gas leak. With a seething hatred glittering in his eyes, he knelt beside me. The *Y* at my crotch caught his attention and he paused. Still thinking about it. I looked up at Faith again, but she was gone. No, not gone. I looked to my right. She was beside me, watching with a calm dread, her chin puckering.

I couldn't let her see this.

The flame from the torch left blue streaks in the air. I could not steady my world, but I couldn't let Faith see this.

"If you'll spread your legs, I'll put this torch out and we'll enjoy the rest of your life together."

"I'd rather burn, thank you." Big words coming from someone so scared, she was about to piss herself, but giving him the satisfaction of seeing the terror trembling inside me was more than I could bear at that moment. Of course, once that pinpoint flame seared a lovely pattern into my flesh, I'd probably change my mind.

"Too bad." He put the torch down. The flame died the minute he released the trigger. Then he rose again, picked something else up, and walked back. "You could have lived another hour or two."

He took a red plastic gas can into both hands and shook it, dousing me in the freezing liquid. Ironic since it was about to burn me alive. Damn it. Nicolette didn't say anything about being burned to death. I curled into a ball and tried to avert my face, to keep it out of my eyes. It stung when it hit the open flesh on my back and buttocks, and I screamed through gritted teeth and closed mouth.

He put the gas can down and picked the torch back up. Lit it with one click of the trigger. Stepped closer. Knelt down.

I'd always wondered, bizarrely, what it would feel like to burn to death. I had seen people set themselves aflame on TV. The act horrified me. Did they regret it once the fire started?

I wanted to apologize to Faith, but my hands were still expertly tied at my back. I had no idea what he'd used, but I could not get out of it.

The torch loomed closer and Faith's eyes grew rounder until I saw her through a sea of fire as I burst into flames.

Chapter Twenty

*I came into this world covered in someone else's blood
and screaming. I'm not afraid to leave it the same way.*
—T-SHIRT

No.

This was not going to happen.

I still had a lot of shit to do.

I gathered what little strength I had, let it swirl and build inside me, then sent it out to swallow the heat like a dragon. I absorbed the fire, breathed it in, reveled as it soaked into every inch of my body. As fast as the fire had ignited, it extinguished that much faster. I thought about waiting for Tidwell's reaction, watching to see if his expression was more surprise or murderous rage. But I figured while I was here, I would finish the job I'd started. I reached out from somewhere deep within, clasped on to either side of his head, and twisted. His neck snapped before he even realized I'd extinguished the fire, and he dropped hard, his face slamming into the train track and bouncing back until he settled in a heap of lifeless flesh and blood.

This would make two men that I'd killed. Two men that I sent to hell. Reyes's dad would be proud.

Faith sprang forward and wrapped her tiny arms around my neck. I almost laughed, but the flesh-and-blood me was back, and pain had permeated every nook and cranny of my body. And my pants were down.

But my heart beat. My blood pulsed. No doubt about it, I was alive. Then the evening hit me. I'd never been quite that close to death—well, me—before. My eyes stung from emotion and from gasoline and I buried my face in Faith's matted, muddy hair. But I was still tied up and the binds were cutting into my wrists. If I didn't know better, I'd have sworn he used some kind of steel cable. So there I lay, half naked and bound. I could break a man's neck, but I couldn't untie myself.

I didn't dare summon Angel, if that were even possible yet. He always wanted to see me naked, but not like this. Seeing me like this would bother him for a long time to come. And I didn't want to summon Reyes, either. I didn't even know if I could. I certainly didn't want Cookie or Gemma here. They would never get over it. No, the only one I could let see me this way was Uncle Bob. We had an understanding, and he would be able to live with seeing me like this in a way the others couldn't. He understood the dangers of the job. He lived with that knowledge every day.

I felt the impression of my phone in my front pocket, more than a little shocked Tidwell hadn't taken it. With Faith clinging to my neck, I twisted my bound hands around, pulling one arm across my back like a contortionist, until I could retrieve it. My dislocated shoulder protested. Pain shot through me until I almost cried out, but I locked on to the phone with thumb and index finger and pulled. Glancing over my hip, I could barely see past Danger and Will. I held it carefully in my shaking hands, scared I'd drop it through the railroad ties to the road below. Then I twisted my head until I could see the screen. It was cracked, but the phone still seemed to work. Faith sat back, balancing on her toes as she liked to do, and kept a hand on my head as though to let me know she was there.

The world had slowed, but my sight was still blurry, my position still twisted enough to make finding Ubie in my contacts difficult. On a scale of one to for-the-love-of-god-this-is-hard, I would've given this a twelve. I scrolled to what looked like the *U*'s and found his name at last. Then, after trying to wipe my eyes on my barely there shirt, I pushed his number, dropped the phone on a railroad tie, and scooted until I could hear him pick up.

"Charley?" he said when I was finally in position. "Did you butt-dial me again?"

His voice caused a wave of relief to rush over me. "Uncle Bob," I said, my voice cracking and weak.

"Charley, where are you?" He was now on full alert, but I'd started crying.

I rested my head against the metal track and said, "I need—" My voice broke, and it took me a second to recover. "I need you to come get me."

"I'm on my way. Where are you, pumpkin?"

"At the bridge," I said, my breath catching in my chest. "But only you, okay? Only you come."

Faith petted my hair as I tried to stay conscious, the fumes from the gas making me even more light-headed.

"Are you hurt?" he asked, and I heard his engine start in the background.

"I killed a man," I replied, right before I fell into darkness.

Over the next twenty minutes, I woke at odd intervals. This had to be the least traveled road in all of New Mexico. I could see between the ties, but the only car I saw pass under me was a faded red Pinto with a chicken coop on top. The other times I woke to the sound of crickets or birds' wings brushing together overhead.

"Charley, talk to me!"

I blinked, tried to clear my head. Uncle Bob was still on the phone, screaming at me. "Okay."

"I called for a patrol car to meet me out here."

Shame consumed me as quickly as the flames had. My pants were down. That was all I could think about. My pants were down. "Only you," I said again, pleading with him.

"I'll get there first. Whatever has happened, we will deal with it together. But I need to know, do I need to call an ambulance?"

"No. I'm okay."

"I'm almost there. I can see the bridge. Can you see my headlights?"

I rolled over and almost cried out at the pain. "Yes," I said.

"What? Charley, where are you?"

I had to endure another roll to get back to the phone. "I'm here. I can see your headlights."

"Black GMC SUV," he said, remembering my earlier encounter with that exact same vehicle. "Where are you?" He had slid to a stop and was running now.

"I'm on the bridge."

His next word was just a whisper. "Charley," he said. It took him a moment, but his footsteps restarted.

And shame engulfed me again. Faith had taken up her post on the bracing as Uncle Bob rushed to me, gun drawn. He first checked Tidwell's pulse. Finding none, he holstered his gun and knelt beside me.

"My god, honey, what did he do?"

"He was really mad."

He struggled to get the binds untied. Lights glowed in the distance. The patrol car was coming.

"Please, hurry," I said, mortification settling in.

"Got it." He pulled the metal wire off my wrists and helped me stand so I could pull up my pants. He had to help with that, too, gingerly lifting my panties into place, then my jeans as hot tears of humiliation slid down my face. "Your back," he said, but I shook my head.

"My shoulder hurts worse."

"Why do you smell like gasoline?" But he'd spotted the torch almost the moment he said it. A gasp escaped him when he realized what he was looking at.

"It's dislocated. Can you fix it?"

"What? No, honey."

"Please," I said as the cop car pulled in beside Uncle Bob's SUV. "I saw you do it to that other cop once. I know you know how."

"Sweetheart, you have no idea what kind of damage has been done."

"Please."

"Okay, lean against the railing."

"Detective?" the patrolman said from underneath us. I didn't know him.

"Up here, Officer. I need you to get the medical examiner out here as well as a few of your closest buddies."

"Yes, sir," he said. He'd focused his flashlight on me. "Should I call for an ambulance?"

"We'll need one, yes, after the medical examiner gets out here."

"What about for her?"

"No," I whispered to him. "I'm fine. I just want to go home."

"We're okay. If you'll just get the ME out here."

"Yes, sir."

"Are you ready?" he asked me.

"Yes."

"Okay, we're going to take this nice and slow. Just relax."

He took my arm, rotated it out, then pulled slowly until my shoulder popped back into place. A sharp spasm shot through me, then relief. It was instant, but with that pain gone, the one in my leg was magnified.

"Okay, now my ankles."

He draped his jacket over my shoulders, then led me back to the ground and knelt in front of me. It took him longer to get the thick wire off my ankles, and I was still dizzy, so I clung to a bracing as he worked.

"Charley, did he—?" He scraped a hand over his face, then took hold of my chin. "Did he violate you?"

I was a little surprised that this seasoned detective would use such archaic language for such a heinous act. "No," I said, my breath hitching. "He tried, but he didn't get far."

Uncle Bob released a slow breath. "Charley, what the hell?"

But I'd had enough of tough Charley. Tough Charley was going on vacation. I was ready to be the little girl he'd taught to ride a bike. The one he took fishing every summer. The one he'd taught about sex, but that wasn't really his fault. I'd raided his porn stash when I was ten. I lunged forward and wrapped my arms around his neck. He cradled my head to him, probably afraid he'd hurt me, and held on for dear life.

"Sir?" the officer said. He'd climbed to the bridge and was waiting for us. "The ME could be a couple of hours, but the ambulance is on the way. Can I get you anything?"

"No, thank you, Officer. If you could section off this area, I'd appreciate it."

"Yes, sir."

He looked down at me. "This might hurt," he said, his expression full of regret.

"It's okay." I kept my arms draped around his neck.

As gently as he could, Uncle Bob lifted me into his arms and carried me down to his SUV. The officer rushed forward to help and assisted in maneuvering us down the steep slope to the road below.

"Is your leg broken?" he asked after he got me settled in the passenger seat.

"I don't know. It hurts. But I want to go home."

"Okay, after the EMT checks you out. Who was this guy?"

"The guy in the bar from the other night. The one who elbowed Cookie. He rammed into me," I said as my lids drifted shut. "He was going to kill his wife."

The rest of the night was a blur. Uncle Bob wanted to call Cookie, but I refused to let him wake her up. She would be livid come morning, but she'd get over it. She always did. The EMT kept insisting that I go to the hospital, but I refused, even when Uncle Bob threatened to have me arrested. I had to remind him that I wasn't like all the other girls in the park. I would heal in a matter of days. He wanted X-rays of my leg, but I had a feeling if it were really broken, I couldn't have put my weight on it. So he took pictures of my back and other injuries for his statement, then brought me home.

The guy even carried me up two flights of stairs.

I would probably have to stop giving him such a hard time for a while. Maybe a day or two. When I asked him about Misery, he shook his head. My Misery. What would I do without her?

So, beaten and bereft, I lay huddled in my bed with a very worried Faith underneath it and a very angry Reyes sitting on the floor beside it, his back braced against the wall, legs drawn, arms thrown over knees, and eyes watching every move I made. Every breath I took. He'd heard us come in and was at my door in an instant. He glared at Ubie, but my uncle, being the gallant man that he was, didn't mind. He seemed relieved to have someone watch over me, since I'd insisted he go home and get some rest.

And while I'd wanted a shower more than I wanted my next cup of coffee, I just couldn't manage it. I didn't have the energy. And I was scared it would hurt. So come morning, my sheets would smell like gasoline even though most of it had burned off, and the whole room would have a singed, crispy aroma to it.

I could feel Reyes's anger, a red-hot rage that simmered just below his steely surface. He probably wanted to sever Tidwell's spine. He certainly had my permission, not that it would do him any good. Then again, he sent Garrett to hell and then wrenched him back out. Just how far did his powers reach?

But that wasn't what I dreamed about when I slept. I dreamed about fire. I dreamed about Kim and her recent hobby. I dreamed about Tidwell and his resoluteness that I burn alive. And I dreamed about the man sitting beside me. His fire. The fires in which he'd been forged. How hot would they have had to be to create such a spectacular being? How bright that initial spark?

And then there was the fire I'd consumed. I'd absorbed it. Bathed in it. Breathed it in and swallowed it.

I was a dragon. Strong. Tenacious. Lethal.

Still, the fucker tried to rape me.

I had to admit, that was a little hard to get past, even in my dreams. But I felt him there, hovering in the shadows. Reyes. Watching over me even in the turbulent realm of my unconscious mind.

When I opened my eyes, his gaze had not wavered. And my hair could not possibly look good. But there was more. I could see the darkness that surrounded him. It swirled like a gathering storm, building and churning. But in the center of it, where Reyes sat, burned a blue fire that licked across his skin like wispy cerulean snakes.

"You shouldn't look at me from that place," he said.

I tried to sit up but couldn't quite manage it. "From what place?"

"From the realm you're in now. You'll see things you probably shouldn't."

"How am I in another realm? I'm right here."

"You're a portal. You can be in whichever realm you choose at any time and be in both at the same time. You should leave it now."

"I consumed a fire tonight."

"Yes, you can do that," he said. He laid his head back against the wall. "And I'm made of fire."

I could see that now. Of darkness and fire.

"Is that how you'll kill me?" he asked.

A zing of surprise darted through me.

"Will you consume me?" he continued. "Extinguish my fire with a breath? Suffocate me?"

"I would never kill you. Why would you even say that?"

A sad smile crept across his impossibly handsome face. "I told you a long time ago you'd be the death of me. Surely you know that by now."

Did he know about Rocket's premonition?

I pondered asking him about it, but another movement drew my attention to a woman standing beside me. Blond. Dirty. But standing. Not curled into herself or rocking back and forth. She was beautiful. African American with long hair that had been bleached to match the landscape at White Sands. She smiled at me as another appeared beside her. Then another and another as all twenty-seven of Saul Ussery's victims stood beside my bed. They surrounded me, their lovely faces full of warmth.

I felt bad that their first impression of me was one of a shivering pile of injuries.

One of them stepped closer. The African-American

woman who smiled. I could see the chipped red paint on the tips of her fingernails. Then I felt something. Her. Her essence. She stepped forward and crossed and in that instant I saw her brother spraying her with a water hose in front of the boy she liked in grade school. I saw her sixteenth birthday cake and the mint green gown she wore to the ball her parents threw in her honor. I saw her first child being born. A boy named Rudy. And I saw her appreciation for what I'd done. I'd caught the man who stole all that from her, and she was grateful.

And Renee, her name was Renee, left me something in parting. As did the next.

I blinked past the dizziness I still felt and watched. Another woman stepped to my side, held out a foot, and dropped as though she were walking off the edge of a diving board. She fell through me, Blaire was her name, and I saw her tie-dyeing T-shirts at summer camp, riding horses on her grandfather's farm, and kissing a boy named Harold under the bleachers at a football game.

Next came a woman named Cynthia. She baked apple pies for her mom when she was little but got into drugs after her dad left them. Lisa had a turtle named Leonardo and dreamed of being a ninja. Emily had been born with a mild case of autism. Despite the obstacles life had thrown at her, she had made it to college. Her mother cried her first day there. She cried more on her thirtieth, when Emily had forgotten her room key and a nice maintenance man named Saul opened her door for her.

LaShaun. Vicki. Kristen. Delores.

I breathed in their gift, and it rushed through me like a tidal wave.

Maureen. Mae. Bethany. One by one, over and over until only Faith stood beside me.

Their gift was strength. They'd given me all they had left, all the power and energy to heal they could conjure, they left it behind for me. It coursed through me, warming and mending.

When all but Faith had crossed, Reyes stood and walked to the bathroom. Faith petted my hair, then ducked back under my bed, unwilling to follow the others just yet. I heard water running, felt his arms as he lifted me, his chest as he carried me. He peeled my clothes off gently. I had some minor burns, but they didn't compare to my back and my injured leg. When I was completely undressed, he lifted me again and lowered me into the water.

I braced myself as it rushed over the slashes along my back. Who knew a belt buckle could do so much damage? After a moment, I realized my fingernails were digging into his flesh. He didn't seem to mind, but I relaxed and released my hold as I sank farther into the water. He took the bar of soap and began to lather his hands. I should have been embarrassed, but I wasn't. His touch was so gentle as he washed me, his large hands roaming over my body, and yet there was nothing sexual about his caress. This time it was nurturing, not demanding. It was healing, not expectant. He laid me back and massaged shampoo into my scalp, rinsed, then lifted me out of the water.

I felt a thousand times better. The gasoline smell had subsided and was replaced with a fresh, fruity blend of scents. The strength of Saul's victims raced through me as Reyes dried me off, wrapped me in a blanket, and laid me on Sophie while he changed my sheets. I just barely remembered being carried back to my room, being slid between fresh sheets, being given a pain medication of some kind.

The one thing that seemed to hold true, no matter the circumstances, was that when I was injured, I got really sleepy. The more severe the injuries, the sleepier I got. So I slept the entire next day, only waking to give Uncle Bob the bare bones of what would become my statement—

minus the whole almost-being-raped thing, which I couldn't talk about just yet—and to chat with a very distraught Cookie, who swore she would never, ever, ever forgive me for not waking her.

But every time I woke up, Reyes was there, sitting against the wall next to me, holding my hand, and giving me room to heal. Artemis kept a watchful eye on me as well. Literally. Like her head sat constantly perched somewhere on my body, and that thing had to weigh thirty pounds. Faith stayed under my bed, and I wondered how she was doing. All her friends had crossed, but when I tried to talk to her about it, she shook her head, signed the word *more,* then scurried back under my bed, so I left it alone.

I needed to contact Nicolette, tell her she was right, someone did die on that bridge. I felt a very strong desire to open her up and study her, but looking through her innards would probably get me nowhere. Still, she could be a valuable asset. I'd have to save her number in my phone. And I had yet to smooth things over with Rocket and Blue. That debacle would take some time.

On the upside, my eyesight went back to normal. Reyes said I could see things from my other realm, the one that I was bound to as a portal. I wondered if I could see *into* that other realm. If I could spy on heaven. I put it on my to-do list as something to try when total boredom set in. Fortunately or unfortunately, depending on one's perspective—that didn't happen often. In fact, boredom might be a nice reprieve from the daily bump and grind that was life as a grim reaper.

Chapter Twenty-one

According to scientists,
alcohol is *a solution.*
—T-SHIRT

Two days later, I was about as spic-and-span as a surly girl with a limp could be. My hair smelled better, and I could almost walk without wincing. Cookie and I went to pay our final respects to Misery, but I couldn't just leave her there. I called Noni Bachicha, who, besides being a gun fanatic and concealed carry instructor, just happened to be the best body man in the Southwest. And he also happened to be the only body man I knew. He said her frame was bent. Apparently, that was bad, but my frame was a little bent, too. I told him we'd be even more perfect for each other. I begged. Pleaded. And I may have thrown in a small fit for good measure. So he picked up Misery for me and took her to the car hospital, where he promised to give her the best of care.

On the bright side, Noni was now a little scared of me.

After that, I'd promised Dad a few days ago I would tend bar for him, so Cookie and I headed back that way. It was nice working almost side by side with Reyes. The room overflowed with patrons once again. Sadly, Jessica was among them. Who knew the best thing Dad could

ever do for his business was to hire a sexy, falsely convicted ex-con?

I glanced up to see FBI Special Agent Carson walk in.

"I thought you worked upstairs," she said, taking a seat
in front of me.

"Yeah, I'm tending bar tonight. My dad's shorthanded.
How's the serial killer thing going?"

She grinned as I continued to wipe down the bar.
"Thanks for solving that, by the way. You sure make my
job easier."

"You are very welcome. Can I get you anything?" It
was nice having her there. She took my mind off the small,
laserlike glances I kept getting from Jessica.

"What's your specialty?"

"Oh, you know. Madness. Mayhem. Debauchery. And
even with all that going for me, I can still make a mean
mojito. Or—" I held up an index finger. "—if you're feeling really adventurous, I make an incredibly decadent
Death in the Afternoon."

Her brows shot up. "Color me intrigued."

I laughed and started preparations for my masterpiece.
"This drink was invented by Ernest Hemingway," I explained, pouring champagne into a fluted glass. "And it
was considered quite avant-garde in the thirties."

"God, I love history."

"Right? Especially when it involves Papa." I took out
an absinthe spoon, set it across the top of the flute, placed
a sugar cube on top of that, and trickled absinthe over the
sugar cube until it dissolved into the champagne. The gorgeous lime green liquid rose to the top, sat there a few
seconds, then slowly emulsified, blending with the champagne until the entire concoction had an iridescent milky
shine. I removed the spoon and handed it to her.

She examined it, took a deep breath, then drank. She

waited. Thought about it. Took another drink. Thought about it again.

"You're killing me, Smalls," I said.

"I like it."

"Don't sound so surprised," I said, adding a grunt. "You'll give me a complex."

"As if." She took another drink. Thought about it. Took another.

I cleaned up my mess and started on a new order before looking down at the file folder in her hand.

"So what's up?"

Her fingers tightened around the file. It was old, its edges frayed, but it wore its coffee stains like a champion. Clearly, it had been read and reread dozens of times. "Remember my telling you I had a few cold cases I wanted you to look at?"

I put out a tray of mixed drinks for Sylvia to deliver, although she hated when I called her that. "I sure do. I thought you were talking about beer," I said, teasing her.

"Well, this is the main one I would love to see solved. It wasn't even my case. It was my father's, and it haunted him until the day he died."

"Uh-oh, now I'm intrigued." I opened the file for a quick look.

"Kidnapping case," she continued, "about thirty years ago. Nothing added up, from the parents' testimony to the suspects to the kid himself. It was just a bizarre case from day one."

"The kid himself?" I asked, even more intrigued. What would be odd about the kid?

"A ten-month-old baby was taken out of his crib while his mother napped."

I perused the file. "No pictures?"

"That's just it. One of the oddities of the case. All photographs of the child were stolen as well."

I eyed her doubtfully.

"Tell me about it," she said, taking another sip. "Nothing made sense. At first they thought a neighbor took him. She kept stalking the family, watching their every move, sending them threatening notes accusing the mother of witchcraft, of all the bizarre things."

"Witchcraft? That was very medieval of her."

"Preaching to the choir. But that still isn't the most unusual part. Even odder were the markings on the baby's body."

"Markings?" I asked, suspicion needling the back of my neck.

"Yes, according to the baby's doctor, there's a rare syndrome that can happen when the mother is pregnant with twins but one of them dies very early in the pregnancy. The surviving twin absorbs the cells of the other and basically has two sets of DNA running through his body."

"Okay, and the markings?"

"Well, sometimes when that happens, the twin's body will have light marks like stripes on his body. But supposedly they can be seen only in a certain light. I don't know. That's the only explanation the doctors could come up with to explain the marks on him."

"They looked like stripes?" I asked.

"Not sure. My dad said they looked more like tattoos."

My lungs seized. After all this time, surely the very case I'd been wondering about for years did not just land in my lap. I had another explanation for those marks, one that involved the son of Satan and maps to navigate the gates of hell, but I wasn't going to tell Agent Carson that. I liked that she thought I was only a little crazy. Bona fide lunatic could drive a wedge between us, and I valued our friendship too much for that. And the fact that she was my only contact at the FBI.

I glanced over my shoulder to make sure Reyes wasn't

listening in. "I would love to take a look at this case. Can I keep the folder awhile?"

"If I can keep this drink for a while."

"It's all yours," I said. "Would you like another?"

"Let me make sure I can walk after this one. I'll get back to you." She searched for an empty table. "I was going to eat. I've been hearing nothing but rave reviews about the food here."

"Yeah, I'm not sure it's the food everyone is raving about." When she raised a questioning brow, I added, "We got a new cook. He's like a supermodel on steroids."

"Reeeeeally?" she purred, looking toward the kitchen. "You know, the FBI takes certain liberties when it comes to kitchen inspections."

Trying to subdue a sudden case of the giggles, I said, "And you can eat at the bar."

"That's true. Can I eat in the kitchen?"

"Charley!"

I jumped and looked over as Uncle Bob charged toward me. What the hell did I do now?

"Why aren't you in bed? Oh," he said, spotting Agent Carson, "hi."

"Detective," she said. "How's business?"

He leaned forward, as though sharing a secret. "Pretty good, if you know what I mean." He indicated me with a nod and winked at her.

She grinned. "I do indeed. We need more of her."

He gasped theatrically, tossing in a hand over his heart and an expression of horror. "Bite your tongue. I can barely handle this one. Speaking of which—" He stabbed me with the scariest, most feared glower in his arsenal. The legendary one that set criminals on edge and made his colleagues giggle behind closed fists while they pretended to cough. It was a thing of beauty. "—what the hell are you doing out of bed?"

"Working."

"Why?"

"It's Dad's fault. He went to my apartment, grabbed me by the hair, and dragged me over here kicking and screaming." I turned to the man who'd just walked up to stand beside me. "Oh, hey, Dad. We were just talking about you."

"Leland," Uncle Bob said, "I don't think Charley needs to be working right now."

"That's what I said. She insisted. Said she was going stir-crazy. Threatened to put a curse on me if I didn't let her."

"That's not the way I remember it."

"Can you do that?" Ubie asked. "Can you put a curse on someone?"

I loved that man.

Flashing him an evil grin, I went back to work, wiping the bar. It seemed like the right thing to do, since I was getting paid to be there.

And here came the last member of the gang.

"Twitter!" Cookie said, pointing at me as she sat beside Agent Carson.

I tossed my rag on the bar and stood up for myself. "Don't tell me what to do, missy!"

"No, that's how all these women know about your man and where he works. He has his own hashtag. It's crazy."

Why that would surprise me, I had no idea. He had entire websites dedicated to him while he was in prison— why should I have expected any less when he got out?

"Does he really have a Ferrari?" she asked.

"A what?" I asked, stunned.

"According to the Twitter-verse, that man is decked out." She waved at the rest of the gang as she settled onto the bar stool.

A Ferrari? Clearly we needed to bang less and talk

more. If he did, where was he keeping it? I would totally have noticed a Ferrari, especially if one were sitting beside Misery.

Uncle Bob quit staring at my receptionist, sat on the opposite side of Agent Carson, and told Dad, "I need that new cook of yours to whip me up some nachos."

"You gonna pay?"

"Do I ever? Oh, and I found out who bought the asylum you've been so worried about, pumpkin."

I'd just picked my rag back up. I stopped wiping the bar again, realizing it was never going to get clean at this rate. "And?"

He handed me a thick envelope and hitched a brow as though I should already know. "It seems you did."

"That's odd. I don't remember buying an abandoned mental asylum. I'll have to look at my bank statement."

"According to this, you're the new owner."

I paused, befuddled, then after a quick succession of blinks that got me nowhere fast, I opened the envelope to find a deed with my name on it. "Reyes," I said, stunned. "It had to be Reyes."

"Reyes Farrow?" Dad didn't know about Reyes and me and our sordid past or even sordider present. If he'd known, I wondered if he would've hired him.

"Yes, it had to be Reyes. Who else? I knew that man had a million dollars. And he drives a Ferrari?" I looked toward the kitchen. "But why would he do this?"

"Well, I didn't know how to tell you this, pumpkin," Dad said, shifting his weight from one foot to the other, "but Reyes Farrow bought this place as well with the stipulation that the offices upstairs be yours. I was wondering about that last part. Is there something you want to tell me?"

"No. And what?" My voice raised an octave. "You sold Calamity's?"

"We were supposed to hammer out the details yesterday, but he said he had a sick friend to look after, so we're going to the abstract company tomorrow."

"I don't understand."

"I'm retiring. And after what he paid me, I can do it very comfortably. I've decided to do some traveling." His gaze dropped to the floor. "Alone."

"Just a man and his thoughts, huh? What about the old ball and chain?"

"I'm sorry to have to tell you this way, but your mother and I are separating." When I pressed my mouth together, he corrected, "Stepmother. We're just— We're going in different directions."

"I don't know what to say, Dad. 'Hurray' just seems wrong." And it did. He loved her. Or at least he did at one time. I couldn't help but wonder how much of Charley went into that decision.

I looked down at the deed in my hands. Surveyed the bar. My offices upstairs. I just didn't know what to say.

"Well, I think a round of nachos is in order," Uncle Bob said, still thinking about his belly instead of my newfound—

Wait. What the heck was I going to do with an abandoned mental asylum?

"We'll discuss this as well as other things later," Ubie added, the threat almost crystal clear, only not because it had a milky film on the top. He shot me his glower again and I had to resort to coughing behind my closed fist.

When one side of the room quieted and a scorching heat crept around me, I turned to watch my man bring two plates out of the kitchen. He smiled and placed two plates of nachos in front of my initiated gang members.

"Enjoy," he said, flashing a nuclear grin when Agent Carson only stared. Who could blame her?

"Mr. Davidson," he said, acknowledging Dad before

leaning over the bar to hand Uncle Bob some extra napkins. His mouth brushed across my ear. "Can you take a break?" He wore a cook's apron. It was the cutest thing I'd ever seen in my entire life, and I fell just a little harder.

"From what I hear, you're the boss, so you tell me." I raised the deed. "What's this?"

He lowered his head as though embarrassed. Reyes Farrow embarrassed? Unfathomable.

"It's yours," he said, fiddling with a small piece of paper in his hand. "I know how important Rocket is to you, so I just thought I'd buy it. Make sure the city doesn't tear it down or anything. We'll need to fix up the outside a little to keep the city off your back, but the inside is all Rocket's."

For the second time that day, I was at a loss for words. Then I remembered the outbuildings. "I noticed you tore down Donovan's house."

He lifted his gaze until it locked with mine. "He's alive because he left town. His house chose to stay. It paid the price."

I laughed. "Fair enough. And you bought Dad's bar?" The astonishment I felt filtered into every word.

"Yeah, about that," he said, hedging, "I'm going to have to charge you a pretty penny for those offices. That's prime real estate. And there are some late fees that will have to be worked out."

"Reyes, I don't know what to say. Did you buy anything else I need to know about?"

"I didn't. But you've been spending money like it's going out of style."

"Why? What else did I buy?"

"You're living in it."

"You bought my apartment?"

"No, *you* bought your apartment. Well, the whole building, actually."

"I have an apartment building?" After a minute, I looked back at him. "I am so raising your rent."

The kitchen door crashed open. We turned to see one of the young prep cooks leaning out of it.

"Um, Reyes?" he said, nervous. "You might want to—I mean there's something—" He pointed into the kitchen.

"I'll be right there," Reyes said—then he looked back at me. "I have to get to work before I burn the place down."

I nodded. "I just don't know what to say."

He closed the distance between us, his heat winding around me like a red-hot ribbon, and whispered into my ear. "Say yes."

He turned and walked away. I watched. He was just ridiculously cute in that long apron. It framed his ass just so.

"Wait," I called out, "do you have a Ferrari?"

He tossed me a wicked grin from over his shoulder. Holy cow, I would say yes to anything that man had to ask, unless he asked about butt sex. I had to draw the line somewhere. Speaking of which, say yes to what? I reconstructed our conversation and came up with nothing. Clearly I missed something. I tended to do that. Freaking ADD.

I turned back to the menial task requirements of my most recent pink-collar position and noticed a sticky note on the bar. The one he'd had in his hands. That man loved Post-its. I read the note, thought about it, tried to absorb its true meaning, its deeper message, then read it again before turning toward the kitchen and shouting, "Marry you?"

Read on for an excerpt from the next book by
Darynda Jones

Sixth Grave on the Edge

Coming May 2014 in hardcover from St. Martin's Press

A blunk is the only thing I draw well.
—T-SHIRT

"A girl, a mocha latte, and a naked dead man walk into a bar," I said, turning to the naked dead man sitting in my passenger's seat. The *elderly* naked dead man who'd been taking up space in my cherry red Jeep Wrangler, aka Misery, for two days now. We were on a stakeout. Sort of. I was staking out a Mr. and Mrs. Foster, so I was definitely on a stakeout. No idea what Naked Dead Man was on. Considering the fact that he looked about 112, probably blood thinners. Cholesterol medication. And, judging from the state of his penis, which I couldn't stop seeing every single time I turned toward him, Viagra. Either that or he was naturally well-endowed. The guy had girth.

"Go, Naked Dead Man."

I gave him two thumbs up then checked the house again, happy to be sitting in Misery. The Jeep, not the emotion. I'd just picked her up from the car hospital two days earlier. She'd had several surgeries to fix her broken girlie bits because a raving lunatic rammed into her. As I was in the driver's seat at the time, he'd knocked her into a state of mangled disrepair and me into a state of oblivion. I stayed in that state long enough for Mr. Raving Lunatic to cart me off to a deserted bridge to kill me. He'd failed and died in the process, but Misery paid a high price for his nefarious machinations. Why did bad guys always try to hurt the ones I loved?

And this one had succeeded. Misery was hurt. Bad. No one wanted to work on her. Said she couldn't be saved. Said to give her over to the scrap yard. Thankfully, a family friend with a body shop and a few incriminating photos which just happened to find their way into my possession agreed, with great reluctance, to try.

Noni had kept her for two long weeks before calling to tell me he'd almost lost her a couple of times, but she'd pulled through with flying colors. When I got the green light to go pick her up, I tore out of my apartment so fast, I left a dust trail behind me. And a flummoxed best friend who'd been telling me about the couple in 3C. They apparently humped like rabbits. But I hurried back to her because I didn't have a car and needed a ride.

When we picked up Misery, Noni tried to tell me everything he'd had to do to her to get her up and running, but I held up a hand to stop him, unable to bear it. This was Misery he was talking about. Not some random Wrangler off the streets. This was *my* Wrangler. My best friend. My baby.

Holy cow, I needed a life.

I had to hand it to Noni, though. Misery was good as new. Almost better than new. It was weird. Her cough was gone. Her sluggish response time was no longer an issue. Her reluctance to wake up in the morning as she sputtered in protest every time I tried to fire all engines was non-existent. Now she started on the first try, no groaning or whining, and she purred like a newborn kitten. How Noni had managed to fix her insides as well as her outsides I'd never know, but the guy was good. And Noni was my new best friend. Well, after Misery. And Cookie, my real best friend. And Garrett, my kind of sort of best friend. And Reyes, my . . . my . . .

What was Reyes? Besides the dark and sultry son of evil? My boy toy? My love slave? My 24/7 booty call?

No.

Well, yes.

He was all of those things, but he was also my almost-fiancé. All I had to do was say yes to the proposal he'd written on a sticky note, and he'd be my fiancé for reals. Until then, however, he was my almost fiancé. No, my soon-to-be fiancé. No! My nigh fiancé. Yeah, that'd do. For now.

I turned back to the naked dead man, stuffed a couple of Cheez-Its into my mouth, and confessed my latest sin.

"I'm just kidding," I said through the crackers, regretting the fact that I'd tempted him and now had no follow-up. No punch line. "I don't know any 'girl, mocha-latte, dead-man' jokes. Sorry to get your hopes up like that." He didn't seem to mind, however. He sat staring straight ahead, his gray eyes clouded and watery with age, oblivious to my charm, to my clever repartee, and intellectual wit. He was ignoring me!

It happened.

"Cheez-It?" I offered him.

Nothing.

"Suit yourself." I dusted Cheez-It gunk off my hands and went back to my drawing. In my attempt to avoid eye contact with Mr. Naked Dead Man's penis over the last couple of days, I'd also avoided several key clues as to its owner's identity. First, he had a long scar that ran from under his left arm, over his ribcage, and down until it ended at his belly button. Whatever had caused it couldn't have been pleasant, but it could be vital in identifying him. Second, he had a tattoo on his left biceps that looked very old-school military. It was faded and the ink had spread, but I could still make out an eagle with its talons gripping a United States flag. And third, right underneath his tattoo was a surname, presumably his: Andrulis. I'd taken out my memo pad and pen and was drawing the tat since I had yet to find a camera that could photograph the departed.

I did my darnedest to draw the tat while balancing the Cheez-It box against the gear shift, within arm's reach, and keeping an eye on the Fosters' house. Sadly, I sucked at two out of three of those tasks. Mostly at drawing. I couldn't paint either. I'd failed finger painting in kindergarten. That should have been a clue, but I'd always wanted to be the next Vermeer or Picasso or, at the very least, the next Clyde Brewster, a boy I'd gone to school with who drew exploding walls and houses and buildings. No idea why. Alas, my destiny did not lie within the lines of graphite or the strokes of a paintbrush, but at the whim of dead people with PTDD: Post Traumatic Death Disorder.

Oh, well. It could have been worse. Clyde Brewster, for example, ended up in prison for trying to blow up a Sack-N-Save. Thankfully, he was better at art than demolitions.

"I know you're not really into baring your soul," I said, eyeing Mr. Andrulis's bare, naked soul, "figuratively speaking, but if there's anything you want or need, I'm your girl. Mostly because not many people on Earth can see you."

I added a shadow on the eagle's face with my blue ink pen, trying to make it look noble, but it didn't help. It still looked cross-eyed.

"And those who can see the departed usually only see a gray mist where you might be. Or they'll feel a rush of cold air when you walk past. But I can see you, touch you, hear you, pretty much anything you."

Maybe if I added highlights on its beak, it would look more like an eagle and less like a duck.

"My name is Charley."

But I was using a pen. I couldn't erase. Damn it. I had

to think ahead. Real artists thought ahead. I'd never get into the Louvre at this rate.

"Charley Davidson."

I tried to scratch off some of the ink, bracing the memo pad against my steering wheel. I tore a tiny hole in the paper instead and cursed under my breath.

"I'm the grim reaper," I said from between gritted teeth, "but don't let that bother you. It's not as bad as it sounds. And I shouldn't have given your eagle eyelashes. He looks like Daffy Duck in drag."

Giving up, I wrote the name underneath the eagle-ish-type drawing, consoling myself with the fact that abstract art was all the rage before pulling out my phone and snapping a shot of my masterpiece. After angling it this way and that, trying to get the focus just right, I realized the eagle looked better when turned on its side. More masculine. Less . . . water fowl.

I saved the best one and deleted the rest as a car pulled up to the Foster house. A nervous thrill rushed up my spine. I put down my pen and memo pad and took a sip of my whipped mocha latte, forcing myself to calm as I waited to see who was driving the gold Prius. The Fosters lived in a modest neighborhood in the Northeast Heights. Mr. Foster owned an insurance company and Mrs. Foster ran the office of a local pediatrician. And approximately thirty years ago, their first son was taken from them, never to be seen again.

I eased forward and pressed against the steering wheel, angling for a better look at the driver when my Aunt Lil's voice wafted toward me from the back seat.

"Who's the hottie?" she asked, her blue hair and floral muumuu solidifying around her as she materialized in my rear view.

I tossed a smile over my right shoulder. "Hey, Aunt Lil. How was your trip to Bangladesh?"

"Oh, the food!" She waved a hand extravagantly. "The people! I was in heaven, I tell ya. Not literally, though." She cackled in delight at her joke.

Aunt Lil had died in the sixties, a fact she'd only recently discovered. So, she couldn't have actually eaten or conversed with the native population. At least, not the living native population. I'd never thought about her visiting the departed when she traveled. Now, *that* would be fascinating.

She hitched a thumb toward my newest friend and wriggled her penciled brows. "You gonna introduce us?"

The garage door raised and the driver pulled inside but didn't close the door. It gave me hope. I just wanted a glimpse. A tiny peek.

"He's not really talkative," I said, squinting for a better view when the driver's-side door opened, "but I think his last name is Andrulis. It's on his tattoo."

"He's got some ink?" She leaned forward and spotted Mr. A's package. It was hard to miss.

"Good heavens," she said, her eyes rounding in appreciation.

Before I could get a look at the driver, the garage door started closing. "No," I whispered, tilting my head in unison with the descending door until it completely blocked my view.

I'd seen a woman's foot as she stepped out of the car before the door closed completely. That was about it.

"He's certainly been blessed," she said.

I laid my head against the steering wheel and expelled a loud breath as disappointment washed over me. I'd been handed a file that could hold many answers to the puzzle that was Reyes Alexander Farrow, my nigh fiancé, and the Fosters were a big piece of the puzzle. Their first son had been kidnapped while napping in his room. Because there was never a ransom demand and no witnesses, the case went cold almost immediately despite a massive search and public pleas from the parents. But the FBI agent assigned to the case never gave up. He'd always believed there was more to the case than just a kidnapping. And so did his daughter who followed in her father's footsteps and became an FBI agent as well. She was also my friend and we'd worked a couple of cases together. She knew about my rep for solving crimes no one else seemed able to, and she'd asked me to look at a cold case that had been the bane of her father's existence.

And that was the day that Reyes Farrow's kidnapping fell into my lap.

"Don't you think?"

I blinked back to Aunt Lil. "Think what?"

"That he's been blessed."

"Oh, yeah, I do." I couldn't help another glance. "But it's just so . . . there. So unavoidable." I tore my gaze away and pointed to his tat. "So the name Andrulis. Does that ring a bell?"

"No, but I can do some investigating. Speaking of which, I've been thinking. I think we should work together." She jammed a boney elbow into my side encouragingly.

"Ooooh-kay."

"Ha! I knew it was a good idea. We probably need code names. And code phrases like, 'The sun never sets in the East.' That could mean, 'Switch to plan B.' Or it could mean, 'Let's grab a bite to eat before the men come over.'"

"The men?"

"Or it could mean, 'How do you get blood out of silk?' Because as PIs, we'll need to know stuff like that."

"I guess," I said, unable to shake out of my disappointment.

"Are you okay, Pumpkin Cheeks?"

"Yeah, it's just . . . well, two hours down the drain, and

for what?" I gestured toward the Fosters' house. "A foot in a sensible shoe driving a sensible car."

She looked across the street toward the house. "What were you hoping to see?"

Her question took me by surprise. Even I wondered what I was really doing there. Did I simply want to see the woman who might have given birth to the man of my dreams? Or did I want a glimpse of the man who might have been his human father?

Reyes was the son of Satan, forged in the fires of hell, but he'd been born on Earth to be with me. To grow up with me. He'd done his homework and chosen a steady, professional couple to be his human parents. He'd planned for us to go to the same schools, to shop at the same stores, and eat at the same restaurants. Sadly, even the best-laid plans go awry.

"I'm not really sure, Aunt Lil."

"Goodness, that won't do. We'll definitely need code names. What do you think of Cleopatra?"

I rested my head against the seatback and gave her my best smile. "I think it's perfect."

"Oh! Trench coats! We'll need trench coats!"

"Trench coats?" But she was gone. Vanished. Vamoosed. I loved that woman. She took eccentric to a whole new level. Still, I had work to do, and sitting at a stakeout just to catch a glimpse of the Fosters was ridiculous. I started Misery, then picked up the Cheez-Its and stuffed a handful into my mouth the very second the phone rang. Naturally. Because when else would it ring?

I hurried and chewed before answering my bestie's ring. Cookie worked cheap, which made her the best receptionist in all of Albuquerque, in my humble opinion. But she was also very good at her job. I'd set her on the task of finding everything she could about the Fosters. She was as fascinated as I was.

After taking a quick sip of my latte, I finally answered. "Do you think if I lived on Cheez-Its and coffee alone, I'd ultimately starve to death?"

"They had another son," she said, her voice full of awe.

I had no idea what that had to do with my question. "Does he eat Cheez-Its?"

"The Fosters."

I bolted upright. "Can you repeat that?"

"The Fosters had another son."

"No way."

"Way." I heard her fingernails clicking on the keyboard as she worked her magic. "Very much way."

"After Reyes?"

"Yes. Three years after the abduction."

"Do you know what this means?" I asked, my awe matching her own.

"I certainly do."

"Reyes Farrow—"

"—has a brother."

Holy mother of bacon bits.